SNAFU

⚕ MEDIVAC ⚕

Also From Cohesion Press

SNAFU
MEDIVAC

Edited by Amanda J Spedding & Geoff Brown

Cohesion Press
Mayday Hills Lunatic Asylum
Beechworth , Australia
2020

SNAFU: Medivac
Amanda J Spedding & Geoff Brown (eds)
2020

Cohesion Press
Mayday Hills Lunatic Asylum
Beechworth, Australia
www.cohesionpress.com

Contents

BROTHER JIM

A few words about James A. Moore

Write the damn book!"
How many times have I heard James A. Moore say this? Not to me. He went a bit further in my case but we'll get to that. But I have heard him say this to many a struggling writer. To folks who were trying hard to get the words on paper but were letting self doubt and procrastination keep them from finishing a novel. And Jim (he goes by Jim) would leap in and tell them to get to work. That he would accept no excuses and therefore they should accept none. And quite a few of those writers did finish what they were working on.

Generosity. In many ways that sums up Jim Moore. He wants you to succeed, and if he can help you he will. I have seen many writers who think success for anyone else somehow subtracts from their own. That other writers are competition and not to be encouraged. Not Jim. He is one of the most generous people I know, both with his advice, and with his time. Just don't waste that valuable time, for he has little patience for people who just want to talk about writing rather than actually doing it.

In my case, Jim didn't just tell me to write the damn book. He offered to write it with me. My first published novel, the first Griffin and Price book, *Blind Shadows*, was a collaboration with Jim. We've written quite a few other things together since, and it's always a good time. He's always claimed that he needed me to write the book with him because I'd read more crime fiction than he had, but I know he also could see that maybe I needed a push to finally finish a novel.

Before I say more nice things about Jim, though, let me tell you that he can be a scary bastard. I've read most of his horror novels and if I didn't know the guy as well as I do, I'd be worried about him. His mind goes down some really creepy paths and brings back some potently horrific images. Human potato stamps anyone? There were times when he and I were working on a book and he'd email me his chapters and I'd read them and go, "Jesus, Jim! What is wrong with you?" And he would reply with his customary EC Comics horror host laugh, "Heh heh heh."

It's not all horror though. Jim's imagination knows few boundaries. In the last few years he's begun to make his mark in the Heroic Fantasy genre, being favorably compared to such greats as George R.R. Martin and David Gemmell. I personally think Jim's horror chops are what gives his fantasy a different spin and gets people's attention. I knew when I read his first fantasy novel, *Seven Forges*, in manuscript, there was something different here. Something dark and dangerous. Less Tolkien and more Robert E. Howard and Fritz Leiber. Heroic Fantasy with teeth.

People often don't know what to make of Jim when they first meet him. In past years he often looked like a lost and possibly dangerous Viking, with his beard and long hair, and his burly physique. A little time spent in his presence would soon cure any concerns that he was about to chop anyone to bits though, and talking to him would soon reveal a quick wit and a ready laugh. He's slimmed down in the last couple of years and at the moment, because of the chemotherapy, his hair looks more like mine. (As in none.)

But the hair will be back and so will the man, because Jim is, above all things, a fighter, and a guy who doesn't give up. Not on others, and not on himself.

Stories I've co-written with Jim have appeared in three SNAFU anthologies so far, and he's been in other volumes writing solo. It's a good fit for Jim because he's a guy who believes you have to stand up to monsters, be they human or otherwise. He's doing that right now, by standing up to cancer, an insidious monster that has taken many lives.

By picking up this book, you're helping Jim with that fight. I know he appreciates it, and I know I sure as hell do too. I need him to get better. He's my friend and my bother. And we have more damn books to write.

Charles R. Rutledge
Atlanta, Georgia
2019

THE ELDON ANGELS

Greig Beck

PROLOGUE

Syria, Idlib Province: Kurdish evacuation – 8 years ago

Captain Mike Taylor and his team crouched as heavy machine-gun fire tore up the ground out at their left flank. *Another day in paradise.*

Three years in med school hadn't prepared him for this, but his Special Forces training had. Mike was a trained killer of evil, but if called upon, he could also heal.

A mortar exploded a hundred feet from them, and he turned his head from the falling debris. He and a few dozen Special Forces were on the ground to assist in creating a safe corridor for the trapped Kurdish and Syrian refugees. But it was turning out to be an impossible task.

In front of him, a few of the Kurdish YPG hunkered down, and one of them, Aiisha, turned to smile broadly back at him. She was like a lot of the Kurdish women who fought alongside their men, as fearless as they were ferocious, and after he'd saved her brother's life, she seemed to have decided she either owed him something or he was now future husband material.

"*Fuck.*"

Another mortar exploded, closer. They were finding their range.

"They're on us; we need to pull back," Henson yelled to him.

And he should have pulled them back, but nothing was achieved without risk. Mike shook his head. "We push through, get under it."

Their current position was described as a blood and bone salad – Syrian forces, Russian Spetznaz, Kurdish YPG, ISIS, Hezbollah, Al Qaida, and too many other small factions to name, and all of them armed to the teeth, and killing, screaming, and dying in equal measures.

It was no place to be a refugee, and that was why he and his unit, the Asgardian Shields, were on the ground. It was a near hopeless task, and he knew the reward for doing impossible tasks and succeeding was just more impossible tasks.

They had one more sniper nest to take down, and they could begin bringing the people through. Mike and two of his Spec Forces buddies moved up to join the small group of YPG. Mike and his guys would draw enemy fire while Aiisha's group would advance and more than likely throw themselves headfirst into an enemy foxhole with gun in one hand and blade in the other. This place was a mad, mad world.

Aiisha turned to smile at him again and put a finger to her lips, and then turned the finger to face him for a moment before making a fist. He nodded and smiled in return – it meant: *this kiss for you, I keep it till we meet again.*

His buddies weren't watching so he returned the gesture. Okay, he admitted it; he liked her too.

He allowed their groups to split, and Aiisha's team advanced fifty feet, staying low. But it was then that the back of Mike's neck prickled. Around him the air became still and everything dropped away to silence. Whether it was a soldier's intuition or a premonition, he knew something was coming. Something bad. He also knew for sure; *I shoulda pulled them back.*

The Russian heavy mortar, probably an M240 that fired a 286-pound shell, landed in the centre of Aiisha and her group. The percussive blast blew a crater 40-feet around and Mike was lifted and thrown backwards to roll like a broken doll until he struck a rocky outcrop. He remembered his face feeling hot and wet, his eardrums screaming, eyes burning, and the salty taste of blood in his mouth.

He didn't know who pulled him out of there. But his military days were over, and Aiisha, and everyone else he knew were gone forever.

CHAPTER 01

Eldon, Oakland County, Missouri – Today
Mike drove the sunny, tree-line roads past fields of long grass dotted with stands of silver maple, ash and oak trees. A sign loomed: *Eldon, population: 1024* – and a turnoff. Houses began to pepper the countryside, then more houses, and then he entered the Eldon town central.

He smiled as he slowed, delighted it looked exactly like its pictures. He felt as if he just travelled back to a time and place where people smiled and waved at each other, the streets were wide, and the sun shone on every corner of the world. Maybe this would lift the depression he'd been drowning in since he'd fucked up, since he'd made that bad call.

He noticed someone behind a window watching him, and gave a small wave, but the curtains were quickly tugged closed. *Well, maybe not everyone smiled and waved.*

Mike chuckled. "Damn outta towners."

He pulled in close to the council chambers and just across from the local museum. He had been given a few contact names: Karen, the vice mayor; Shelly, his soon to be assistant nurse, and doctor Ben Wainright, seventy-nine years old, looking to retire, and the reason Mike was here.

There were no parking meters and no street signs, which made him grin. This was definitely an advantage over big cities where cars were seen as the enemy and parking them was a luxury for the rich or the lucky.

He looked across the street. "Vice Mayor Karen first it is then." He shouldered open his door and crossed the near empty street to the chambers. It was a square 1960ish building, one of the few that was painted totally white. Mike headed to the woman on the phone at the front desk. An oak staircase that could have come straight from the set of *Gone with the Wind* rose beside her.

"Hi." He gave the receptionist his most charming smile.

She returned his smile, winked, and held up a finger as she finished her phone call. "Doctor Taylor." It wasn't a question and her eyebrows travelled halfway up her forehead.

"Guilty." Mike held his hands up but was still a little surprised she recognized him.

"I'm Gladys, and we've been expecting you." She beamed like a schoolgirl. "You're as nice as in your pictures."

"Thank you." Mike chuckled. "Ah, is the vice mayor in?"

"Yes, but might be in a meeting. I'll check if she's free." Gladys pressed a button on her phone system, spoke softly for a second or two, and then turned to nod to him. "She's coming down."

An upstairs door opened and closed, followed by the click of heels on linoleum. For some reason Mike automatically sucked in his stomach.

Karen Powell came down the steps, her dark eyes were on him, and she didn't smile until she stepped right in front of him. She was tiny, standing no more than around five-feet-four, give-or-take.

She held out her hand. "Doctor Taylor, pleased to meet you in person."

"Thank you, and likewise." Though her hand was small, her grip was firm. Also, rather than the soft skin he expected, the palms seemed a little calloused – *gym junky or rock jock?*

She tilted her head. "So, you found our little oasis without problem?"

He grinned again. "Yes, and Eldon is as beautiful as I expected, and it's my pleasure to be here, Vice Mayor. Oh, and please call me Mike."

"Only if you call me Karen." She watched him. "Just popping in to say hello, or is there something I can do for you?"

"Just on my way to say hello to Doc Wainright, and let him know I've arrived. As I was passing by, I wondered if you were in."

4

"Good," she said. "You'll like Ben. he's been my family doctor for years, so I guess I'll be seeing you in the future."

"You and the family?"

She shook her head. "Yes, but it's just me and Benji – Benjamin – my twelve-year-old son."

He waited for her to elaborate but she didn't, so he just assumed it was too early for him to know those sort of private details. Mike waited a moment more and then jerked a thumb towards the door. "So, I better, ah, get going then."

She continued to watch him with that small smile of hers, before suddenly having a thought. "Hey, this weekend the Mayor is having a send off for Ben, so you're here at the perfect time. Be worthwhile you coming along, meet all your prospective patients."

"Okay, yeah, sounds real good." He gave her a small bow and quickly glanced at Gladys who was on the phone but still watching him like a hawk. "See you, Gladys."

She crinkled her eyes at him, while carrying on with her cheery phone conversation.

Back in his car he read the sign of the closest cross street to get his bearings. It was Friday and he had planned on checking out his practice on the weekend but found that Wainright's clinic wasn't that far away. He could drop in on the old boy first, and then if he needed any supplies – food and medicines – before opening mid week, he still had the afternoon to get everything sorted.

He pulled out and headed down the street to the first turnoff at Dugdale Street, then motored on past antique shops, general stores and a few empty coffee shops. Finally he came to a neat little house with a brass plate out front: *Ben B. Wainright – Medical Practitioner*.

Mike sat in the car for a moment admiring the small cottage that was painted in deep blue, with gloss white for the fencing and balustrades. It looked well maintained and it was obvious Wainright took pride in its upkeep. Always a good sign.

He stepped out of his car and smiled. "One day all of this will be yours."

The spring-hinge on the gate groaned a little as he eased it closed and he took a moment to admire the garden before approaching the open doorway. He stepped in and smelled lavender and alcohol.

Behind the desk a young woman had her head down with earphones in. Mike assumed she was transcribing medical notes for Doctor Wainright, but as he neared her desk, music leaked from the earplugs and he saw she had a magazine open.

He leaned on the counter. "Shelly Horton, I presume?"

She looked up, and her eyes suddenly went from bored to alert. She flapped the magazine shut and flashed him a brilliant smile as she pulled the plugs from her ears. "Hi there, sorry, can I help you?"

"I think so." Mike smiled back. Even though he didn't like the idea of his potential new receptionist ignoring patients, he guessed if the practice was quiet, then he could cut her some slack.

"I'm Doctor Michael Taylor... is Doctor Wainright about?"

She rose to her feet. "Michael, Doctor, Wainright, yes, yes he is." She stuck out a hand and leaned forward over the desk counter, making the front of her uniform strain. "I'm your receptionist, Shelly Horton."

He shook her hand and she held on. "Nice to meet you, Shelly. Pretty quiet, huh?"

She nodded vigorously, still holding onto his hand and coming around the desk. "Some days, yes. The Eldon folk here are generally pretty healthy. Unless it's flu season."

"Well, that's no good." He grinned and eased his fingers free. "How am I supposed to make a living if no one ever needs a doctor?"

She giggled, and her eyes flashed at him. She pointed one slim finger towards a side door. "Would you like me to get him? Doctor Wainright."

"Sure. I'm only popping in to say hello for now."

"Then *hello*." She waved with both hands and smiled broadly. "I'll wake him up." She heading to the consulting room door and leaned closer as she rapped twice. "Doctor Wainright?"

"*Come.*"

The voice was deep but weary. Shelly waved him on as she pushed open the door.

Inside Wainright pushed to his feet. He was thin, stooped, and slightly grey faced but his smile was warm, and though slightly rounded at the shoulders now, Mike bet that the man would have been tall and striking.

Mike crossed to him quickly. "Ben, so nice to meet you face to face at last."

"Likewise," Wainright said, shaking his hand. The hand and fingers were soft and the bones felt like sticks under the papery skin. He stood examining Mike for a few minutes and then dropped his hand.

"I'm glad you came." He stared into Mike's face, his own now deadpan. "Mike, everything I did here, I did for the benefit of the Eldon community." He straightened his narrow shoulders. "But I guess history will be my judge."

Mike frowned a little. "I think it'll be the judge of all of us."

Wainright grunted and turned to his room. "Just tidying up some redundant files for you."

Mike noticed the neat piles of folders and filing cabinets hanging open. All except one. Tucked away in a corner was an older wooden cabinet, solid, and the only one with a padlock on it.

Ben noticed where he was looking. "Don't worry about that one as I plan on getting rid of it. It's just information about the old Angel Mine."

"The disaster?" Mike asked. "I read about that; a dark day. The mine flooded; quite a few deaths, wasn't there?"

"There were." Ben turned watery eyes on him. "But this is just some details of residual cases of skin irritations and other things from the mining chemicals of the day. Nothing important."

"Something called Angel syndrome, wasn't it?" Mike pressed, recollecting a few references when he was researching Eldon. But there was no real description of what that even meant. "I'd be happy to look it over, just to—"

"*No.*" Wainright's voice cut across him.

Mike raised his eyebrows. "No big deal." He turned back to look at the old cabinet again.

"We should have blown that damn mine up," Wainright muttered.

"*Huh?*" Mike turned back, not sure he heard right, but Wainright waved it away, signaling the conversation was closed. "This way, Doctor."

"You never told me what you plan on doing after you've retired. Have you got family around these parts? Going travelling, or just going to spend more time fishing?"

Ben Wainright shook his head wearily. "No, I think I'll just go back to where I came from. I've been waiting for you for a long time. Thank you for coming in, Mike."

"Oh, okay." Mike shrugged. *That's odd.* "My pleasure." Wainright must have been waiting on someone, anyone, to take over.

The old doctor steered him towards the door. "I'll finish up now."

"Guess I'll see you at the Mayor's this weekend," Mike said brightly.

"Enjoy the practice." Wainright ushered him out and headed back into his office, leaving Mike and Shelly alone.

Mike turned his receptionist. "Where he came from?" he said. "He's been here all his life, and he's going home? To where?"

She shrugged. "I've worked with him for two years, and he keeps a lot to himself. We mind our own business. It's what we Eldoners do."

CHAPTER 02

Mike headed toward his car, still thinking about the Angel Mine. The historical reports he'd read stated many had died in the initial underground collapse, and then there was some site contamination. It was the one mystery about the place that intrigued him. Odd that Wainright blew it off as being just a few minor skin irritations.

His boarding house was on the outskirts of town and if memory served, not all that far from the mine site; maybe a twenty-minute drive on an empty road. This time of day, a piece of cake.

It had just gone three in the afternoon; he could probably take a quick run out there, and be home in time for dinner.

"Let's do it."

Mike jumped in his car, checked his maps and then drove out of town, heading back along the highway and passing only a few trucks and SUVs.

He didn't really know why he had an interest in the mine; curiosity maybe. *Angel syndrome*. As a medical man, his interest was piqued. And the filing cabinet in Wainright's office was one of the few repositories of information he knew of, and yet the old doc wanted to destroy it. *Something a little off there.*

Mike slowed at a rusted gate, checked his maps once again, and guessed this might have been the turnoff. There were no signs, nothing to indicate this was once one of the largest and most prosperous limestone mines in America.

That was then, he guessed. It was more than half a century ago, and not exactly a tourist hotspot. The metal gate was propped upright, and Mike got out and simply lifted and laid it out of the way.

Ten minutes later he came to a stand of stunted trees around an open patch of ground. There were a few abandoned railway carts, or jerry carts he believed they were called, plus a stack of rusting spare rails.

When he got out of his car, the acrid, dry smell of chalk and limestone assailed him. But there was nothing else; no birdcalls or the background *zumm* of crickets and cicadas. It seemed not just people had abandoned the mine.

Mike was about to head off when he stopped and returned to the car to rummage in the map compartment, then the middle box, and finally the door slots.

"Shit."

The flashlight wasn't there, and for the life of him he couldn't remember removing it.

"Just when you need it."

He sighed as he straightened. "Lucky I have the night vision of a cat." He chuckled, hitched his pants and headed towards the mouth of the mine.

Old, rusted cyclone fencing was strewn around and he carefully stepped over it. As Mike moved closer to the large opening, he noticed a few scrabby and twisted trees that had long surrendered to the lifeless dirt. There were also columns of stone about and these, too, were twisted into weird shapes.

He stopped before one and narrowed his eyes, unable to tear his gaze from the odd thing. Perhaps it wasn't stone; it looked like ancient tree bark. And if you looked at it from just the right angle, it could have had facial features carved into it.

Mike crossed to another of the petrified pillars, and peered even closer. The features and detail were beginning to weather away, but whoever had done the work had been quite skilled. They also had an eye for the macabre. The face seemed twisted in torment.

"Creepy as fuck," he whispered, and finally turned away.

The mine's cavernous mouth opened into a shallow basin, a dark hole sunk into the ground at its end that led down at a gentle slope. He eased down into the recess and walked towards the far end.

"Damn." It was blacker than the darkest night inside. He squinted, waiting for his eyes to adjust, but it made no difference. Only a few dozen feet in and there was simply not enough light even for a shadow. No human eye would ever adjust to that.

Mike tried to breathe slowly through his nose. Though the water had long receded down to the depths of the mine, he was still wary of the contamination Wainright had mentioned. And he certainly didn't like the idea of starting work covered in some sort of weird rash either.

He didn't know how long he stood there staring into the Stygian darkness, but he knew it would be useless to go further without a light. Useless and dangerous.

People had died down there, and he couldn't remember reading whether their bodies were ever recovered. If not, then it was a mass grave.

"Hello-ooo!" he shouted.

His voice bounced away into the dark tunnel and echoed several times until silence finally returned.

He grunted and was about to turn away, when he thought he heard what sounded like a small dragging noise from deep in the caverns.

He spun back.

Waited.

Mike concentrated so hard his head begin to throb. His hand went to his hip, reaching for his gun; it wasn't there anymore, but old habits never died. He continued to stare, frozen to the spot. Something was moving in there, he was sure of it.

He'd done nighttime incursions before, but they'd had night vision goggles, and he'd been armored and armed to the teeth. Now he had nothing but his wits.

Mike was about to call again but suddenly realised he didn't feel like making any noise, and he was certainly not venturing any closer to the mineshaft. He didn't like the odds.

I'll come back with a light. He backed up a few steps, keeping his eyes on the impenetrable darkness of the mouth of the mine.

As he made his way back to the car he noticed a sign lying in the dirt.

WARNING – No swimming, no bathing, no drinking. Ground water contaminated. By order of the Eldon city council, Oct. 1978.

Mike exhaled and turned back one last time to let his eyes run over the mining grounds.

No, he didn't think he would come back with a light. In fact, he didn't think he'd come back at all.

CHAPTER 03

Eldon, Missouri, 1977: Angel Syndrome – first cases
"I'm sure it's just the flu, Mary. It's the start of the season after all." Doctor Ben Wainright smiled reassuringly at the woman, who hung on his every word as if he'd just climbed down from the Mount with a stone tablet under each arm. But he knew that in a small town, the local doctor's opinion mattered, and was only one step below that of the Lord.

The young mother was widowed and struggled to look after her ten-year-old son, who now sat silently, staring straight ahead.

The boy had presented with symptoms Wainright had been seeing quite a lot lately – listlessness, sleeplessness, loss of appetite, and unlike a fever-heat, the kids had the opposite – their core temperature was on the low side.

The only worrying symptom he couldn't account for was a roughening of the skin on the lower back, thighs, and hands. Right now, those tiny hands grasped the armrests of the chair, and to the naked eye only looked a little darker than his normal skin tone

"Aspirin, orange juice, and early to bed." Wainright smiled as the woman nodded and helped her son to his feet.

Wainright turned to a large jar that held plastic-wrapped lollypops and lifted out a red one and green one. "Billy, which one?" He held them out.

The boy didn't even turn.

"Billy?" he moved them in front of the boy's face.

The boy's hand lifted slightly, but then hung in mid-air for a moment before he shook his head, dropped his hand and turned away.

"*Hmm.*" Wainright kept the calm smile on his face, even

12

though a kid refusing candy was a huge red flag. "When was the last time he had a good meal?"

Mary seemed to search her mind for a moment. "Yesterday. No, the day before, when he had a cookie, but that's all."

"Okay, you've got to try and get some food into him. He needs his energy to fight this bug." He looked down at the kid. "Will you help your mom out there?"

Billy nodded dreamily.

"Good boy." He shook her hand. "And call me in a day or so to let me know how he's getting on."

"Yes, Doctor." Mary guided the boy to the door, and Wainright opened it for them.

He caught sight of his waiting room and was surprised to see it filled with anxious-looking parents and their children, with a few lone adults scattered amongst them. Whatever it was, something was going around. He closed the door and quickly jotted down some notes.

The days rolled on, and then the weeks. The first flurry of parents bringing in their children dwindled and then stopped. He wanted to believe the bug – or whatever it was – had burned itself out. Thing was, he hadn't seen a single one of the people who presented with the original symptoms.

Zero follow-up was too good to be true, and then Margie told him the local schools were only half full – those kids were probably still at home. Curiosity and a local doctor's desire to care for his community overwhelmed him.

"If the mountain will not come to Muhammad..." He got to his feet and packed his leather satchel. "... then Muhammad must go to the mountain."

Ben got in his sky blue Plymouth Duster and groaned, immediately wishing he had parked in the shade. He quickly wound down the widow to release some of the furnace-like air from the interior. He would have done the same on the opposite window but couldn't be bothered reaching across. *One day they'll have machines to do that for us,* he mused.

It was a short drive to the Hepworth place. Though the tarred road ended a while back, the dry weather of late meant at the dirt road was solid; rutted, but solid. He pulled up out front and tapped the horn twice.

He got out and stretched his back, feeling the wet shirt unglue from his body. He was a tall man and regarded as being quite dashing. He'd come unannounced, so waited a moment in the sunshine expecting Mary to appear on the front porch and forgive him for the unexpected intrusion.

When no one appeared, he walked briskly up the front steps and twisted the bell. It rang loudly inside the house.

He gave it another minute and then peered through the glass panel and saw Mary coming slowly down the hallway. She wiped her hands on a cloth and tucked it into the waistline of her skirt before opening the door.

The pretty young mother looked drained of color, and her eyes were red rimmed from either lack of sleep or crying. Ben guessed, both.

"Ben." She made his name sound like a lament.

"Mary?" He stared for a moment. "Ah, I came to check on Billy. Is everything okay?"

After a moment she shook her head and her voice was little more than a squeak. "Not really."

"May I come in?" He stepped closer.

"*Um…*" She wrung her hands for a moment, but her head was down as she nodded then shuffled aside.

Ben stepped through the doorway and pointed to a closed door. "Second on the right?"

She nodded again and he proceeded down the hallway to Billy's room. "Follow me please," he said over his shoulder.

He slowed as he neared the door, reached out a hand. A tingling grew in his stomach that hinted at a nervousness that shouldn't be there. He shook it off, twisted the knob and pushed the door inwards.

The first thing that hit him was the smell – fish, methane and excrement. He'd never actually smelled what a fish shit out of its body, but he bet it smelled like this.

"He had an accident," Mary whispered.

14

It was dark inside, and he reached for the light.

"Don't," she said.

He paused with his hand raised. "I need to see what I'm doing. I'm sorry." He flicked the light on.

The scream that came from the mess of soiled bedcovers made the hair on his neck rise. It was an animalistic screech of pain and torment, and held hardly any human notes. It continued to fill the small room.

"*Billy*," Wainright said forcefully.

The boy immediately quietened but had burrowed down below the covers. Wainright glanced around the small room; on the bedside table were numerous plates, many still piled with spoiling food. A few looked to have been at least nibbled at, but just the meat.

There was also a bedpan tucked under the bed that had a few tiny logs of dry feces piled inside. It probably didn't help the smell in the bedroom. He nudged it to the side and the sat on the edge of the bed.

He looked up at Mary. "I'm going to examine him now, is that okay?"

She just stared, not at him, but at the rumpled mound of blankets.

"I'll take that as a yes." Wainright reached out. "Billy." He laid a hand on the mound. "Billy." He felt the hardness beneath and was surprised by the sharpness of some of the edges on the boy's body. Rather than a ten-year-old kid under the covers, it felt like someone had thrown a blanket over a tree stump.

"I'm going to have to pull the covers back now, Billy."

The mound shook violently for a few seconds, so he paused.

"Does the light hurt your eyes?" he asked.

There came something like a nod from the top end of the mound.

Wainright sighed, determined to press on. "I need to examine you, so just keep your eyes shut."

The mound jiggled violently again, and there came a sound like a coarse exhalation that devolved into a sibilant hiss.

Wainright had had enough. "Sorry, Billy, I'm just here to help." He yanked the blankets back.

He sucked in a breath and leapt to his feet. The boy was naked, but from his head to his groin the skin was totally grown over by some sort of hardened growth.

The boy looked up at him with a face that was as horrifying as it was pitiful. Small yellow eyes glared as his mouth opened, showing a line of needle-like teeth that seemed to travel all the way down the gullet and would have been more at home on some deep-sea predatory fish.

Billy mewled and placed hands that has encrusted claws over his face. Wainright swallowed with a dry throat, and steeled himself as he carefully sat again. He lifted a hand and reached out to place it on the boy, but froze – *infection*, his mind screamed.

Wainright drew his hand back, stood once more and leaned forward. He licked his lips. "Ah, Billy, tell me where it hurts."

There came a soft mewling again and then a rasping sound. Wainright leaned closer. "I didn't catch that, Billy."

"*Alllloooverrr.*"

"All over," Wainright repeated. "It hurts *all over* your body?"

"*Yesssss.*"

A knot of anger grew inside his stomach, and he straightened and turned to Mary. "How long has he been like this?'

She shook her head for a moment and he noticed her eyes were wet as she stared at her son. "Days."

Wainright scowled. "He's been in this condition for days? How could you—?"

"He wouldn't let me." The words came in a rush and her eyes slid away from her boy's to his. "It started weeks ago as a course rash. It got worse, then this started growing on him." She bustled in closer. "He wouldn't let me tell anyone. Made me promise."

"I'll need a sample." Wainright reached into his bag for some gloves and found a disposable hypodermic needle. He gently laid a hand on the boy's upper arm, and felt the strange texture beneath his fingertips. It didn't feel like skin at all, more like exposed bone or maybe even something akin to tree bark.

"Just stay still for a moment, Billy." He pressed the needle into the arm, but the point wouldn't penetrate the skin. "Damn." He drew it back, looking at the tip. He'd have to find an area that wasn't calcified.

Wainright looked back at the boy who had pulled the blankets back over himself. He went to peel them back again.

"I haven't quite finish—"

The boy lunged at him.

Wainright yanked his hand out of the way just as the needle-sharp teeth came together where his fingers had just been. "My God." He leapt to his feet, staring.

The boy pulled back beneath the blankets, his small yellow eyes glaring. Wainwright's heart thumped in his chest. The kid looked like some sort of vicious animal retreating into its burrow.

Wainwright swallowed noisily. "I'll, ah, need to do some analysis, Mary. Right now, I have no idea what it could be. I'll consult the medical texts when I get back, and also make a few calls. I still need…" He quickly crouched to grab Billy's bedpan. "… this."

Billy grumbled as he retreated fully into his nest of blankets, and Wainright looked briefly into the bedpan at the small speckled logs. He was confused, bewildered, and a little frightened.

"Mary, do you know if he ate anything, or came into contact with anything strange?"

She seemed to search her mind for a moment, and then looked up. "The mine. All the kids go and swim at the mine. It's the first time it's been flooded in years. Billy said when the water dried on him it made him a little itchy."

Wainright knew the place; the Angel Mine was just outside of town, and though home to a disaster just on twenty-five years ago and all closed up, sometimes the ground water percolated to the surface and created an oasis. It was rare, but it would be irresistible to kids on a hot day.

"Okay." He started for the door and, once outside with Mary, he pulled it shut. He lowered his voice. "We'll need to send him to the hospital. Get professional care from experts, and some decent food into him. We can't have him lying here like this all day."

"But he doesn't," she whispered. "He goes out at night."

"Goes out? Like that?" His head jerked back on his neck. "How? Where?"

She looked up at him, moon-eyed, and slowly shook her head. "I hear the window open... about midnight."

He waited but she just went back to wringing her hands. "Okay. Ah..." He held the bedpan and looked around. "Do you have...?"

"Yes, yes." She bustled away.

Wainright looked down at the boy's bowel movements. They were dry, oval and had white flecks through them. It reminded him of coyote scat.

Mary returned with a cloth that she draped over the pan. It wasn't sealed but he didn't think it'd make a mess as long as he kept it upright.

She then led him to the door and stood to one side watching him. With his medical bag in one hand and the bedpan in the other, he could only nod and give her a benign smile. "Don't worry, Mary, we'll sort this out."

She nodded. "Please..."

He paused.

"Please help us," she whispered.

Wainright sat back for a moment and pondered his next move. There were other children affected. Lots of them. Now it seemed to be some sort of outbreak of... *what*? He had no idea, but after examining Billy's excrement, he found it contained animal bones. Looked like the boy's nighttime foraging was where he was getting most of his meals.

18

His filing cabinet was now near full of cases, and he knew it was time to admit defeat. He pulled out the small, black leather-bound address book he had in his top drawer that all physicians possessed. Emergency numbers for everything from fires and flooding to nuclear bomb fallout. It also had the number for the Communicable Disease Center (CDC) that had been around since the mid '40s, and one he never thought he'd ever have to call.

He circled the number and lifted the phone. This was out of his hands now.

Wainright was there when the vans arrived – dozens of them – all black. He felt like some sort of informer, identifying the families, where they were, and then assisted in allaying their fears when they were rounded up for detailed medical treatment at a facility in the big city.

Most went willingly, some fearfully, but all hoping for answers, a cure, or perhaps just an end to the horrifying ailment afflicting their children.

Not all the kids were found. Some were assumed to have gone feral and simply melted away into the countryside. Or worse. Rumor was they all disappeared into the depths of the Angel mine.

Long after the vans had gone, Wainright headed out to the mine and saw that a line of cyclone fencing had been erected with multiple warning signs. The waterhole the flooded mine had created had drained away again, perhaps back to the subterranean lake where it originated.

He stood in the sunshine for some time, the heat of the noonday sun stinging his neck. He imagined the whoops of delight from kids leaping into the water – boys and girls, freckle-faced, sunburned cheeks and bronzed shoulders.

They were all gone now, contaminated, and those found were herded away in the night – all on his say-so. He felt sick in the heart as he headed back to his car.

CHAPTER 04

Eldon, Missouri – today

Saturday morning and Doctor Mike Taylor had time on his hands and decided to wander into town. It was his first weekend and he was excited. Everything was new and interesting, and he loved exploring.

Mike looked up and down the main street deciding on his exploration plan. He'd go down one side and come back up the other, doing a bit of window shopping, and maybe introduce himself to a few of the shopkeepers.

Opposite the council chambers was the Eldon Museum. It certainly wouldn't hurt to bone up a little more on his newly-adopted home's history.

Mike finished his coffee then began his walk. At the single-story barn-like building with the glass double doors, he cupped hands to each side of his face to peer inside. It had just gone 10am, and though there was no 'Sorry we're closed' sign hanging on the door, he didn't know if they even opened on Saturdays.

There was a flicker of movement inside and he grabbed the large brass doorknob and turned it. The door opened smoothly and he pushed into a smell of mustiness and dry air-conditioning.

"Hello-*ooo*." The musical greeting made him smile and a woman bustled toward him with hands clasped in front of her.

She pointed. "It *is* you." She beamed. "You're our new doctor."

Mike raised his eyebrows. "My notoriety precedes me."

She laughed softly. "You had a write up in the *Eldon Gazette* just a week back. You look just like your picture." She held out a hand. "It's nice to meet you, Doctor Taylor."

"Nice to meet you too and please call me Mike, Ms...?" He returned the smile.

"Alston, Samantha Alston. And thank you. I'll call you Mike out here, and Doctor when I'm visiting. Okay?"

"Works for me." Mike grinned back.

She leaned a little closer. "I'm also president of the Ladies Bridge Players Club."

He nodded, trying to appear impressed. "Nice."

"So, you've come to take in some of our history?"

"Sure have."

"Then let me take you on a personal tour." She rubbed her hands together and turned.

The museum wasn't large; maybe in the past it had been a house, but now its one floor had been partitioned into open display rooms for each of the period themes.

She pointed out certain relics, pictures or artifacts, and gave him a brief overview of each. Samantha was pleasant, knowledgeable, and quite entertaining. Mike was enjoying himself.

She paced as she kept up her stream of information about when Missouri was first settled, the state's oldest town, founded by French Canadian colonists in 1735. Then she stopped and gave a tiny shrug. "But our little town of Eldon never made an appearance until 1882 and is a relative newcomer to the landscape. It's said that it was the old stories apparently that stopped a lot of people from settling here."

"Stories?" Mike asked.

"Yes," she declared, then frowned a little. "Well, maybe *legends* is a better word. In those days, superstitions and belief made a huge difference."

"What sort of legends?" Mike asked, intrigued.

"Well, though Eldon is a young town, and Missouri is only just on four hundred years old, its history is far, far older." She half turned. "Well beyond our history."

Samantha led him into the back of the museum, and switched on some lights. "There were seven ancient tribes in the area of what is now called Missouri: The Chickasaw tribe, the Illini, Ioway, Missouria, the Osage, Otoe, and the Quapaw tribe."

She stopped before a large case that held what looked like several statues. "And these are some of the mysteries of the area. The history of the Black River area goes back to the Paleo-Indians, the ancient peoples of the Americas who were present at the end of the last ice age. They camped and hunted along the Ozark Rivers, perhaps as long as fourteen thousand years ago."

"Wow, that *is* old. I never knew." Mike blew air between his lips. "And they made these?"

"We believe so, but we don't exactly know how. Or even where the unique material came from." She briefly turned to him. "It's petrified wood, you know. But from no tree anyone can identify." She peered in at the statues. "It's been dated to around 10,000 BC... twelve thousand years old."

Mike stared. The statues were intertwined with roots and slightly eroded now, but the detail was still unbelievable. There were several men, women, and even a child. Their fingers, and even hair could be picked out. But it was their faces that pinned Mike's attention – they wore ghastly expressions of horror.

He recognized them. "You know, I think I've seen something like these before. Down near the old Angel mine. There looked to be very weather-beaten versions of these out front at the mine's mouth."

She tilted her head. "Why would you go there?"

"Um, well..." He gave her a lopsided grin. "I was just exploring."

"I don't think it's safe. I've never been out there... and never will," she added. "Might be similar, but I doubt it. Probably just some weird geology or a sand-blasted old tree stump produced by some of our harsh summer gusts."

"Yeah maybe." Mike looked back at the agonized faces. "Not exactly uplifting images."

"No, not at all," she said with a shake of her head. "And the conundrum is that the first American Native Indians who lived around these parts led a Stone Age lifestyle, meaning they only had stone tools and weapons. So it's still a mystery how they even worked the petrified wood, or what they were meant to represent with their visages of pain and terror. The one thing all the tribes had in common was the name of a powerful god: *'Adotte Sakima'* – the tree king."

"*Adotte Sakima.*" He tested the words as he continued to stare, and the more he did the more unsettled he became. There were small physical perfections like scars and blemishes that were beyond anything he'd seen before, and especially from an artist that created them so long ago.

One of the men had a slightly balding pate, the woman had a small adornment through her earlobe, and the child held something in its tiny curled hand that could have been a toy.

"What could generate such fear?"

He hadn't seen that level of sculpting complexity even on statues from the ancient Romans, and perhaps only from sculpting masters like Michelangelo.

"Men only fear God and the Devil," he whispered, then turned to Samantha. "Where were they discovered?"

"Deep below the ground in some limestone caverns just after the town was settled. We can only assume the early peoples must have taken them down there."

CHAPTER 05

The send-off for Old Ben Wainright was an afternoon cookout at Mayor Keith Melnick's large house that sat just out of town. Mike was looking forward to the formal goodbye for Ben, but his main interest was talking to Karen again.

He stepped out of the shower, toweled himself down, and then used his fingers to brush his hair – he still looked passable.

Mike worked out and was in good shape but the shrapnel wounds to his chest and shoulder – purple circles and strokes and some surrounded with reddish flesh – still ached when he worked out. As a physician he knew what that meant; he'd pay for it when he was older. But that was something he'd worry about another day.

Thirty minutes later he was pulling into the driveway of Melnick's house set on a huge expanse of very manicured lawn. Fruit trees lined the fence, creating a never-ending bounty that glowed red, orange, and purple in the warm sunshine.

There was a good crowd already, and fronting up he spotted the town attorney, Ralph Gillespie, chatting to Karen who stood beside a boy that looked remarkably like her, so it was safe to assume it was her son.

Melnick spotted him and waved. Though he felt like a bit of a small fish amongst the town heavyweights, he guessed as he was their soon-to-be doctor, he'd end up knowing all their secrets soon enough.

"Michael, glad you could make it." Melnick toasted him with an ice cool looking highball style drink and grabbed his arm. "Got some people for you to meet. Settling in? Found everything you need? How do you like Eldon so far?"

Mike grinned, knowing all the questions probably weren't expected to be answered. Just the obvious ones.

"I love it here. I'd say it's just like home, except this is better."

Melnick was satisfied with his answer and grabbed his forearm and steered him towards a group of older people as he motioned for a waiter to bring him a drink.

"They're mai tais." He winked. "My own recipe. Got a bit of a kick to them."

Karen caught his eye and he waved. She made a show of waving back and nodding, and she obviously used it as an excuse to extricate herself from Gillespie and headed towards his group, dragging her son with her.

Ralph Gillespie tagged behind, but the look he gave Mike said he didn't like the intrusion.

"Mike, meet Benji. Benji, meet Mike," Karen said, looking from her son to Mike. "Mike is our new doctor."

Benji stuck out a small hand and grinned. "Please to meet you, sir."

Mike gripped the small hand. "Likewise. And its just Mike to my friends."

The boy smiled and continued to study him for a few more moments before half-turning to his mother. "He looks like Batman doesn't he, Mom?"

Mike chuckled at Karen who now also scrutinized him. People had often said he reminded them of a young Ben Affleck... except with a few scars. He could certainly live with that.

He leaned closer to Benji and put a finger to his lips. "That's because I am Batman. So don't tell anyone."

"Great, we now have a doctor who's a superhero." Karen grinned as Mike took another sip of his mai tai and grimaced.

"*Yech.*" He stuck his tongue out, much to Benji's amusement.

Mike was enjoying himself and found Karen to be interesting and charming. He hoped she felt the same. But Mayor Melnick soon muscled in amongst them.

"Okay, Mike, what have you done with him?" Melnick smiled good-naturedly, but it was clear that this entire expensive event was for Wainright, so the guest of honor better front up. And because Mike was the guy taking over the practice, Ben had somehow become his responsibility.

"Anyone called him yet?" Mike asked.

"I'll do it now." Melnick pulled out a paper-thin phone and examined his contacts before letting it dial. He waited, and then his brows drew together. "That's odd." He looked up. "It says the number is no longer in service." He frowned. "He's still in town, right?"

"Sure is, I just met with him yesterday," Mike replied. "I haven't seen him since then, but he didn't say he was leaving. Well, not immediately."

Shelly, his receptionist barged in, having overheard. "He should be here. He's very punctual."

"Well, even if you've left town, you don't cancel your mobile phone." Ralph Gillespie had joined them, and a small crowd was now gathering.

"He should be here." Shelly folded her arms.

"Do you think he's all right?" Karen asked.

Mike felt in his pocket. "I've still got his spare house keys. I can take a quick run out there."

"I'll come," Shelly piped up. "Maybe he just has car trouble, and now that his phone isn't working, he can't tell us."

"That must be it," Melnick agreed. "Mike, go get him."

"On it." Mike strode to his car, and though the party continued, it had formed into clumps of whispering guests.

Mike cracked the window to let in some fresh air and relief from the clouds of Shelly's perfume. He glanced at his receptionist. "Had Ben, Doctor Wainright, been feeling okay before he retired? Acting normally?"

She hiked her shoulders. "He didn't talk that much to me in the office. But he was always polite, just a little sad, distant sort of."

Mike came off Newton Street, and turned into Mills street.

"There it is," said Shelly, pointing. "Number twenty-one; that's Doctor Wainright's place." She craned forward. "Ooh, and he's burning rubbish at this time of year – very naughty."

They pulled in at the column of smoke. It was a well-kept cottage with a slatted fence, vines growing through it, and a rusted post box just peeking over the top.

Mike was first out of the car, and he immediately smelled the chemical stink of plastics burning. "I don't think he's burning leaves." He walked briskly up the path and then bounded up the few steps to the landing and pressed the bell.

"Just open it." Shelly came up quickly behind him.

Mike turned. "Just give him a second." He waited.

Shelly peered in through a window. "Nothing moving inside." She came back and stood on the other side of the doorframe. "Come on, he might have fallen down. He's old, remember?"

"Yeah, okay." Mike sorted through the keys choosing one that looked like a front door key. He stuck it in the lock, and it turned first go. He pushed the door open and peered around inside. "Hello Ben?"

Mike concentrated, yet there was nothing but the heavy *ticktock* of a large clock somewhere further in.

"*Doctor Wainright.*" Shelly's raised voice flooded the cottage, but after a few seconds there was still nothing but the clock. "Come on," she said and led Mike in.

She quickly went from the living room to his bedroom, opened a closet door and found it empty. Same for the drawers as all the clothing and personal items were gone.

"Strange; looks like he's all packed up." She turned slowly. "Try the kitchen and washroom," Shelly said, obviously speaking to herself, as she sped out of the bedroom.

"Slow down." Mike tried to keep up.

The house looked like it had been vacated and even the refrigerator was empty.

"What's he been living on?" Shelly pursed her lips and stood with hands on her hips for a moment. She then quickly crossed to the window over the sink and peered out into the backyard.

"There's his bonfire, and also the only place left to look – the shed." She pulled open the backdoor and stepped down the few steps and marched across the fifty-feet of grass to the shed.

Mike followed and saw that the rubbish pile that was still smoldering and giving off toxic chemical gasses had the remains of jackets, pants and even leather shoes. There was also a laptop computer, and something that could have been a melted mobile phone.

And there was another set of keys. Mike crossed to the smoldering pile and carefully reached in to grab them. "Ouch." They were still hot.

"Hurry up," Shelly hissed over her shoulder.

"Something is very wrong here," Mike said as he caught up.

Shelly grabbed the large door handle and turned to him. "Maybe he already left." She tugged open the peeling paint door that skidded on the ground. Now wider, it allowed the single room to be flooded with light.

Shelly gasped, eyes bulging. Mike looked in over her shoulder, and even though he had seen horrific things as a military medic, this took him by surprise.

Ben Wainright was hanging by the neck; face black and tongue protruding like a fat, dark slug from between his lips. A small stool was overturned below him along with a small pool of fluid, undoubtedly urine.

"Ah, shit. Stay there." Mike rushed inside to grab the body. Immediately, he felt the cold and stiffness of rigor mortis in the cadaver and he let it go for a moment where it now swung, making the rope stretch and squeak.

Shelly hadn't moved but finally managed to close her mouth. "He... hanged himself? Why did he hang himself?"

Mike righted the stool and was about to step up, but then thought that it was a good question. Though the probability was he *did* commit suicide, in the event it was something else, he should avoid disturbing the body.

He backed up, bumping into Shelly. "I don't know, but we better not touch anything. Let's call the sheriff." Mike grabbed her arm and led her out of the shed, but she kept looking back over her shoulder as if expecting Wainright to jump out at them.

Mike sighed, and knew he'd need to make calls to the sheriff, mayor, Karen, and all this while they're back their sipping on mai tais and waiting for their guest of honor, who was now rudely swinging from a damn noose.

Sherriff Kehoe was on his way, and the mayor would have to break it to the party that their beloved Doctor Ben Wainright wouldn't be making it. Ever.

"Shelly, as the resident medical professional that has to act as both physician and coroner, I have to hang out here for a while. But you don't. Do you want me to drop you somewhere? I doubt the party will be continuing now."

She looked back towards the house and slowly shook her head. "I want to know why he killed himself." She folded her arms. "I'll wait... with you."

It was barely ten minutes more before Sherriff Kehoe arrived. The man was alone and as he exited his car, his face was grave.

"Show me," was all he said.

CHAPTER 06

Eldon, Oakland County, Missouri – 2 weeks later
The ground began to shake.

Mike had just come into the practice and was right in front of Shelly's desk when he stopped to hold his arms wide a little like a tightrope walker.

"Whoa." He looked up, newspaper in one hand and coffee in the other. "What was that?"

She smiled and shrugged. "Probably a little 'quake. We get 'em now and then. I heard they come from down deep and are due to some big old caverns collapsing, and not when the planes or plates or something moves. Nothing really to worry about."

"Tectonic plates," Mike added. "And you mean the mines?"

She wrinkled her nose and shook her head. "No, I think I remember it was more like the big sinkhole type ones deep down. Eldon sits on ground that's a little like honeycomb. The deep limestone melts away leaving big holes."

Mike raised his eyebrows. "Good for spelunking."

"What?" She grinned. "Spunking?"

"*Spel-un-king* – caving," he said on his way to the office.

"Oh, that." Her mouth turned down. "I'd hate that 'cause I hate dark places."

"Yeah, not really on my bucket list either." He lifted his chin. "Appointments?"

"Yep," she read from the schedule on her screen. "Mrs Abernathy at nine, John Jamison at nine-thirty, and Mrs Oswald is bringing in her son at eleven."

"Good." He meant it. He needed work as a distraction following Ben's suicide.

As coroner, he'd checked the man over, and it was straight-forward strangulation. Jumping from a stool doesn't break the neck, so death doesn't come quickly; instead it's just a slow choking. Without his hands tied behind his back, it takes will power to go through with it. Ben must have really been determined to check out.

"How you doing? About Ben I mean," he asked Shelly.

She bobbed her head from side to side for a moment. "A bit bummed. But okay. And you?"

"Yeah, yeah, just... confused by it all."

When Mike had first come into the practice following the suicide, he'd found a stack of letters addressed to many of them – himself, the mayor, Karen, Ralph and most of the other councilors and town elders. They all contained just two words: *forgive me.*

Forgive him for what? His suicide? Maybe. Or was there something else? Some other thing he had been carrying around; some industrial-grade guilt that finally overhwlemed him.

Mike turned in his chair to look at the large antique and formidable wooden filing cabinet in the corner, and sat staring at it for several moments. It was the only thing he hadn't got around to investigating.

He crossed to it and ran his hand over the exterior – oak probably and he bet it weighed two hundred pounds and maybe another hundred fully loaded. He pushed it a little and it didn't budge even a fraction.

Mike pulled at the top drawer and that also didn't shift. "Yep." He stuck his finger in one of the brass keyholes in the drawer face. He knew it'd take a large old-style Mortise-type key with the rounded barrel. And he'd just found one in the top drawer in his desk. He snatched them up, and knew before he even tried that it was going to be the right one.

It was time to find out what secrets Ben was trying to hide.

CHAPTER 07

Eldon Sparkling Mineral Water Company, Eldon.
"Boss, Well-24 has just gone dry. And 25, 26, and 27 are running dirty so we shut em down." The engineer looked up from his clipboard. "The quake."

"Shit-damn; knew it." Harry Reith was the owner and president of the company, and there was one thing he hated about working in an area riddled with limestone, it damn well moved, and when it did, it sometimes swallowed their water.

It could drain away, be cut off, or silted up for years and rendered unusable as it clogged the pumping machines. Though they did significant testing to ensure no contaminants got into the water, like heavy metals, silicates, or composite toxins, the upside of their wells being so deep, was there was little chance of water-borne bugs in it.

"What about the new well? Site-30?" Reith asked.

The engineer scoffed quietly. "Funny thing that. When the geologists first identified Site-30, it looked to only have a few hundred mega-liters of water. But after that little shimmy we just had, they tell me that it now stands at several gigaliters."

"So, that's where all our water went." Reith shrugged. "So, tap it."

"Might be a little dirty." The engineer tilted his head.

"You already tested it, right?" Reith asked.

"Yeah, when we first found it, but…"

"You know what we sell, other than water?" Reith half smiled, and didn't wait for his engineer to respond. "That's right, nothing. So pump it up, scrub it, and let's go. We got orders to fill."

The engineer snapped the note board shut. "On it, chief."

CHAPTER 08

Benji's pushbike was raising dust as he just kept pace with his pals. The day was hot, and the four boys and two girls peddled like demons.

Out front were James and Kenny, followed by Isabella, him, and lagging behind was Gemma and finally big Alf, puffing hard as his stomach bounced as he navigated the small bumps and pits in the old roadway.

It was a brutally hot day, and the small group headed out to the old limestone mine to investigate the stories that had intrigued them following the quake. If true, their summers were about to get a whole lot more fun.

"Here." James swerved off the road and onto the disused track. The kids all skidded, peddled on, and stood in their seats to pick up their pace again.

It took another twenty minutes to get to the first fence whose lock had long since corroded. They headed in, carefully threading their way around old machinery, disused railings and rusting jerry carts.

They'd all been out here many times in the past and it was dry as chalk dust, and just as uninteresting. There had been a few gnarled stumps of weird looking rock trees, and dust covering everything. They'd tried to venture into the mine once, but after only a few dozen feet they gave up as the darkness had scared the shit out of them.

But when the small group arrived at their destination and stopped in a line, their mouths dropped open and then curved into grins.

"It's like one of those places in the desert... you know," Alf wheezed.

"An oasis," Benji provided, letting his eyes move slowly over the landscape.

The once dry and scrabby ground out front of the mouth of the mine was set in a shallow depression a few hundred feet across and just two to three deep. Dry, cough-inducing and boring. But not now.

Now the depression was filled with a huge pool of sparkling water. It had a slight greenish tinge, but it was so inviting, it screamed at you to *come on in*.

The quake had only happened a few days ago, but amazingly, the surrounding plants had improved. The twisted trees didn't have leaves, but their bark was ribbed, glossy and more, muscular looking. There were also patches of thick grass that had sprung up and even small fern fronds touched on the edge of the water.

Benji smiled. "Oasis." And that's exactly what it was.

James got off his bike and let it fall with a clatter. He started to pull off his shirt. "I'm in there."

"Wait, what?" Isabella pointed to the rusting sign with barely legible writing. "You saw that contamination sign, right?"

"No, yeah, whatever. That was a hundred years ago or sumthin." James' narrow chest was now bared to the sunshine and he began to undo his jeans. "C'mon... everyone, *c'mon*."

James, Kenny, Gemma and Alf, walked carefully across the scrabble, until they made it to a grass verge. James turned back to where Isabella and Benji still sat astride their bikes.

"Chickens." He tucked his fists under his arms and flapped stunted wings for a second or two, before turning back to the magnificent water, finding a deep spot and leaping in.

Harry Reith was down in the Eldon Spring Water testing facilities and his scientists looked concerned. And if they looked concerned then he was concerned.

"Looks a little green." He held the glass of water up to eyeball it for a moment before sniffing the top. "And there's an odour. What is it?" he asked his lead guy, Pete Coughlin.

Coughlin took the glass from him. "Zero bacterial count, normal mineral count, and been run through various filters leaving nothing toxic behind." He sniffed the glass as well. "It just seems to be some sort of residue. Might be organic, but probably safe though."

Reith exhaled through his nose and raised an eyebrow at his technician. "Let me be frank; it stinks like shit. I wouldn't drink it." He looked up. "And this is from the new well, Site-30, right?"

"Yep. Maybe the tremor stirred it up a little." Coughlin shrugged.

"A little? It's fucking soup," Reith scoffed. "Doesn't look like mountain spring water to me and more like something you'd get from draining a fish farm."

"We could put it through micron filters or use evaporation methodology to take out any of the microscopics, but that's time consuming and expensive. It'll cost you more than what you can sell the water for. For now, that's as good as it gets." Coughlin stuck both hands in his coat pockets.

"Shee-it." Reith exhaled through clenched teeth. Looks like he had three choices: dirty water, overpriced clean water, or no water. He sighed. "We'll need to find another goddamn well. We'll miss our delivery dates."

Coughlin began to grin.

Reith scowled. "Okay smartass, what?"

"Well, I was just thinking that seeing it's safe to drink, so for all we know the unknown residue might be good for you." He shrugged. "It's just a little stain and a little smell. So what? We can mask the odor with a few drops of lemon flavoring. Then we sell it as a mineral health drink."

Reith's brows slowly began to rise. "But no artificial stuff, right? Pure health tonic."

Coughlin nodded. "Of course. We use citral; comes straight from lemon oil extracted from the peel. Natural as your granny used to make."

Reith rubbed his chin for a moment, his vision turned inward. "And you're sure it's safe?"

"I'm betting as safe as any of our products. And as safe as our testing can assure us."

Reith thought about the implications, and then the opportunities. He spun back. "Brilliant. Make it happen." He headed for the door. "I'll be up in marketing getting the guys to knock up some labeling." He turned as he got to the exit. "If this sells, I'll give you a bonus that'll put a smile on your face bigger than Texas."

"Thank you, sir." Coughlin gave a small bow, and then turned to clap his hands. "All right people, we've got some work to do."

CHAPTER 09

Mike sat staring at the pile of brown, nondescript folders on his desk labeled with nothing but dates and sometimes numbers.

Inside there were notes; pages and pages of the small, tight writing style of Ben Wainright. Some had Polaroid photographs, and they dated from early 1977.

Many were headed: *Angel Mine Syndrome* with a case number, and Mike tried to get his head around the story they told, especially considering the man had said there were only a few minor instances of infection and skin irritation.

But the reality was back in '77, there was some sort of horrifying outbreak that primarily afflicted the children. Over twenty boys and girls fell ill to a horrifying condition that drove gross deformities in the skin, muscle, and skeletal structures and also seemed to affect their thinking, making them exhibit psychotic behavior. The children were incongruously labeled: *angel children,* or just, *angels.*

The first case was of Billy Allson who didn't live that far from where Mike lived now. His mother, Mary, had brought him in with a rash on his lower back. In a few days it had progressed to significant crusty extrusions that coated most of his body and much of his face.

There was a shadowed and grainy photograph that showed a small figure in bed. Mike squinted and was sure the eyes were yellow – not like jaundice yellow, but almost a glowing, nocturnal stare.

"Je-zuz," he whispered.

Pictures of the other afflicted children were impossible to comprehend. Maybe because of the poor camera equipment used, but as far as Mike could make out many didn't look like children at all but instead some sort of creatures assembled from bony plates and tree bark. And some were worse.

There was nothing Mike knew of any time or anywhere that could do that to people. Even severe mutagens that scrambled DNA and cell structure acted slowly, and usually ended with the body simply corrupting with cancerous cells, and not looking like it was trying to remake itself into… into something else.

Wainright had been understandably overwhelmed and had called in the authorities. The CDC arrived first, and then some other government types that Wainright noted he never discovered who they really were.

The children, all of them, had been evacuated. From what Mike read and understood from the notes, none of them ever returned. Not them. Not their families.

Wainright blamed himself for informing on them, but what else was he supposed to do? He had no chance of curing or even diagnosing what was happening to them.

Mike had so many questions, but the only person who could have answered them had just taken his life.

He felt sorry for old Ben Wainright, keeping this to himself all these years. Mike knew guilt, and it was a burden that weighed heavily on a person, sometimes, crushingly.

CHAPTER 10

Eldon, the Adam's residence

"I've got a headache... and a sore throat." Ten-year-old James Adams grimaced as he demonstrated swallowing for his mom.

Joanne lifted the small flashlight again. "Say *ahh*." He did so and she peered in. "It's very red in there." She gently laid a hand on his forehead.

"Ow." He winced.

She pulled her hand away. "That hurts?"

He nodded and swallowed again. This time she actually heard it make a dry clicking sound in his throat.

"Does your head hurt on the inside or outside?" her brows knitted together.

"Both."

She shone the light in her son's eyes, and he screwed them shut. His forehead hadn't felt hot to the touch, but she did see some odd bumps and marks appearing like the beginning of a pebbly rash. "Okay, no school and I'll make an appointment to see the doctor."

"*Yes.*" He settled back into his soft pillow. James frowned as he reached up to trail his fingers over the top of his head.

"Lumpy."

His fingers came away covered in hair.

CHAPTER 11

Harry Reith held up the bottle of mineral water. The label showed the Eldon brand and also had the words '*super health tonic'* in green calligraphy blazed across images of a crystal clear lake, waterfall, and trees with colorful birds. The bottle's glass was also green to hide the pale green tinge of the liquid, but as they had called it a health tonic, it didn't really matter.

"Looks good." He turned to nod to the assembled marketing, sales and technical teams. "I'd buy it."

He twisted the top, and heard the hiss of escaping gas. He sniffed, and then shrugged. "This is where the rubber hits the road." He lifted it to his lips and sipped. And then sipped again, longer this time.

He lowered the bottle and grinned. "This is good. Just a hint of lemon that combines with whatever shit was in there to give it quite a unique flavor." He chugged down some more. "We might be on a winner here."

Reith took a few steps towards the window that looked out over the carpark as his mind worked. He spun back. "Okay, let's go with it, full scale. I want full production, ten thousad units per day to start. We'll do a sample population test right here in Eldon, and if it works, we'll move it out to all the regular big buyers."

"You got it, boss."

"And get to work on some slick ads we can run nationwide. This could be the next big thing – and we don't even need to add caffeine or sugar – it'll be the healthiest drink on the market."

He tipped the bottle up and drained it. "This is damned good. Well done everyone." He headed for the door but paused. "I want it in everyone's icebox by week's end."

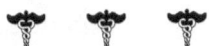

Just before dawn, the morning deliveries were being made to the many cafes, restaurants, convenience and corner stores. In amongst their usual deliveries of milk, soda, and alcoholic drinks, was a crate of brilliant green bottles.

On the side of the crate were the words *'Eldon Spring Water – super health tonic'*. The samples were free to the retail outlets, and before noon all had been sold on to the public, or tasted by the shop owners.

The new spring water was a hit.

CHAPTER 12

Marshal Simmons wiped his hands on a rag and jammed it into the back pocket of his blue coveralls. The sun was down now, the last of his mechanics had gone home and he was getting ready to shut up shop.

There were a few vehicles waiting for some minor work, but business was getting tough. The new cars these days were basically computers on wheels. They hardly ever broke down, and you didn't put your head under the hood to see what was going wrong, you simply plugged them into some other computer thingy and let it run a *diag-nos-tic* over the entire system, from its air-conditioning to the transmission. It then told you what work it needed.

He sighed, there wasn't enough in the kitty to afford one of those things, and so for now, he relied on the old timers like himself to bring in their aging autos.

Marshal didn't have any kids to leave the garage to, so when he retired or died, the garage would die with him. *That's progress*, he thought glumly.

The smash of glass from the rear of his workshop dragged his head around.

"Who's there?" He stared into the darkness.

The sound wasn't repeated, but a sixth sense told him he wasn't alone anymore. Marshal padded softly to a workbench and grabbed up a long silver wrench, and then walked between two cars and towards the dark rear of the shop. He immediately regretted not flicking the overhead lights back on, but that'd mean backtracking now.

There came a skittering sound, and he wondered whether there were raccoons in the building. If one of his mechanics had been leaving food in the bins, he'd skin 'em alive.

"Garn, *git!*" he yelled.

The workshop remained silent.

Marshal had two options: he could flick on the lights and spend hours doing a search of the workshop for some critter making mischief in here. Or, he could leave it until tomorrow morning when the sun was up. Easy decision.

"See you tomorrow." He tossed the wrench onto a bench top and turned away.

The thing that landed on his back was damn heavy, and hard, and felt like it was made of rock as its fingers or claws dug into the meat of his neck while hissing like a boiling kettle.

"Get offa me," he yelled while waving his hands over his head.

His flailing left hand got bit, crunching bone and making blood spurt. Marshal wailed as the thing then started to drag him, its claws digging deep into his flesh like daggers.

He skidded across the floor and managed to catch sight of himself in the glass doors – it didn't help – the thing that had hold of him was basically human shaped, but it moved weirdly like an insect, and had skin that was all horny and rough.

"*Help!*"

And it was enormously powerful, dragging him as if he weighed nothing. It leapt up onto a bench and went straight out through a broken window, taking Marshal with it.

"*He-eeelp!*" he yelled again. But no one came. No one heard.

My garage is dead now, he thought, as he was quickly drawn into the darkness of the woods.

CHAPTER 13

The days rolled on and soon became weeks. Mike had treated Karen for an ingrown toenail, and though he was busting to ask her out, knew that it wasn't good form to ask out patients, especially while treating them.

Luckily, Karen asked him over for dinner with her and Benji.

He smiled as he put his tie on – he had no idea of whether he would be overdressed or not, but he could always take it off.

He continued knotting, unknotting, adjusting, and then reknotting his tie as he listened to the radio. The local news was informing them that the search was continuing for the missing families. It seemed small groups of people were vanishing or leaving, and oddly, not telling anyone they were going. Not even relatives.

The next report was on the livestock attacks in the outer areas of town, and given there were grey wolves in Missouri, they were being looked at as the culprits.

Mike checked himself one last time in the mirror – still looking good, though a little tired around the eyes. Maybe he'd look better if Karen's lighting was a little dim. He snatched up the bottle of red wine and headed for the door.

Karen and Benji lived the other side of town, but given Eldon central only covered a few square miles, he'd still be there in under ten minutes.

Saturday evening was warm and dry, and the streets had a few people wandering to the cafes, restaurants, and probably the only cinema in town. Turning off the main strip, he wended his way to the northern outskirts and quickly found Karen 's neat little two-story cottage.

He pulled up out front and saw that her Jacarandas were in bloom. The South American trees had lilac flowers that when they began to fall created a carpet of soft blue in her garden. In through the windows he could see the golden glow of candles making it warm and inviting.

As he stepped out, Mike sucked in a deep breath, feeling the tingle of butterflies going mad in his belly.

Come on, buddy, you're thirty-six, not sixteen.

He walked up the steps, stood outside for a moment to smooth his hair, and then reached towards the bell just as the door was pulled inwards.

Benji was grinning, his hair slicked down, and his probably bestest ever clothes on. He turned and in his earsplitting outside-voice, yelled: "Mo-*ooom*, Batman is here." He turned, grinning even wider.

"*Coming.*" Karen's voice floated down from upstairs.

Mike waited. "Is there a password?"

Benji nodded.

"Gotham." Mike lifted an eyebrow.

Benji stood aside. "That was it."

Mike stepped inside and the boy shut the door. "This way."

He led Mike into their living room that was lit with candles, and he looked up at Mike and then rolled his eyes. "We have lights and don't always use candles. But Mom wanted to do it tonight. Do you like candles?

"I do. Reminds me of a birthday party," Mike observed.

Benji looked around, nodding. "Yeah, it does sorta." He turned back. "She spent all day cleaning."

Mike chuckled. "Best leave some secrets."

He looked up at Mike, surprised. "It's no secret." He waved an arm around. "Look how clean it is."

"Halooo." Karen breezed in wearing a tight cotton dress, hair immaculate, and all finished with old sandshoes.

"You look magnificent," he said, meaning it as his heart leapt in his chest.

She lifted a foot. "The ultimate in sensible shoes."

"On you it looks good." He chuckled. "And the toe?"

"Much better." She dropped her foot. "But I desperately wanted to wear nice shoes, and tried some on – painfully bad move."

He nodded. "Give it another few days."

"That's the plan." She spotted his wine and held out her hand. "For us?"

He handed it over. "Yeah, it's red, is that okay?"

She looked at the label. "Very nice." She turned. "Benji, grab us the two wine glasses from the table."

He scampered off and came back with two enormous glasses. She took one, and Mike the other, and then she opened the wine and poured them both a good splash. She held out her glass. "Thank you for coming."

He clinked her glass. "My absolute pleasure."

She pointed at the couch. "Sit down while I finish up in the kitchen. Benji, keep our guest entertained." She vanished down the hallway still holding the wine bottle and glass.

Mike sat, sipped, and put his glass down. He saw the boy sipped something red as well. "What's your poison, buddy?"

Benji grinned and held it up. "Blackcurrant juice. Mom doesn't let me drink soda, as she says this has more vitamin C and doesn't make your teeth fall out." He hiked slim shoulders. "It's okay."

"It certainly is." Mike made small talk with Benji about school, his friends, favorite holidays, and anything else he could think of. In turn Benji wanted to know about the grossest things he had ever seen as a doctor.

In another moment, the aroma of chicken filled the air and Karen called them to the table.

"I warn you, cooking is not my forte," she said with a crooked smile.

He looked at the table and the huge pot in the centre, still bubbling with something red and hearty inside. Small crusty rolls were on each of their plates and the silverware was laid out.

"Chicken and bacon pasta, with spinach and tomatoes."

It smelled as good as it looked. "Fantastic." Mike inhaled again, feeling his stomach rumble.

"Is it your favorite?" Mike turned to Benji.

"I don't know; I've never had it before." His eyes travelled over the pot. "Smells good though."

Karen laughed softly. "Yeah, okay, cats out of the bag; we're road testing it tonight."

The meal was good, and Mike was delighted to only end up with a few spots of tomato on his tie. Dessert was hazelnut chocolate pie and ice cream, which was even more to Benji's liking.

In between mouthfuls, he kept up his conversation. "Mom, Mike was telling me about the grossest things he's seen as a doctor."

"Probably not great dinner table conversation," Karen replied.

Benji was undaunted. "Tell her about the old man with the giant wart on his nose." He looked from Mike to Karen. "It was as *big* as his nose."

"Gross, no thank you." Karen sighed.

"Comes with the territory, I guess," Mike said. "At least it wasn't as bad as the stuff that came out of the Angel mine."

"What?" Benji frowned.

Mike nodded. "Finally got to read old Ben Wainright's notes. About fifty years ago, seems there was some sort of contamination outbreak that came from kids swimming in the flooded mine."

"They got sick?" Benji's eyes were wide.

"Yeah, real sick," Mike said. "Not good. He kept the details in a locked filing cabinet. It was really horrible."

"Just from *swimming* in it?" Benji's voice had risen.

The boy looked pale and Mike started to regret bringing it up.

She stared for a moment. "I never knew. I guess it's a good thing that it's dry now. And has been for decades."

Benji put his spoon down. "No... it isn't."

Mike took a drive out to the mine site first thing next day with Karen. Benji had twisted his mother's arm to tag along. He retraced his steps to get to the main shaft area, and was soon stopped in his tracks.

"Holy crap," Mike said. "Oasis is right."

"Told ya," Benji extolled. He then marched up to the large green-tinged pond. "It's even bigger now. And there's more trees."

"Don't get too close," Karen warned. She sniffed; frowned. "Smells like a beach at low tide."

Mike agreed. "Could be some methane gas that was in with the limestone, I guess. Looks pretty clear though. But that's exactly what Ben..." he stopped, remembering what else Wainright had included in his notes. "Let's take a look."

He walked closer to the pond edge and fished in his pocket for the small plastic sample jar he had brought with him. He crouched, unscrewed the lid and dipped it in half filling it.

Mike held it up towards the sun and then shook it. "No particular matter, except for a slight green color. But could be chemical residue, plant material, maybe even bacterial, fungal, or even viral." He sniffed it. "Yep, something unpleasant though." He screwed the cap on.

"My friends swam in it. But I didn't. Neither did Isabella," Benji said in a solemn voice.

"Good," Mike said and turned. "Who *did* go in?"

"James went in first, then Kenny, Gemma, and also fat Alf."

"Don't call him fat." Karen frowned. "He's just well fed."

"No wonder you're in politics." Mike winked up at her, and then turned back to the pool and scanned the ground at its edges. "So, four kids, huh? Lot of footprints for just four of them. When did you say you went in?"

Benji stepped closer and rested a hand on Mike's shoulder as he looked around. "Last Sunday, when it was hot. Maybe they came back or it was some other kids. Everyone knows the pond is full again now."

"Well that's just great," Mike muttered.

"We need to warn people. Get the water tested as well," Karen said.

"Yeah we do. We're not going to be popular, but this site caused a lot of problems all those years back." Mike turned to Benji. "Hey, have you seen, uh, James, Gemma, or any of the others since?"

Benji tilted his head and his brow furrowed. "Nah, not for a while."

"Not even at school?" Mike frowned.

"It's school holidays," Karen said.

"Oh yeah, right." Mike looked around slowly. "Maybe I should visit them then, just to check they're okay."

"I could come... show you where they live," Benji said.

"We should go on the way back from here," Karen suggested. "If it was Benji, I'd want him checked out like yesterday."

44

"I agree, but it might panic Mom or Dad if the town doctor turns up with the vice mayor."

Karen snorted. "I know just about everyone in the town. *You're* more likely to scare them than me."

Benji shook his head. "He's not that scary, Mom." He swung to Mike. "She can stay in the car, and we can go and see them. They all know me."

Mike grinned. "Hey, maybe your mom and I should stay in the car so just you can examine them."

"Sure. Can I wear one of those listening things around my neck?" Benji immediately was onboard with the idea.

"It's called a stethoscope. And the only people who wear them around their neck are actors playing doctors." Mike wiped his hands on his trousers. "Anyway gang, let's go and say hi to some people. I also want to check out this sample under a microscope."

CHAPTER 14

"That one." Benji pointed. "The one with the big tree in the yard."

"Got it." Mike pulled in at the manicured streetscape. In the front yard of No.12 was a pushbike on its side, and a football rolled under a huge oak tree.

It was still just before midday, but as Mike stepped out his stomach rumbled as his appetite told him it thought it was lunchtime even if his watch didn't.

Karen joined him and Benji maneuvered himself to be in front.

"James parents are Joanne and Gary Adams," she said. "Nice couple, and James is an only child."

Mike was first up onto the porch and knocked on the door. He turned to face Karen and Benji. The boy kept his eyes on the door as though trying to see through it.

"*Hello.*" The soft voice floated through the wooden door, and in the slats of the glass panels they saw there was a shadow there

"Jo, it's me, Karen. I've got Doctor Mike Taylor with me."
She turned to face Mike. "We're just following up with a few
people on some general community things and it's your turn."

They waited for several moments, but there was no
movement. Karen frowned. "Can you open up please, Joanne?"

They waited a few more moments. And then the latch was
drawn back and the inside handle squeaked. The door was
pulled inwards a crack. A woman, probably mid thirties stared
out. Mike noticed that the eye was red rimmed with a dark circle
beneath it.

Karen stepped a little closer "Joanne, are you okay?"

The eye stared back for a moment more before the door was
pulled open.

The first thing Mike noticed was the smell. He turned to
Karen, lowering his voice. "Like at the mine site."

Karen went to the woman standing so still in the darkness
she might have been a shadow. "Joanne, what is it?"

The woman sucked in a deep breath, held it, as she bit both
her lips for a second or two. Her eyes screwed shut as she talked
in little more than a squeak. "They're gone."

"Who? James? Is James gone?" Mike asked.

"And Gary as well." She looked up, but Mike couldn't see
her clearly in the darkness.

"May I?" Mike reached for the light switch and flicked it on.

The woman cringed, holding her hands over her head as if
warding off a blow and kept her eyes shut tight. That was weird,
but it was her look that alarmed Mike most. She had a pebbly
rash all over her face and her hair looked to be coming out in
clumps.

"Oh, Joanne." Karen winced, but didn't move to touch her.
Instead she pulled Benji back a step.

"Mrs. Adams." Mike came and held the woman's forearms
and stared into her face. "Did you go swimming at the mine?"

She shook her head.

"Okay, okay." Mike continued to stare, but she had lowered
her gaze and just seemed defeated. "Where did they go?"

"James ran away. Gary went too." Her throat sounded course and painful. She looked up, and Mike could swear her eyes had a yellow tinge.

"Were they sick?" Karen asked.

Joanne seemed to think about it, and then she nodded as her face crumpled. "Yes, very sick. And they've… changed."

"Has James changed?" Benji frowned in confusion and crept forward. "Into what?"

Karen leaned over to grab his shoulders. "Wait in the car please. This is important."

"Aww." Benji scowled up at his mother. "But James is my friend, and I know I can help if—"

"Now." Karen stared.

"*Awww.*" Benji shook his head and turned. "I get to do nuthin interesting." He kept muttering all the way outside.

Mike looked around the house and saw the disheveled state of the place – dirty clothing, food packets and empty spring water bottles colored a brilliant emerald green. He noticed the clothing Joanne wore was expensive but filthy with sweat and stains.

"How long… have they been gone?" he asked.

She tilted her head back, and opened her mouth. "Days ago; I'm waiting for them." She grit her teeth and made a small sound in her throat.

Karen reached out to her. "Are you okay?"

"It calls." She held a hand to her head. "I can't…"

"Who? What calls?" Mike ducked his head as he tried to see into her eyes, but she kept them screwed shut. He reached for her and grabbed her upper arms now, but instead of feeling soft skin, he felt something hard, like tree bark through her top.

He let her go, remembering Ben Wainright's description of the affliction, and of the angels.

She tilted her head back. "So deep."

"It's the mine," he said, half turning to Karen but keeping his eyes on Joanne. "Joanne, we need to get you to hospital." He reached for her again. "We'll come back for James and Gary, okay?"

47

Her head was tilted far back on her neck now and her mouth hung wide. Mike noticed her throat and teeth looked strange.

Mike tried to drag her to the door, feeling the bark-like substance over more of her skin, but she started to moan and her mouth opened even wider. Impossibly wider.

"It calls. I have to *go-ooo*."

She tugged her arm, but Mike held firm. Karen also reached for her other arm, but then Joanne lunged at Karen, mouth open, and Mike dragged her back before she could bite. In turn Joanne rounded on him, jaws snapping.

"Goddamn, Joanne. Stop that."

He pushed her away, and she went to the floor. But she was only down for a moment, before she was up and skittering away, on all fours. She moved fast. So fast. And unnaturally. Maybe it was the bony extrusions all over her body, but she moved like some sort of hard-shelled insect.

"Jesus, she's having a psychotic episode." He grabbed Karen and pulled her out of the way.

In another moment, there was the crash of breaking glass. Mike and Karen went after the women, but arrived to find the kitchen window broken and nothing but an empty yard beyond.

"What... what just happened?" Karen blinked several times. "I know Joanna, she's normal."

"Infected," Mike said softly.

"Infected? By what?" Karen's face creased.

He turned to her. "The mine. Has to be. It's like what Ben Wainright wrote about." Mike spoke the words yet still didn't understand it. "But he didn't say anything about it being contagious." Mike began to think out loud. "There could be dozens of infected and contagious people wandering around out there."

"Out there?" She stared up at him for a moment. "Benji!" She sprinted for the door.

Mike followed Karen out and saw her run around the car, peering in the windows, and screaming her son's name. But there was no one inside, and the front passenger door was hanging open.

She turned to him, eyes wide and hands curled in fists. "He's gone. *He's gone!*"

"Benji!" Mike did a broader circle around the car. He tried to remember the details from Wainright's notes. Many of the angel kids were rounded up and taken away, but some were said to have escaped into the countryside and never found. One theory was they entered the mine, and went down deep.

"Could he have gone home?" Mike asked.

"Yes, but why would he leave us?" She shook her head. "He wouldn't."

"James," Mike said.

"Yes." She spun to him. "He wanted to help find James. Maybe he went looking for him."

"Or maybe he saw him." Mike exhaled through pressed lips. "Look, there's a chance, *uh*, that he might have gone to the mine."

Karen slowly turned. "To the mine; *in* the mine. Why?"

"I don't know why, but it's a hunch. It's also where Wainright thought a lot of the missing kids went all those years ago.

She opened the car's front passenger door. "Then that's where we're going. *Now*."

"No, we check your home first to make—"

"*No*, the mine." She bared her teeth in panic.

"And what if he's waiting at home? What if we get trapped somehow and he's left alone?" Mike reached across to lay a hand on her arm. "It'll take us ten minutes to swing by your home."

She looked like she was going to explode with impatience, before she exhaled. "Okay, okay. Let's go."

As Mike sped, it took them no time to return to Karen 's house, and just a single minute more for her to go careening through her place, screaming her son's name.

"Grab another light," Mike yelled while he stood on the front porch, yelling Benji's name.

Karen came barreling out. "The mine," was all she said.

"Okay, but call the sheriff. I want someone to know what's going on." Mike climbed in as Karen dragged out her phone.

It took them fifteen long minutes to reach the Angel Mine turnoff, and after a few minutes traversing the rutted track, Mike pulled over and they climbed out.

He reached into his map compartment and retrieved his Glock. He hoped he wouldn't need it, but as the old saying went: better to have it and not need it, than need it and not have it. He also grabbed his flashlight he had remembered to replace.

Karen saw the gun, and just nodded. Mike tucked it into his belt at the small of his back, and together they headed up.

At the top of the hill they stopped.

"It's dry," Karen observed.

"It's all drained away again." Just like what happened back in the 70s, Mike remembered. It seemed this stuff bubbled to the surface, infected people and then returned from where it came.

Mike stood staring. Returned to where exactly? And what was in it that caused the infection, and, alterations in people?

The afternoon was late now, and the shadows were lengthening. It was dry, but there was something else different about the site that Mike couldn't quite put a finger on.

"Those petrified trees are gone," Karen said, frowning. "Someone took them?"

That was it. "Maybe," Mike said, anxiety twisting in his gut.

Mike wasn't sure when the water had drained, but already the outside ground was dry again, and in the dusty earth there were numerous tracks.

"People went into the mine; lots of them," he observed.

He peered into the solid darkness of the mine mouth. He didn't want to go in but knew there was no way he wouldn't if there was a chance Benji was down there somewhere.

"Benji!" Karen yelled and walked a few paces closer to the mine entrance. She cupped her mouth. *"Benji!"* This time so loud she went a little hoarse and his name bounced back at her several times before fading into nothingness.

But there was no reply.

She held her hand out to him. "Give me the flashlight."

"Where's yours?" he asked.

She took the flashlight. "I haven't got one; only candles. She fished in her pocket. "All I could find was this." She pulled out an old silver cigarette lighter. "My ex husband's."

Mike groaned. "Okay, give it to me." He took it and tested it, producing a small orange flame.

"He's in there; I can feel it." Her voice trembled.

He nodded to her. "Don't worry. If he is, we'll find him."

They stepped into the darkened maw.

CHAPTER 15

"Slow down," Mike demanded. She ignored him.

In little more than thirty paces, the light from behind suddenly seemed a long way back, and up ahead it was nothing but impenetrable darkness. The flashlight beam was quickly reduced to a pipe of light that only illuminated a few dozen feet, and Karen had to keep sweeping it from left to right to light their path.

The mine entrance was quite large and probably had seven feet of height, but Mike still had the urge to crouch.

"Wait up," he said softly, not knowing why he felt the need to whisper. "Point the light at the ground."

She did as asked. Footprints. Lots of them. Coming and going.

"Plenty of traffic," he said.

"*Shush.*" She paused, concentrating, and then slowly shook her head. "There's nothing, not a sound. Maybe they all left." She turned back to the darkness of the seemingly endless tunnel and sucked in a deep breath. "*Benji!*"

Her yell made Mike cringe, and he pulled his gun from his back and stuck it in his side pocket. The echoes bounced back at them for another few seconds until the air dropped to silence again. The pair waited for a few more moments but there was no response.

"Perhaps he's so deep he can't hear us," she said hopefully.

"Yeah maybe. The footprints go in further," Mike said. "We're here now so should check it out. But we really should be outside for when Sheriff Kehoe arrives."

She nodded and turned back. Mike noticed the light wobbled in her hands. Oddly, there seemed to be a breeze blowing in their faces, and there was the pervasive smell like from a stagnant pond – fish, methane and a general slimy rottenness.

Mike thought that maybe they'd find where the water level had retreated, and their way would be blocked. But looking down again he saw the ground was already quite dry.

Karen headed off, and Mike stayed right on her shoulder. He had that tingling feeling in the back of his neck he used to get on night missions in the forces. The last time he had it like this, people died.

Not today, never again. He pushed the memory down.

"Look," she said. "The walls."

She raised the flashlight but the beam was far from steady. Where she illuminated, the walls were covered in what looked like tree roots. But they were glisteningly wet, almost like arteries and veins.

"Roots this far down?" she asked.

"It'd need to be a redwood or maybe giant fig tree." Mike frowned. "Weird." He stepped a few paces closer. "Hold the light up."

She did so.

"And they look like they're growing up from below." He quickly checked his watch. "Come on, let's keep going a little deeper."

They continued on a few hundred more feet, and the walls were now totally ribbed by the roots. The silence was suddenly broken by the crunch of feet on gravel.

Mike pulled his gun and dragged Karen to the side of the mineshaft.

"*Hallooo?*"

Relief washed over him. "Sherriff?" Mike let Karen go and tucked his gun away.

The footsteps got louder, and the tunnel became illuminated by two powerful flashlight beams.

"Doctor Taylor, vice mayor." Kehoe touched his hat and thumbed over his shoulder. "Deputy Anderson." The young man nodded.

Mike and Karen quickly updated him on their search and what happened at Joanne and Gary Adam's place. The sheriff's brows knitted ever deeper as he listened.

"And you think they swam in this bad water and got some sort of... mental sickness?' Kehoe asked.

Mike wanted to keep it simple. "Yeah, I think so, but maybe it's contagious now, so we need to be careful."

"What? Shouldn't we be wearing protective clothing?" Deputy Anderson asked.

Mike was sure the young deputy still had a few blushes of pimples on his cheeks that reddened even more.

Mike shrugged. "I don't know yet. But for now, we need to be careful."

Kehoe hitched his belt and shone his light further down the mineshaft. "Well, let's look for Benji. Marty, get up here close by me."

They headed further in and the deeper they went they found that some of the walls had crumbled, exposing new tunnels. There were also a few huge blocks of stone that had collapsed from the ceiling to the shaft floor.

"Can't go much further, I'm afraid," Kehoe said. "Getting a might dangerous."

"The kids did, and so did some of the adults." Mike pointed at the ground.

"We'll give it another few hundred feet, but it's a cave-in risk; you can see that too, right?" Kehoe didn't wait for an answer.

Karen held up her flashlight trying to get in front, but after another few minutes they all slowed, becoming more careful as dust rained down.

"Goddamn stinks in here." Deputy Anderson gagged.

"Just stale air, is all," Kehoe replied.

The air was becoming so thick, Mike could almost taste it. As they crossed by an alcove Karen screamed and fell against him. Her light went haywire for a moment and Mike grabbed her arm to steady it, while also drawing his weapon.

In the side tunnel that looked more like a natural cave that had broken open perhaps by the force of the water, stood one of the petrified statues. Karen held the wobbly light on it for a moment.

"What is *that* doing here?" She looked briefly up at him, her breathing coming fast.

Mike lowered his gun. "I don't think it's like the ones from outside."

Kehoe looked at Mike's gun and grunted.

Mike ignored him and took the flashlight from Karen and moved a little closer. He was right; it was and wasn't like the ones outside. This one was wet looking and the features more distinct. In fact, it was a work of art, and if not for the rough wooden surface, was terrifyingly life-like.

Oddly, the roots were twined around it, growing up from the floor and embracing it. The other difference was instead of having a visage of agony, the face of this petrified statue made it look like the subject was in ecstasy.

"Amazing," he whispered. "Did someone bring this down here, or was it always here?"

Karen edged closer. "It looks like it's growing down here. How is that possible?"

"Or taken root," Kehoe said.

"Was this here before? Does anyone know?" Mike asked.

Kehoe shrugged. "Never been this far in. Never had a reason to."

Karen went up to the thing and peered into the upturned face. "It seems... familiar." She held up a hand. "I could swear it looks like Marshal Simmons, the garage owner."

Kehoe squinted. "It does look a little like old Marsh."

"Simmons is on our missing person's list, boss," Deputy Anderson said softly.

Karen reached up with flashlight to prod at the statue. "Hard, but not quite petrified hard."

Kehoe shone his light around at the walls. "Pretty damp down here. Damn roots everywhere."

Mike followed his gaze; Karen and Deputy Anderson did the same.

"No more statues. Thank god." She turned her light back to the single statue. "Just this one... *hey!*"

Mike spun back.

"Has this thing...?" She turned to Mike, frowning.

Mike knew what she was getting at. The statue's face seemed to have turned a fraction. Before, it was facing up towards the cave ceiling, but now was a slightly angled towards them.

"Please tell me it's just a trick of the light." Deputy Anderson's voice was strained.

Mike felt a tingle run up his spine. Kehoe's light went from the thing's head down to it base, and he saw that it also seemed to have slid along the ground.

"Yeah, we should probably leave now." Kehoe lifted his light to the statue's face. Its eyes flicked opened.

"*Shit.*" Mike raised his gun.

The twin orbs were a brilliant yellow and shone like lights in the darkness. Then to everyone's horror, it screamed, a sound so animalistic and ear piercing it stretched their nerves to breaking.

"*Its alive!*" Kehoe yelled.

It took a step towards them and its arm rose.

"Move, move, move," Mike yelled.

Deputy Anderson was first out of the side cave, followed by Mike dragging Karen with him. Kehoe kept his gun trained on the thing as he backed away.

Out in the main shaft, Kehoe went to lead them out, but Karen stopped dead.

"No." She swiped Mike's hand away. "We are *not* leaving without my son."

"We need backup," Kehoe said. "This is beyond us."

As the trio debated their next move, from behind them came

a gurgling noise, and Mike spun to see the deputy being held by another of the statues.

Kehoe and Mike raised their weapons, but the thing had the deputy between itself and the line of fire.

"Get out of the way," Kehoe yelled, his gun up and steady.

Karen shrank back, but towards the cave depths. As they watched, the statue thing leaned forward to fix its mouth to Anderson's neck, and as the young man screamed, the hard-crusted lips burrowed in.

"*No shot, no shot,*" Kehoe screamed. "Anderson, get out of the fucking way."

Mike didn't have a clear shot either but fired anyway. His bullet struck the side of its head, blasting away a fist-sized piece of the overgrown skull.

Even after the damage, it didn't let go and in the glare of the light its eyes fixed on him, he could see inside the open skull – just a mad tangle of what looked like fibrous roots.

It ripped its mouth from Anderson's neck long enough to hiss like a snake, and Mike fired twice more. This time most of the top of the head was blown off.

Even with that gone, the thing didn't go down. Instead it dropped the deputy and stumbled away into the darkness. Kehoe rushed to Anderson as he fell, holding his neck as blood pulsed through his fingers.

"Gotta get him out." Kehoe lifted his deputy.

Karen screamed behind them, and Mike spun.

She was gone.

"*Karen!*" Mike shouted. "*Karen!*" He roared again and then jogged a few paces further in.

"Goddamnit," Kehoe said between clamped teeth.

Mike tore part of Anderson's shirt free and wrapped it as best he could around the deputy's wound.

"Sorry Mike, got to get my deputy topside before he bleeds out."

Mike nodded. "Go." But then spun back to the sheriff. "Wait." He ran to snatch the deputy's large black flashlight from his belt.

Kehoe held his deputy under his arm, and then nodded to Mike. "Good luck, Doc."

"You too," Mike said. "See you soon."

Mike went fast, gun held firm in front of him and the flashlight underneath, trying to cover every inch of the mineshaft.

The tree roots were everywhere now, like ribbing, and making the shaft seem more like the gullet of a large animal. Several times he came across the standing statues, and even though some slowly turned on creaking necks to watch him pass, none moved from where they had rooted.

This was what was happening to the infected of this town. Perhaps to begin with they were like feral creatures like Benji's friend James, but once they made it to the mine, they began to complete their transformation.

And the others? He wondered whether the other people who had disappeared were changed? Or they were just snatched and brought down here? He just hoped they weren't killed immediately. He had to save Benji and Karen.

Mike moved farther, deeper into the cave, into the darkness then stopped to listen. The sound of water up ahead. After a second debating the pros and cons of making any noise, he decided.

"*Karen*?" his voice boomed and then echoed away. He was about to call again, when a tiny scream came back – it was her – Mike launched himself forward, running hard now.

After another few hundred feet the rotting, fishy smell took on a more distinct odor. Methane gas.

Mike slowed as the tunnel became wetter and more fetid. The walls were moving now almost in peristaltic waves like the inside of a gut. He felt like he was being swallowed alive, soon to be digested.

The tunnel had ended, and he moved through raw tumbled rock, obviously where the miners had broken through into the water cavern all those decades ago. He had to breathe shallowly as the gas was starting to make his head and vision swim.

Mike entered a large cavern that seemed to have no end. He stood high atop a slope, looking down on a dark lake of bubbling liquid. The methane gas was percolating from below to pop in little explosions of vapor. Hundreds of feet out from the shoreline there was some sort of island and on it was a single massive tree-like thing.

"*Adotte Sakima.*" Mike remembered the name of the first people's powerful god; it was real.

As he stared, the roots constantly moved, snaking about and curling over objects that it snatched up and fed into itself. Hanging from its withered branches were pendulous bulbs that writhed and jiggled and threatened to birth monstrous things.

Mike slid down the slope holding his light up. The powerful beam only just reached to the tree, but he saw there were people floating in the disgusting water, some face down, but others being dragged out towards the waiting tree – it was these poor souls the roots delicately picked from the water, and stuffed into one of many red-lined orifices on the mighty trunk.

"Ah shit," Mike whispered. This was the thing the Paleo Indians had tried to warn them about all those millennia ago. This was the plant god that lived below them all. Perhaps thousands of years ago the waters had surged to the surface and its spores infected people, turning them into some sort of quasi-plant beings to do the bidding of a living, sentient tree. The rest of the people were captured and herded down here as nothing more than plant food.

"*Karen!*"

"Mike."

His head swung to the voice. He saw her then. A group of the petrified-looking beings dragged several people towards the water. Karen was there, clinging to a smaller body, which lifted his spirits a fraction. *Benji.* Karen had found her son.

He reached for his gun but realized he could never fire it in here, not with the methane gas. So ran towards them, not having any plan at all.

As he did the branches of the tree stopped their sinuous movement as though the massive growth became aware of him.

In seconds, from the fetid lake, from the walls, and lifting from the earth, strange figures began to rise. If they had once been people, they were nothing like that now. Decrepit creatures of twisted limbs, spiked growths branching from them, and glowing yellow eyes that were all held together by slimy mosses.

They screeched and whined and scuttled towards him. Some came on broken limbs, others dragged themselves, but more came incredibly fast.

Mike charged towards Karen and Benji, and as he closed in on them he lowered his shoulder and smashed into one of the beings holding her, knocking it backwards a dozen feet.

He swung the heavy flashlight like a club, smashing down and crunching away chunks of the petrified skin and head. In seconds he had freed them, but only temporarily as hundreds of the things were coming at them. Fast.

"Can you run?" he asked her.

She clung to him and nodded jerkily.

"And Benji?" He lifted the boy's chin. Benji nodded more slowly and it seemed the methane was fogging his mind. It would happen to all of them soon, and then they'd either be fed to the tree god or changed into monsters.

"Gotta move, Benji. We have to run fast. You gotta keep up with your mom, okay?"

Benji nodded again, and put a hand on Mike's shoulder to lift himself to his feet. He opened glassy eyes wider. "I dreamed you'd both come get me." He gave them a hazy smile. "I want to go home now."

Mike turned to the approaching horde. He knew they'd never be able to outrun them all.

"I'm going to slow them down." He handed Karen the gun. "Don't fire this until you're out of this cavern. And *don't* stop running for anything, okay?"

"No." She shook her head, eyes panicked. "Not without you."

"I'll be right behind you. Don't stop for anything. Go! Save your son." Mike pushed her. "*Save Benji.*"

Her eyes were wet, but she nodded and then the pair began a staggered run to the mouth of the cavern.

Mike turned back towards the horrifying beings surging towards him. It looked like someone had opened the gates of hell. To his horror he saw that some began to run towards Karen and Benji, trying to head them off.

He waved his light at them. "*Hey!* Here I am, you ugly bastards!"

Mike snatched up a slimy stone and hoisted it at the group; managed to strike one, but it didn't even flinch. He picked up another rock and this time threw it with all his might towards the tree. It fell short, sending up a splash of mucousy water. But even the failed attack prompted a response. Immediately all the things turned towards him.

And only him.

"Here goes." Turning he saw that Karen and Benji had vanished and he began to edge backwards. There was so many, he knew they'd cut him off before he made it to the opening. And some were running a lot faster than Karen could manage – they'd be chased down before they reached the surface.

"Fuck it." His mind was becoming foggy from the gas and his thinking clouded. Flashbulbs of light began to go off behind his eyes and he suddenly remembered another woman who had died in his place on the battlefields of Syria…

"Not this time."

He reached into his pocket for the cigarette lighter, drew it out and held it up. He looked out towards the tree and saw that it had gone back to feeding human beings, some struggling, into the many maws along its trunk. It obviously felt it had won.

"Go to hell."

Mike flicked the wheel.

CHAPTER 16

Karen staggered out of the mineshaft mouth, dragging her son with her, and sucked in a huge breath. There was no one waiting for them. The sheriff had obviously taken his deputy to hospital.

Benji wheezed as he recovered from the methane saturation in his lungs. Karen lifted him out of the small depression in front of the mine mouth just as she felt the ground rumble beneath her feet. In another second an orange hurricane burst from the shaft to roar like a jet engine and incinerate the twisted trees and everything else before it.

She threw Benji down and covered him with her body, and with luck she was to the side of the gout of flame. After another minute she slowly sat up, her eyes glistening as she realized what it meant.

Benji coughed. "Where's Mike?"

"He stayed..." she whispered, "... to save us."

"I knew he would," Benji said.

She nodded, staring back at the mineshaft. The flames were dying down, but there was still an orange glow coming from deep down in the mine's throat that made it look like the entrance to Hell.

"Thank you," she whispered. "Thank you for saving us both."

EPILOGUE

Minneapolis, Minnesota – Population 453,325
"What have we got here? Desmond Morrison was President of Landers Supermarket Chain that had stores in every state, bar Alaska. And he was working on that.

He looked at the crate of emerald green bottles – Eldon Spring Water: *Super Health Tonic,* was printed on the label in stylized green calligraphy and blazed across images of a crystal-clear lake, waterfall, and trees with colorful birds.

Danny Barker lifted a bottle free and cradled it in his hand. "It's the next big thing, and free samples for our new customers. It tastes great and contains no caffeine, sugar, or artificial flavorings. Natural mineral-infused water from the pristine underground lakes of Eldon. With just a hint of lemon zest." He held it out. "Try it."

Desmond eyed him suspiciously for a moment and then took it, twisted the cap off and sniffed. He seemed to approve as he tilted it to his lips and drank. He kept going until half was gone.

Danny worked to suppress his smile; he knew he had him. In sales it was called: *getting the prospect to take ownership*.

"We're only doing a hundred thousand units per day, so numbers are limited for now." He shrugged. "It's a little more expensive than our usual products, but I think you'll agree it's well worth it."

Desmond lowered the bottle and looked at the label for a moment more. "The next big thing, huh?"

"Bigger than goji berries and coconut water combined." He grinned and waited.

"Volume discount?" Desmond raised his chin.

Danny's face became serious. "Not really, but for you, I can knock off two percent if you take ten thousand."

"Five," Desmond countered.

Danny shook his head. "Three percent; best I can do."

Desmond eyeballed him for a moment, then stuck out his hand. "Done. Organize the paperwork."

"You got it." Danny gave him a firm I-mean-business handshake. Truth was, he'd closed every deal today with the new drink. It was proving a big mover, and the test run they'd done in the hometown of Eldon had shown an overwhelming approval rating. *Eat your heart out, candy cola.*

"I want it on the shelves first thing Monday morning." Desmond got to his feet. "Let's make everyone in the country as healthy as they are in Eldon."

BLANK WHITE PAGE

James A Moore

Lucas Slate sat astride his dark horse and stared into the sprawling affair with little or no expression on his gaunt face. He looked upon the collection of hastily assembled buildings and well-used tents with eyes half-lidded. An unwary sort of soul might have thought he wasn't paying attention, but he was.

"It occurs to me, Mister Crowley, that this place looks too much like other areas we've both seen in the past."

The air had a hard bite to it. The wind was dry and cold and cutting. Winter was well and properly on its way and the people in the small town knew it. They were shilling their goods with a sort of cheerful desperation that said at least a few of them could think of better places to be. He wondered if any of them would succeed in finding those better places before the winter came properly.

Jonathan Crowley, who was riding his own horse and sitting only a few feet from Slate, allowed himself a small smile and shook his head. "And, what, exactly, is it that you think we're going to find here, Mister Slate?"

Slate did not bother turning to the sound of Crowley's voice. He knew what he would see. The same lean, plain features and brown hair, brown eyes. Same offensive smirk on the man's longish face, though at the moment it was hidden behind almost a month's worth of beard growth. They'd ridden across half the Arizona territory, riding past patrols of Cavalry and Indians alike, because something inside of Lucas Slate told him he had to be here, but he had no idea what that something was.

He just knew it chewed at him.

Only a short time ago he'd been quite a different man. His

hair white, and his skin was as pale as snow, same as always. He was an albino, after all. But beyond that there was remarkably little that was the same.

When he'd lived in Carson's Point, Colorado he'd stood at least eight inches shorter and he'd been told more than once that he had the face of a woman. True, a few of the folks who'd made that claim had been drunk and desperately lonely, but he knew that his face had been different, as surely as his body had changed.

Slate stood over six and a half feet now, and while he still sported the same hat he'd taken to wearing as the local under-taker – a fine old hat that served him well and looked somber enough for funerals – he could no longer fit in his old suits and had been forced to buy new shirts and new pants as well; rawhide in this case because the damnable cold would have sunk through anything less.

He had always been thin. Now he was gaunt, and his muscles were cords of leather under skin that had long since stopped being supple and soft. No one would ever mistake him for a woman these days. Instead they'd contemplate whether or not someone sharing his old profession should have buried him. He was not dead. He just looked the part.

He had always been soft spoken, but these days his voice was lower and seldom seemed to want to come out as much more than a whisper. The only thing that had not changed was the cultured southern drawl that moved through his words. "I'm intending to find answers, Mister Crowley."

Crowley nudged his horse closer. Slate looked toward the man and considered the beard he was growing. Jonathan Crowley did not look like a man who should have a beard to him. It didn't seem to fit his long face. "I am very fond of answers, Mister Slate. But I have to ask, what, exactly, is the question?"

He looked at Crowley. The man was dressed in fine clothes. A cotton shirt, a charcoal, pinstriped suit with a vest, and over that a great duster that kept the cold and wind from touching anything under it. He sported a gambler's hat on the top of his head, and a heavy wool scarf of a dark, somber red hue.

Slate offered a thin-lipped smile of his own. "I believe the question is the very one you've been contemplating since we started riding together. What, exactly, am I becoming?"

Crowley nodded. "That is a question worth answering."

"Indeed it is, sir."

You could hardly call it a town, really. More a collection of shops and brothels all shoved together and becoming a town already called Silver Springs, Arizona. The place was an assortment of thieves and whores and criminals, as could be expected in a boomtown. The rumors of silver had driven herds of people into the area and the fortunate few who had struck solid claims guaranteed they'd stay. There were white folk, red folk and black folk, all of them in the same area. Crowley imagined if he looked around he'd even see a few Chinese as well. That seldom happened in places that were properly called civilized. There were too many who considered the other races as enemies for that. Here, where money was more important than opinions, there was less need of being selective.

Crowley rather liked that part of the situation. He'd never much cared for the need to believe one people were better than another. One on one, most of them seemed all right. It was only when you gathered any of them in groups they tended to be stupid.

The ground was as dry as the air, which is to say most of the folks in the area would be getting their water from wells, or from the barrels a few enterprising people were bringing with them. It was a commodity. The Verde River was a few hours ride from the area, and he had already seen a group of men at the edge of town working on figuring the best way to get the water from there to here. What they lacked in equipment they seemed to make up for with enthusiasm.

He could see that Lucas Slate was tense. Slate, who seldom

seemed bothered by much of anything since he'd begun changing. Slate, who calmly and methodically followed through with some very grisly work was currently as taut as a bowstring.

"We have traveled through Indian territories and been shot at several times, Mister Slate. Who do you think is most likely to be of assistance to us in this situation?"

The two of them were still at the edge of the crowded area. Someone, somewhere, had claimed they found silver in the area. A week later the first building seemed old. Now? Now the crowds kept coming and the buildings kept popping up like mushrooms after a rainstorm.

Slate looked slowly over the area and then finally shook his head. "I'm sure I have no idea."

Crowley smiled. "Look around us, Mister Slate, and tell me what's different about the people here?"

"Nothing that I can see." He spoke even as he once more scanned the crowds. "Ah. I see it now."

"What do you see, Mister Slate?"

"The Indians. They're more afraid of *me* than they are of *you*."

Crowley chuckled. "Well now, don't you think that deserves a bit of investigation?"

Slate took off his hat for a moment and ran long, pallid fingers through his long, thin, white hair. "Indeed I do, Mister Crowley. Indeed I do."

They rode forward at a leisurely pace, two men who scared most people without even trying.

Silver Springs wasn't old enough to be on any maps. The town had been hastily assembled and that tended to make navigating the structures challenging. There were no rules, really, except the ones people managed to force on each other. Most of the folks who saw the strangers eyed them warily, rather like one might contemplate a substantial rattlesnake that was minding its own affairs but was looking at you with one ophidian eye.

To be fair they struck quite a few notes that qualified them as unusual. The gaunt man rode on a pale grey horse that didn't seem to breathe. It did not snort, nor did it whinny. The beast seemed oblivious to most of the other animals in the area, though the same was not true in reverse. A good number of dogs made it a point to be elsewhere when the horse got too close, and they made certain to bark their dissatisfaction just as soon as they were far enough away to assure the great horse could not easily get to them.

The man riding with him seemed of particularly good humor, with an eager smile that did not sit well. More than a few of the faithful crossed themselves when they saw his broad, even teeth. When Crowley was not smiling he was hardly remarkable, but there was something inherently wrong with his grin. There was something about the way he moved, the way he looked at folks, that left them a mite worried that he could just possibly take note of them. His horse was only remarkable in that it did not run from the larger grey beast the gaunt man rode.

Both men sported weapons, but that was hardly unusual in this area. The gaunt man had a long rifle draped across his saddle, held in place by the weight of his hands. A shotgun rested near his leg, and a careful eye would make out the two Colt Navy revolvers tucked into saddle holsters. And knives? There was a knife hilt at the top of each boot and at least one large blade strapped to his hip. He carried enough weapons to promise mayhem, even if his deathlike face and grim pallor hadn't already advertised a penchant for destruction.

Crowley slipped off his horse with an unsettling grace. He didn't bother stretching or adjusting his posture as so many did. Instead, he seemed perfectly relaxed and comfortable. Lucas Slate dropped down with substantially more difficulty and looked around the area with hooded eyes.

"You're not feeling well, Mister Slate?"

"Something's wrong. I don't quite know what, or why, but I'm feeling decidedly ill at ease."

Jonathan Crowley adjusted his wide brimmed gambler's hat and looked around carefully. "In the time I've known you I've run across remarkably little that put you under the weather."

"Indeed, sir. It is a rarity." Slate's soft southern drawl was more pronounced. "And one I daresay I do not enjoy."

"Close your eyes, Mister Slate."

The man did as Crowley suggested.

"Now, tell me what you feel both in your body and outside it."

To most, the conversation would have seemed foolishness, but Lucas Slate knew better. He was changing and his changes included some very devilish alterations to his senses. He could often see past the lies that presented themselves to most people, and he could occasionally feel much more than he should have been able to consider.

"Well now…"

Crowley said nothing, but he watched the man very carefully.

Slate turned his head slowly to the left and tilted his ear higher, as if trying to catch a sound. "Well now," he repeated. "That's something, isn't it?"

"What might that be, Mister Slate?"

"I can hear something. Sounds almost like music, but nothing that makes sense."

Crowley nodded slowly. All around them people were going on about their business and giving a wide berth to the two of them. "Then I might suggest you investigate. Shall I come with you?" He made the offer already knowing the answer.

"Not at this time, Mister Crowley. Though perhaps I could count on you to remain within shouting distance."

Crowley nodded again. "I expect I can make myself available to you, should the need arise."

Crowley turned his horse away and started on a parallel course. The smile dropped from his face as he merged with the people moving about the bustling area.

***

Crowley knew that if you sit long enough, people tell the most amazing stories. It wasn't hard to find a place that was selling food, but finding one where the food wasn't dubious was more of a task. Still, Crowley managed well enough.

There was a tent not far from the first stable that had slices of roast beef, a thin gravy, and potatoes for a few pennies. A single penny bought a plate of beans from a pot that looked diseased. The establishment also had a bar, and that almost always guaranteed conversation. Crowley bought his food and settled in to listen.

Most of the people were talking of only two noteworthy things. The first was the silver in the area – amazing how many wanted it and how desperately they were willing to search for instant wealth. The other major topic of conversation was the ongoing Indian wars.

War might have seemed too harsh a word for some, but Crowley didn't think so. There were soldiers moving through the area, and they were there for the main purpose of pushing any red men they saw onto the reservations they had set aside.

Crowley had no idea why. Until a little over a year earlier he'd made a very strong point to stay well away from human beings in general, and while he was once again obligated to deal with people, he had no desire to get involved in their politics. One thing hadn't changed in his time on the planet: people got together and made messy political situations and then other people came along and tried to fix them. In the process there was normally a great deal of bloodshed. He didn't worry about politics. He worried about the things that tried to break into the world and take it for themselves.

A man standing a few feet away from him was speaking. The man was short, stout, and stank. He needed a bath far more than he needed a whiskey, but the drink was what he was after and what he was enjoying.

"Big as a bear," Stinky said, "and white as snow, and looking around like he's waiting to kill something."

Crowley could guess whom the man was speaking about.

The man pouring whiskey was taller, leaner and looked about as friendly as an executioner. Still, he nodded and poured and listened.

"Thing is, all the Indians is looking at him like he's gonna kill 'em and cook them up for dinner." The thickset man smacked his lips noisily and slurped down his whiskey like it was water. His mustache, desperately in need of a trimming, trembled as he spoke. "Far as I can see that would be an improvement."

Crowley kept his tongue. Ultimately, he didn't much see a need to involve himself in the discussion. Still, it was interesting to hear.

When the bartender finally spoke it was softly, but with an edge. "Don't much care for the Indians, but I'm just fine keeping the army out of here, too."

"Oh to be sure," Stinky said. He had a sloppy smile on his face and he nodded his head so hard Crowley wondered how it managed to stay attached. "Any ways you look at this situation, I prefer to avoid having a hundred soldiers coming along and shooting the hell out of everything again. I already had that problem in Maryland, Virginia and in Alabama. I'm done with men in uniform."

Crowley snorted at that, not even trying to suppress the noise.

Stinky looked his way. His brow knitted. "You think soldiers are a good idea, mister?"

"No. I just don't think men in uniform will ever go away."

"How you figure?"

Crowley cut a piece of beef and chewed on it for a moment before answering. "You have silver mines here. People are staking claims and digging and some of them are making money. Those people are going to want to protect what is theirs, so they'll either hire men in uniforms to protect it, or they'll demand men in uniforms to protect it. Either way, you're going to get men in uniforms. Then you have your Indians, who maybe don't care about the silver and maybe do, but either way probably don't like getting pushed from place to place. They're going to get upset sooner or later and they're going to push back, and sure enough, more men in uniforms will come along to stop that from happening. I believe that's why you currently have men in uniforms heading in this direction."

Stinky looked at him for a long moment and then a smile broke on his face. He had a good smile. It made his face round and cheery. "Mister I like you. Let me buy you a drink."

"By all means," Crowley said. "But I'd ask you to do me the kindness of standing downwind. I'm still eating and you have a ripe odor on you."

Might be that some people would have taken offense to that, but stinky did not. Instead he laughed. "It's been a long few days riding to get here. Haven't found the baths yet."

The bartender pointed. "That way. Three doors down."

Crowley finished his meal and Stinky, who had forgotten all about the offer of a drink, went to get himself cleaned up. Really, that was better for everyone involved.

Captain Henry Folsom looked around the settlement and glowered from under the brim of his Hardee hat. The men with him were tired and hungry and they needed supplies. He wasn't overly fond of the way the place looked, but they would simply have to work with what they had available.

There were Indians moving among the people in the camp and he didn't much care for that. His job was to make sure the Apache stayed where they belonged and that was a task he took very seriously.

"Sergeant Barnes," Folsom spoke clearly, with a hard, barking note in his voice that perfectly matched his disposition. "Find stables and a spot upwind from this filth."

"Upwind, sir?" Barnes asked.

Barnes was one of those people Folsom always found offensive: they'd all been on the road just as long, but Barnes was neat and clean and not a hair was out of place.

"I have no desire to smell the people here if they reek as badly as the area looks."

Barnes snapped off a hard salute and broke away from the men.

When Folsom slid from his horse's saddle and landed, it was with remarkable agility. "Sergeant Fowler?"

"Yes, sir?"

"Take your squad and ride a circuit around this cesspool. I want to know how many Indians are here and why they are here."

"Yes, sir!"

A moment later the commander of the Seventh Battalion strutted toward one of the only solid structures he could find in the town. It was two stories of wood rot and sagging boards, but it was an actual building and that had to stand for something. The man who walked beside him was not Indian, yet he was not a proper white man, either. He said he was from China. All Folsom knew for certain was that Chi Chul Song was a better tracker than anyone else he'd met and that the fellow worked hard for a small wage. He did not speak to Song and the Chinaman returned the favor, but Folsom was happier with the man beside him than he was without. Song stood next to him with his muscular arms crossed over his broad chest and continued to say nothing while Folsom commandeered the Silver Springs Hotel for himself and his soldiers.

Lucas Slate felt the tugging at his body and soul like iron shavings might feel the pull from a magnet just exactly too far away to make them move. He could have resisted, but part of him did not want to. Part of him wanted this, needed to know what was behind the silent summons. What bothered him was he couldn't decide if that part was what he liked to think of as himself, or as the thing that was changing him. There had been a time when he could tell the difference with ease, but familiarity was not being kind to him.

What had once been a distant voice inside his soul was now a part of him, much as he hated the notion. The endless whispering influence that had already changed his body was now better positioned for chipping away at his mind. He still knew who he was, but recent events argued that he might not stay that way too much longer.

One nameless town, one odd beastie – odd enough that Crowley had never heard of it before – and the thing inside him had taken over, nearly drowning him in the dark waters of his mind. The change had happened so quickly that he couldn't fight it off. One moment he was himself and the next something else had controlled his actions. It had worked out to the benefit of Slate and Crowley alike, but it had put a strain on their relationship, and though Crowley did his best to act as if nothing was different, Slate's mother hadn't raised any fools.

His horse clomped along as calmly as ever. The dogs in the area, and there were a goodly number of strays, barked and raged and backed away. The horse did not care. It wasn't really a horse anymore, of course. It had been snake bit a while back, when he and Crowley were in the middle of the badlands. The horse had reared up and run a hundred yards and then fallen on its side. By the time he'd reached the thing, it was dying. The muscles in its body were shuddering and the beast was soaked in sweat, surely as good as dead. Crowley had come along, moving at a leisurely pace. He'd stopped long enough to shoot the snake dead and then followed, but the look on his lean face said he knew what Slate knew: the horse was a goner.

And for only an instant, that dark whispering voice that seldom spoke loudly enough to be noticed on a conscious level had reached out and taken control. Slate had leaned down and grabbed the dying horse's head, wrenching it roughly around until the animal's open mouth was aimed at his face. He'd leaned down and exhaled a powerful breath into the horse's mouth and then held it closed with his hand.

He stayed that way until the animal shuddered and then shook him off. A minute, perhaps two, and the horse was up and fine and Crowley was looking at him with a calm that was even worse than the man's damnable smile.

Something needed to be done about what was happening

inside Slate's body and his soul. He had no idea what that something might be, but he believed with every fiber of his being that the answers were somewhere near him, somewhere in this place. Just then he saw the palest man he had ever seen. Deathly white, actually. An Indian, that was obvious, but there was nothing natural about his hue or his demeanor. The man walked past him in the middle of a crowd, hunched over to the point where he looked easily a foot shorter than he should have. He had a shawl drawn over his head and if Slate hadn't felt that something was wrong, he'd likely have dismissed the shape as an old squaw.

The face that peered from under that shawl was drawn and ancient, thin and angular. The eyes were hidden in shadow, but he could feel them scrutinizing him just the same. The man stood up quickly and let the old cloth fall from his head and his shoulders, dropping it to the ground. Around them, most of the people paid no mind, but every Indian backed away as surely as if they'd been hit with boiling water. A few of them screamed, to boot.

When he smiled, it was worse than Crowley's. He spoke words that were not English. Slate should not have been able to understand them, but he did. The old man said, "I know you."

Slate shook his head. He spoke in English but knew the man understood every word. "I have never met you before. I'd remember you."

"You will know me better soon."

It was at that moment the Cavalry riders broke through the crowd. Slate had been so busy looking at the pale man that he'd lost track of everything else. The soldiers came on horses trained to bull their way through crowds. One of them had an old Indian woman by the wrist and was dragging her along beside him. Another had rope around the wrists of three younger women, also Indians, who were crying and trying to keep up with the rider and his horse.

Slate felt that other presence slither through his mind, but did not take the time to pay it any attention. He had other concerns. He was not fond of men who mishandled women. As a half-breed himself, he didn't much care what race they were.

He rode his horse four paces toward the first of the riders and allowed himself a very small grin of satisfaction when the horse reared up and threw the rider. The horse didn't like Slate's mount. Most animals did not. As he rode forward a little more the rest of the horses grew skittish and backed up, despite their riders' urgings.

The first of the soldiers looked up from where he'd landed on his tail end and glowered at Slate. Slate looked back down and kept his face deliberately expressionless.

"Watch where you're going, you damn fool!" The old woman backed into the crowd as the soldier stood. Slate supposed he should have known the man's rank in the Cavalry, but he did not. He had never much cared for the soldiers he'd met and the feeling had always been mutual.

"I did nothing, sir, but continue on my way."

The man had risen to his feet and was still scowling, at least until he saw Slate's face a little better. As he shaved himself when he needed and looked at the changes in his features with a sick fascination, he knew what the man saw and that it was not particularly pretty.

"Well you've interfered in a military operation!"

"Wrangling squaws is a soldier's business these days?" Slate kept his voice as calm and soft as ever. Oh, he'd been riding with Crowley far too long. "I'd have thought you might actually try to find a few braves to fight instead of simply stealing their women."

"Get off of that horse, you bastard. You'll be coming with us."

Slate looked at him for a long moment and rested his hand on the grip of his rifle. "As I am neither a squaw nor a brave, I believe I will stay exactly where I am."

In the distance the other cavalrymen had managed to calm their horses – while successfully moving several feet back – and were watching what happened carefully. Apparently the man who dragged old women around was in charge.

"That's a direct order!" He was furious, the soldier, but he was not very wise. He came toward Slate with one hand holding to the butt of his service revolver.

Slate spoke softly, his expression remained calm. "I am not now, nor have I in the past, been a part of your army, sir. I do not answer to you."

"Are you a Confederate, boy? Is that the problem here?"

The man was likely a few years younger than he was. Not that it much mattered.

"In fact, sir, I was on the side of the North in the conflict, though I was not a soldier. I agreed with the notion that all men are created equal. I should think that would include red men, would it not?"

"What?" The soldier scowled and came closer still. Slate suspected he intended to sneak up and attack. He lacked in subtlety.

Slate sighed. "I am not a Confederate. The war is over, by the by. I am a gentleman. You might have run across a few in your journeys, though I fear it is just as likely you've never run across anything but gutter trash."

That seemed to be enough for the soldier. He stepped forward with every intention of pulling Slate off of his horse. His gloved hands grabbed at the reins of the horse and tried to lead it roughly away.

The horse did not move.

"You'd do well to leave my mount be, sir. He doesn't much like you."

"Piss on your goddamned horse!"

Slate sighed and climbed down from the saddle. The great grey beast looked at him with only the mildest interest.

Rather than bother with the horse Slate took hold of the cavalryman's ear and pulled savagely. The man screamed as cartilage snapped. While he was howling in pain, Slate punched him across the jaw and broke bones.

The next of the soldiers was already drawing his firearm.

Slate looked at the man and did the same. "Don't. It won't go well for you."

The man did.

It did not go well.

Stinky came back a while later. His actual name was Owen Napier, and he was a man without much purpose in his own estimation. "I come from a family of lawyers. They make a good living and I am fortunate enough to share in that, but I don't much like the law. Thought I might come this way and find something more interesting to do with my time."

"So you decided to try mining?" Crowley considered shaking his head at the notion because Owen-the-less-stinky didn't strike him as a very physical man.

"Lord, no!" Napier shook his head hard enough to rock his jowly face. "I figure if anything I might report on what happens here. Send articles back to a friend of mine in New York."

"Not a lot of money in that, is there?"

"I have a family. They'll keep me fed." He patted his belly. "As you can see that's not much of a consideration for me. Besides, they're glad to have me out here. I can't get in the way and I might have useful information for them, too." For a man who was carefully not admitting to being sent away from the family as an embarrassment, Napier seemed cheerful enough. When he patted his belly it also showed the bulge in his vest where he was smart enough to hide a small two-shot Wesson. It only took one bullet to kill a man if you were fast enough.

"So where are you from, Mister Crowley? I can't quite place your accent."

Crowley looked at his new acquaintance and smiled. "Here and there." Before Napier could ask any more questions, Crowley turned the tables. "What is it you have against Indians?"

"Hmm? Oh, nothing at all. But I keep hearing about raiding parties burning peoples' homes down and taking their women. That's a godless thing to do."

"Are you a scholarly man, Mister Napier?"

"I like to think so." He nodded. "Yes, I am."

"Look into your history a bit better and you'll find that raiding parties, houses being burned down, and women being taken from their families are not at all new notions. I don't believe there's a part of the world where it hasn't happened for as long as there have been people."

"Well, certainly not among civilized folks."

Crowley smiled again and Napier got a nervous look on his face. "Whatever makes you think a few buildings brings about a civilized human being?"

Before Napier could answer, Lucas Slate walked into the room, looming over everyone in the place. Most of the conversations died in an instant. Slate's voice remained as soft and cold and low as ever. Napier looked toward him and blanched. "Mister Crowley, I believe I'm going to need your assistance."

From outside the tent a slowly growing sound caught Crowley's attention. It was a noise he'd known for many, many years and one he never had much affection for: the sound of many men on horseback. Like as not, they were men in uniforms and their intentions would not be much to his liking.

"What have you gotten yourself into, Mister Slate?" Crowley did his level best not to smile, but it wasn't easy for him.

"There were a few men in uniform decided they had to take some ladies from this area without their agreeing to be taken. I intervened."

Outside there were the noises of commands being barked and repeated, horses coming to a halt and whinnying their displeasure, and a few dozen men working quickly to become organized in a chaotic situation. In other words, soldiers in action.

Crowley sighed and placed his hat on his head. "And did your intervention result in injury or worse to the men?"

"Indeed it did, sir."

"Well now, this should be something."

The man pouring whiskey looked uninterested. Napier seemed eager to hear more. He also studied Slate with wide eyes. He stopped when Slate turned quickly and stared back just as hard. Might be things would have gone wrong from there, but a collection of Cavalrymen came into the tent before things could get worse.

Of course, them coming in rather took care of worsening matters all by itself.

Folsom looked around. They were an unpleasant lot to be sure. The tent was filled with people, and most of them were unwashed and underfed. Folsom looked at the crowd and found the man his soldiers had reported with amazing ease. The gaunt albino was as tall as he was thin and looked like death. He was dressed like a savage in rawhide, sported a coat made of some sort of animal fur, and carried two large pistols on his hips. Despite his uniform and the men behind him, Folsom hesitated for a moment. Then the Chinaman, Song, moved a bit to the side and a few more soldiers stepped into the tent beside them both.

Having an audience never failed to make Folsom feel the need to be brave. "You!" He stabbed a finger at the albino. "What in the name of God did you do to my men?"

The gaunt man looked at him. Next to him a smaller man with a feral smile looked in his direction with nearly feverish eyes. Most of the people were looking toward him, but what made those two different was simply that they were not afraid of him. Not in the least, and that was a worrisome thing.

The albino said, "I did nothing to your men that they did not provoke, sir." He had a southern accent. Little existed that was more contemptible in Folsom's eyes.

"I have four dead soldiers and a handful of men who swear you killed them. Attacking a soldier is a hanging offense." Folsom stepped forward and Song moved with him, a graceful, silent man with the eyes of a cat. Song always looked like he was ready to pounce, to kill, though Folsom had never once seen the man strike first.

"And I repeat, Mister Crowley, I do believe I'll need your help." The albino murmured to the smiling man next to him, seemingly unable to speak louder than a whisper.

The man with him slipped forward and stood between Folsom and his prize.

"Don't make this concern you, mister."

The stranger's smile grew broader and ice rimmed the inside of Folsom's stomach. He had no idea why, but the man scared the hell out of him. Still, there were the troops to consider and justice to be handled.

"I know you. Henry Folsom. How's your mother? Ruth, I believe?" The man did not speak. He purred. Folsom felt that cold in his guts spread. His mother had passed when he was only ten. How the man could possibly know her was a mystery. Still, he seemed familiar,

"I do not believe we've met before."

"I know you. I know your father, Alexander. Your mother, Ruth. I knew your sister as well, Loretta." The lean man looked away for a moment, his eyes staring past Folsom toward something only he could see. Folsom barely remembered his older sister. She'd been involved with a man in Boston. There had been a scandal, of course, though his father did his best to hide it. Loretta died and died badly. The thought was enough to twist his heart into a knot.

"And your name?"

The stranger smiled. "I'm Jonathan Crowley."

Folsom backed up, his eyes growing wide. That was impossible, of course. He remembered Crowley. The man had seemed a giant to him when he was a child. He'd been tall and lean and he'd had the most terrifying smile.

"Good Lord." Folsom's lips barely moved. "How is that possible?"

Crowley's smiled dropped as fast as it had shown itself. He ignored the question and countered with, "I expect your men might have told you one version of the tale. Why not hear the other version before you decide how to handle the situation, Captain?"

The request was reasonable enough, but Folsom did not like the tone of voice any more than he liked that damnable smile. He didn't like the fear that seeing the man caused in him, either. "Your friend will have a chance to tell his side of the story when he stands trial." He wanted to dismiss the man, planned to, in fact, but the man stayed where he was and damned if that smile didn't come back and grow broader still.

Crowley's brown eyes regarded him for a moment and then he shrugged. "He won't be standing trial. He has things to do and so do I." That was the end of the argument as far as Crowley was concerned. His tone said as much. Folsom looked closely at the man for the first time and shook his head. "Sir, you should take yourself away from this situation before it grows any worse. I have witnesses that say a man with skin as white as snow killed four of my men. I see exactly one man with skin as white as snow in this area, sir. In fact I'd hazard there are no more albinos for a hundred miles in any direction."

"Would you indeed, sir?" The albino's face crept into a strange smile as he spoke. His eyes glittered under lids at half-mast.

"Have you seen yourself?" Folsom asked. "Your skin is as white as milk."

"Indeed it is. Has been my entire life. I did, however, have a conversation with another man not long before I saw your men, and he was just as pale as me."

The smiling man laughed; it sent shivers down Folsom's spine. "Well now, I would hazard a guess you might be mistaken, Captain." His tone was dry and mocking and Folsom found him distasteful in the extreme. That damnable laugh, however, echoed in the back of his mind, brought back thoughts of his sister, and how he'd felt when he found her body.

No. The past was just that, and he'd not let the grinning fool confuse him with what had to be half-truths or blatant lies. How he knew about Folsom's family was irrelevant.

He had every intention of brushing the nonsensical claim aside, but before he could the man he'd observed pouring shots of whiskey spoke up. "Saw him myself. He's a little shorter, a lot thinner, and looks like he's an Indian, but his skin is just as pale."

"Nonsense." Folsom shook his head. "Corporal Bridges, kindly put that man in irons." He pointed toward the gaunt man.

Bridges nodded and took a step forward. The corporal was a burly man, large and heavyset and capable with his hands. He'd knocked several men larger than him down a few sizes in his time and he would likely do so again.

The smiling man shook his head and blocked Bridges. "Let's not make a mistake here, gentlemen. My friend and I are perfectly willing to leave town right now and end this without any additional troubles."

"Are you deaf, sir?" Folsom's voice was as harsh as a whip crack when he spoke. "I have dead soldiers on my hands!"

"Your soldiers died trying to shoot me down." The gaunt man's voice remained as calm as ever, but the expression on his face belied his tone. "They were a mite bit offended, seeing as I stopped them from taking a few squaws to have their way with."

Was that guilt in Folsom's chest? He tried to tell himself that it was not, but he also remembered his sister and the scandals she'd been involved in and that feeling bloomed inside him. With an effort he crushed the emotion down. "It is our duty to curtail the growing Indian problems in this area. And in addition to confessing to killing my men, you've just confessed to interfering with that duty." He looked away from the gaunt man and barked at the corporal, "Bridges! Lock that man in irons!"

Bridges nodded and started forward. Before he could take two steps, the smiling man moved forward and struck him a solid blow that dropped the larger man to the ground.

"That's enough of this!" Folsom grabbed at the pistol strapped to his hip.

By the time he'd drawn, several of the soldiers with him were doing the same, and the two men he was facing had both managed to draw as well.

The smiling man had two Peacemakers. One of the large

bore barrels was aimed at Folsom. The other was pointed at Song, who was crouching slightly and looked like he might well enjoy taking a bite out of the gunslinger.

The albino aimed a heavy shotgun at the whole lot of them. He'd swept the damned thing from under his coat with ease, and was looking hard at Folsom.

"Anyone pulling a trigger might well wish they'd reconsidered, gentlemen." A round-bellied man walked forward. His voice shook, but he had a pleasant enough smile on his round face. "Might I suggest we put weapons down and come to an understanding before anyone else is killed?"

Folsom didn't like him. He spoke like a lawyer. Still, he offered a chance to the captain not to get his head blown off by two different men. Outside of the tent several of his men let out bellows of anger and shock. The ground trembled lightly and while he feared taking his eyes off the two men aiming at him, he risked a look around to the entrance of the tent.

"Would someone kindly tell me what the hell is going on out there?"

Private Bronson called out loud and clear from the other side of the tent flap, "Captain! We got injuns coming our way! A lot of injuns!"

The smiling man laughed again. It was a humorless, bitter sound.

There was a point where no more could be tolerated. That point had come a long time ago as far as Alchesay was concerned. His parents had been murdered and scalped when he was a boy. His wife had been taken only a few years ago. His family had been attacked and slaughtered again and again over the years, first by Mexicans and now by the round eyes. Enough.

Several of the tribal elders wanted peace, but that time was past. They came into the area and looked for silver, and when they found it, they started digging. Most of the *Dilze'he* were already stuck in this desert land, forced here by the white man, and now they were being told to move again.

And maybe they would have. Maybe even Alchesay would have accepted this – though he was not truly sure if he would or not – but now these fools had come and dragged several women from the town. They thought the women did not understand their words, but they were wrong. His sister was among them and she'd heard what the men intended to do.

And according to her, a Skinwalker had saved them.

Whatever the case, it had only taken the word of his sister to send him toward the town and because many of the men were just as tired of being pushed and pushed, they came with him.

There would be no more of their women raped or scalped by the white men.

The men in blue uniforms were gathered in one area when Alchesay charged into town with his men. In numbers they looked to be stronger, but they were all busy looking at one tent and before they were aware, Alchesay and his men were in range.

The first rifle shots cracked through the air before the soldiers did much more than look around with open mouths. All around the area people of all colors were running, wisely clearing away from the charging horsemen. Four of the bluecoats fell before any of them considered attacking in return. Two of their horses fell too, shot by who knew. Men and horses alike screamed.

And then the soldiers turned and grabbed for their weapons.

Alchesay had planned for this. Instead of staying at a long range, he and his men charged their horses into the enemy. Flesh fell before the hooves of his mount. Men screamed and fell, and the horse stumbled but kept its footing. He was too close to shoot, so he swung his rifle and hit whatever he could with the butt of the weapon. Someone fired from nearby and a bullet cut past his head. He had no time to consider that. Instead he hit another bluecoat and felt bone break.

There were screams, of course. And then there were battle cries. He called out for his men and they called out as well. The cavalry recoiled as if hit by boiling water.

He charged forward.

The tent was closer now. And the time was finally here. He would kill them all, every last one of the soldiers. They would all pay for what they had done, what they had planned to do. There would be no mercy.

Unfortunately, the men in the tent felt the same away.

There were more of the soldiers than he'd expected. They came from inside the large tent and started shooting and they were far enough away that they could still aim and shoot and kill.

Beside him Mangas stopped his battle cry when a bullet tore his skull away. He fell from his horse and into the tide of men being crushed, and that was the last Alchesay saw of his lifelong friend.

The bluecoats kept coming, and Alchesay jammed his heels into the horse's flanks and charged forward into the crush of soldiers.

And men screamed.

And men died.

And Alchesay roared his challenge for all of them. His skin felt hot. His bones were blades of ice. His heart thundered in his chest and his eyes shook in his skull.

And then the change came, and Alchesay roared his challenge a second time as his teeth grew and his body twisted into a new form.

Halfway across the camp he'd crouched in the dirt and made markings with one pale finger. His other hand had poured colored sand into the markings and filled them in.

The Navajo called his kind Skinwalkers. It was as good a name as any, but he knew better. There was more to them than just changing shapes. Most of his kind were gone now. They tended to kill each other off. It was not something they could, or wanted to control. Like the weather or the stars, it was simply what was supposed to be. They felt a dislike for each other that could seldom be set aside for long. The one he'd seen earlier was a child, barely born into the world and likely knew nothing of himself.

He probably wanted to know more about what he was. And why he existed. The old one could have told him, but that was not what he planned this day.

What he planned was violence and carnage and blood and suffering, the things he fed on best.

And so he'd finished his simple spell and looked at the characters he had drawn in the dirt and then at the Apache charging into town. They had plans, too, and those plans were of blood and violence.

So the old one helped them along.

His hands had scooped up the colored sand and dirt and held the mixture out and blew it at the Apache as they rode past.

He did not hit all of them, but he'd hit enough.

He waited until they were engaged with their enemies and the bloodshed had begun before he said that words that made the spell awaken. And just that easily, the anger within the warriors was given a face and a form.

The old one settled down and watched and waited.

Soon enough he would feed.

Crowley shook his head as the cavalrymen turned away from him and from Slate alike. Slate stared at them with an expression that was either shock, outrage or both. Whatever the case, it made Crowley chuckle.

"You find this situation amusing, Mister Crowley?" Slate looked his way with an expression of disappointment.

"Not at all, Mister Slate. I find you amusing."

"And why would that be?" Damned if Slate didn't sound offended.

"Because you look so very annoyed that the men who want to hang you are no longer bothering with you."

Slate blinked and a quick, embarrassed grin flashed on his face. "Yes, well, when you say it like that."

"We should leave."

"I agree." Slate pointed at the men flowing out of the tent. "But there are men in our way."

"This is a tent, Mister Slate. We can climb out from under it if we must."

The bartender looked at them and shook his head. "Could just go out the flap at the other side, too."

Crowley smiled and tossed the man a coin.

And as they were walking away from the soldiers, ignoring the screams and the gunshots, a deep roar shook through the air and the tone of the screams changed from anger and pain to deep, abiding terror.

And he knew before it happened of course. It was inevitable, really.

Someone out in the front of the tent let out a shriek and someone else called out, "Help me! Oh, Lord, help me!"

Crowley shook his head.

"You don't have to, you know." Slate's voice, as soft as a whisper.

"Oh, but I do." He shook his head again. "Can't you feel it? Whatever is out there, it's not natural." He spoke as if he regretted what was going to come next, but still the smile pulled at the edges of his lips and his heart beat faster in his chest.

"Well then, shall we do this?"

Crowley spun hard and nearly ran for the men at the opposite end of the tent. Many of the soldiers were coming back in, their eyes wide and frightened. He could understand that. There were a lot of things out in the world to be afraid of.

Folsom had planned to come out with guns blazing and eliminate the threat before it could become something larger. He'd half expected to run across a few of the savages in town, but when he heard the horses, and the sound of Apache battle cries, he felt a cold knot of dread in his stomach.

Had he, perhaps, turned a blind eye to his men having their way with the squaws? Yes. Why? Because happy soldiers performed better. What he had not truly considered was what might occur when the red skinned brutes found out about what was happening with their women. That was the very first concern when he heard the sounds of his men screaming. It shouldn't have been, but truth be told the guilt had been gnawing at him for a while.

The guilt went away the second he saw the monsters.

He'd pushed through the crowd of his men to assess the situation and was looking directly at the Indians when they changed. Not all of them, only a few, but it was enough. The man at the front of the charge was a stocky brute in leathers. He wore a canvas coat that had seen its best days a few years earlier and was coming apart at the seams, and his rage was a brutal thing to behold.

The coat tore itself apart, shredded right before the captain's eyes, and the clothes beneath it did the same, peeling away even as the man continued charging forward on his horse. One pace and the fabric was splitting. Another step forward and the horse was knocking two soldiers aside. A third step and one of the soldiers fell to the ground while the other kept his balance. A fourth step and Folsom was drawing his weapon, intent on killing the fool horseman. A fifth step and everything changed all at once. The horse let out a shriek and lost its balance falling forward and crashing to the ground. He was a horseman himself and knew instantly the beast had broken its neck. The rider fell forward and *blurred* as he caught himself on his palms. That was the only way he could think of it. The fabric on his body was torn apart and so was the flesh beneath it. Folsom looked and his eyes refused to see properly. Great flakes of flesh and hair split away from the shape of the man and when he moved forward, standing instead of sliding across the ground, which seemed an impossibility by itself, he was not a man anymore but something entirely different.

The thing still had two legs and two arms, yet beyond that he would have been hard pressed to say what might seem humanoid about it. The body was wrong. Too broad, and covered in wiry fur. The head seemed to grow directly from the torso, and while he knew the thing must surely see, the only features that made any sense were the teeth that filled a mouth far too large for the rest of the hellish shape.

The thing roared again and Folsom aimed and fired, and then fired twice more. His aim was true, and a hole blossomed in the center of the demon's chest. It stepped back and then fell back and landed in the dirt, rolling and thrashing, slamming into the shuddering, dying horse, which once again let out a scream of panic and pain.

His men did their best to get away from both shapes, but even as they tried to escape the other horsemen were coming and they, too, changed. While Folsom was busy trying to kill the first nightmare a pack of equally-unsettling things dropped from their horses, snarling, bleating, screaming, and attacking the members of the Cavalry.

They were none of them the same. Each was a different form of nightmare; some thickset and low to the ground, others long-limbed and far too tall for a human. The horses fled, kicking and screaming up a hellish noise, crushing everything that got in their way as they made as much distance as they could from the hellish things.

The only thing they had in common was that each and every one of the nightmares was, indeed, as white as the snow. They were ghostly, horrid things that scared him to the point he thought he'd piss himself.

The thing he'd shot got back up. It wasn't completely white anymore. There was a lot of blood spilling from the wounds he'd put in it, but that didn't seem to be enough to stop it. There was no face, just that damnable mouth full of fangs as it screeched and leapt at him.

And then the pale white man he'd been ready to lock in irons pushed past him and fired a shotgun blast into the open mouth of the thing. The barrel was just past Folsom's face and he felt the detonation as much as he heard it. After that he wasn't hearing much of anything. His ears were too stuffed with cotton to make sense of the words spoken.

Just the same, he understood the gesture when the albino swept him aside and fired the second barrel of his weapon. The thing he shot did not get up again. They were tough, but they were not indestructible.

Crowley was next, moving past him with no sign of a weapon in his hands and that mad grin of his spreading across his face.

His hearing was coming back enough that he heard the words from the smiling man's mouth. "What are they, Mister Slate?"

The gaunt man shook his head. "No idea, Mister Crowley, but I believe they are connected to whatever is drawing me here."

One of the things, too thin and too tall and reaching for a private who was screaming and staring down at the stump where his hand had been, turned its attention to the man named Slate and let out a sound like a cat hissing, if that cat was the size of a bear.

Crowley stepped around the gaunt one and blocked the oversized hand that reached for the albino. He struck hard enough that the nearly skeletal thing reared back in shock. It was almost twice as tall as a man and had a face that was stretched and thin and filled with teeth the size of knives.

"No. I don't think you want to do that." Crowley kept smiling.

Folsom shook off his confusion and decided to handle the matter. The revolver kicked when he pulled the trigger and he watched the left half of the thing's neck explode in a gout of crimson that splashed both of the men.

Slate flinched as the thing screamed and clutched at the wound. That made Folsom feel a little better about his own fear.

Crowley stepped in closer and kicked the spindly leg of the

thing with the heel of his boot. Bones snapped and the ghostly white demon fell as surely as if struck by an axe.

Folsom felt something touch his leg, and almost shrieked. He looked down and aimed his Colt at the source of whatever was touching him. It was Song. Half of the Chinaman's face had been carved into bloody red trenches and his eye was missing. He clutched at Folsom's pant leg and let out a sound. And then he died.

Folsom shook his head, angrier at the loss of the heathen than he would have ever expected. "That's enough of this madness!" he roared, and all around him the soldiers stopped their panic, or at least calmed it down. They were soldiers and they were used to combat. What they needed, what they always needed, was someone to lead them. "Kill these damned things!"

To make his point he aimed at the next of the things close enough for him to hit, and fired. The shot went astray and only clipped one overly large ear on the beast. When it looked at him, really looked at him, Folsom knew he'd made a horrible mistake. He'd have apologized if he could have found the words, but it was on him far too quickly. Folsom let out a yelp as clawed fingers ripped into his coat and the beast lifted him into the air, baring impossible teeth and roaring directly into his face.

Folsom aimed his weapon and fired, and nothing at all happened.

He tried again.

Nothing.

"Well, damn." It was all he could think to say.

The captain was staring at his death, and Crowley was tempted to let it take him. As a boy he'd been a scared, confused little thing. As a man he smacked of too much cocky attitude and too little common sense. Worse, he was actually making himself useful. It was easier to ignore men who were useless and cocky about it.

Still, at the moment there were other considerations, like the damned things chewing their way through a dozen soldiers. They were monsters, yes, but nothing he'd ever seen before. They did not reek of the demons he was used to, and they were not spirits in any sense he was familiar with.

When he'd come to the New World he'd done so to study these exact sorts of creatures. There had been a definite excitement in finding new and interesting beings in a land he had never been to before.

That excitement had not changed. Adding to it was the sheer variety of shapes that these creatures took. They were, he had no doubt, of similar ilk. They had to be.

Even things that ran in packs seldom liked to mingle with creatures.

That was the part that made him smile.

Lucas Slate grabbed the thing holding the captain and hauled it backward by the scruff of its bullish neck. It let out a yowlp of surprise and so did the Cavalryman. The good news for the captain was that it let go of him. That was also the bad news for Slate. The thing he was holding onto moved like a sack of cats held over a roaring fire. It twisted and whipped its arms in wide arcs and screeched as it turned on Crowley's companion, and both of them stumbled back and fell.

Before Crowley could get to them, they were lost in the crush of people.

A soldier aimed for the area where they'd fallen and Crowley knocked him aside, throwing off his aim as he waded into the crush of flesh. People moved and thrashed and pushed in and out of his view. Crowley ignored them all, save to push them aside. Somewhere ahead of him, not but a few feet to be sure, but in the press of struggling bodies it might well have been miles, his companion was down on the ground and fighting.

When the bullish thing flew through the air, it was as limp as a sack of horse dung. The thing trailed blood, and as it rose into the air, Lucas Slate stood, covered in the same crimson stains and looking truly enraged.

His shirt had been torn apart and deep cuts ran along the left side of his muscular chest. Those cuts bled, a reminder that he was still at least partially human despite his appearance.

Slate looked around and stooped long enough to grab his fool hat from the ground. That hat had seen better days and likely would have been thrown away by most people, but the battered old thing with its dusty band and the broken feathers sticking from the same went back on Slate's head before he looked around and the rage faded from his expression.

It was a calmer expression he wore as he reached for his Navy revolvers and started aiming.

Crowley had the good sense to stay well away from the man as he pulled the triggers. The first bullet blew a hole through a white, scaly thing with too many eyes, and also took the hand from one of the Cavalry. The creature flopped to the ground and twitched. The soldier fell to his knees and screamed. By the time those two things had occurred, Slate had turned his attention to the next target and fired with that same dead expression on his face. *Boom!* The creature fell. Slate's mouth twisted into a feral snarl and he fired again. The bullets from his weapon were a reminder that death could be sudden and violent. Another explosive noise and the Indians and the soldiers alike were quickly backing away from Slate. He stood taller than any of them and he looked like the Grim Reaper ready for the harvest. The only things that didn't run were the white nightmares around them. They should have fled but it seemed beyond them to reason that well. Instead they charged toward Slate and he fired again and again until the last of them fell at his feet.

Through it all, Jonathan Crowley watched with his eyes narrowed to slits and a grin frozen in place.

When the final beast had fallen, Lucas Slate looked at Captain Folsom and shook his head. "I do not currently feel inclined to go with you for trial." Both of the weapons were still in his hands and the barrels of the Navy six-shooters were smoking in the cold air.

Folsom stared at the spectre before him for ten heartbeats without responding and then finally he said, "Currently, I do not feel much inclined to argue the matter, sir. We have all of us had a day already."

"Indeed."

Folsom called for his men to gather the dead and the wounded. His voice was weaker than before and his hands shook. That did not make him a coward in Crowley's eyes. It merely made him human.

He rather envied the soldier that.

Folsom sat in his newly-appropriated office in town. He thought about the day's events. All told, if you counted the Chinaman – and he did – he had lost seven men, and the number of wounded was higher still.

Somehow he had avoided getting injured himself. The men looked up to him and none of them had missed that he was in the heart of the combat. They knew he hadn't stood behind the lines and watched them take the damage. No, he had come out to the assistance of all when the damned Indians had attacked.

Being as he was in the middle of town when the attack took place he should have expected some sort of coalition of towns-folk, but he was caught flatfooted. The men who came before him were dressed, as gentlemen should dress, in proper suits with vests and with matching shoes. That was an accomplishment at least half the time; at least it had been since he crossed into areas across the Mississippi from home. That said, they needed a good wash and not a one of them seemed familiar with the idea of shaving. The facial hairs were long and the facial expressions were dour.

They'd been droning on for a while now, long enough for him to get the gist. They wanted the soldiers gone. Or they wanted assurances, or they wanted the Indians dead. Something of that sort.

When he'd heard enough he raised one hand and the conversations stopped. "What exactly do you gentlemen want? Pick one thing. I haven't the time to listen to every complaint you have. I need to report the deaths of my soldiers and I need to prepare your town for any more possible Indian attacks."

A black haired man sporting the most impressive mustache Folsom had ever seen, spoke. As his lips moved, his mustache jittered and jumped. It was nearly mesmerizing. "There wouldn't be any Indian attacks if you'd left well enough alone." The man leaned forward and planted his hands on the long oak table the captain had commandeered to act as his desk. "We had us an understanding. We didn't piss on them and they didn't come along and try to kill us. You notice how they only went for soldiers? There was a reason for that."

Folsom stood and gave the man his best hard look. It was a good one because the fellow took two paces back, shaking his head. "Do you know who I am, sir? Do you even begin to know why I am here? I'm here because I was called here by one of your own. A telegram was sent to Washington, D.C. and that in turn was considered and then acted upon. I am the result of that telegram."

"And who the hell sent it?" The mustache trembled with righteous indignation. Folsom knew the man he was speaking to had eyes, but he had not yet been able to focus on them enough to consider the character they might reveal.

"Allucius Sheppard." Folsom reached into his jacket pocket and fumbled out the original paper. "Says here he's the mayor of this town."

The mustache tightened for a moment and then trembled even more. "Al? Al Sheppard not only isn't the mayor of anything, he'd dead!" Several voices murmured their agreement. "The damned fool drank himself to death. Passed out and choked on his own regurgitation. And besides, he was never in charge of a damned thing around these parts."

Folsom felt a flush run into his cheeks. "Be that as it may, I have my orders to get rid of the red man in this area and I intend to follow those orders." He leaned onto the table and heard it creak threateningly under his weight. "I've spent time listening to your concerns, gentlemen. Until I hear otherwise, my duty is to remove the Indians from this area and keep your town safe. Good day."

"We were already safe!" Mustache shook his fist and looked like he might even consider using it against Folsom but decided at the last moment not to get himself shot. "Leave us to our own devices, sir! We have to live here when you're done with your damned orders."

The man turned his back and stomped away before Folsom could respond, and after a brief hesitation the rest of the sorry lot followed suit.

Folsom settled back behind his newly acquired desk and started composing his explanation of the day's events. Colonel Hartshorn would want to know what had happened and he'd need to offer a proper defense. The loss of so many and that on top of being caught unawares, was not going to sit well. Folsom dreaded the shit storm that would surely be coming his way.

He had no idea.

Lucas Slate squinted at his reflection in the dusty mirror. The clothes were nice, a gift from Crowley, and they fitted properly. The tailor had a suit that was supposed to be picked up and never was – the man had died apparently – and while it took a bit of waiting while the adjustments were made, the final result was worth the patience.

Crowley eyed him critically enough to make him wonder if the man had ever spent time as a tailor himself. Finally he nodded his satisfaction and counted out coins for the man who'd sold the suit.

"There is a haberdashery at the edge of the saloon over that way." The tailor pointed vaguely, which, as the town had no proper streets, was the best that could be managed, "should you like a new hat as well."

Slate stared at the man for a moment and then simply shook his head.

Crowley walked for the door of the shop after thanking the tailor.

Slate watched Crowley break into one of his smiles. "What?" Slate was slipping his hat in place and almost managing a scowl.

"I have seen men less devoted to their wives than you are to your hat, Mister Slate."

"And had I a wife, perhaps I'd care less about my hat, sir."

"I should rather not consider the ramifications of that statement."

Slate reared back as if slapped and then chuckled. "You've a vile mind, Mister Crowley."

"Now, tell me about the pale thing you saw before everything went mad."

"He was tall and thin and pale. Looked to me as if he might be an Indian, but as washed of color as me." Slate looked away. "He spoke to me in some language I have never heard, but I understood him. He said we would meet again."

"You were pale when we met. You are an albino, after all, but you are a different sort of pale now."

"How do you mean?"

Your skin lacked pigment before. Now it has more color to it, but that color is white. That's really the best way I can put it."

Slate nodded and pursed his thin lips. "He was too thin."

"What do you mean?" Crowley looked puzzled.

"I mean I am thin, but I am still a possibility. He was taller than me and thinner than me. He looked impossible. His body is too thin and his arms and legs so very long and his head shape was thinner even than mine."

Crowley stared at him for a long moment and finally nodded. "That thing we dealt with in Carson's Point was a bit like that. But only a bit."

"I never truly saw the thing but towards the end, and frankly I was a bit too unsettled by what was happening to me to much care at that point."

"You touched a stone. The stone went into you. We've discussed that before, of course. We know that the stones were put into the – whatever the hell it might be's – chosen victims and they changed, but it wasn't the same as these things. These were sudden and the bodies didn't stay changed."

Slate looked at him. "Did they not?"

"No." Crowley looked back just as hard, his face impossible to read past that damnable grin of his. "They became what they once were when they died. They were Indians, but we knew that."

"Why do you suppose they attacked?"

Crowley shrugged. "I neither know nor care. Humans do stupid things to humans all the time, Mister Slate. I don't allow myself the luxury of paying much attention."

That was a lie and Slate knew it. They discussed many things on their travels and inevitably what they talked about most was the state of the world around them as gleaned from various newspapers. Crowley bought them and read them insatiably. Still, he did not call the man on his lie.

"And the soldiers? How do you feel about them being here, Mister Crowley?"

"I've never much taken to soldiers. Been one before, fought in my share of wars and followed orders, but I've never liked it. Soldiers are expected to follow orders, no matter how foolish those orders might be."

Crowley paused a moment and then asked, "And you? Do you side with the Indians?"

"No sir, I do not. I side with the people on the streets who are getting caught up in this conflict. I knew what those men intended when it came to the squaws." He shook his head. "I do not believe that women should be misused."

Crowley nodded.

"And you, Mister Crowley? Do you side with either group?"

"The Indians were minding their own business. The army was sent by someone. They do not, as a rule come without orders. They are summoned. So one is doing what they have always done and the other is following orders from elsewhere. I can't say as I much care either way."

"You keep saying that sort of thing, and yet, here you are, grinning and wading into conflicts."

Crowley's voice dripped with sarcasm. "My pale companion has gotten himself into trouble and asked for my help. What is a man to do?" His plain face looked around the shop for a moment and then back to Slate. "How does the suit feel?"

"Like proper clothing, and I thank you for it, Mister Crowley." Slate ducked his head briefly for a moment, feeling an unaccustomed flash of shame. "I fear I cannot possibly pay you back any time soon."

Crowley waved it aside. "I have the money to spare and you have lost all you owned before we met. As we are traveling together for the present time, I can hardly expect you to settle into life as an undertaker again, though I imagine you could have made fair compensation this particular day."

"Just the same."

"Should I decide you owe me, Mister Slate, you may rest assured you'll be informed of such debts. Until then, merely accept that under our current circumstances I do not mind investing in your clothes." He snorted. "Besides which, you were beginning to look too much like an Indian and I need to not confuse you for any other white-skinned Indians we might encounter."

"Do you suppose that's a strong likelihood?"

"You've run across one already and I am fairly certain you are looking forward to a second encounter."

"What makes you say that, Mister Crowley?"

"Because you have a need to understand your place in the universe, Mister Slate."

"And you don't?"

"I have known my place in the universe for a very long time, Mister Slate. And we are still looking into your position."

Neither spoke of what might happen when that position was known.

Finding rooms proved challenging, but not impossible. Apparently having a giant albino looming over your shoulder made people more willing to find space for a man in a negotiating mood. The rooms were comfortable enough, and as an added bonus seemed bug free.

In the morning, Crowley looked at the growth on his face, and trimmed the hairs down to manageable levels rather than shaving them away completely. He knew it wouldn't last but for the next few days at least he had a neatly-trimmed beard and mustache to fight off the cold.

When he came downstairs, Slate was already waiting for him, and the small gathering of tables were all filled except for the one where the albino waited. His hat had been mended and looked mostly like it had in the past. Crowley chose not to feed into his obsession and ignored the thing completely. Within twenty minutes they'd eaten and after ten minutes more they were on their way.

"Where are we going, exactly?" Crowley asked, though he already knew the answer.

"I'm off to find the other one like me. You are along to keep me out of trouble."

Crowley nodded. "I seem to remember something about that."

"As it was your idea, I should hope so, sir."

Despite the violence of the day, before the crowds were moving about, many of them looking to buy wares and others looking to sell. It was distinctly possible that there were even more wretches moving into the town.

There were soldiers everywhere they looked, though for the moment none of them seemed to be causing too much trouble. Crowley had no doubt that would change soon enough.

Folsom had made clear his intention to clean the Indians from the area for the safety of all involved, regardless of how the people felt about that. As it had been Indians starting the shooting the day before – excluding what Slate had accomplished all by himself – it seemed perfectly reasonable to expect the captain and his men to be as prepared as possible.

A pickpocket tried to steal from Crowley. He stopped the attempt without causing a scene. It was a bad time to be a thief and a worse time to be a child. He decided to let someone else deal with handling the young boy with the grabby hands. The things they'd been bothered by the day before were far more worrisome. Besides which, Crowley kept most of his money hidden where it would never be found. A moment later he changed his mind, and contemplated going after the kid and teaching him a lesson, but it was too late. The would-be thief was long gone.

He watched the other Skinwalker from a distance, and noted the man who walked with him. They were both powerful, as was expected of any Skinwalker, but the one with him, the smiling man, he was a different sort of powerful. He carried himself with confidence and he smiled at almost everything. Not a pleasant smile but a baring of teeth, a warning that the man was deadly beyond most people's reckoning. Where they walked, people scattered away from them, perhaps without even being aware of it.

The Skinwalker was aware, of course. That was why he was following them. They were dangerous and they could well be dangerous enough to cause him harm. He would find out soon enough.

The wind blew and whispered its secrets and he listened as he had learned to long ago. The stories of the wind were all about the Indians coming toward the town. There had been a great deal of blood spilled and the Apache in the area wanted to settle the matter. They did not wish to talk any longer. There is a point where anyone can lose hope of a simple resolution and that time had come and passed.

All around him people moved and milled and sought desperately for what would make their lives complete. An urchin moved toward him, furtive and worried. He bumped into a man in front of the Skinwalker and plucked a few coins from his victim's pocket. A moment later he was bumping into a young woman and apologizing even as he lifted a small item from her bag. And then he bumped into the Skinwalker, mumbled an apology and continued on with a small silver nugget the Skinwalker had been carrying for the last three days.

The silver meant nothing to him. He had taken it from a dead man he found on his way to the town. The corpse had been torn open by what at first glance appeared to be wolves, but the Skinwalker knew better. He could smell shapechangers and found the notion amusing.

The fact that the boy took it merely meant that he had managed to catch the old sorcerer's attention. That was enough.

A whispered word as he crouched and grabbed at the soil. The arid earth crumbled in his hand and he spat into it, rubbed it between his fingers and his palm until it became a doughy mass. He stood just long enough to throw that simple lump at the thief, striking him on the back of his neck. The boy reached reflexively for what hit him and the old man smiled and continued on his way. Only a few seconds later the screams started as the boy fell to the ground, swelling and choking and trying to breathe. It was not the first time he'd spread a sickness and it would not be the last. This was a minor one and would only kill a few, but it would leave them all afraid.

Somewhere behind him a woman screamed as the boy's flesh rotted away and spilled his bodily fluids into the street. Up ahead, far enough along that they did not seem to notice, the other Skinwalker and the strange creature walked on.

Crowley noticed Slate cock his head to the left. "What is it?" he asked.

"That damn song again," Slate replied. "Every time I hear it something goes wrong."

"You are hearing a summoning spell. Whatever this thing we're looking for is, it summons energies and what I can only call demons, even if they don't feel like the ones I'm used to."

"Then how do you know?"

"I've been testing your limits, Mister Slate. Seeing what it is you might be capable of, but I have my own abilities."

"You've never much discussed what they are."

Crowley cast a sideways look in Slate's direction. "We don't much talk about what happens if I decide you are a threat. We both know the answer already, yes?"

"Of course." Slate nodded, but his voice remained soft and dry. "I might be a threat and you might need to eliminate that threat. We've already seen a little of what something like me can do. If I don't maintain control, I understand what you'll have to do and I condone it."

"Do you?"

Slate looked at him and his mouth trembled for a moment. "I've no desire to become the sort of monster I was raised around."

"You were raised around monsters?"

"I was raised an albino and a mulatto in an area where many considered that a sign of the Devil, sir. Had my family not had a certain level of influence I'd have been killed. As it was, I remained locked inside my house most times to avoid a beating. There are all sorts of monsters, Mister Crowley. Not all of them cast spells or have fangs."

Crowley nodded. "Agreed. Very well, Mister Slate. A few facts for you. I can see the dead. I can communicate with them. Mostly I choose not to."

"Why is that?"

"Because the dead are not of interest to me. They are dead, and often they make demands when they know they can be heard. I am not interested in their demands and I have no desire to be plagued by them any more than I have been in the past." Crowley's face grew troubled for a moment.

"Are the dead around here?"

"Some. Not as many. Not too many have died here yet, though I imagine that's to change soon."

"Are there any dead around us now?"

"Oh, yes." He looked past Slate's shoulder at the faint ghostly image of Molly Finnegan and nodded slowly. She looked at him, implored him, would have begged if there was enough of her left, but there was not. Something had stolen most of her away in Carson's Point, not too long ago, and left just enough to ensure he was haunted by her. He had not yet resolved to destroying that remnant or sending it on to whatever lay beyond this realm. If he didn't think about it, he could tell himself she wasn't suffering. Sometimes, most times, really, he didn't much like himself. He promised himself that he would release her soon. Very soon. Just not yet.

"What else to you see that you do not speak of, Mister Crowley?"

"I see a lot. I hear just as much. I heard the spell that was cast. I'm still trying to understand it. I know that it came from behind us, but so do you."

Slate nodded in agreement. "I do indeed. I've been trying to decide how to handle it."

"Well, perhaps you should confront your enemy and be done with it."

"Is he my enemy?" Slate's voice carried an uncertain note.

Crowley stopped walking and stared hard at him. "I should imagine he is. He's killed several people with his actions, and a few moments ago he killed a young boy who was seeking enough to stay alive in this hellhole."

"Did he?" Slate shook his head. "How do you know that?"

"Because currently the dead boy is standing over his rotten remains and screaming his rage into the skies. You cannot hear the dead, Mister Slate, but I can and I do."

Slate closed his eyes and nodded. "Then I suspect he is, indeed, my enemy."

Crowley heard the sound of gunfire and screaming from the far side of the small town, same as they had the day before. The screams were not pain or suffering. They were war cries. "Well, things are likely to get confusing right about now." Crowley spat the words, but again his smile crept out.

"I suspect you are right, Mister Crowley. And should I confront my enemy or wait?"

"It might be that the fighting won't reach us."

Slate nodded again and spun hard on his heel, moving back the way they'd come.

Crowley watched him, watched the crowd that had turned toward the sounds of dying, part before Slate as easily as calm waters part before a ship's prow, and watched also as the small shape he approached unfolded itself from a stooped position.

Lucas Slate was taller now than most of the men around him. He was taller than Crowley by a few inches, though they had only recently stood almost the same height. Crowley had once stolen a suit of the man's because it fit well enough to allow it. As tall as Slate was, the thing that stood before him was taller by almost a foot. How it had hidden itself in so small a form was a mystery that Crowley would try to solve later.

The thing was the same color as Slate, a white that seemed too vibrant for the cadaverous shape. It had long white hair tied back in a braid, and wore clothes that looked like rawhide but that Crowley knew immediately were human flesh.

It had a very long body and a long face, eyes as dark and black as pitch and as shiny as polished glass. When the nightmare smiled his gums were gray and his teeth an unpleasant shade of yellow.

Slate and the thing spoke to each other, and Crowley listened and understood not a word of it. In the distance a dead boy kept screaming his outrage at being murdered and further away still, the gunfire continued in sporadic bursts.

The Indians came in hard and fast, and this time there were more of them and they were better organized.

Folsom's men were doing their duty, guarding the town, and none of them took their task lightly. The day before had been reminder enough that their work was dangerous.

So when the red men came, the alarm was quickly called. Folsom stepped outside and prepared himself for the battle. The men were ready and so was he and by God, he'd see the savages pay for their bloody assault.

The men rallied quickly and he called for them to assume the various posts he'd laid out the night before. They were ready and they were more than willing after seeing their companions taken down. One or two might well have been worried about whatever sort of monsters the Apache had brought with them the day before, but they rallied just the same and he was proud of them.

Captain Folsom walked away from the hotel and headed for the sounds of combat, his heart pounding with the thrill of combat. He was not afraid. The Lord had blessed him with a brave heart and a noble purpose. He would see the day through and take no prisoners. The savages had earned a quick death for their troubles.

Up ahead of him, Sergeant Barnes had taken a position on top of a two-storey mercantile, firing as quickly as he could into the crowd below. The man was hell with a rifle, and with each shot, an Indian dropped, but damned if it didn't seem there were endless numbers of them this time around.

He had dealt with the Lakota before but never with the Apache until the previous day. They did not seem cut from the same cloth. They seemed more determined to stand their ground and take whatever it was they wanted.

"Fowler! Where is Sergeant Fowler?"

"Sergeant Fowler is on the other side of town, standing his ground and waiting, sir!" The man that spoke to him was just out of his sight, but he recognized the voice of Private Herbst. The voice was as distinct as the man himself, a red haired brute nearly as strong as an ox. He turned to bark an order at Herbst and saw the private's body jerk twice, saw the blast of meat and bone that came off his left shoulder and then saw the man hit the ground, screaming.

Damned foolish of him to look away from the conflict. He looked back toward the crush of Indians charging into town and the chaos of people getting away from them. The civilians ran, as well they should. The soldiers stood their ground.

Folsom drew his revolver and took aim at the closest savage, a lean old man on a black horse. The old man saw him and charged, riding hard to reach him. The bullet Folsom fired caught the old man in his thigh and blew through the leg and the horse under it with ease. The old man screamed, the horse screamed, and both collapsed in a sliding heap. Neither was dead, but he intended to remedy that. One step closer, and the bullet from the next Indian caught Folsom in the chest, tearing through the rib above his heart and then through the organ itself. He tried to aim his weapon but his traitorous fingers dropped it. The pain, when it showed up, was as large as a mountain and crushed his chest in its grip. Folsom tried to scream, tried to do anything at all, and managed only to fall backward and land hard on the ground. The horse and rider stomped over his body as they continued into the town, followed by several other natives.

Crowley watched on from a distance, his face calm and almost expressionless, his eyes intensely focused. Slate did his best to ignore the man, which, considering the nightmare in front of him, was not that difficult.

"You have questions," the thing said. It was a statement rather than a question. Again it was spoken in a language other than English, one completely unknown to Slate, but he understood just the same.

"What are you? What am I?"

Those vile teeth flashed and the impossibly thin, tall man chuckled. "You were given a seed. It was planted in your body. I do not see it." It stared for a moment and then pointed to the small bump almost perfectly centered in its own forehead. When he touched it the skin parted like an eye blinking and for just an instant a greenish-gray stone showed before the skin sealed itself again. "It would be similar to this, but not exactly the same."

Slate remembered touching the stone, feeling it; remembered that pebble, too, had a song to sing. He nodded but did not speak.

"That seed is what you are. What you are becoming. We are not many, there have never been many, but we are powerful."

"What do I do about it?" Slate asked.

"Embrace the changes. I fought mine and in the end it caused me nothing but pain."

"What is the song I hear?"

"That is magic trying to tell you how to grow and become strong."

"Do you hear that same song?"

The thin man looked at him with a cold, sly expression. "I am the song."

"I don't understand."

"We are a part of the world. This world and others. We can listen to the song and we can sing notes from the song and create wonders. But we must feed if we listen to the song."

He wasn't sure if the thing was being deliberately vague or simply lacked the ability to explain itself. Either way, he was starting to dislike the thin man.

"What do we have to feed on?"

"Mostly pain, and others like ourselves." That smile grew larger.

Then the thin man reached for him and placed a hand on his chest and something inside of him pulled and twisted and shook through his body like a tree's roots being ripped from the ground. Lucas Slate tried to step back, tried to break free, but the thin man's hand on his chest burned at him and left him unable to move a single muscle. He stared at the yellowed teeth in darkened gums surrounded by white, smiling lips, and felt hatred rip into his heart.

In a lifetime full of predatory people who thought he was easy prey Lucas Slate had proven more than his share of people mistaken. He could not make his body move. He could not make his anger known by any of his previous methods. He could not, by God, even call out to Jonathan Crowley a dozen strides away. Instead he listened to the song that called to him and tried to understand the things it was saying.

The pain fought for his attention. The song had been trying to get his notice for longer.

He let the song win.

Crowley stared hard at the two pale men, waiting as they stood face to face and spoke. He could not understand a single word they were speaking and that, too, was something he was unaccustomed to. He did not understand because the words were new to him, but they were also not words, not exactly. Damned if it didn't sound like to two of them were harmonizing.

As a counterpoint to their song, the battle raged close by and drew closer. The Cavalry was fighting against the invading Apache and by the sounds of screams, cries and gunshots; the conflict was in a full fury.

Crowley stared toward the sound of battle and saw the soldiers retreating, heading at a slow crawl toward where he stood and watched another war taking place.

Sometimes the conflicts seemed impossible to escape.

The gaunt man facing off against Lucas Slate slapped Crowley's companion in the chest and Slate started jittering where he was, standing still and twitching, seizing again and again. The usually calm face pulled down, drawing into a pained expression and Slate's eyes raged silently.

Crowley'd planned on doing nothing at all about this. He made it a habit not to get involved in several different sorts of situations, not the least of which were cases when one monster fought another.

Did he think Slate was a monster? That was the question.

Not far away the dead boy kept screaming his anger to the skies. He refused to be placated by whatever it was the afterlife was supposed to offer him. From the corner of Crowley's eye he could see the vaporous spectre of Molly Finnegan, dead since the previous winter, buried by none other than Lucas Slate, and whose body once pushed itself out of the ground at the behest of whatever sort of creature Slate was becoming.

Behind Molly a Cavalryman's head snapped back violently and he flopped to the ground without making a sound that could be heard from the distance. Molly looked at the body expectantly. Crowley looked away.

Helping Slate would be a hideous mistake. The events of the last summer had proved that beyond a doubt. The man had muttered words and shattered the ground at his feet. He was no longer human.

And yet, as Slate asked for help in the tent earlier, Crowley was still allowed to respond now. He was freed from his usual constraints when asked for assistance by a human being.

And he was freed when asked by Lucas Slate.

"Damn me," he muttered.

The gun was in his hand in a second. He cocked the hammer, aimed and fired. Aimed, fired. Aimed, fired, and then again.

All four bullets slammed into the thin man. The first shot surprised him. He had apparently forgotten Crowley was there. The bullet tore his right arm apart, dragging it from Slate's chest. Slate staggered backward, gasping. The second bullet took the thin man in the left shoulder blade and spun him where he stood so that he was looking toward Crowley's feet. The third round punched into the thin man's chest and blew a hole through his left lung. The fourth round hit him in the stomach and doubled him over as sure as if he'd been kicked by a horse.

The thin man gasped and grunted and then fell to his knees, trying to balance himself on his hands. He bled from each wound, streams of blood flowing to the ground. Crowley took three strides forward and looked down at where Slate lay on the frozen soil. Slate looked at him then sat up, wincing. Where the thin man had touched him, his shirt was torn and the skin underneath was already bruising, showing an amount of red that would have been alarming on most people, but for all

Crowley knew, the color was perfectly normal in an albino who got himself bruised properly.

"I wasn't sure if you were going to help me or not." Slate's voice was more raspy than usual.

Crowley did not answer. To his left he saw the thin man getting to his feet.

"Mister Crowley!" Slate's eyes grew wide.

The thin man was looking hard at him and he was scowling. His face, already long and thin, grew longer still as he opened his mouth to speak. What he said meant nothing at all to Crowley. It was just gibberish. Just the same he felt his body hurled backward and did his best to prepare himself for impact.

The good news was that he landed on a canvas surface. The bad news was that a cast iron stove was under that canvas. He felt his ribs break on impact, and his right arm snapped in three places. He did not black out. He was not that fortunate.

The Skinwalker looked at his prey and smiled again. The wounds hurt, but he would heal. He would take from the younger, weaker Skinwalker and he would feed on the essence as had been done for as long as there had been Skinwalkers. Each was born, each created their seeds, each offered the seeds to worthy humans and then left. Later, after the seeds had a chance to grow, they came back and harvested their children. This one was not one of his, but that did not matter. He would feed and he would feed well. If the one who created this one took offense, he would feed on the progenitor as well.

The young Skinwalker stood, shivered. His chest was an angry red mass. The bruising was no doubt painful. The seed was deep inside this one's chest, near his heart. That was why he'd grabbed him there. Most Skinwalker's chose to place the seeds in the forehead. It made it easier for their children to see with their new senses and it also made harvesting them easier.

"I will kill you now. If you stay still I will try to make your death simple." It was a mercy he was willing to offer.

The young one nodded and said "Fuck yourself." The shotgun rose and both barrels of the weapons fired at him.

The Skinwalker had been alive for a very long time and he was familiar with European weapons. Familiarity, however, did not prepare him for the pain. A hundred tiny pellets rammed through his flesh and burned into muscles, into bone. One of the tiny shots tore open his right eye and the agony was greater than he had felt in lifetimes.

He yowled and fell back, clutching at his face. He had planned to be merciful. That plan was finished.

He looked through his good eye in time to see the young one breach the shotgun and pull out the hot shells. As he watched two more were inserted and the gaunt man came closer, scowling down at him.

He raised one arm and sang. His right arm was ruined and hadn't had time to mend, but his left worked well enough. His fingers clenched the air and he pulled with his song, with his mind, willing the seed deep in the other to come to him, to tear free of its moorings and come to him.

Lucas Slate dropped the shotgun and clutched at his chest. Was this a heart attack? He had no idea, had never felt one before. The pain grew larger and he fell to his knees, crying out.

Had any pain ever been this large? His hands held tight to the front of his chest, and under the palm that touched his pallid skin he felt something moving, twisting. He remembered the day he'd swallowed the oddly carved pebble he'd been given as a gift. It was a memory he'd done his best to forget, a fevered dream he never wanted to recall.

Much like the pain tearing him in half.

Lucas Slate screamed, something he hadn't done since his transformation had started. The sound was not remotely human.

For three seconds Crowley had a fantasy about Molly. Her body was next to his and she whispered in his ear, a warm breath that tickled pleasantly. Then the pain kicked in and took him from his reverie.

There was magic about and while he often hated that notion, Jonathan Crowley was healed by the presence of the supernatural. His skin ached and his bones shrieked a symphony of pain, then the agony faded into a deep fiery itch as they pulled themselves to where they belonged and healed within him.

Crowley opened his eyes and stared at Slate and the thin man. Both of them were on their knees, straining and bleeding and locked in some sort of silent struggle. Slate did not seem to be winning. He would rather Molly whispering in his ear, but she was dead and the past offered him little solace.

"All right then," he moaned. It took only a moment for him to stand.

The sounds of gunfire grew closer, drowning out the cries of the dead pickpocket and the unsettling scream coming from Slate.

Crowley started walking, heading for the two of them.

The first of the Indians came into view and almost immediately reined in their horses. They stared at the thin man and Lucas Slate with expressions of dread that were nearly comical, and grew almost as pale as the two of them.

He had no idea why the Apache were so afraid of the pale men and he did not care. What mattered at that moment was that the whole marauding lot of them watched for all of five seconds, and then their leader let out a command that had them turning tail and leaving the area at high speed.

As Crowley had witnessed, the Indians in the town had been scared of Lucas Slate. Apparently two of his kind in the area was a bit too much for them to stand. Crowley smiled at the notion, even as he looked back to Slate and the thin man.

Slate screamed again and blood spilled from between the fingers clamped over his chest. His eyes were wide and his mouth moved like a trout out of water seeking a gasp of proper breath.

"Move your hands, Mister Slate!" Crowley bellowed the words and the thin man ignored him.

Slate looked at him and managed a puzzled expression. "I am... I can't. What do you need?"

"I need to see what he's reaching for inside of you."

Slate stared at him for a moment and slowly, carefully let his hands fall away. The lump that was revealed was the size of an apple. That Slate's chest had not exploded was something of a miracle in Crowley's opinion. Heavy lines of red stained a great deal of his body and in addition to the heavy lump trying to tear free of him, there were other lines, other things moving under his skin. All of them seemed connected and all seemed determined to come out.

Crowley looked away from Slate for only a moment to assess the thin man. He'd been beat down a good bit. Four holes from the bullets Crowley himself fired and more still from a shotgun blast or two. Only one eye remained and it stared only at Slate.

The bastard was smiling.

Crowley hated when other people had a reason to smile. Well, at least when they were enemies of his. He walked closer, scrutinizing the thin man's face.

One eye was gone. One remained. Centered above them was a small opening in his head, and that at least was something Crowley was familiar with.

He had seen similar stones in Carson's Point. They had caused him no end of troubles.

Two fast steps had him picking up his pistol. Three more strides and the barrel was one inch from the center of the thin man's forehead.

As he cocked the hammer back the bastard finally noticed him and his one remaining eye opened wide. Crowley pulled the trigger and ripped the top of the thin man's head away with one shot.

The thin man launched backward and slammed his ruined head into the frozen ground. Deep within his skull a collection of grey things wriggled. They all seemed to be seeking something that was no longer there.

114

Crowley looked at the body for a moment and then checked the remaining portion of the skull. The bullet had managed to destroy that damned stone, whatever it might be, and though he couldn't be sure, he suspected that was a mighty fine thing, indeed.

Slate fell forward and caught himself on his hands again, whimpering.

The sounds of combat were gone. The noise of people screaming had died as well, though in the distance a dead boy wept with less fervor, perhaps one step closer to accepting his fate.

Crowley put his weapon away and helped Lucas Slate to his feet.

"Are you well, Mister Slate?"

"I am not, sir. But I am alive and I thank you for that." His voice was fainter than usual.

"You'll have to be well enough." Crowley squinted as he looked around. "You take the Indians and I'll handle the soldiers."

"What do you mean?"

"I intend to stop this damned fighting before one or both of us is killed."

Lucas Slate nodded, hefted his shotgun and looked toward the direction the Indians had gone, the direction of most of the fighting.

As he walked, he murmured under his breath, words to a song that no one else in the vicinity could hear or understand. The furious red marks on his torso rapidly faded, first to pink and then to the same color as the rest of his flesh.

He was learning. The song had many, many notes and Slate suspected he would not know them all for years, but for now he learned how to heal himself with the song and it was a start.

Crowley found Sergeant Fowler and his men gathered near the far side of town, following orders. They were there to make sure the Indians didn't storm in from the other side of the area, and likely to clear a path should it become necessary to flee Silver Springs.

Crowley walked directly up to the sergeant while the man watched warily.

"Sergeant?"

The man nodded and came toward him with caution. There was no telling where a man might stand on the Indians. Most agreed they should be sent away, but wise soldiers didn't take that for granted.

The spell was simple, and one of the very first he'd learned ages ago. Crowley didn't like using sorcery on human beings, but if he had to, he made exceptions.

"Sergeant, I'm sorry to inform you that your captain and most of the rest of your soldiers are dead. They were killed by the Indians, who are fleeing even as we speak. You've won the battle, but the cost was high."

There was truth to his words, but only as much as he needed. He could have told the man that it was the heart of Summer and he'd have agreed. That was how sorcery worked.

"I'm sure they fought bravely." The sergeant's voice was slightly slurred.

"Of course they did. They fought valiantly and they won. But wouldn't it be best if you returned to your base camp and reported in? If more Indians should come back they might see your presence as a challenge and you can't do your duty if you're all dead."

The sergeant looked around uncertainly. There were seven men with him. The rest were elsewhere or dead.

"Yes, of course. We'll head for home."

"An excellent idea, Sergeant. You have to make sure your men are safe, after all."

He finished the incantation. The sergeant would forget having seen his face. The men around him would remember only that the sergeant had been informed of their pyrrhic victory and nothing else.

A short walk had him reuniting with Slate and with the man who stood near him. Stinky Napier was clean and sober, his eyes haunted by the sights that Crowley didn't need to see to understand. There were dead men up ahead and likely a lot of them if the sounds from earlier were anything to be judged by.

Crowley smiled broadly for him. Napier flinched a bit but stood his ground.

"And is the town still alive, Mister Napier? Or are we the only survivors?"

"Oh, there are more, Mister Crowley. The Indians only wanted the soldiers. They were good about not shooting anyone else." He frowned a moment. "Can't say the same for all the soldiers. Some of those boys shot anything that moved."

"Still think the red men are all heathens?"

"Absolutely. Doesn't mean I have to hate them. I just know they do not properly worship Jesus Christ."

Crowley shook his head and said nothing. That was a story he was wise enough not to touch on.

"Your friend is very persuasive." Napier's voice caught him off guard.

"How so?."

Slate chuckled to himself. He was looking remarkably healthy for a man whose chest had been nearly broken open twenty minutes earlier.

Napier eyed him dubiously but continued on. "Walked right up to the Indians where they were getting ready to have a bit of fun with the soldiers and put a stop to it."

Crowley's grin was quick and savage. "And what did you say to them, Mister Slate?"

Slate looked directly at him. "Leave." He shrugged. "They left."

"So the Indians are gone and the soldiers are leaving." Crowley nodded, a satisfied expression crossing his features and feeling decidedly alien there.

"Can't be that many soldiers left." Napier's frown deepened and he looked around. "I don't reckon that's a bad thing just now."

Slate spoke up, his voice still pained. "Might we be on our way, Mister Crowley? I'm feeling a bit faint."

Mister Napier opened his mouth to say something else, but one look from Slate silenced him.

When the morning came the two men claimed their horses from the stables. A surprising number of the Cavalry's horses were gone, despite the lack of riders, but no one was foolish enough to try for theirs.

Outside, the remaining soldiers were gathering together, preparing to head northeast, toward Camp Woodbine, if Crowley was remembering properly.

"Where are we headed today, Mister Crowley?"

Crowley looked at his companion and shrugged. The weather was hideous, but that was hardly unusual. "I took the time to listen to a few men chatting last night, after you had gone to sleep. The men were French and talking about *Loup Garou*."

Slate frowned. "Werewolves?"

"You speak French, Mister Slate?"

"Not as well as I speak English, but I can manage. Spent a bit of time in Louisiana and dealt with my fair share of Cajuns."

Crowley nodded. "We're heading west, Mister Slate. We shall discuss what happened here when you feel more inclined to discussing the matters, but we are heading west to see if there are, in fact, werewolves hiding somewhere in the region."

"You don't suppose it's merely wolves?"

"No. In my experience, wolves very rarely attack wagon trains."

Slate nodded. "Well then, I imagine this will be an interesting journey." The man seemed distracted and Crowley simply nodded. Let him have his time to think.

As they rode, Lucas Slate listened to the song that always played for him and, in listening, began to comprehend.

TAKING DOWN THE TOP CAT

R.P.L. Johnson

Night fell in the jungle: greens sinking into blacks, shadows growing up from the valley floor like a dark liquid pooling in the deep places of the world.

Sergeant Jared Naylor scanned the compound through his binoculars as he waited for the rest of the team to make their way up the narrow game trail. From above it looked like a holiday resort. The main house nestled into the wooded hillside, its sprawling size artfully hidden by sculpted gardens that led down to the river. A helipad and boathouse on the river completed the picture. It looked more like an eco-retreat for detoxing celebrities than a drug lord's stronghold.

"Man, I am in the *wrong* business," said Garcia. He gave out a low whistle as he stared down at the luxurious compound.

"Well today's your lucky day, Private," Naylor said. "I hear there are going to be a few vacancies opening up in his operation pretty soon."

Germaine McDowell lumbered past, toting the heavy MG4 as if it was a kid's BB gun. "Of course that would mean you'd have the mighty fightin' Delta Force bearing down on your ass right now," he said.

Garcia shrugged. "I heard they ain't so tough."

Mac gave him a friendly shoulder check as he walked past. "Some of them ain't," he said.

"Zip it," Naylor said. "Save the bull session for the ride home. I want it tight and quiet from here on in."

He checked his watch; they were right on time. Not bad after a ten-mile hike through dense jungle. This hadn't been a usual infiltration. Their target was Hernando Ramirez, head of the infamous Cascajal drug cartel. Ramirez was notoriously

120

paranoid, and his compound was miles away from any road and well off any commercial flight path. They couldn't afford to give him any warning, so they had been dropped two valleys away with the rest of the journey being made on foot. Other squads were hiking in from the south, and under Emcon Alpha, full radio silence, timing was everything.

"There's the boathouse," Jim Lowe said, the last man in their four-man fire team.

"I see it," Naylor replied.

The boathouse was their way out. Getting away from the compound had to be as fast as their approach was stealthy. This operation was strictly off the books. The chain of command went from Naylor to his Captain straight to the commander of Delta and then to a D.C. suit. Naylor had been working operations like this for years but still got nervous when he thought about who was ultimately in charge. A Mexican drug lord might kill you, might even torture you first. But those Beltway cats would sign your death warrant with no more thought than swatting a fly if they thought it was in their interests. They couldn't afford to get caught in Mexico. If they did, the unofficial war on drugs could become an international incident.

Fortunately Ramirez's lavish lifestyle extended to a collection of motorboats in his private boathouse. That was Naylor's objective: hold and secure their way out while the other squads took out Ramirez and his key lieutenants.

They made their way down the hill. If anything the undergrowth was even thicker on the south-facing slope and they were forced to hack their way through the bush.

Naylor swung his machete against a particularly tangled knot of vines when the blade struck something hard. He pulled the vines and they came away like a living tapestry, an interwoven blanket of tough, woody tendrils. Behind was a huge boulder of yellowish green rock just like the outcroppings they had seen during their hike. But this wasn't just some slab of bedrock protruding through the topsoil, it was a huge stone head.

"Well, would you look at that," Garcia said. "Olmec, I reckon."

"Listen to him," Mac said. "Just 'cus his gran'pappy swam the Rio Grande forty years ago, he thinks he's some kind of expert on Mexican history."

Naylor examined the huge artefact. The features had been smoothed by time but Naylor could still make out the broad, fang-filled mouth of the Olmec jaguar God.

"Well in this case, I think he's right," he said. "This is Olmec country, and they liked their carvings sure enough. I even saw one like this in a museum in Guadalajara one time."

"You know, I heard Ramirez was into all this shit," Lowe said. "Collects artefacts, even makes out like he's some kind of champion for the native Olmec Indians."

"Yeah, I heard something similar," Naylor said. "Seems like being a drug lord with more money than God isn't enough for him. Ramirez likes to pretend he's some kind of mystical badass, Lucifer and *Sante Muerta* combined. I guess it helps to keep the locals in line: stops the coca farmers from selling the crop to the other cartels. It's all bullshit designed to keep the locals away from his pleasure palace."

"Pleasure palace," Garcia repeated. "I like the sound of that. Like I said, I'm in the wrong business." He patted the giant stone head as they walked past. "I'm going to tell Ramirez about this, he might want to add it to his collection."

They hit the boathouse at the stroke of 2:00am. There were two guards on patrol, both were chatting and smoking on a small jetty that jutted out where the river widened in front of the house. Both caught three rounds each from the supressed MP5s carried by Lowe and Garcia. They collapsed in unison, hearts shredded, blood pressure crashing and pitching them into a deadly faint while the rest of their body caught up to the fact that they were dead.

Naylor ghosted forward to secure the bodies, afraid one of them would pitch over into the lake, raising an attention-getting splash. But they both crumpled into their own footprints, empty eyes staring up at the sky.

Naylor crouched over the bodies, scanning the boathouse through night vision goggles. There was no sign of movement, and no sign either of the simultaneous attack Naylor knew would be happening right at that instant on the main house.

That was good. Silence meant things were going to plan.

"Mac, get that SAW up here. Garcia, start prepping the boat."

The two men moved with smooth, practised efficiency. Mac heaved a crate onto the jetty and set the big machine gun up on its bipod while Garcia started to check over the motor launch Naylor had picked.

"Lowe, give me an overview," Naylor said.

"On it."

Lowe took out a small drone, a quad-rotor hardly bigger than his outstretched palm, and pitched it into the air like a softball. At about twenty feet its four tiny propellers spun to life with no more noise than a family of mosquitos and Lowe flew it towards the house, controlling the tiny drone with what looked like a wireless game controller with a built-in screen.

Naylor know what to expect, but he asked anyway.

"How's it looking?"

He could see Lowe's smile as his teeth flashed green in the night vision.

"Sergeant, when this is over we can sell the video to the Stockade to train new Operators."

"That good?"

"Textbook."

"Hey Garcia," Mac hissed, "you still want to join the cartel?"

"I've changed my mind," Garcia replied. "I hear the retirement plan's kinda rough."

Gunfire, coming from the main house. Naylor recognised the distinctive agricultural clatter of AK47s and in reply, the faster buzz of a Delta machine gun. Sounded like the cartel had finally woken up. Well, that was to be expected eventually.

"Stay tight," Naylor said. "Garcia, how are we going with that boat?"

"Two minutes, Sergeant."

"Damn," Mac said. "I could throw a rock in downtown Jersey and hit three guys who could jack a boat faster than you."

"Can it," Naylor ordered.

He crept over to where Lowe was still piloting the drone. Its night vision camera clearly showed the main house. There was no sign of the other Delta squads, but staccato flashes of light strobed in the windows in time to the clatter of gunfire on the night air.

More gunfire now, mixed with screams. Animal sounds ripped from human throats. The night was alive now with movement and noise. The old dance – predators and prey.

Something wasn't right.

A voice came on the secure Delta short-range network, breaking radio silence with a garbled scream.

"Holy shit! Get back, get back, get b—"

The fast, pneumatic flutter of suppressed gunfire swamped the panicked voice: not a controlled burst, but a full-auto spray that emptied the clip in seconds. Then the screams cut short with a wet, ripping sound that reminded Naylor of his mother de-boning a chicken.

A growl. Naylor tried to imagine what could be done to a human throat to make such a noise, but failed.

The screaming carried on the still jungle night. Naylor stared at the drone's screen, willing it to show him what was going on. But whatever it was, it was happening inside the main house.

He listened closely. He had heard his share of gunfire and screaming, but this was different. The screams had a panicked edge, not cries of pain, but animal yells of terror. The gunfire was wild and sporadic. He expected that from the cartel guards, but he could hear the familiar crack of Delta-issued Berettas. The two squads that had stormed the house had ditched their rifles and were using their sidearms. That was bad.

The comms was alive with voices now: radio silence forgotten. Naylor heard desperate pleas for help and snatched fragments from open microphones.

"What the fuck was that?"

"Oh, God... Oh, God...."

"Where d'it go? Where d'it go?"

"What the fu—"

"Fall back! Fall back!"

The roar that echoed across the compound was as loud as thunder.

"Boat's ready, Sarge," Garcia said.

"Okay." Naylor broke radio silence to send the coded signal that their way out was ready. He didn't know what was going on at the main house, but now they could complete the mission and exfiltrate down the river as planned.

His call was answered by another chorus of shouts and curses over the radio, punctuated by gunfire.

"Get ready, people," Naylor said. "Whatever's happening in there, they'll be coming in hot."

"Copy that," they said in unison. They had all heard the pandemonium over the radio. They knew that whatever clusterfuck the mission had turned into over at the main house was about to descend on them.

They waited: trying not to listen to the cries on the radio; trying not to picture the fire fight, the dark, confined corridors of the house lit by the deadly strobe of muzzle flashes, the bullets, ricocheted fragments and splinters ripping into flesh. And definitely trying not to picture whatever it was that was making that fucking roar!

The noise grew even more chaotic, if that was possible. The gunfire had almost completely stopped and the shouts had turned to sobbing screams. But throughout it all, unchanged, was the deep-throated roar and that other noise: the chicken-bone sound of tearing flesh.

Finally, even the screams died away until there was only one voice, breathless and pleading.

"Please... please..."

Silence.

"Sarge?" Mac asked. He was still scanning the path back to the house through the holographic sight of the MG4.

"I know, I know," Naylor replied. If anyone was coming back to the boat, they'd be there by now. Instead there was only silence. Even the radio was quiet.

"Boat's ready, Sarge," Garcia reminded him.

Naylor knew what he should do. He should pack up and leave, get his men out of there. Those were his orders. But just as he knew what he should do, he also knew that he couldn't do it.

"Mac, you stay here with the SAW. Guard that boat. The rest of you, on me."

Naylor led the way up the path to the house. If anything, the silence was worse than the screaming they had heard just moments before. Lowe had placed his drone into a hover. It would keep station there without any human control, giving them an overview of the battlefield. But it wasn't telling them anything. The house still looked quiet. There was no sign of movement, not even from the cartel's guards.

"I got a body," Garcia said. "Not one of ours."

Naylor looked at the corpse as they passed. It was indeed one of Ramirez's men; he was still clutching his rifle, but didn't look like he'd got a shot off before his throat had been cut. Naylor appraised the work with a professional eye. He was starting to put together a picture of what had happened. The approach had been good, the guards taken out swiftly and silently. Whatever had gone wrong had happened inside the house.

They reached the main door. The black cavity stood like an entrance to another world.

"Hey, Lowe," Naylor said. "How good are you with that drone?"

"You want to go inside?"

"You got it?"

Lowe broke out his controller again and the three men took cover behind the stone carvings that flanked the main entrance as Lowe flew the little craft inside.

He was good; the drone flew steadily along at about head height, giving them a real picture of what it would be like to walk down the corridor. At first there were no signs of trouble, the house looked just like Naylor expected from their briefing: an opulent villa with broad corridors lined with paintings and statuary that reflected its owners love of the local, Olmec culture. Small versions of the stone heads they had seen in the jungle sat on mahogany tables; tapestries and jade masks hung from the walls. Everything was painted in a palette of jungle greens and deep black from the drone's night vision camera.

"Back up," Naylor said. "There, just there."

"We got a casualty," Lowe said. A broad staircase led down to a basement level. At the top of the staircase a soldier lay slumped in a puddle of his own blood.

"Gunshot to the throat," Lowe said. "He never stood a chance."

So far, so bad, Naylor thought. But casualties were to be expected. What else had happened? What else could make two fire teams of hardened soldiers descend into panic?

"More bodies," Lowe said. "Bad guys mostly. Looks like quite the fire fight."

Naylor nodded. Delta had come in, taken out at the guards at the cost of one of their own and pushed on into the house. But that was about as good as it had gotten. Lowe stopped calling out casualties after the first half-dozen. They lay where they had fallen, cartel guards and the Delta operators. The walls were daubed with blood, and doors and doorframes shattered by automatic gunfire. Instead of an expensive villa, the lower level looked like a war zone. The expensive tapestries and artwork was smashed, fragments on the floor amid the brass of discarded shell casings. Here and there grenade damage had started fires amongst the wreckage. The flames glittered green in the night vision giving the place an otherworldly, eldritch air.

"What the hell happened here?" Lowe asked.

Naylor looked at the bodies. They had been torn apart.

"Grenade do that?" Lowe asked.

"Don't think so," Naylor replied. "I'm not seeing any blast damage. Looks like they were cut."

"What the fuck?" Lowe said. "Who the hell were Ramirez's bodyguards? Ninjas?"

"I heard one time, this guy in Columbia, he kept a whole zoo. He had lions and all kinds of shit," said Garcia.

"You think animals did this?" Naylor said. "Think maybe Ramirez let them out?"

"Well I've never seen a bullet open a guy up like that."

The drone pushed on down the corridor.

"Signal's getting weaker, Sarge. I don't know how much farther I can go without losing the drone."

"Copy that," Naylor said. "Keep going."

The little quad-rotor flew down another short flight of stairs; the only sound in the house was the whine of its tiny electric motors. The stairs opened into a large room – the biggest they had seen – but instead of Garcia's zoo this place looked more like a museum. Glass cases lined the walls, most of them shattered and cracked, their contents indistinguishable from the shards of broken glass and debris that littered the cabinets.

There was movement at the edge of the screen. A black shape that Naylor had thought was a shadow suddenly slipped away out of the frame.

A figure moved behind it, a soldier, lying against the wall, one leg stretched out in front of him, the other folded beneath him, broken or dislocated or both.

Naylor watched the man's eyes as he tracked the departing shadow with a look of barely contained horror. He was alive.

"Shit! It's Miller," Lowe said.

Miller saw the drone. With a quick, desperate look back at the departing shadow he mouthed, *Help me!*

Miller's eyes darted to the left. A split second later a black shape moved in front of the camera and the drone was swatted from the air. It tumbled into the wall and the screen went dead.

"What now, Sarge?" Garcia asked.

Naylor didn't answer. He had seen something. "Lowe, give me a playback of the last few frames."

Corporal Lowe rewound the last few seconds of the tumbling drone until the image stabilised.

"There!" Naylor jabbed at the screen. An instant before the

drone was hit it had caught an image, a pattern of blotchy black rings."

"What is that?" Garcia asked.

"Jaguar," Naylor replied. "It's a jaguar."

"So what do we do now?"

"What do you think?" Naylor asked. "We go in."

They followed the route the drone had taken, the scene looking eerily familiar through the green night goggles clipped to Naylor's helmet. They descended the stairs, checking the vital signs of the bodies they passed, but there were no more survivors. Perhaps there were more inside. Perhaps it was just Miller. Either way, Naylor was going to find out.

"Holy crap! Just look at this place," Garcia said as they descended the second flight of stairs.

It was the room they had seen with the drone. Ramirez had created his own museum inside his house. Naylor had seen this kind of thing before. Some of these guys had collections that rivalled anything in the Smithsonian.

Ramirez's taste ran to Olmec artefacts and guns. Stone heads of various sizes lined one wall of the room along with fragments of frescoes and larger carvings. Each was lit with tasteful up-lights and labelled with a small plaque. The other side of the room looked like a cross between a jeweller's front window and an armoury. Naylor had never seen so much gold. There were gold plated rifles and matched pairs of jewelled pistols. There were older weapons, lovingly restored and, just like the Olmec masonry, each item was labelled with obsessive care.

Garcia whistled. He picked up a gold-plated 1911 semi-automatic with mother of pearl grips.

"Stay focussed, Garcia," Naylor said. "We don't have time for rubbernecking."

"I know, I know. But man... just one of these things could set a guy up for life. And two... Well I'd—"

It hit Garcia high, springing from the shadows four-footed like a cat, although Naylor had never seen any cat that big. It was bigger than a jaguar. It was more like a bear, although slimmer and sleeker and faster.

It sprung on Garcia, knocking him sprawling with its speed and sheer weight and riding him to the ground, crushing the breath out of him. Garcia didn't even get a chance to scream before it bit down with its huge jaws. There was that noise again: the wet, crunch of snapping bone. Naylor squeezed the trigger on his MP5, more out of instinct than conscious thought and the muzzle flash lit up the green-black flank of something squatting on Garcia. It ignored Naylor's shots. He saw the muscles bunch under its sleek pelt as it worked its massive jaws, twisting and pulling and then it was gone, leaping away through a doorway leading to another wing of the museum.

"Holy shit! Garcia!"

Naylor was at his side in a second while Lowe covered the doorway with his MP5. But Garcia was already dead. His head lolled at an unnatural angle, his neck half torn away by a terrible wound that had opened him up from chin to collar bone.

"What the fuck was that?" Lowe shouted.

Naylor didn't know. Some kind of animal, Garcia had been right about that much. A tiger maybe? He could think of nothing else with that combination and size and speed and predatory savagery.

"Just watch that fucking doorway," Naylor said. "You see any movement, you light that fucker up, you hear me?"

"Copy that," Lowe said through clenched teeth.

Naylor quickly padded the last few metres to where Miller still lay slumped against the wall. He was unconscious. As well as his broken leg he was bleeding from four parallel slashes across his chest. Naylor slapped him, hard. It barely roused him. He stared past Naylor with unfocussed eyes.

"Wake up, Miller, dammit," Naylor said and slapped him again.

That seemed to work.

"Out! We've got to get out," Miller said.

"No shit," Naylor replied. "How many of those things are there?"

Miller grimaced as Naylor helped him onto his good leg. "Just one."

"One!" Naylor thought of the bodies littering the upper levels. "You're wrong. Ramirez must have had a goddamn zoo full of those things. No way one animal could do all this."

Naylor hefted Miller onto his shoulders in a fireman's carry, ignoring the man's cries of pain.

"You don't get it," Miller said. "That's no animal. We took out Ramirez's guards, followed him down here when he ran. I... I saw him change. That thing is Ramirez."

Delirious, Naylor thought. Stress and blood loss. They would have to get him back to the boat and stabilise him. Get some saline into him to get his pressure back up before they could get any real answers out of him.

"Jesus Christ, I saw him change!"

Naylor started back towards the stairwell feeling naked without the comforting weight of his MP5 in his hands.

"Contact!" Lowe shouted and fired a short burst down the corridor.

"Just keep it off our backs. We're outta here," Naylor replied, grunting with the effort of carrying Miller.

Suddenly Lowe was firing. The room lit up green from the light of the muzzle flash on full auto. Naylor saw movement: he caught a glimpse of something tall filling the doorway, walking on two legs like a man but the head and thick, powerful neck were anything but human. A second later something hit him from behind. It felt like he'd been hit by a truck. He fell into one of the shattered cabinets, felt an immense weight crushing the wind from him and grinding his face into the glass shards. He could feel its claws ripping, snagging in the tough webbing and pulling him left and right with immense, animal strength. Then suddenly the weight was gone and Miller's screams were echoing down the hallway.

Naylor rose shakily to his feet. Miller was gone.

"It just took him," Lowe said. "I emptied a full clip at it and it didn't even slow."

"Which way did it go?"

He didn't need an answer. The creature's deep, rattling roar rang out from somewhere behind them, chilling Naylor to the marrow.

He raised his weapon and stood back to back with Lowe. *Let's see you sneak up on us this time.*

"We're leaving," Naylor said. "Stay together, keep it tight, all the way back to the boat and we're gone."

"Copy that."

The roar sounded again, closer now.

"It's picking us off, one by one," Lowe said.

"So stay together. Don't give it that chance."

They stumbled through the debris-strewn room towards the stairwell. Naylor nearly tripped a couple of times but didn't dare take his eyes from the holographic sight of his rifle and the arc he was scanning back down the hall.

He saw movement, a subtle shifting of the shadows. Whatever this thing was, it had a jaguar's stealth. The shadows embraced it, pooling around it like a liquid cloak. He saw the gleam of yellow eyes and loosed a few rounds at it, drawing out another roar, a deep animal noise that plucked a bass note in his guts. Suddenly he became very aware of his place on the food chain and knew that it was not the top.

The old dance, predator and prey, but this time they were on the wrong side.

"We need to go faster," Naylor said.

The creature rose onto its hind legs. This was no jaguar; this was like no animal Naylor had ever seen before. It had the head of a big cat complete with yellow eyes and snarling lips pulled back to reveal long, interlocking fangs. But the head and powerful, sinuous neck rested atop human shoulders and long, muscular arms. Naylor could see the muscles on the thing's chest. It was built like a power lifter, but under the sleek, black fur the musculature was human. Only below the hips did the cat-like form reassert itself with long, seemingly double-jointed legs ending in huge paws.

It roared, jaws opening impossibly wide, fangs glistening.

Naylor fired; he flicked his MP5 onto full auto and mashed the trigger. The creature hardly seemed to notice. Lowe turned around and opened up; Naylor could see the creatures flesh rippling where the rounds struck it, but they were as ineffective as a handful of thrown pebbles.

It kept coming.

Naylor's gun ran dry; he quickly popped the magazine and slammed a new one home, knowing as he did so that it would do no good. Eleven men had tried to kill this thing and eleven men had failed.

The creature swiped at them with one clawed arm. Naylor heard Lowe scream, felt blood splash hot against his skin and then the creature's follow through picked him up and hurled him into a broken display cabinet. Splinters of wood and glass stabbed into him and his desperate, outstretched fingers stubbed painfully into something heavy lying in the shards.

The creature stepped over the moaning form of Lowe as he writhed on the floor and reared up before Naylor. He could smell it now: a warm, animal smell, like the steam off the jungle floor after rain. He could see the rosettes of its mottled fur, black against the deep purple of its pelt. He saw its yellow eyes on him and its paw raised, claws extended for the killing blow.

"Get down!"

It was McDowell. He was standing at the base of the stairs, cradling the big MG4. The muzzle flash stabbed out into the darkness and tracer rounds hammered into the creature. It screeched in rage and covered its face with one huge arm. Naylor could smell burning hair where the hot tracer rounds hit it, but just like the nine-millimetre slugs from the MP5, McDowell's barrage didn't seem to be penetrating at all.

Naylor had to get out from under the thing. He clutched the weight under his hand, not caring what it was, and swung upwards. Gold glittered and the thing in his hand carved a bright arc upwards through the green-tinged darkness and bit into the creature.

It screamed with rage and clutched at the bloody stump where its right arm had been. It looked at Naylor with an expression of pure hatred and then it was gone.

"What the fuck was that thing?" McDowell asked.

"That was Ramirez," Naylor replied. Crazy as that sounded, he was certain it was true. Naylor had seen some weird shit in his time. He knew the world wasn't quite the way most people thought it was, but the differences could only be seen around the edges, in extreme situations in off-the-grid locales. The kind of places he found himself in more often than he liked.

Miller had not been delirious; Ramirez had changed. Somehow after his guards had been defeated the cartel boss had become that creature. He had killed the rest of the squad and now he was after them.

McDowell helped Lowe to his feet. His uniform was shredded from hip to shoulder, the ragged torn edges were soaked in blood. The creature's claws had bit deep into the muscle of his chest and stomach, but he was still alive.

"Good job," Lowe said nodding towards the thing Naylor still clutched, white-knuckled in his hand. It was a knife, a golden knife. Blood flecked the ornate curved blade, as rich and as red and the rubies that studded its hilt.

"Looks like you hurt it," McDowell said. He was right; the creature's severed arm lay where it had fallen among the splintered remains of the display cabinet. Only it wasn't really the creature's arm. Naylor looked at it closely: the fur was patchy and dry, flaky leather showed though the many bald patches. It was smaller, too; a dry, desiccated thing, quite unlike the powerful, vital creature that had nearly killed him.

Naylor picked it up. The skin came away in a roll and a human arm fell out onto the floor, leaving him holding the paw and tanned hide of a jaguar's forelimb. The skin tingled in his hand. Naylor could feel the power in it just waiting to be set free again.

"What the fuck!"

Naylor quickly searched the shattered display cabinet. So far the golden knife had been the only weapon able to injure the creature. Maybe there were more. He found nothing but torn velvet cushions and broken glass.

He searched the floor until he found what he was looking for: a laminated card about eight inches by six, the label from the display case. It showed a picture of the knife and what looked like a full jaguar pelt, complete with fanged skull and paws.

"It's an Olmec artefact," he said, reading from the card. "Olmec shamans worshipped the jaguar and wore its skin during their religious rituals. It was said that some shamans could use the pelts to become skinwalkers, manifestations of the Olmec jaguar god."

"Are you saying we're fighting a god?"

"You saw that thing. Bullets just bounced off it. So far the only thing able to hurt it has been a three-thousand-year-old ritual skinning knife. That thing is Ramirez!"

"God or not, we've hurt it. We need to get the fuck out of here before it comes back."

Naylor flexed his fist around the golden knife. He thought of all the good men lying dead on the villa's upper floors. He thought of all the evil Ramirez and his network of drug dealers had done. Yes, he had hurt it and it had felt good. He wanted to hurt it again. He wanted to go back and report mission accomplished. He wanted Ramirez's head on a plate. The jaguar pelt tingled in his hand. Maybe now they had the chance to do it.

They hurried out of the museum. There was no sign of the creature, but that didn't mean it had given up. The jaguar was a stealth predator. It hunted in silence, pouncing on its prey.

The night seemed lighter now. Naylor flipped up the night vision goggles and found he could see pretty well without them. They were getting close to the exit: he could smell the scent of the jungle wafting in through the shattered front door. It smelled like... like everything. He could smell the moisture in the air and tell you how long it had been since the rains. He could tell the season from the type of pollen on the breeze, he could smell the myriad creatures of the jungle night. If he listened closely, he thought he could hear them, hear their nocturnal burrowings and scurryings. He could almost taste them. The old dance again, but this time he was the hunter.

They made it outside. Naylor could see the path to the boathouse as clear as day. He could smell the sweat on his companions and hear the pulse of their beating hearts as McDowell helped the injured Lowe towards the boat.

And he could hear something else.

Something was stalking them. Ramirez had got out. He was here.

Naylor pulled the pin on an incendiary grenade and tossed it into the house. It exploded inside the building. Soon it would be engulfed in flame. Ramirez's millions in stashed cash, his priceless artefacts, Garcia and the bodies of Naylor's fallen squad mates would soon all be nothing but ash. The only trophies were the golden knife Naylor still clutched in his left hand and—

"Contact!" McDowell shouted.

Naylor saw it; saw the bulk of the skinwalker silhouetted against the sky as it slunk along the roof of the covered boathouse walkway.

"He's mine!" Naylor shouted and the words came out funny: deeper, with a rattle along the edge that was just short of a growl.

He flung off his helmet and MP5, tossing them into the burning house along with the rest of his grenades. He sprinted towards Ramirez, covering the ground with easy speed. He was aware of everything: the sounds of the night, the route to the boat and how long it would take his friends to get there. He felt like he could close his eyes and find Ramirez by scent alone. He had never felt so alive.

The Ramirez creature dropped in front of him but Naylor was ready for it. He swung the golden dagger up towards the creature's throat. His hand thudded into Ramirez's leathery paw as the creature blocked the knife with contemptuous ease. Its claws extended, slicing into Naylor's captured hand like five switchblades.

Naylor roared – a brutal animal roar of pain and rage ripped out from between his fangs and only then did the Ramirez creature notice the change.

Naylor swiped upward with his right hand, the hand bound in the fragment of the skinwalker pelt. Only it wasn't his hand now; it was a sleek, black javelin of sinew and claws. The one-armed Ramirez had no defence. Naylor's claws raked up his chest and tore out his throat.

Naylor tasted blood as the last beats of his prey's heart sprayed its lifeblood over him as it fell.

He lifted his head to the night sky and roared.

The motor launch chugged away down the river. Behind them, the compound blazed in a red and gold mirror of the sunrise that was just beginning to creep over the hills behind the house.

Naylor closed his left eye, the human one, and marvelled at the rich colours.

He looked over at Lowe who lay against the gunwale, swathed in bandages from the boat's first aid kit. "You look like hell," Naylor said.

Lowe looked back at him. "You can talk," he said.

Naylor smiled, feeling the unfamiliar length of the incisors on the right side of his mouth. He looked down at his paw: the black jaguar fur reached halfway up his bicep before giving way to human skin. But the changes didn't stop there. His right eye was bright yellow with a slitted pupil, his right ear was pointed and wouldn't keep still. It kept moving, searching out sounds on the riverbank.

"That was some mission," McDowell called back from the wheelhouse.

"Yep," Naylor replied. He hefted the rest of the skinwalker pelt he had taken from Ramirez's body. "But I reckon they're going to get a lot easier from now on."

THE DEMON LOCKE

Alan Baxter

You have got to be shitting me."

"The Demon Locke has protected humanity for centuries, Mr Clay."

"Sergeant Clay, please. Mr Clay was my father and I have not earned that title yet."

"As you wish, Sergeant. But regardless, I am not shitting you."

The woman, Sister Agatha, smiled softly, condescendingly Clay thought. In her long, plain grey dress, she looked kind of like a nun, but without a wimple of any sort. Her hair hung long and straight, ash blonde.

He shook his head, trying to decide whether maybe there was a hidden camera somewhere in the old castle. "Okay, let me get this straight. You have a Most Important Nun–"

"The Demon Locke, yes."

"Right. And she stops demons from getting out."

"Yes."

"But she's sick and we have to get her back down the mountain to the hospital you've had set up in the old school on the edge of town."

"Yes. You passed it on the way here, you were supposed to log its location."

"We did." Clay frowned. "But you really need the SAS to move one nun?"

Sister Agatha sighed. "I was told you'd simply follow orders."

"You are not my CO, lady. Explain it to me like I'm five. Why not just take her down in a damn wheelbarrow or something if it's that important?"

Sister Agatha interlaced her fingers and rested her chin on them for a moment in thought. "Let me give you an abridged version of the story," she said, looking up again. "Centuries ago, humanity came under attack from beings best described as demons."

"Like, demons from Hell?" Clay said. "You're telling me Hell is real?"

"Well, at the time, that's what they thought. These days we think maybe it's not so simple, and perhaps it's more like another dimension that interacts intermittently with our own, and these creatures are of that dimension. But let's say demons from Hell just for brevity's sake, yes?"

Clay inclined his head, gestured for her to continue.

"Very well. So, our Order was established with ancient knowledge, to find a way to banish these demons. There were various magical and occult options open to the ancient Sisters, and other groups helped them. It's a very complicated process, but in essence a system was developed. A person, The Demon Locke, is able to prevent these beings from getting into our dimension by closing all access into herself." Agatha pursed her lips a moment and Clay had impure thoughts, then felt slightly guilty. Then again, was she even a nun really?

"Imagine a powerful magnet," Sister Agatha said. "So strong, nothing can escape its pull. It gathers everything metal to it and holds it in place. The Sister who takes on the role of the Demon Locke fulfills a purpose like that, only she pulls to herself and holds onto all the possible connections between our dimension and the other. Hell, if you will. So all the time the Demon Locke is in place, the demons can't get through."

"Hence the name."

"Correct, Sergeant. Hence the name. Now, that's obviously a very dangerous position to put one person in, so they have to be protected. This castle is that protection. The rest of us keep the castle secure with powerful wards, the Demon Locke remains safe, and she keeps the demons from invading our world. That's why the castle is so remote. But now that very remoteness is causing a problem, as the Demon Locke is sick and requires immediate medical attention."

Sergeant Clay nodded, thinking. "Okay, assuming I buy all this Halloween shit, let me ask a couple of questions."

"If they're quick."

"Right. Okay, one: Why isn't there another Locke woman? Seems dangerous to only have one."

"Indeed. As soon as the new Locke is appointed, she begins training her apprentice. Usually there are decades, and it only take a few years to train the successor. But our current Locke is young, and unexpectedly sick. The apprentice is not yet ready."

Clay nodded. "Something to think about there, huh? Maybe train up a few at a time?"

Sister Agatha sighed again. "In fourteen hundred years this has never happened." She held up a hand as Clay opened his mouth to speak. "But yes, your observation is erudite."

"Is it now? I've never been called that before. Okay, second question: Why don't you bring the medics here?"

"A fair question. Do you see any power outlets in these stone walls, Sergeant?"

"You know there are generators and shit? Or run a power line up here?"

"Of course, but for fourteen hundred years we've been self-sufficient. And a generator isn't stable enough. The Demon Locke has reached a point where she requires daily dialysis. That is not possible here. We have organised everything in the old school, just six miles from the foot of our mountain, where there's a stable power supply, doctors on hand, medicine, and so on. We need your help to get her down the mountain, and along six miles of road to that location. There we have set up the wards like the ones here and once she's inside all will be well. It's moving her that's the problem. We can't maintain moving protections. From when we leave these walls until we get her inside the school, the demons will try to get her. That's where you come in."

"They won't just run rampant, these demons?"

"We don't think so. Their priority will be to kill the Locke, thereby freeing themselves more permanently."

Clay sniffed, sucked his teeth. "This is the most mental medevac I've ever heard of."

"Nevertheless, here we are."

"We have to fight off demons?"

"Yes. They will manifest in any way they can. Once we move the Locke and her power is interrupted, they will come. They will manifest near her, as she will be able to hold some degree of control, but not enough to keep them out entirely. And we cannot protect her while she's moving."

"A shame we can't get our Land Rovers up through all these trees. The path down is pretty narrow. You planning to carry her?"

"We have a plan to mover her."

Clay nodded. "You know, in the SAS we have a saying. Kiss."

Agatha frowned.

"It's an acronym. Keep it simple, stupid. Would it be fair to say that the simplest interpretation of this medevac is for my men to travel with you lot to the new location and kill anything that comes near us along the way?"

Sister Agatha smiled. "Yes, Sergeant Clay. That would be perfect."

"Okay, you grunts, listen up. We have about two miles of winding path through this forest, back the way we came, until we reach the foot of the mountain. At the base will apparently be a truck, where we left our Land Rovers. We and that truck will drive six miles to our target location. The Sisters will be travelling in that wagon." Clay pointed to the long, narrow canvas-covered wooden wagon in the castle courtyard. "We stay in formation around it and murder with great prejudice anything that comes near. And I mean anything. Even a fucking ant. Any questions?"

Corporal Patel raised his hand.

"Yes?"

"Why not horses?" Patel's face was scrunched in a mixture of discomfort and disgust.

Clay looked at his seven Operators, saw variations of the same expression on each of their faces. He had decided not to ask, but now the subject had been brought up, he couldn't ignore it. He should have known better than to ask them for questions.

He turned back to the wagon, standing before the closed wooden gates, and realised his own face had twisted to match Patel's. The Demon Locke, her apprentice, and Sister Agatha were inside, hidden by the canvas sides. In front, where there really should be horses, six more Sisters stood in two lines of three, leather harnesses jury-rigged to fit around their torsos. They leaned gently into their harnesses, ready to haul the wagon along. Clay hoped they were fit nuns – two miles was a long pull. Then again, it was all downhill, zigzagging along the well-trodden dirt path between the trees. The six women returned his gaze with unself-conscious equanimity.

"Why not horses?" Sergeant Clay called out.

Sister Agatha poked her head out of the canvas flaps at the front of the wagon. "Because the demons will manifest through any living thing. A horse, a bird, anything. The only thing they cannot subsume is a human being, as our minds are too strong. Normally one horse would pull this narrow wagon up the mountain when we re-supply in town. We thought six Sisters would probably account for one horse."

"Demons, Sergeant?" Patel asked.

Enough of this. Fuck all the nonsense, the essence of this job was simple. "No more questions, squad. These crazy ladies are going to run a wagon down to a truck, we kill any beast that comes near." He frowned. "Got it?"

"Yes, Sergeant!" they yelled in unison.

He looked over the group. Two patrols. Half a troop. Eight soldiers including himself. He had a wave of concern, suddenly wondering if they would be enough. Demons? Really? They didn't even have their captain here and Clay wondered if command had seriously underestimated the importance of this mission. Had Clay and his men been sent purely to humour some crazy religious order? What if all this was real? But it was too late to do anything about that now.

They all carried C8 Carbines with plenty of spare ammo, and each had a Sig Sauer P226. Between them there were a bunch of Flash-Bangs and a decent supply of L109A1 HE Fragmentation Grenades hanging in their webbing. Despite that, Clay suddenly felt decidedly underdressed. A two-mile run and a six-mile drive. It would have to be enough.

"Patel, Farley, over to the left side of the wagon and stay there the whole way," he shouted. "Dillbury and Canton, you take the right side. East and Stephenson hold the rear. Brown, you're with me in front."

The group ran to their positions, immediately tensed and ready, carbines held at port arms.

"We're ready when you are," Clay called out.

"We've been ready for some time," Sister Agatha said, poking her head out again. She looked up to two sisters at the gate. "Let's go!"

Those sisters each pulled hard and opened both sides of the gate. The six women in the harnesses strained forward and the wagon creaked, then began to roll. The soldiers jogged along-side, holding their positions, eyes everywhere. A more bizarre assignment Clay could not imagine, but it all sank away in favour of training. The path up the remote Scottish mountain was familiar to them, having hiked it earlier in the day. It wound its way down to a gravelly area of level ground where the truck would apparently be waiting. Two Land Rovers were already there, having brought Clay and his men that far. They would use the Rovers to escort the truck the last bit along the road. Simple, right?

He glanced back to six nuns driving their shoulders into harnesses, legs pumping under their flowing grey habits, and shook his head. There was nothing simple about any of this.

They cleared the gates and started along the hard-packed earth of the mountain path. Another perimeter fence surrounded the entire castle, signs on the outside that read *Private Property – Keep Out*. Clay and his men had let themselves in there that morning and left the gate open. Within moments they were bearing down on it but Sister Agatha's voice cut through Clay's thoughts.

"It begins!"

He glanced back and saw her pointing up ahead of them. Turning back he jumped to see the sky filled with birds, a dark cloud of crows swooping in over the treetops.

"Kill every fucking bird!" he yelled and lifted his weapon.

Eight carbines burst into life and the sight was hard to believe. As they raked fire through the flock, the birds burst into flames when hit, spiralling down like WW2 Spitfires. They began to shriek and wail, a sound unlike anything he'd ever heard from a crow before. Unlike anything he'd heard from any creature.

The birds wheeled to the left, went up and away, and Clay was about to relax when they came back around, diving once more. This time they seemed to flex and pulse in the air, growing exponentially larger, stretching the frames of their bodies. Feathers burst free, but they flew on. The troop began firing again and the swollen, twisted avians exploded in fire and smoke, filling the air with their flames and their screams.

Then one broke through. Clay tried to track it as it came low over the nuns in the harness.

"Beware crossfire!" he yelled, then the bird struck the centre nun on the left full in the face.

She wailed and staggered, blood flooding her face. For a moment she stumbled and was dragged by her harness, then with an incredible show of strength, she found her feet and ran on. Farley ran wide as the crow that had attacked her came around and he crouched low to shoot up at it and not risk hitting any of the nuns or soldiers. The crow exploded, a stink of sulphur and something far less pleasant. Fire rained down from it and two nuns beat furiously at their hair to put out the embers and the wagon rolled on.

"What the fuck is this?" Stephenson shouted from the rear of the group.

"A job," Clay called back. "It's a deployment like any other. Don't sweat the details, kill everything!"

"Two o'clock!" Canton called and all eyes turned.

"Again," Clay muttered under his breath. "You have to be shitting me."

Dozens of red deer came galloping through the trees. Some with huge antlers, some without, but all with bright red, fiery eyes. Their maws split in howls to reveal unnatural rows of sharp white fangs. As they drew nearer, their spines arched, shoulders popped out in grotesque slabs of muscles. They grew and stretched to the size of cattle, but the eight soldiers were already firing.

Clay pulled a grenade free and lobbed it past the front wave with all his might. It fell just behind the advancing herd, red fur and bloody meat spraying up into the air along with dirt and grass and leaves.

Where bullets struck the demon deer, blood poured out thick and black. Flames licked back from their faces, those burning eyes singeing the fur of their heads to charcoal. As they fell under the heavy ordnance, some stumbled and went own, others leaped and bounded with the speed and grace of savannah gazelles. Except these were now the size of shire horses.

If the screams of the crows had been disturbing, the howls emanating from these beasts was truly disarming. The sounds turned Clay's blood to ice, made his stomach roil and his knees weak.

"This side too!" East roared as the first herd drew near and Clay glanced back to see more Hell-deer catching up behind the wagon. East and Stephenson ran backwards, raking fire as they went. They would have to manage. Patel dropped back a little from the other side to assist them, Farley moving forward of the wagon to fire across and assist Clay and Brown.

Clay looked at Brown's face and saw the man's eyes stretch wide. He turned back to the front in time to see the foremost giant deer was upon them. He went full-auto at point-blank range, shredding the beast's shoulder and ribs, but not before it had Brown by the face in its fang-filled maw. The soldier screamed as he was lifted off his feet and carried away.

Clay turned, still firing, and finally the beast stumbled and went down, rolling over Brown as it did so. The soldier's body was jelly as it was crushed and flipped. He landed beside the dead deer, his face gone, just red mince from the base of his neck up.

The wagon rolled on.

A nun screamed as another deer got close. Clay and Farley emptied cartridges into it from either side, but it got to the front right nun first. It grabbed at her shoulder, shaking its head like a crazed dog, ripping her arm free. The nun shrieked, blood geysering from the hole where her arm had been. Their bullets took the deer down and it thankfully fell to one side, the nuns managing to haul the wagon to the right just in time to avoid crashing over its carcass.

The one who had lost her arm stumbled, face white as marble, and fell. Hanging in the harness, she was dragged along, feet bouncing behind, her habit billowing like a windsock. The woman on her left, in the other front harness, reached across with a face set in determination, and yanked at a leather strap. The dead nun fell from the released harness, the two behind jumped her as she rolled, then the wagon wheels *bump-bumped* over her body and she was left broken and bloodied on the trail.

Clay looked over to the middle row, to the nun who'd lost an eye. The front of her habit was dark with blood, her face pale where it wasn't scarlet, but she ran on, teeth gritted in a snarl of effort. He shook his head. These women were something else.

"The truck!" someone yelled, maybe Farley.

Clay looked up, relieved to see the trees opening out and the gravelly ground ahead. Their two Land Rovers stood side by side where they'd left them. Not far away, a 7-tonne box-back truck waited, the roller door at the rear open. Clay saw two nuns in there waiting, a third leaning out of the driver's window, brows tight in concern.

The nuns in the harnesses turned sideways and got the wagon as close to the back of the truck as they could. They yanked on their quick release straps and ran to the side of the wagon. All except the one who had lost an eye. She collapsed, waving her compatriots on.

Sister Agatha threw aside the canvas covering. She and the apprentice in there with her lifted a third, looking weak and thin, her face grey as ash. The Locke, Clay presumed. With care, but speed, they hefted the sick woman and jumped clear across from the wagon to the truck. Had they practiced that manoeuvre? The women who had run with the wagon clambered in behind.

"You are shitting me!" Dillbury said.

Clay turned to look and saw a flock of giant, swollen sheep hammering across the heath. They looked like storm clouds rolling along the ground, but for their black faces and rage-red eyes. Each the size of a car, legs grotesquely swollen, their bleats echoed with ear-piercing ferocity.

The soldiers lobbed grenades and fired in sweeping, controlled bursts, exploding the first wave in sulphurous flames.

"Get to the Rovers!" Clay yelled. "I'm in front, Canton in behind the truck!"

Before the demon sheep could get too close, the soldiers ran for the Land Rovers. The roller door on the back of the truck banged closed and the truck roared, wheel-spinning as the nun driving it peeled out.

Clay leaped into the driver's seat of his Land Rover, trusting Patel and Farley to get in and start firing. He was immediately deafened by their carbines and knew they were on it. Brown should be there too, but his corpse was crushed back in the forest.

Canton would be in the driver's seat of the other Land Rover, Dillbury, East, and Stephenson riding with him. Clay accelerated hard past the truck, saw the driving nun's teeth bared in determination as she hunched over the wheel. He pulled in front of her and matched speed, saw sheep all around exploding in bursts of sulphurous flame from his men's bullets. Their bleats were piercing screams that tore at his eardrums even over the almost continuous gunfire.

"In front!" he yelled, appalled at the sudden appearance of some fifty demonic, over-sized sheep blocking the road. Why the fuck did Scotland have to have so many godsdamned sheep?

In the rearview mirror he saw Patel stand up through the open top of the Land Rover, an M72 LAW compact anti-tank rocket launcher resting on his shoulder. Clay smiled as the rocket whooshed over the Land Rover's cab and sent demon flesh and wool up in a billowing cloud. Taking no chances, Patel reloaded and fired again. The Land Rover shot into the swirling smoke, bouncing over pieces of sheep and broken road. Through the roiling haze, Clay watched in the rearview and let go a sigh of relief when the nun's truck burst through, jouncing crazily, but still heading fundamentally straight ahead.

The journey stretched into a surreal mayhem of continuous assault. Canton would frequently pull up alongside, East matching Patel with his own M72 LAW, blowing flocks of Hell-sheep into the dark beyond. The others kept up a furious rate of fire, taking out any beasts that got near.

At the five-mile mark, another flock of fiery birds came in, tried to assault the group from above. Most were shot, some managed to hit the truck, but even in their swollen state they didn't have the power to get through the hard metal shell of the truck's box.

We're gonna make it. Then Clay cursed himself for jinxing the operation.

From the right side, about one o'clock, the heath was churned into dust by a herd of Highland Cows, their long red fur streaming in the wind as they ran, curving horns grown to ridiculous proportions. They came at a furious pace, on a direct collision course with the truck. Demonically expanded to the size of small trucks themselves, there was no way the nuns would survive that impact.

As they barrelled along the small country road at close to eighty miles per hour, Clay desperately tried to think of a plan. How did anyone stop something like that? Then he saw Canton's Land Rover coming up beside the nun's truck. Staying in front, letting Patel and Farley keep the road ahead clear of sheep, he watched as Dillbury, East, and Stephenson clambered up from the Land Rover and jumped onto the roof of the speeding truck. They held on for dear life as Canton swerved the Land Rover to the right, putting it directly between the truck and the stampeding Highland cattle.

"You mad fucking bastard!" Clay cried with glee as he saw the flames licking out of the back of the Land Rover. The amount of ammo, grenades and rockets in that vehicle made it a bomb of significant proportions.

"Get clear you fucker!" Clay yelled at Canton, who was clearly too far away to hear a thing, especially over the roar of engines and the barrage of gunfire. Sheep exploded in front of Clay, but he largely ignored them when he saw Canton launch himself out of the speeding Land Rover. The lunatic flew backwards and managed to lob a grenade back into the vehicle, then he hit the heather and rolled crazily. The Land Rover reached a few metres in front of the Highland cows, and went up in a burst of light and an ear-splitting explosion that sucked away all other sound. Red fur flew, long, curing horns span up into the air. Other cattle around the edges of the racing herd were blown off their feet sideways, still more pitched into the crater made by the exploding vehicle.

With a whoop of joy he couldn't hear, Clay roared on, the nun's truck tight on his arse, and they saw the large building ahead that had been converted ready for the Demon Locke. It was surrounded by a chain link fence, two nuns standing ready at the gate.

"How many of these bloody women are there?" Clay wondered aloud, as they hauled the gates open and he drove straight in, the truck right behind. They skidded to a halt and the roller door of the truck went up.

"Get her inside," Sister Agatha said. "You know what to do, the doctors are waiting."

Clay climbed out of the Land Rover as his men jumped off the roof of the truck. He walked up to Agatha, but she ignored him, watching the skies, the land outside the compound. She frowned as a huge cloud descended from the north. A cloud of birds, Clay realised, oversized and grotesque, bearing down on the building. Sister Agatha pursed her lips, Clay saw her hands tighten into fists.

"We're safe in here, right?" Clay asked.

"We're inside the wards, yes. But if they can't get in here, they'll go elsewhere while they can."

The neat formation of birds suddenly stuttered and fractured. Some tumbled from the air, others twisted and shrank, then flew off in random directions.

Sister Agatha smiled. "The Locke is in place," she said quietly. "She's okay." She turned and walked into the building.

Clay followed her, immediately assailed by the smells of a hospital. The small, pale woman from the wagon was the centre of fervent activity, doctors and nurses moving busily around her. She leaned sideways to see Clay and smiled.

"Sergeant," she said, her voice weak, strained, but her eyes glittered with alertness. "Thank you."

Clay nodded. She seemed anything but the single human being holding hordes of demons at bay. "You're okay?" he asked.

She smiled so sadly that it cleaved his heart a little. "No, not really. But I'll live long enough now to ensure the safety of the world. And maybe a little longer, if I'm lucky."

"You're..." Clay paused, pursed his lips. "You're doing it now? Stopping the demons?"

"Yes. It's a state of being, Sergeant Clay. It's complicated." She smiled again, more good-naturedly this time. "I know I make it look easy. It's not, but I do my best."

"We'll leave you to rest," Sister Agatha said. She gently put a hand to Clay's arm, guided him back outside. As they emerged into the warm, fresh air, she turned to him and smiled genuinely for the first time. Her face softened with it, kind and friendly. "Thank you, Sergeant. And I'm sorry for your loss."

"You too. And you're welcome. We're all done here?"

"Yes, you saved the world today, Sergeant. You and your men."

"All in a day's work."

"And while we're here, we'll train more than one appren-tice." Sister Agatha gave another smile and squeezed Clay's shoulder, then turned and went back inside.

"Hey," came a voice from outside the fence.

Clay turned and saw Canton, bruised and bloody, heather stuck in his webbing.

"Who wants burgers for dinner?" Canton asked, pulling grass from between his teeth.

SHOW OF FORCE

A Jack Sigler/Chess Team Short Story

Jeremy Robinson & Kane Gilmour

"Show of force operations are designed to demonstrate resolve.
They involve the appearance of a credible military force
in an attempt to defuse a situation."
—Joint Publication 3-0, *Joint Operations*

1

The helicopter set down a half mile from the raging storm, which made the desert look as if it were being sucked up into space. A twisting cloud of dust, sand, dirt and snow spiraled into the sky and covered a region that stretched for miles, engulfing most of the so called 'Great Gobi B Strictly Protected Area.' Six bodies slipped from the rotary-winged vehicle and began a fast march toward the howling blizzard.

The region had been set aside as an International Biosphere Reserve in 1991, but in practice, that just meant there was very little there. Mongolia had agreed to the classification of the rarely-used land in exchange for developmental aid. Stretching over 3000 square miles, the place was a combination of drab-colored desert steppe and low, craggy, arid mountains.

The paramilitary team arrived at the leading edge of the storm, and was swallowed by the blinding whiteout conditions. Bursts of sand and ice particles, propelled to 100 mph by roiling winds, blasted across the landscape in thick, nearly solid slabs, buffeting their bodies. Unwavering, the soldiers pressed on. The radio earpieces and speakers inside their helmets, hidden beneath hoods, blocked external audio unless they were switched on. Without that block, they wouldn't have been able to hear each other over the mechanical, high pitched whine of the rampaging weather.

When the gusts of the storm periodically cleared, they could see each other in their full-body, white environment suits, trudging across the patchy scrub-grass-coated ground. The suits looked like the bastard children of environmental hazmat suits and yetis. With full-plate face masks, and tight, fur-coated hoods, they might have easily been mistaken for small polar bears missing their snouts – polar bears with plastic-coated automatic weaponry. The synthetic fur on the exterior of the suits repelled the sand and snow. Each member of the team also wore a tactical climbing harness that covered chest and pelvis, which could be used for rappelling or climbing, but more often was used for attaching equipment to the body. Underneath the outer suits they wore gel-heated full-body wetsuits to help maintain a comfortable internal body temperature.

Outside the environment suits, the mercury would be hovering around -40 degrees Fahrenheit, without the windchill. Scrubbing filters could provide exterior air if their self-contained tanks ran out, but they anticipated being on the ground for less than twenty minutes.

The land was barren rock and jutting hardy grasses – until unexpectedly, it wasn't. The hard ground gave way to treacherous sand dunes, and then just as seamlessly merged back into more crumbly rock and clumps of pale green vegetation.

"Charming. Like New Hampshire in the spring," one of them said, breaking the silence on their internal comms.

"Nah," the burly man in the lead said. "Spring is mud season. It would be like this, but we'd be caked in mud, too."

The slightest of the group groaned and said, "Golf alpha romeo." It was shorthand for 'get a room.' It was a common thing for the man and woman to bicker while in the field, but the other team members all knew how they really felt about each other.

"Hold up here," the slim man in the rear said. He squatted,

and the others paused in their march without protest, dropping into similar crouches. They all held specially-designed, plastic-coated FN SCAR rifles, capable of withstanding the grit from extreme sandstorms. Even the weapons' muzzles were covered in a thin layer of plastic that would be ripped away once they opened fire, should it come to that. But they expected it wouldn't. This mission would be a cakewalk compared to what they normally faced.

The slight man, carrying a simple M-21 sniper rifle, also wrapped in white plastic, approached the thin man who had called a halt. He squatted and brought his weapon up in the direction his leader was looking, straight into the thick maelstrom. "King, you see something?"

The team's leader, King, stayed motionless for another full minute, before he replied. "No, Knight. Sorry. Just getting used to the complete lack of visibility and exterior sound. We don't know what's out here, so everyone stay sharp." Jack Sigler, callsign: King, stood up and headed out, into the howling storm.

Named for pieces on a chess board, each of the other members – designated Chess Team – stood and followed. The team was formerly with the US Army's 1st Special Forces Operational Detachment – commonly known as Delta. Then, for a time, they had operated as part of a freelance organization, Endgame, stopping threats that politics and time constraints prevented other Delta groups from engaging. Now the Chess Team were fugitives from the US government, but they still fought the good fight across the globe. Each member of the team played a different role, and their callsigns designated those positions.

The burly man in the front of the group, Stan Tremblay, callsign: Rook, was their heavy weapons and ordinance specialist. He had armed the team for this mission with a special weapon that operated like an underwater spear gun, but what it fired were short javelins with radio-controlled explosive rings around the shafts. They could be fired from a distance, arcing into the ground, and then detonated later from a safe distance. In addition to a rifle and a spear gun, he also lugged an M240B machine gun.

Behind Rook in their line up, as they penetrated the storm, was a woman, callsign: Pawn. Anna Beck had formerly been the team's security specialist, when they were a part of a larger organization. Now she functioned as a spotter for the team's one-eyed, Korean-American sniper, Knight. She also held her own in a fight either with her FN SCAR or in hand-to-hand combat.

Shin Dae-jung, callsign: Knight, moved up beside Beck, and kept pace with her. After an injury in Africa had taken his eye, he'd learned several tricks to deal with the loss of depth perception, and he had even briefly used an artificial, computerized implant, but the thing had given him sizzling migraines. While the implant was still there, it was turned off. He was using old-school techniques until the pain-causing kinks were worked out. Pawn was always by his side, to prevent his limited vision from causing him problems. She spotted for him when he was sniping, covered his back during incursions and held his hand in their down time, as his lover and friend.

A few paces behind them, another small figure trudged through the howling snow and ice. At just over 5'6", Bishop was the second of three women on the six-person team. Asya Machtcenko, a former Russian soldier, and King's sister, hauled spare drums of ammunition for the M240B Rook carried. The huge weapon was also covered in plastic, although the vents on its barrel assembly were covered with a thinner layer, which could be quickly punctured with a pin, should the shooting need to start. The weapon needed to vent its heat. Bishop and Rook would take turns using it, if there was a need.

"It had to be during a *Zud*," she said.

"A what?" Queen, the final member of the team, asked. Zelda Baker was the team's medic, and also its most deadly hand-to-hand combatant. She stalked through the storm just behind Bishop, carrying yet another FN SCAR rifle, and several more ammunition canisters for the big gun.

Before Bishop could answer, the team's handler, a man named Lewis Aleman, who communicated remotely with them from a hotel room in Beijing, replied, "She means the winter. It's a Mongolian term for a particularly bad one. Entire herds of livestock can perish when these Siberian anti-cyclone storms keep temperatures plunging to forty below." Aleman, callsign: Deep Blue, orchestrated matters from afar, providing whatever satellite intel he could for the team's missions, although their resources were not what they used to be.

"This gorilla suit is keeping me plenty comfortable," Rook said.

"Pretty sure she meant the lack of visibility, numbskull," Queen retorted.

"It's going to be hard enough to find this terrorist base," King spoke up, "with them being dug in underground somewhere."

"Sorry I couldn't get you better intel, guys," Deep Blue's disembodied voice replied. "All we know is the Bright Tomorrow cell is operating out of the area. Military sat coverage didn't show anything, so they must be concealing heat signatures and working out of a tunnel system or a cave or something."

"We'll find them," King said, determination filling his voice and lending the others hope.

"I don't think that's going to be a problem," Rook said. "I think my Aunt Mabel's half-blind dog could find them."

The others reached Rook's position, where he had stopped in his tracks. As they looked up, another hard gust of wind blasted into them from the north, pushing away a wall of grit and white, extending their view to over a hundred yards and revealing what appeared to be a huge castle.

2

"Can you believe this, Blue?"

"I can't see it, King," Aleman reminded him. While Aleman was used to having a video feed, on this mission he did not. The others quickly described the structure to him.

"Okay, you're right. I don't believe it. There was nothing on sat scans. Nothing on Google Earth or half a dozen geographic aerial photos."

As Aleman spoke, the others melted back into the edge of the storm cloud behind them, until the building was no longer visible, and they were concealed from any prying eyes on the tops of the battlements, the style of which reminded King of the Great Wall of China. The sloped walls, constructed from rammed-earth, brick and stone, had crenellated tops, all supporting four corner watchtowers. He had glimpsed it only for a moment before moving back into the cover of the raging storm, but that was enough for him to question his location, since the nearest segments of the Great Wall should have been almost 400 miles to the southwest.

"Are we at the right coordinates, Blue?" King asked.

"That's confirmed. My best guess would be that the Mongolians built it to be modeled after the guard tower sections along the Great Wall, which they would have been familiar with. Why? Beats me. The top must be painted in local camo patterns to conceal the structure from sat photos. And the area is covered in clouds or outright storms, like you're dealing with, for much of the year. It's still amazing nothing showed it being there."

King lay flat on the snowy ground with the others. If the particulates in the air were swept away by another gust, their suits would camouflage them somewhat. All of them kept their weapons trained toward the strange building in the desert. "Sounds like the perfect place for Bright Tomorrow to operate out of. But I wonder why none of the other teams found it."

Aleman had tasked the team with finding the terrorist command camp after several attempts by US and joint European teams had failed to locate the headquarters. Most of the special forces teams sent into the stormy region of desert had simply not returned. Those who had come back alive complained of supernatural creatures in the sand that had killed or eaten entire squads of men. The stories had been conflicting and unbelievable – exactly the sort of thing Chess Team faced on a regular basis.

Although the team had been surprised by the sight of the building when they had been expecting caves, King was already strategically assessing the situation. "Bishop, take the 240 and break right. One hundred yards, and set up there. Crawl forward until you can just barely see the building. The edge of the storm probably won't hold here, but you should have some cover."

Bishop collected the big gun and slipped away into the white gloom.

"Rook and Queen, break left." King didn't need to elaborate any further. "Knight and Pawn, the back. Find a way in. Those towers look like good overwatch."

"Visibility would be crap from up there, but we'll find something," Knight replied. He and Pawn were up and following Queen and Rook to the left. They would then circle around the left side of the structure to the back. That left King to cover the front of the building – a hundred yard long wall with a massive twenty foot-high set of banded wooden doors in the middle, closed against the rage of the storm.

He crawled forward in the blinding snow and sand, noticing for the first time that the grit scraping across the full faceplate of his helmet was actually scratching the plastic. If this went on too long, they would be blind, even when the wind cleared the air. Another of a thousand small variables he filed away in his head for later.

"Blue, how long until you can get us infrared coverage?" King asked Aleman.

"Another twenty minutes – and that's if I can get in. It's a DARPA satellite, and their encryption is crazy."

"Do what you can. I'd like to know if someone's coming up on us from behind, before they actually step on me."

"It's not that bad," Knight mumbled.

King recalled a report from a mission Knight had been on in Uganda, where a soldier had actually been standing on Knight's concealed sniper position – had actually been standing on Knight's arm, completely oblivious to the danger he was in. If that was the only time that ever happened, King would be happy.

He felt a twitching sensation at the back of his neck, and quickly whirled around, scanning the swirling white and tan haze. The base looked abandoned, but King's instincts told him it wasn't. Not being able to see or hear in the field was as limiting as wearing a bag over his head. With the helmet keeping in heat as well, he couldn't even smell an attacker sneaking up on him. The only thing the team had going for them *was* the weather. It was unlikely any Bright Tomorrow security would be outside in this mess – and the building looked pretty sturdy against attack. Between its remote location, the camouflaged roof and the extreme temperatures and low visibility, they probably had their forces set up inside the outer walls of the building. It would be enough. That's how King would have done it.

"Knight, are you in position in back?"

"We're up top, in back. Place is totally deserted. Looks like no one has been up on these walls all winter." It didn't surprise King that Knight and Pawn would have taken the initiative to scale the back wall without reporting on the lack of posted guards. They all knew each others' strengths and played to them.

"North and east are clear," came Bishop's thick Slavic accent.

"South is… wait. Do you feel that?" Rook said.

King was about to reply when he did feel it. A tremor in the ground. Aleman had briefed them about the region, which was prone to mild earthquakes and aftershocks. After a second, the rumbling sensation faded. "Just a quake. Moving on the door. Watch me."

King stood in a low crouch, waited for a strong gust of wind and then sprinted forward, toward the looming doors of the big building. He zig-zagged as he ran, hoping to throw off the aim of any guards Knight and Pawn might have missed. They were at the back of the square, castle-like base, and the length of each wall as over 100 yards, so even with Knight's keen eye, they might have missed someone in the front. But with Rook and Queen on one side of him, and Bishop on the other, King felt safe in making the dash to the wall.

When he reached the sloped surface next to the looming

doors, he turned his back to the stone, sweeping his SCAR back toward the snowstorm. If there was a threat above him on the fortress wall, Bishop would have him covered. He was far more concerned about the concealment the storm afforded anyone circling behind the team. And if he was honest, the rumors of supernatural creatures had him on edge—he'd faced things that shouldn't have been possible on more than one occasion.

He turned and faced the door, prepared to plant one of Rook's explosive spikes in the dirt in front of the threshold, but at the last second he had an idea. The doors had massive circular iron rings for handles, about the size of dinner platters, hanging at King's shoulder height. He guessed most of the much shorter Mongolians would have had to reach up for the handle. King just reached straight out and grasped the ring in his gloved hand.

He tugged, and the door opened, as if it's hinges had been oiled at least sometime in the last week—otherwise all the grit in the air would have jammed them up.

"The place might look abandoned, but someone's here."

3

Knight hurried along the edge of the crenellated wall, running his hand along the edge of the parapet for balance. He knew Pawn would be on his blind side, doing the same. The wind was worse up on the forty-foot-tall wall, and the snow and sand blew so hard that he couldn't see more than a few feet.

They had been lucky to get one of the gusting bursts that had cleared the air temporarily, so they knew they were alone on the top of the wall. As they raced to the nearest corner watchtower, they stayed low, but speed was now more essential than stealth. With the snow untouched on the walkways along the walls, and on the pagoda-like central building inside the outer wall, anyone even glancing out this way during a clearing in the storm would see the new footprints.

"This feels all wrong," Pawn said, speaking directly to

Knight on a separate sub-channel they had between them, for additional communication. It was another subtle tool they used to compensate for the loss of Knight's left eye, but they rarely needed it for that purpose. Instead, they used it to talk privately, away from the ears of the others. The system was set up so that if anyone spoke over the network, they would hear the exchange in their left ears. If Pawn and Knight wanted to speak exclusively to each other, they would hear the replies in their right ears. A toggle switch allowed them to choose on which network to broadcast. So far, they hadn't mixed up the channels.

"I agree. I know it's brutally cold out here, but they don't even have any cameras," Knight said, as he reached the doorway into the corner tower.

"Sand would probably scour the lenses on the first day," Pawn observed.

"Front door's open. Going in," they heard King report from the front of the building. "Stay frosty. The hinges have been oiled recently."

Knight felt the need to get deeper inside the building than King, and faster. He knew it wasn't necessary to compensate for his injuries with his actions, but being sneaky and fast was something he had done even before the loss of his eye.

Pawn didn't need him to explain the plan. They had become like one human in two bodies over the last few weeks. She would anticipate his moves, learning his style and his intentions from simple gestures. Pawn was fast enough to anticipate what he would do, and to keep up with him.

He grasped the door to the tower, and tugged on it. It opened a little stiffly, as if it, too, had been oiled, but grit from the blowing storm had still found its way into the frame and the iron hinges. Pawn covered his entrance, then they leap-frogged positions into the unlit stone stairwell. Knight pulled the door closed after them, plunging them into darkness.

"Blue, do you copy?" Knight asked.

"Crystal clear," came Aleman's reply.

"We're inside the southwest tower. What's the temp in here?"

Their suits, which Aleman had appropriated for them on the black market, had temperature sensors inside and out, allowing Aleman to monitor their bodies in the frigid climate, but also so they would know if the temperature outside the suit warmed up enough for them to remove it.

"Ten above," Aleman said after a brief pause. "It'll be chilly, but you can remove the helmets."

"'Bout damn time," Pawn groaned, slipping the helmet off over her head.

Knight did the same, and instantly he heard the roaring of the wind outside the thick wooden door. The sound was somewhat muted, so he was able to listen for sounds in the darkened stairwell. Convinced they were alone, he donned an AN/PVS-14A night vision monocular, and Pawn did the same. The devices strapped over their heads and amplified the available light. In this case, there wasn't any ambient light, so Knight activated an extremely dim LED at the sole of his boots. The light was so slight and diffuse that an unaided human eye could see it, but not be able to pinpoint its exact location. That wouldn't help them much while in the confines of the tight stairwell, but once they were down at ground level, the space would open up, and they would be able to hide in the darkness. Also, at the first sign of contact, Knight could douse the dim light, switching it to a pulse mode. It allowed he and Pawn to see the walls and the steps of the twisting spiral stone passage, and he quickly descended, looking for tripwires or other security devices as he went. So far, he was disappointed in the security, but terrorists weren't known for their adherence to norms, and he supposed with the remote location and the climate, they really wouldn't need too much to dissuade visitors.

"There should at least be a guard dog, or something," Knight said softly, over the open comms.

"Perimeter report," King asked.

"All clear, Boss," Rook said.

"Nothing," Bishop added.

"We're approaching the ground level," Knight said.

"Warmer inside, but still no tangos," Pawn said. "This doesn't feel right."

"Agreed..." King said, and then he lapsed into silence. Knight could tell from the way he had said it that he was considering calling the operation off. It wouldn't have been the first time King had done so, and he tended to be the most cautious of the team now. Knight continued down the steps, waiting for the call.

It didn't come.

Oddly, neither did the ground floor.

The stairs kept circling down, and Knight was sure they had descended close to sixty feet now. The ground level would have been at forty.

"These stairs keep going down, King. We're investigating."

"Roger," King said. "I'm checking the main floor, but it looks deserted here, too."

As Knight and Pawn descended, they noticed the shades of green in their monocles brightening. Knight switched off his boot LED and found he could still see. "Light source," he whispered, speaking only to Pawn. She made a soft grunting noise he knew to be an acknowledgment.

After a few more steps, the stairway opened up onto a catwalk in a dimly lit, wide open space. The lights were far below, but bright enough that Knight removed the monocular entirely. They stayed in the shadows of the doorway, stowing the assistive devices, before Knight belly-crawled to the edge of the metal catwalk, and peered down into the chamber forty feet below him.

"Shit. King," he whispered on the team network. "This looks like a bio-weapons lab. All bright white walls and glass down here. We're forty feet below the surface level. I'm seeing large glass vats with nuclear green liquid and bio-hazard symbols on them. A few people milling around in white lab coats."

"Deep Blue?" King asked, irritation audible in his voice.

"Everything we have says it's a simple terrorist command center. I have no intel on labs or chemical weapons."

"The brief is the same," King said. "Plant your bomb-spikes. We get out and blow the place sky high. No matter what they're cooking up here, the remote location will prevent it from spreading and the sands will cover this place up."

"Damn, remember those guard dogs you wanted, Knight?" Rook's voice came over the net. "We've got a roving patrol here. I don't think they've spotted us. Looks like six men. They're all bundled up like hairy brown pillowturds."

"Still nothing on this side," Bishop added. "I can't see anything."

Welcome to my world, Knight thought, still rueful over the loss of his eye.

Then he saw a dozen men, armed with AK-47 rifles, come rushing out onto the floor of the lab below. He crept backward across the metal suspended floor, toward the door to the stairwell. Pawn was already there in the shadows. She raised a finger, pointing at the far side of the catwalk that surrounded the entire lab space. Over eighty yards away, on the opposite wall, was another doorway, most likely to another guard tower.

Eight men rushed out of the doorway, their boots clanging on the metal catwalk. They were bundled up in what looked like rags and furs, and they were each armed with a rifle. The men circled the catwalk, heading right for Knight and Pawn's doorway.

4

Queen slipped through the snow like a wraith. While Rook attempted to cover her position from where they had been keeping an eye on the south and eastern sides of the building, she followed close behind the roving patrol of men as they moved along the south wall. She briefly switched on the audio for the outside of her helmet, listening for any noises over the howl of the storm, but all she heard was the constant, roaring whine of the wind.

Feeling confident in her approach, because the storm would cover any noise she made, Queen rushed toward where she'd last seen the man, before they disappeared into the blowing ice crystals. The whiteout was thick, but she pressed on blindly, hoping to catch the men and dispatch the entire patrol before anyone was the wiser.

Instead, she ran right into a wall.

Of fur.

In the split second it took her to realize that the men on patrol had performed a 'Crazy Ivan' technique, suddenly turning to ensure no one was following them, the man she had run into, covered in rags and furs, and carrying a fur-wrapped AK-47 rifle, began to raise his weapon. Queen's wasn't in position. Her rifle was angled off to her left after the unexpected impact. So she lunged upward with it, the side of the SCAR smashing into the man's gauze-covered head. She figured he could barely see through the layers of cloth anyway. After the weapon impacted his head with a dull thud, the coverings were displaced upward, blinding him.

She didn't know if a gunshot would be audible over the screaming wind, but she didn't want to chance it. She dropped her SCAR, and it swung down to her side on its sling. Her hand came up with a SOG SEAL knife instead. The blade was seven inches long, making it a monster of a weapon. She normally preferred a shorter 4-inch blade, but in this environment, where she expected any opponents to be wearing thick layers of clothing, she had thought it best to go with a longer knife. As the blade rammed home into the man's throat, and continued straight back to sever his spinal cord just above his second thoracic vertebrae, she congratulated herself on the choice. The wide man, looking like an overstuffed brown pillow in his thick clothing, tumbled backward. She held tight to the handle of the knife, and it sluiced out of the guard as he went down.

She was just starting to turn, to keep her own system of Crazy Ivans in the blinding white, when she saw the barrel of an AK-47 emerge from the white fog to her right. With no time to fully turn, she lunged her whole body in that direction, mashing the barrel of the weapon away from her, even as it lit up, spewing 7.62mm death in an uncontrolled burst. She only hoped the man, whose finger had clenched in surprise, managed to mow down some of his fellow guards. Then she and the man were tumbling down toward the ground.

Moving the fight to the rocky soil was a bad enough turn of events, but just as she and the second man hit the hard, frozen ground, something worse happened.

The wind abruptly stopped.

And the blowing snow and sand that had been obscuring her from view, vanished with it.

"Fight or flight?" Pawn asked, sheltered in the shadow of the doorway.

Knight waited a beat before replying to her. "Option 3. Rook style." He dove forward, rolling out onto the catwalk. As he went low, Pawn came out behind him, aiming high and firing at the oncoming team of guards. Her three-round burst hit the first man, spinning him, and her second burst hit the next man in line. As the two victims fell sideways, the third man on the narrow catwalk was revealed, and a second later, he was impaled.

Knight had fired one of Rook's tailor-made spear gun-like bomb-spikes. The compressed-air weapon was strong enough to send the metal spike across the catwalk to drive itself deeply into the man's chest. Pawn could see the small red LEDs on the ring of explosives around the shaft were lit already, indicating that the bomb was armed. As the man fell backward into the others still standing, Knight and Pawn took off running the other direction along the catwalk.

The remaining three men opened fire on them, bullets pinging off the metal catwalk near their feet as they ran. Suddenly the wall to their left began sparking from additional bullet impacts, and Pawn swept her SCAR over the railing to her right, firing several blind shots down at the floor of the lab, where she assumed the other guards were standing. She knew there was a risk of hitting the vats of fluid down there, and she had no way of knowing what they contained. But since the mission was essentially to *break everything*, she figured it would all work out okay.

As Knight reached the corner of the catwalk, and another doorway to their left—most likely to another watchtower, he darted inside, holding his arm up to show her that he held the transmitter for the bomb-spike. He was going to flick the switch.

Pawn darted into the doorway, just before the pressure wave ripped along the metal floor, nipping at her heels. As soon as it was done spewing shredded fabric and shattered, blood-stained chunks of rock their way, she darted back out onto the catwalk, which was now mangled and on fire at the end. She leaned over the railing and fired a bomb-spike from her own spear gun down into the lab. The spike implanted in the ground right next to the largest vat of lime green fluid. Pawn then pulled back and swept her SCAR up to cover Knight. He had reloaded his own spear gun and leaned over the rail, as she had done, firing his spike to a far corner of the lab's floor. They took turns, laying suppressive gunfire and launching their deadly cargo, until Knight had loosed four of his seven remaining spikes and Pawn had fired all eight of hers.

Wordlessly they turned to ascend the darkened stairs of the new tower, hoping there would be an exit, because the space behind them was about to erupt in a fireball of chemicals, pulverized stone and slivers of metal and bone.

"What in the name of Michigan J. Frog happened to the friggin' storm?" Rook asked, scrambling to his feet and racing toward the distant brawl between Queen and one of the patrolling guards.

With the air suddenly clear of ice and grit, he could see she had already taken one of the men down, but while she grappled with another, there were four more men. Two had turned already and were rushing toward their fallen comrades.

Rook loosed a controlled burst of fire from his FN SCAR, dropping one of the men, and winging the other. He kept running toward them, firing again as he got closer. He dropped the second alarmed guard, just as Queen plunged her huge knife in the chest of the man she had on the ground. Rook kept advancing and was pleased to see the last two guards hadn't even turned yet.

Queen climbed to her feet. Rook was still half a dozen yards from her position and heading for her at a run. He was about to fire on the last two guards, when one of them turned and the other simply dropped. Rook raised his weapon to fire on the turning man, but he dropped as well.

Queen felt the ground trembling again and then saw Rook heading her way, aiming past her. She turned back and saw the last of the guards fall down. Then she and Rook both understood what had happened to the men.

King, approaching from the back of the building, he had taken both men down with single shots from his rifle, as he'd come around the corner.

But something was wrong. He was running toward them, and moving full out.

"King, what's—" Rook started to ask.

Then Rook noticed the vibration beneath his feet. At first he'd written it off as another of the tremors Aleman had mentioned. But it was stronger now, and the ground was bucking and jumping, as if this earthquake was going to be a huge one.

Then the source of the quake became clear, as a monstrous thing followed King around the corner, hissing and frothing.

5

King ran faster than ever before, but it still wasn't enough.

Once he'd heard there was a bioweapons lab concealed

underground, he'd planted four bomb-spikes—one in each corner of the ground-floor courtyard inside the outer wall, then he'd headed out a rear gate. That was when the trembling had begun. He'd sensed that it was closer than the rumble they had experienced the last time, and that its force was increasing at an exponential pace.

He had wondered if it was something Knight and Pawn had set off underground, but then the wind died. He could see. A hundred yards behind the building, the soil had erupted, as if a mole twelve feet in diameter was burrowing up from underground. He had thought of the giant 250-foot-diameter sinkholes that had opened in Siberia months earlier.

But the thing that fired out of this hole like a breaching whale was no mole, and the hole had not been a sinkhole, but a tunnel. The creature was ten feet in diameter, and rose up out of the hole straight into the air, at least twenty feet high. It had shiny, wet skin, blood red and covered with cascading rains of dirt. Its long, tapering body was ribbed into segments, and the front end of its tubular shape opened into a huge gaping maw.

It's a worm, he had thought. *It's huge!*

And then the mouth had opened wider, and a plume of purple vapor shot out, making the rocks and soil that it hit steam with wavering fumes.

And... King had thought, *Time to go.*

As soon as he'd started running for the southwest corner, the massive thing had begun to chase him. He reached the corner and took down two guards, but he didn't slow.

"King, what's—" Rook was starting to say.

King had no time to answer him, and the man would get an eyeful in just a second. "Bishop! Going to need that 240, southwest corner. Coming in hot!"

Rook and Queen were already turning to run as he approached them.

"Why am I not surprised it is you who started the big rumbling?" Bishop replied from the other side of the building. She hadn't said so, but he knew she would be hauling the machine gun to the location he had specified.

"Yeah, count on him to find the one thing out here bigger than a damn rabbit. Knight, Pawn. We're leaving in a hurry," Rook said, running side by side with King.

"We're already on the roof. What the hell is that?" Knight said.

Then King, who had opened his exterior microphone, heard the small man take three shots at the pursuing worm with his sniper rifle. "Didn't even slow it," Knight said.

"Slow what?" came Aleman's disembodied voice. "What are you dealing with?" He was used to being able to see everything the team saw through high tech lenses and video feeds, and he was clearly at a loss with no visuals.

"Seen Tremors or Dune?" Rook asked.

"A giant worm?" Aleman said, disbelief coloring his words.

"Yep, but redder than a Doberman's wanger."

Queen had taken the lead in the sprint and was veering toward the corner of the building, just as Bishop rolled on the ground from the opposite direction, coming to rest prone and planting the 240B on its bipod legs.

Queen nimbly leapt over the long weapon and Bishop, and she rounded the corner of the structure. Rook was right behind her, and hopped over Bishop, too. King dove to the ground, next to his sister, just as she opened up with the chugging big gun. He added his FN SCAR to the process, unloading a full magazine at the giant slithering thing heading their way. The ground trembled slightly as the monster approached. King assumed the full on earthquakes were from it tunneling under the soil and rock.

"*Kakova hera*," Bishop swore in Russian—*What the fuck?*— while pounding the approaching worm with a withering torrent of 7.62 rounds, highlighted with the occasional tracer shot of brilliant orange, so she could adjust her vector of fire. The concentrated fusillade chewed a ragged hole through its side, just to the right of its black, gaping maw, but the beast's approach wasn't halted or even slowed.

"Pick up," King said, buttoning out his magazine and quickly inserting another before blazing away at the worm again.

Bishop scooped up the machine gun and ran. King turned to follow her around the corner of the building, just as the rumbling thing spit at him again. This time a burst of the purple liquid arced forward out of the cloud of vapor, dashing against the side of his environment suit. He saw his left arm start to smoke, but he didn't slow down his pace.

Bishop, Rook and Queen had all set up at the northeast corner of the building, past the big, wooden front doors. While Bishop inserted a new drum into the machine gun, the others were firing above King's head at the pursuing creature. The worm had continued well past the corner. It clearly couldn't turn effectively, and King was grateful for the brief reprieve.

"Boss, your suit's smoking, like it's gonna melt," Rook said.

Bishop opened fire on the creature, this time able to strafe the worm's full forty-foot-long side, as it slowly arced around the open desert floor.

"It sounds like a Mongolian Death Worm," Aleman said over their comms.

"Oh that's helpful," Rook said. "It couldn't be the Mongolian Fluffy Rainbow-Pooping Worm?" He dropped a magazine and slotted a fresh one into his SCAR, but then let the weapon hang. It wasn't doing any damage to the giant ribbed creature. He'd wait until it closed the distance, and then he'd try his 'Girls'—a pair of IMI Desert Eagle Mark XIX Magnum .50 caliber semi-automatic pistols. He'd had several pairs over the years, some getting lost in different skirmishes. He hadn't yet come across anything, no matter how big, that wouldn't feel a few slugs from the handguns at close range.

"He has a point," King said, perturbed. "How to kill it would be better than a name."

"It's a mythical cryptid. Supposed to be about four feet long," Aleman said.

"Bigger," Queen said. "Much bigger. Twelve foot diameter. Forty feet long."

King pulled free his KA-BAR knife, a 7-inch blade like Queen's, and slid it into the boiling, formerly fur-covered sleeve of his environment suit's fabric, slicing it open, then he dropped the smoking knife on the ground. He'd tried to cut away the burning part of the suit, but had failed. "Rook."

It was all he had to say. As he flipped off the helmet and hood of the suit, breathing in the freezing air, Rook moved forward to grab the outer fabric of the suit in places where it hadn't been coated in the creature's deadly venom. He pulled the fabric taut as King disentangled himself from the outer garment, being sure to lean as far from the smoking side as possible.

Rook instantly saw King's breath add a cloud of vapor to the already rising ribbon of steam from the cooking fur on the ruined suit.

"It's supposed to be able to spit venom," Aleman continued.

"Think we can confirm that one," Rook said.

Queen fired a sustained burst with her SCAR as Bishop reloaded the machine gun. The creature had finished its wide loop and was homing in on the team, at their new location.

"We need a plan," Queen urged.

"There's nothing about how to kill them. No one has ever even had a confirmed sighting of one..." Aleman sounded frantic.

"Then give me some other intel," King said, his teeth beginning to chatter. "How long do I have in just the wetsuit in temps like these?" He had shed the outer garment, and it now lay smoking on the ground, like a dead animal on a charnel heap. He wore just the under-suit, which was a special gel-heated neoprene, and he had been able to salvage his boots and the furry gloves from the outer suit.

Rook thought he looked strange in white, fur-clad boots and gloves, but a black body suit and hood. Like some kind of snow bunny at the Winter games, but this one had an automatic rifle and was collecting the bomb-spikes for his spear gun from the pile of quickly discarded equipment.

"Your suit? Oh crap. Um...if you keep active, any part or your skin that's exposed might be able to withstand frostbite for...around ten minutes. Maybe less."

King turned to see the approaching worm was just a few yards away, and it was beginning to rise up in the air, like a cobra poised to strike.

6

"There!" King pointed the barrel of his SCAR and fired an unrestrained, fully automatic burst, holding down the trigger. "Under its neck."

The others instantly saw what he was targeting. Just under the rim of the creature's black mouth, which lacked teeth but had short one-foot-long wriggling tentacles, like insect feelers or kelp waving in an undersea current, was a small metal box affixed to the creature's crimson skin. It looked to be the size of an old metal lunchbox, and King's bullets pounded the can, pinging off of it. Then Bishop opened with a sustained burst from the 240, and the box, as well as the slick, wet-looking skin below it, disintegrated.

The giant worm dropped down from its attack position, its heft slamming into the ground and sending a shockwave under foot. Then it turned and headed away from the building, and the surprised team.

"Control mechanism?" Queen asked.

"Possibly," King said. "Blue, we need a pick up, ASAP."

"They can't, King." Aleman's voice was apologetic. "The chopper is still on the other side of the storm. It's no longer blowing where you are, but it still stretches for forty miles. No way for them to get to you. You'll have to hump it out to the LZ."

"Knight?" King asked.

"Proceeding. We'll catch up."

Knowing he had to keep moving, and even then his time was limited, King made the decision. "Move out."

The team picked up and headed toward the distant cloud that marked the edge of the storm, back the way they had come. The wind had stopped blowing in their location, but they could still see a far off wall of white and swirling brown. They double-timed it for the raging storm, keeping an eye on the receding worm, as it wandered aimlessly south and then west again, back from whence it had come.

The team made it halfway from the castle to the edge of the cloud when the rocks around them pinged with the ricochets of missed rifle fire. They each dropped, and rolled to the sides, then faced back toward the strange brown fortress. But the shots hadn't come from that direction. They were coming from a small team—maybe ten strong—of additional guards to the north. They were still a few hundred yards away, their rifles only just inside the effective firing range.

Queen glanced at King and saw that he wasn't reacting as quickly as she would have expected. His lips hadn't turned blue, but they had lost their color, and his face looked pale against the black neoprene hood lining. "Rook, Bishop. Take this. I'm getting King to the LZ."

Rook raised his SCAR and fired off a few rounds at the approaching men. The weapon had a much longer range, but at the distance, any kills would be simple luck. "Watch out for the Jumbo Fire Turd."

"Nice," Queen said, grabbing King by the arm and starting to run with him toward the nearby wall of the storm. "You kiss *me* with that mouth, remember."

"Only because you ask me to—" Rook started to say, before his body was violently flung to the ground. Bishop had opened up on the approaching guards with the machine gun, but she stopped immediately and turned to Rook. The left arm of his suit's fur was a deep maroon. "Shit in the milk carton! That stings like bastard."

Bishop started opening a portable med kit they each carried, which was strapped to their stomachs, over the environment suits, but as she unzipped it, Rook spoke again.

"Just a through and through," he growled. "I'll be alright."

Bishop lunged back to her trigger, trusting Rook's self-assessment. They had all taken minor grazes from bullets—or worse—at this point in their careers. She laid down a suppressing fire that had the new group of guards diving for cover or simply dropping dead with tufts of crimson mist staining the white clouds around them. She counted ten men, but their number was dwindling under her constant stream of automatic fire.

Rook rolled over, pulling up his rifle and adding his bullets to hers. They had the guards, all of them wrapped in their brown furs, pinned just behind a small ridge of rock. But then two things happened at once.

The wind picked up again, the storm having shifted enough to cover them in waves of sand and snow. Their visibility was lost completely.

Then the building, so reminiscent of China's greatest architectural accomplishment, detonated. The chemical reaction made the explosion far stronger than the bomb-spikes should have done alone.

A howling burst of flame ripped horizontally across the ground, with a pressure wave so strong that it rolled Rook's body across the rocky ground, crushing him into Bishop's prone form, and the two of them slammed into a low ridge of crumbling rock. The wall of flame came next, flashing across their bodies and whipping across the fur coatings on their environment suits until they were singed clean. The shrieking wind carried the rest of the destruction away.

"I think I just got a tan," Bishop said, shoving Rook's body off of her.

"You got off light," Rook complained. "I think I just lost my nut hairs."

"Aww, both of them?" Bishop said. She started to look for the machine gun, but found the barrel had been coated in small pebbles and sand, the grit having invaded the open gas ports. Attempting to fire it now would result in a misfire at best or another explosion in her face at worst. She left it, and hauled Rook to his feet. As she did, a huge wall of red flashed by on her right, just where she had been laying.

The death worm had returned.

The massive creature worked its way past them like a shark blitzing past its prey. It was so close she could reach out and touch it. It blurred by like a subway car if she had been standing too close on the platform. She could see the ragged gouges and holes in its scarlet hide, where she had riddled it with the 240 earlier.

The blasting wind slowed, and she could see once again in the direction of the small group of pinned guards. She wished she couldn't. The worm ran straight for the men, snatching one guard up with its black tentacles, and flipping him into the air. The beast rose up again, close to twenty feet straight up in the air, like it was performing an old Indian rope trick. Then it grabbed the man before he reached the apex of his flight, and swallowed him down in one gulp. Again, Bishop was reminded of a shark.

She saw one of the other guards banging his heavily gloved fingers on an oversized remote control with a three foot long silver antenna. It reminded her of the controllers she had seen boys in Russia use on remote controlled toy cars. "They *are* controlling the worms."

But then the worm flopped down onto the man, mashing him and two of his fellow guards into the ground, before another gust of wind obscured her view with a river of white snow. The gust curved down toward the ground and then straight up into the sky, like a geyser.

"I've got nothing you can fight them with," Aleman said over the comm, "short of immense doses of electricity or dousing the region with chemicals from above—things we don't have. Get out of there, Bishop."

"We have one more thing that can do the trick," Knight yelled, as the ground rumbled.

Rook turned in time to see—and then side-step away from—another giant worm. This one looked fatter, but shorter than the first. Twenty feet at the thickest part, just past the head, and then tapering down to ten feet in diameter, over forty feet away, down by its tail end. It was a darker, richer red than the first. Not as shiny, and without as many defined ribs. This one also had another unusual feature.

Knight was hanging from its side.

With one hand, he clung to one of the bomb-spikes, which he had manually impaled in the creature's side. The worm was moving fast, and Knight was fifteen feet off the ground, as the creature rushed past, spiraling higher, so that Knight was lifted up and on top of it.

7

Anna Beck raced after the runaway death worm and its precious cargo. The thing was moving at a good clip, and the ground—covered with random clumps of hardy vegetation or craggy rocks—made for treacherous footing.

The plan had been simple. Knight had raced after the second worm, bomb-spike in hand. He hadn't had a chance to load it into his launcher, and instead had run on foot toward the side of the massive creature. He should have impaled it and dropped away, so she could detonate the bomb once he was clear. Instead, Knight had held onto the spike, and been hoisted for a ride on the top of the charging worm.

"What the hell are you doing, Knight?" she asked, huffing, as she ran full out behind him. "You were supposed to spike it and get off, not go all rodeo."

She knew the transmitters for the detonators on the jury-rigged spikes had a limited range, so she needed to be close enough to the creature to kill it, but she needed to get Knight and herself far enough from it that the blast didn't injure them, too.

"Getting elevation," he said. "There are more of them."

She heard the distinctive crack of his sniper rifle go off, over the howl of the wind on her exterior speaker. Then she turned her head and saw a third worm—this one a mottled brown and white—suddenly veer away from its previous course. Knight had just shattered its control box. If he hadn't, she never would have known it was pursuing her until it was too late. Now the brown creature made a lazy turn heading back toward the destroyed lab.

"How many more?" Aleman asked in her ear.

"Enough," Knight said, his voice terse as he concentrated on firing again. Beck knew his voice well enough to tell when he was aiming.

"Team, if you can kill those things with the bomb-spikes, you need to do it," Aleman said, hesitating as he said it, as if he were doing three other things on the computer at the same time.

"King said to bug out, Blue," Rook said over the comms. "Bish and I are already moving toward the LZ." Everyone knew that King made the final calls when the team was in the field.

"Those things already have a taste for human flesh, if the guards have been using them for security. If even one of them survives, it could rampage across the countryside, devouring nomads—or worse, it might pilgrimage to a population center like Beijing."

"Blue is right," King's voice came over the comms, his teeth still chattering. "We're nearly at the chopper. I'll be fine. Sending Queen back for support."

"I'll take the brown one, then," Pawn said, changing direction and pursuing the large mottled worm. As she ran, she mounted one of the two bomb-spikes Knight had handed her into her spear gun. She planned to chase the thing into range and then simply fire the weapon at it, but the lumbering creature turned instead of continuing straight. It performed a slow loop back to the north, and then in the direction Knight had gone, riding on the back of the brick red worm.

The ground shook with each leaping step she took, and she found it easier to run in the patches of loose sand than on the vibrating rock. As the thing changed direction again, cutting across her path, her distance to it was shortened, and she soon got within spear-gun range. As she loosed a spike from the weapon, the visibility increased yet again, and she saw the brick worm, Knight squatting on its back, charging straight for her mottled brown worm. The two would either attack each other, or pass right next to each other, like speeding trains. Unsure of which it would be, and what Knight would need, she continued racing for the collision site.

As she ran, she saw Knight stand up.

Then at the last second, the two speeding worms altered direction just slightly, and she could see that they would pass right next to each other. Knight leapt from the reddish worm to the brown one, rolling on the back of the latter. Pawn altered her trajectory to follow the brown worm. As the red worm's tail cleared the brown's tail, Knight activated his transmitter, and the speeding red beast's front end exploded in a gout of thick white fluid and chunks of brick red skin. Much of the obliterated head was involuntarily swallowed by the hollow, fast moving cylinder of its body, before the creature ran out of steam and seemed almost to deflate, finally stopping its momentum.

Pawn chased the brown worm as it fled into the storm with Knight now surfing on top of it. "Brick red one's down. That leaves the brown one Knight's on and the one you guys filled with lead," she announced on the open channel. "What next, Knight?"

"Run along side," Knight told her. "I'll lower a rope."

"Why not just get down?" she asked, frustrated that he didn't get off the thing. How could she blow it up, if he was still in range?

"This one is going our way."

"The first one is still out there," she pointed out. "We need to get them all."

"Nah," she heard Rook's voice say, followed immediately by a resounding boom. "Queen and I just took care of Chuckles, the Swiss Cheese Worm. That just leaves yours, Knight."

Pawn ran as fast as she could, but she didn't think she would catch the fleeing brown worm and the man riding it. The ground rumbled hard under her feet, making every leap and hop treacherous. Her boots had slid more than once, and she was afraid she would turn an ankle. She was also starting to sweat and overheat in the warmed suit.

"Guys, I'm seeing a much bigger Richter pattern than before. The seismic readings suggest a full on earthquake is coming. Maybe all the tunneling from the worms?" Aleman sounded uncertain. "I think you should bail. You can re-arm and come back for the last worm."

"Shit," Knight blurted.

"What is it?" came King's voice. His words no longer stuttered from cold, and Pawn assumed he had reached the helicopter and a spare environment suit.

"It's turning," Knight replied, and just as he said it, Pawn burst through a cloud of swirling snowflakes and grit that gusted so hard it almost knocked her backward. She saw the brown worm turning. It would cross her path if she didn't hurry. Getting stuck between it in front of her and an earthquake behind her, with the helicopter on the other side of it did not appeal to her. She poured on the speed, intending to run past its head, like racing a train, and continue through the storm. She had already seen the thing was slow to corner, so she wasn't worried it could change direction at the last second and maul her.

"Time to get down, Bronco Billy," she said, as she raced past the thing's black-tentacled mouth. As she passed it, she saw Knight slide down the creature's ribbed side like it was a playground slide. Until its curvature stopped at its widest spot, a good ten feet off the ground, and dipped back under the fast moving beast. Knight dropped those last ten feet into a sand dune and rolled in the dirt, his furred suit flinging a spray of grit in the air like a car's tire spinning in mud.

Pawn veered toward Knight, but he was already rolling to his feet and running toward the distant helicopter on the other side of the storm's whipping frenzy. He wasn't waiting on her to catch up, so she forced herself to sprint faster.

When she felt they were far enough from the receding brown worm, she activated her transmitter, and the sky behind them filled with an orange ball of flame and smoke, billowing from the last worm's split open center. The massive creature rolled across the ground, out of control.

The ground shook hard, and Pawn realized it wasn't from the explosion, but from the earthquake Aleman had mentioned.

"Don't look back, Anna," Knight called. "Just run!"

Her eyes grew large inside her faceplate as she realized what he was saying.

It wasn't an earthquake.

She really didn't want to know how big this one was.

She really didn't.

But she looked.

8

"Report," King's voice came over the comms.

"Umm," Rook said, taking aim with his spear gun. He pointed it up in the air like an English longbowman, and Queen, to his side, picked up on his intent and did the same with hers. "Knight and Pawn are being chased by the biggest friggin' large intestine you can imagine."

With that description to King, he fired, and Queen did likewise. The twin bomb-spikes arced through the air and over the heads of Pawn and Knight, who were running toward them full tilt. Behind them was a massive death worm. This one dwarfed the others, with a diameter at the head of forty feet. As far as Rook could see, the thing's body trailed behind it a hundred yards.

The spikes implanted themselves in the top of the thing's neck, and Rook loaded another spike. Then he turned to run toward the edge of the storm, where King and the helicopter pilot, a retired Marine named Woodall, waited ready to take off at a moment's notice.

"We'll be coming in hot with the giant shit garage on our six."

"Taking it too far," Queen said, berating his disgusting description, while twisting in the middle of her run to fire another bomb-spike backward in an arc. This one implanted in the creature's back, ten yards further down from the first two. Then she continued her twist until she was facing forward. She kept running.

Knight and Pawn were catching up to them, and the megaworm kept twisting through the storm on their heels. It was so large that even when the gusts of snow blew through the air, mostly obscuring Knight and Pawn, Rook could still see the bright, shiny red of the thing's skin and the dark waving tendrils at its mouth through the blizzard.

Knight pulled alongside him, as Rook bunny hopped clumps of pale grass and stunted shrubs growing from rocky patches in the ground where they had sunken roots deep and found a source of water. Looking over, Rook saw that Knight carried a rope bag in his left hand and an empty spear gun in his right.

The bag held a neatly coiled 11mm climbing rope, and it was designed so the tip could be pulled out one end, and the rope would keep feeding out of the bag without tangling. The team carried two such rope bags. Knight had one and Queen wore the other strapped across her back. Rook wondered if they could lasso the giant slithering creature, but he quickly discarded the thought and poured all his energy into running for their one and only escape route.

As a larger, heavier man than the others, Rook was a slower runner. Pawn and Knight soon pulled in front of him, and he could no longer even see Queen in the distance. He glanced over his shoulder at the massive oncoming freight train of tendrils, the mouth of the worm yawning open like a dark cave that was chasing him. He found a second wind and began stretching out his strides.

"Hurry up, ma puce," Queen said over the comms. "We need to leave. The pilot says the storm is getting worse. If we don't take off in the next two minutes, the engine might get borked from the sand."

Even with the new burst of speed and Queen's encouragement, using her pet name for him, Rook didn't think he was going to be able to make it. Each step he took rattled his bones, as the pursuing giant worm shook the earth. He didn't even know if the few bomb-spikes they had planted in the thing would be enough to stop it. This one was twice as thick as the last one and many times longer.

What if the bastid splits in half from the explosion and turns into two worms?

Then he burst out of the boiling cloud of snow and sand to find he was running across clear, open, sandy ground. The sudden lack of wind resistance almost pitched him forward onto his face, but his legs awkwardly pinwheeled until he regained his step.

Two hundred yards away, the helicopter's rotor was already spinning up to speed. The pilot wore an environment suit like the team, so he could keep the side door open and waiting. Pawn was tossing her FN SCAR rifle into the interior and clambering up. Knight was right behind her, slinging his rope bag and empty spear gun inside. Queen was aiming another spear gun in Rook's direction, but at an upward angle. King, wrapped in a spare, white environment suit, was reaching down to haul Pawn into the doorway.

The sight of his teammates gave him hope, and Rook found yet another burst of speed, his legs beginning to burn, and a cramp forming in his side, just above his right hip.

At one hundred and fifty yards, Rook saw Queen launch her bomb-spike, and then scramble to load another. King was hauling Knight into the open bay, and Pawn was fumbling to load another spear gun.

It was the frantic handling of the weapons that made him look back.

The ground vibrated and rippled beneath his feet, as Rook twisted to see the pursuing creature. The Mongolian death worm raised its head up as it came, looking like a huge, fast-moving wave of surf, ready to crash down on him. Its mouth was a gaping black void around a brilliant, scarlet skin that glistened in the sudden sunlight at the edge of the blowing storm behind the thing.

The creature, like all the others, had no visible nose or mouth. It was just a long, ribbed tube with a dark tendrilled opening at one end and a tapering diameter at the other end. But this worm was so big that the spaces between the ribbed segments on its sides were so deep, Rook thought he could stand inside one without the sides of the segments touching him. He tentatively planned to try just that if it came down to it.

He faced forward and threw the last of his energy into a final press of speed toward the helicopter, which was just beginning to hover. In his quick look, Rook had seen that the storm was closing almost as fast as the giant, hungry cylinder.

The ground shook so hard that rocks the size of baseballs skittered across the jagged landscape. He didn't have to look behind him to know that Mighty Joe Worm was gaining on him. The fact that all five of his teammates were firing spear guns over his head now was all the indication he needed that his time was almost up. When the pilot raised the helicopter another foot, and started to bank the craft even further away from his frantic dash, it underscored the point for Rook.

When he glanced back one more time and his boot caught on an unforgiving shrub, he felt himself pitch forward, overbalanced. Rook knew it was the end.

9

King saw that Rook was going down. He leapt out the still-open helicopter door and raced to meet the man. Rook had almost made it, before he had tripped, just thirty feet away. King cleared half that distance before Rook actually hit the ground. Either to his credit or due to his sheer momentum, Rook continued forward on the rocky soil, rolling forward on the ground, even as King skidded to a halt next to him.

Together, they got Rook to his feet and ran the last of the distance toward the black helicopter. To the pilot's credit, he had angled the vehicle closer in, toward the men, the pursuing hell worm and the raging whiteout wall.

King simply dove head-first into the belly of the cargo area, willing Rook to follow him. He slid across the floor of the angled craft and his hand grasped a cargo strap, just as someone else's hand latched onto his wrist to hold him in place.

The helicopter banked away, still rising off the ground. King was worried that the tips of the vehicle's blades might scrape the rocky soil at such a steep angle of departure, but the pilot was top notch.

When he turned to look back out the open side door, King saw the massive worm was just below them, but rising up off the ground, pursuing the rising helicopter. The pilot was gaining altitude, but only at a slightly faster rate of gain than the death worm. The black maw followed them into the sky like a pirate ship intent on doing them ruin.

Rook had indeed made it into the craft, and he was now sitting with his back against the bulkhead. He'd formed a figure eight knot on the end of the rope from Knight's bag and was clipping it to the front of his harness with a black, anodized aluminum carabiner. King expected he would clip the other end of the rope onto the body of the helicopter for safety, but he never got the chance.

As the helicopter began to pick up vertical speed, the worm fell farther from the open door until Knight judged the distance enough. He flicked the switch on his transmitter, holding it up so everyone could see him deliver the coup de grâce.

Nothing happened.

"Son of a bitch," Rook called. "Try this one." He reached out the hand of his bloodied arm and slapped the switch on his own transmitter, which was attached to the front of his gear harness.

Again nothing happened.

"We're too far away from it now," Queen said, reminding them all that the devices had a limited range. She called to the pilot. "We need to drop altitude a little."

"Screw that," Rook said, standing and pulling his twin Desert Eagle pistols. "Somebody get the friggin' rope."

With that he leapt head first out the open door, and toward

the still rising void of the death worm's mouth.

Five sets of hands scrambled for the rope bag and the black climbing rope that rapidly unspooled from its depths.

Rook sailed straight down through the air, head first toward the oncoming ring of waving tendrils. He could see that the creature had raised almost half of itself straight up off the ground, chasing the rising helicopter with unrestrained hunger.

He had no question in his mind that the others would secure the rope, preventing him from falling to his death. Instead he worried that his plan to get close enough to the bomb-spikes that the transmitter would work might be flawed. He couldn't do the math quick enough to determine when his plummeting body would meet the rising worm. He'd always hated those kinds of problems in school.

Instead, he focused on what he knew how to do best.

Time to break shit.

He fired his huge pistols at the inside of the worm's mouth, blowing huge chunks of skin apart, even from that distance. Then the rope caught taut above him, jerking his descent to an abrupt stop, and he felt the last meal he'd eaten, hours ago, try to leave his body through the top of his head. Then his body flipped upside down, because the attachment point on his harness was in front of him. He was now hanging in the air with his back facing the lunging creature and his stomach facing upward at the bottom of the helicopter.

As the vehicle swung him over the edge of the worm's mouth, he twisted in his harness, looking down at the outer side of the beast. He could see one of the bomb-spikes implanted in its flesh. He figured he was close enough to the creature now. He slapped a hand still holding a Magnum against the switch of the transmitter on his chest, but the bombs still refused to explode.

"Monkey fucker-noodle!"

A boiling cloud of purple vapor bellowed out of the creature's mouth, and Rook knew they had just a few seconds before the death worm spewed a stream of poison at him and the helicopter. The edge of the storm had found them, too, suddenly whipping the rope, and Rook's dangling body.

He raised both pistols and fired both magazines dry at the single bomb-spike he could see on the side of the worm's slick body. He quickly ejected both magazines and slotted in a single new one for the pistol in his right hand. He took a single steadying breath as the raging wall of white began to cover up the creature's body, just feet below the silver of the bomb-spike's surface. The purple cloud coming out of the creature's mouth was billowing back past the creature, as its mouth still rose into the air. The thick viscous fumes further obscured the explosive spear nailed into the worm's hide. He started to worry that the acidic nature of the fumes could incapacitate the detonators on the bombs, but then he let the thought fall Zen-like from his mind as he aimed, released his breath and squeezed the trigger.

The effect was instant.

Although the explosive compound in the spears was hardy enough to take a shot from a bullet without exploding, the small detonators on the spikes were not. The bullet impacted the detonator, and the smaller explosive it contained went off, taking the larger explosive with it. The bomb-spike's explosion then activated the others embedded in the creature's thick hide, all over the front half of its body. The entire upper half of the giant beast turned into a maelstrom of orange fire, black smoke, purple venom, red skin fragments and white swirling snow and ice.

The helicopter rose abruptly, tugging Rook with it, but his suit still got splattered with gore. Smoke rose from parts of his formerly white covering, melting from the viscous goo that now coated him.

"I'm gonna need a new suit fast," Rook said over the comms. "And an aversion therapy doctor with a gallon-sized bucket of sour gummy worms."

"Copy that," Aleman said. "Are you clear?"

Rook looked up as he was tugged from above. The team

pulled him up as King looked down for visual confirmation of Rook's situation. Rook gave a thumbs up. "Aside from the melting, we're golden."

"We're done here," King said. "En route to the safe house."

"Actually," Aleman said. "The safe house is compromised."

"Admiral Ward?"

"Uh-huh." Aleman said in almost a groan. "Better come to me instead."

"Will do," King said, adding his muscle to the rope pulling effort. "But then we're going to have a chat about what to do about this thorn in our side."

HUNGRY EYES

Seth Skorkowsky

15 July, 2009

The second one is coming up now," I said into the radio. From my vantage point, crouched behind a rooftop wall, I watched an orange basket stretcher emerge from the manhole. It stopped as it reached the tripod straddling the opening and swung there, dangling above the pit. Blue-uniformed officers carefully pulled it out and began unstrapping the black body bag secured inside. Colored lights flashed atop the response vehicles, parked to shield the grisly work from the view of onlookers pressing against the nearby barricades. Shouts in French echoed up from the crowd and the police trying to contain them.

Nick's voice came though my ear bud. "Colin, you in position?"

"Aye," Colin answered.

"Mal, keep us posted, but stay out of sight," Nick ordered, his Armenian accent muddling the words.

"Roger that." I wiped the sweat from my forehead, wishing a cloud might block the summer sun. Below me, the men lifted the bag and set it down on the concrete beside the first.

"They're going for the third one." I tucked lower behind the wall as the men sent the now empty stretcher back down into the abyssal hole. In the distance, the distinct *nee-noo-nee-noo* of a police siren echoed though the Paris streets. The line running from the tripod stopped.

Two minutes later, a worker flipped the tripod's winch and the spool began to coil.

"They're reeling it up," I radioed.

"Let's get ready, people," Nick said.

Nervous excitement tingled across my shoulders as I

watched the spool grow larger and larger. Finally, the orange stretcher emerged up from the catacombs sixty feet below. "It's up."

"Distraction coming in fifteen seconds."

I tightened my jaw, fighting the urge to ask, but knew better. Nick loved his surprises as much as he loved reminding me that I'm the new guy.

"Ten seconds."

The workers pulled the stretcher onto the ground. The crowd behind the barricade, pushed harder, cameras flashing as they strained to see. Police stepped between them and the body, forming a human shield.

"Five."

I held my breath.

A loud boom thundered two blocks away. Car alarms erupted, accompanied by screams. Another boom sounded a moment later.

The police and medical workers shot upright, peering that direction like startled meerkats. White smoke billowed from the direction the sounds had come, filling the narrow street.

Several police and paramedics charged in that direction as others ordered the crowd to disperse. It didn't take much to persuade them, and then the police ran after their companions. One stopped, just beyond the far barrier, his back to the bodies and ear to his radio.

"Clear," I said. "Still one nearby."

"Keep an eye on him," Colin said. He slipped out from between a pair of emergency vehicles and hurried to the bagged bodies, his copper hair hidden beneath a dark ball cap.

Licking my lips, I watched the lone policeman. I stole a glance to Colin to see him peel open the first bag, recoil at unleashed sight or stench, then lift his camera.

Shouts continued down the street as the thickening white cloud spread. What the hell had Nick done? Was anyone hurt?

"One." Colin zipped the bag and moved to the next.

The lone officer shifted back and forth on his feet but hadn't moved. One by one the shrieking car alarms began to silence.

"Two." Colin said. "These things are weird."

"No commentary," Nick ordered. "Mal, how we look?"

"Some of the officers are headed back," I said. "Block away."

The lone officer started toward the trio jogging out from the smoke.

"Colin, be quick," Nick said.

"Just a few more seconds."

The policeman slowed as he met his companions. They spoke with wild moving arms, pointing toward some unseen thing down the street. Two of them broke off and headed toward the vehicles.

"Get out of there," I said, my voice a whispered yell.

Colin looked up from his camera. Quickly he zipped the bag and hurried away before the police noticed him.

I blew a long breath, a wash of relief pouring down my body. "He's out."

"All right," Nick said. "Extract. Meet at the hotel."

I sat on the bed, laptop before me. Scouring a map of the catacombs, I marked where the bodies were discovered, and the best places we might gain access. Colin sat at the small table across the room, working on his own computer. He hadn't spoken much since he arrived, only transferring his photographs over and giving the occasional grunt as he scrolled through the images.

The room door clicked and Nikoghos Tavitian stepped inside, his trimmed black beard framing his ear to ear smile. His olive knapsack rattled as he dropped it beside the door. He nodded to Colin. "Doctor," and then to me, "Doctor." With a flourish, he set a paper bag on the bed between us and withdrew a brown bundle. "Dinner is served."

Colin, who isn't actually a doctor, having joined the Order before completing med school, never liked being called that. Nevertheless, Nick always addressed us that way when he was in good spirits, and terrifying an entire city appeared to have pleased the Armenian immensely.

Nick underhand tossed a bundle to me. "Good work, Malcolm."

I caught the crinkly roll, feeling the warm bread inside. "What the hell did you do?"

"Distraction." Nick removed his own sandwich. "Needed something big enough to get everyone out of there. Just a pair of flash bangs and a smoke grenade in an alley. No one was hurt. Though…" He chuckled. "I think one woman did shit herself."

"You realize that this could wind up on world news?"

He shrugged, his smile dimming. "Back page stuff. They'll write it off as a bad prank."

Colin nodded to his monitor. "It'll make the front page if police see what did this."

I stood and peered down at Colin's screen. The image of a mottled purple corpse, its teeth and cheekbones gleaming out through ragged holes. Blood-caked lashes framed the pits where its eyes should have been.

The image flipped to another, a girl with curly blonde hair. Her throat was torn out and grimy bite wounds covered her bare shoulders. Blue eye shadow crested the black pits of her empty sockets. I no longer wanted my sandwich.

Nick took a bite of his. "So what do you think?" he asked around a mouthful.

Colin unwrapped his own sandwich, unleashing the smell of fresh bread and meat, completely inappropriate for the horrible images. "Look to be cataphiles."

"Cataphiles?" Nick asked.

"People who explore the catacombs," I answered. "The old mines are strictly off limits, but people still go down there to explore, or party. Several even live down there. Three hundred kilometers of tunnels and chambers. Plenty of room for everyone."

Nick shrugged. "Not for them it seems. So, Mal, you're the Librarian. What do you think got 'em?"

I looked back at the screen, this time a young black man with his face mostly chewed off, his grisly skull framed in jagged skin. "Ghouls. Archives show that they've made their home down there several times before. Last known infestation was during the war."

Colin nodded. "I agree. Blood wasn't drank. Bite marks correspond."

"What else does it tell you?" Nick asked me.

"There's at least four of them, either ghouls or ghouls and their undead familiars." I answered, resenting this thinly veiled pop quiz.

"Why?"

I looked away as the image changed to a close-up of the black man's mouth. His tongue had been torn out. "Ghouls only attack if they outnumber the victims or if the victim is injured or ill."

"What about the eyes?" Colin asked.

"What about them?" I asked.

"They're gone."

"Ghouls must have torn them out."

"I don't think so." Shaking his head, he scrolled to a close-up of the girl's face. "You can't pop an eye out without tearing the skin around it. At least not without tools. But the skin is unmarked. Same with all of them. It's like they were sucked right out."

Nick leaned in over Colin's shoulder. "What could do that?"

Colin shrugged. "No clue. Something else? Took the eyes and left the rest for ghouls to eat, maybe?"

They both looked to me.

I studied the picture, and then the next. "I don't know."

"Don't know?" Nick asked. "Your job is to know them."

I shook my head. "I don't recall any demon that sucks the eyes out."

Colin gestured to my laptop still open on the bed. "Then search the records."

"Only ten percent of the Valducan Archives are digitized. I'd have to go back to the chateau and search the books."

"We don't have time to go to HQ," Nick said. "The authorities are going to be scouring the catacombs for whoever killed these people, which means they'll probably get killed themselves. We have to eliminate the threat now. So think, Doctor."

A sharp spike of anger shot though my gut at Nick's scolding. But he was right. I was the team's Librarian. This was my job. Closing my eyes, I searched my memory for anything that targeted eyes and didn't leave a mark. Even beyond the Archives, my experience as an anthropologist gave me a wide knowledge of folklore and supposedly mythical monsters, the main reason I was selected for the job. Other demons ate eyes. Wendigos loved eating them. But surgical removal? "I can't think of anything."

Nick frowned, but only for a moment before his grin returned. "A holy weapon will destroy them, regardless."

"We're in Paris," Colin offered. "Maybe the eyes are French cuisine to ghouls."

We laughed as Nick pulled his duffel from the closet and dropped it on the bed. "We guess ghouls from the initial report. So, Mal, what harms ghouls?"

"Obsidian," I answered.

"Good." He withdrew a box of ammo from his bag and pulled out a round. "If things get hairy, these will drop one." He held up a nine millimeter with a black gem nose, prongs holding it in place like a goth girl's engagement ring. "We don't want to be shooting much down there," he said, continuing his rooting. "Yes, the glass tip will cut down on ricochets, but closed quarter shooting is always dangerous. I ever tell you about that vampire nest we rooted out of the Moscow Metro?"

"Every time you drink vodka," Colin answered.

Nick paused. "I do, don't I?" He shook his head. "Don't answer that."

"What about my sawed-off?" I asked. "I have some obsidian shells."

"You and that fucking sawed off," he said. "Yes, it'll work. No, don't shoot it. The other problem with shooting down there will be report. Give us all some permanent hearing loss. We'll need to run suppressed and even then, it'll still be loud as hell."

"Then why bring guns?" Colin asked.

"Cause I'd rather be deaf than dead," I answered.

Nick nodded in approval. "That's my boy."

"So what's the plan?" I asked.

"Three hundred klicks leaves a lot of room for them to hide. The sooner we begin the better. I say 2200 hours we go in. So rest up."

The night was still and humid as Nick and I exited the van, gear in hand. My sacred charge Hounacier, a bone-handled machete, hung at my waist. Nick's holy nadziak, a Polish war pick named Ozkareen, clanged from the black plastic ring at his belt. Colin drove off the moment the door was closed, leaving us alone on the empty street.

We stopped at a metal door set into the sidewalk and lit by a single light post, orbited by moths. We heaved up the door and a caged screen beneath that, revealing a landing four feet down and steel rungs descending into the darkness below.

Nick drew a milky plastic tube from his vest pouch and cracked it in one hand. Orange light ignited within like liquid fire and he dropped it. The glow stick fell and fell, tumbling past more steel rungs until finally bouncing out of sight twenty meters below. He stabbed a finger downward and I swung my legs through the opening and dropped onto the landing. Nick handed me a heavy pack which I set at my feet before moving to the rungs.

I clicked the lamp affixed to my caving helmet, unleashing a beam of crimson light. With a final nod to Nick, I started the climb down. Dizzying patterns of multi-colored spray-paint and marker covered every inch of the walls. Symbols, names, professions of love, and illegible slogans scrawled in dozens of different languages all stating the unspoken truth – *I was here before you.*

The heat of the summer night quickly vanished, the temperature dropping with each rung downward. The sweat on my neck grew colder, bringing a chill. Colin's whispered voice sounded above me as he returned, the van now safely parked. I looked up to see his silhouette pull the door shut, sealing us in with a metallic thud.

The shaft around me opened up, revealing a long passage, the floor peppered with cigarette butts, spent batteries, empty wrappers, and burnt matchsticks. Nick's glowsitck burned at my feet, casting its light across the graffiti-etched walls. I shone my light either way up the passage, seeing only a short way down each before the darkness swallowed it up. Dust rained down from my companions' descent and I stepped aside. I brushed the grit from my face, a pointless endeavor, I knew, as there would soon be so much more to wipe over the next few hours.

Nick was grinning as he reached the bottom, his white teeth glowing red in my light. "Reminds me of Moscow," he said with approval.

Colin's voice echoed down from above. "Reminds me of a carnival house into hell."

I glanced over at the giant pentagram spray painted beside me, its disproportionate goat's head leering out from the inverted star. I knew that Colin, the ever devout Irish Catholic, was going to hate this hunt.

He reached the bottom and curled his lip at the painted symbol.

"Welcome to hell," Nick said. I wasn't sure if he was merely being dramatic, or translating the French words scrawled above the goat's image.

Colin snorted and touched Saighnean, the holy anthropomorphic Celtic sword at his waist. "Fuck this place."

"Which way?" Nick asked, turning to me. Joviality was gone. Only the cold steel seriousness of a Valducan knight remained. He was a different man when he hunted.

I pointed down the eastern passage. "Bodies were found that way."

Nick drew his torch, clicked on a bright red beam, and started down, taking point.

We followed the winding tunnel, past small chambers

littered with spent candles and empty beer cans. One room was still lit with burning candles, but there was no other signs of the occupants. The air was still, completely unmoving, and when we did stop, the absolute silence was more unsettling than I cared to admit. More than once, the low passages forced us to crawl like worms to continue and I was grateful for the helmet as I banged my head into the rock above.

After two hours, the smell of decay tickled my nose. We turned into a small room. Dark splatters, almost black in our red lights, marred the pale limestone walls. Dried bloody mud covered the floor, broken and dusty under booted footprints. The stink of ammonia prickled my nose somewhere deep below the stench of dried blood and spilt intestines.

"Here we are," I said. Taking a moment, I removed my water bottle and washed the dirt from my mouth with a healthy swallow. My left hand burned from the numerous nicks and scrapes, and I wished I'd worn a glove on it. But the warding eye tattooed on my palm would be useless if covered and taking the time to remove a glove might not be an option if I needed it. The tattoo, one of several on my body, was a gift from Hounacier, a blessed medal to commemorate a special kill.

Nick walked into the center of the dried stains and looked around, searching the ceiling and walls for some hidden secret.

"Wish we could have seen what it looked like," Colin said. He ran a gloved finger around one of the sharp holes left by tripod feet dotting the cracked floor, remnants from where the workers had recorded the gruesome scene before moving the bodies.

"So Malcolm," Nick said, his headlamp's light falling on me. "Where to?"

I removed my tablet and winced as the screen came on, shining in my eyes like a floodlight. My night vision, previously preserved by the crimson lights, was gone in a painful cinching of pupils. Through slitted eyes, I studied the catacomb map and highlighted the path we'd covered. I pointed to an arched doorway. "That will lead us to a lower level. My guess is that the nest is deep."

"All right," he said. "You be sure to keep track of where we are. I don't want to get lost."

I flipped off the tablet and stored it away. "Follow me."

We headed through the passage, gradually sloping down further beneath the Earth. Once we had to climb down a near vertical stretch until reaching an arched passage. Standing water filled many of the halls, forcing us to wade thigh-deep through it to continue on and leaving us cold and wet. I imagined unseen hands grabbing us from below the murky surface, yanking us down to be drowned and eaten. I wanted to rush, but the threat of unseen pits hidden beneath the water forced us to move slow. More than once I felt what I was sure to be a bone crack under my boot.

Eventually, we stopped in a room with benches hewn from the stone walls and I checked the map. Five hours, and we'd barely begun to cover the catacomb's length.

"I think this is good for tonight," Nick said through a mouthful of cereal bar. His coating of chalky dust left his beard gray, giving him the appearance of a statue come to life. "We should head back. Continue tomorrow. I don't want to stay down here."

"I completely agree," Colin said. "But let's find these bastards soon. I don't want to spend all summer crawling around in this shit."

"Let's hope the next hunt is somewhere warm and sunny," I said, flipping off my tablet and returning it to its plastic bag.

We headed back, Colin taking the lead. The journey felt longer than it should have, my perception of time warped by exhaustion and the impatience to breath fresh air. While I frequently turned to check behind us, I couldn't help but shake the feeling we were being followed. Unseen eyes watching us from the blackness. Once, I even stopped the others, convinced I'd seen a shadow move at the edge of my light, but there was nothing there.

"You're tired," Nick said. "Just stay alert. Never assume it's in your head."

The paranoia continued to mount until we finally crawled back up that painted shaft and back out onto the streets and into sunlight.

16 July, 2009
We headed down at 2100 hours from a new location, a locked and rusted gate along the Seine. This time I wore rubber waders and carried dry socks stuffed into bags. Three hours later, we reached the room we'd stopped at before.

"Look here," I said, shining my light onto the dusty floor. A bare footprint, its long toes resembling a hand with their length and positioning, marked the very center of one of our own old boot prints. "I knew I heard something behind us."

"They knew we were here," Nick whispered, his hand moving to the war pick at his belt. "Biding their time for an opening. Stay sharp."

I sympathized with Theseus, hunting and being hunted by the Minotaur in Minos' labyrinth. I sniffed, a faint and familiar smell tingling my nostrils.

"Ammonia," Colin said, reading my face.

We continued on, searching the tunnels for any signs, that tickling at my nape that we were being watched now fueled and unstoppable. Three times we wheeled around, believing something behind us, but there never was.

We'd rounded a corner when Colin, in the lead, brought up a clenched fist, telling us to stop. He motioned to his ear.

Holding my breath, I listened. Only silence. I opened my mouth to whisper a question when a distinct grunt, like from some large rooting animal, echoed from the darkness ahead. Then the sounds of splashing water, followed by another grunt.

Nick looked back at me, his hand lowering to his war pick. I drew Hounacier and we moved forward, silent as we could.

The passage sloped downward, turning twice before opening into a long, vaulted room, its floor completely submerged in milky brown water. Nick's bright torch reflected off the surface, throwing its shimmering glow across the ceiling.

Another splash brought the light down on a onto a vaguely human shape twenty meters away at the far end, standing before an arched doorway. The ghoul's eyes reflected the light from their deep sockets. Wild black hair crested its simian head and down its hunched back. Wet rags, the remains of whatever clothes the owner had worn when the demon had taken them, hung in shredded tatters, dripping on the landing on which the creature stood. The ghoul's lips curled back as it growled, long and steady.

Colin began swinging his sword beside him, the blade quickly gaining speed. He took a step forward.

"Stop!" Nick hissed.

Colin looked back, but kept Saighnean's spinning.

Nick nodded to the floor. "We have no idea how deep that is."

As if in answer, the ghoul let out a howl and slammed its fists into the floor.

"He's right," I whispered. "It's not coming at us." I scanned the water, searching for any sign of a floor or movement beneath. I didn't know if ghouls even needed air, but their undead familiars wouldn't.

The ghoul roared and hopped, but didn't advance.

"Just keep at it, asshole," Nick said. He dropped his holy weapon into his belt loop and drew his pistol. The black suppressor made it look like a cannon.

The ghoul slapped at the water and took a step forward, obviously unconcerned by the gun.

The shot cracked though the room, louder than I would have expected. The round caught the demon in the thigh. It howled, stumbling back, blood pouring down its leg. Nick fired again, this time blasting a hole in the wall behind it.

The ghoul scrambled back through the doorway. The obsidian-tipped slugs couldn't harm the demonic spirit, but they'd definitely kill the possessed body. It leaped for cover as Nick's third shot rang out.

We stood there for a solid minute, listening.

"Cheap trap," Nick said, holstering his pistol. "Lure us into some sunken pit. Let us drown and eat us." He turned to me. "Is there a way around?"

Giving the water a wary glance, I stepped back into the passage before sheathing my machete and opening the map. "Yes. Take us about an hour."

We headed back and circled our way around, eventually making it back to the flooded chamber from the other side. The ghoul's blood still spattered the ground, but didn't lead us far before ending at another submerged hallway with no way around.

After nine laborious hours, we returned to the surface, tired, bruised, and frustrated.

17, July 2009

"We'll get them tonight," Nick promised as we started down the manhole on our third night. "I promise."

"You said that last night," I said.

"But tonight they'll get aggressive. Their trap didn't work, so they'll make their move. We just have to beat them to it."

"If you're wrong," Colin said, his voice echoing up from below. "You owe me a drink."

Metal and concrete grinded above as Nick slid the manhole cover into place. It thudded, pinching off the light from above. "Deal."

The ladder ended in a circular brick chamber. Shards of broken bottles gleamed from a mound piled along one side. Three arched doorways lead from the room. Above one, stenciled in metallic paint, read Dante's immortal line, *Lasciate ogne speranza, voi ch'intrate*, the words framed with winged skulls.

"All right, Doctor," Nick said as he reached the bottom. "Which way?"

I nodded to Dante's door, "Abandon all hope, you who enter here," and we headed through. We followed the passage past several antechambers, each decorated in its own style. In one, a support pillar had been carved into that of a long-haired maiden, a rotted green blanket wrapped over her shoulders like a cape, and a hundred empty tea light cups laid out on the floor before her. I took comfort that none of those candles were burning.

The passage continued on, shrinking lower and lower until we had to crawl. Nick cracked another glow stick and hurled it ahead. It skittered and fell into a room at the far side. "Is there another way around?"

I shook my head. "No. Not unless we doubled back three kilometers. That should empty into the hall we want."

He shined his light onto the ceiling, revealing a wide crack running the length. One good bump might easily bury us forever. "Stay low." He continued forward.

Something moved past the light ahead, casting a shadow. Icy fear shot down my spine. There was no way to draw our weapons and fight in this tiny space, and whoever crawled into that room would be open to attack, helpless.

Scratching came from ahead, like fingernails desperately trying to dig their way through a chalkboard.

"Back!" Nick whispered though clenched teeth. "Back! Back! Back!"

We scrambled backwards. Colin cursed as my heel nearly took him in the eye, but I dared not slow lest Nick's back-scrambling boots hit me. Heart pounding, sweat ran down my face and into my eyes. Finally, my feet made it back to the opening of this death trap and I nearly screamed as hands gripped me from behind, yanking my belt.

"Gotcha," Colin said pulling me out.

I rolled onto my knees and helped pull Nick out from the hole.

I peered down the empty tunnel, seeing orange glow the far side, but nothing more. "Did you see it?"

Panting, Nick shook his head. "No. But, it...growled."

"Shit." I looked back down the shaft. "You think it's waiting?"

He blew a long breath. "Possible. If it is, whoever sticks their head out of the passage first is a dead man."

"What if we go close to the edge and pushed each other through at the end?" Colin asked.

"Not willing to risk that. Not if there's another way."

"Three kilometers," I said.

"Then we need to hustle." Nick cracked another stick and dropped it on this side of the shaft. "Keep your eyes and ears open. They're hunting us now."

Taking point, I led us back down the passage, past the cloaked maiden, and through another hall. Steps led down into gray water, leaving narrow ledges on either side. Straddling the flooded passage, our backs against the arched ceiling we continued on, our red-hued reflections staring up at us.

Twice we stopped and listened for sounds behind us, but heard nothing. Each time, we dropped another glow stick so that we might see any pursuers following us past that point. After two hours, I turned down a passage and saw an orange glow ahead. Cautious, we drew our weapons and crept forward.

The glow stick rested on the floor, nine inches beneath the square passage in the wall. Hounacier ready, I removed a telescoping inspection mirror from my belt and held it out, making sure the tunnel was vacant, then peered though. Fifteen meters down, I could see the light of Nick's second stick. "Clear."

"Look at this," Colin said, kneeling beside me.

More bare footprints, like those from the previous night, marred the dusty floor. They crisscrossed back and forth across the side entrance.

"At least two," Colin said.

"And one in shoes," I added, nodding to a set of sneaker tracks mixed in with the other prints.

"Which way?" Nick asked.

I motioned ahead.

"So let's find 'em."

We continued on, following them as best we could until reaching bare stone. We stopped in a cathedral-like chamber with four other exits. After checking the map, I selected one. Nick left a fresh stick on the floor as Colin and I built a line of empty cans across the passage entrance.

We made it twenty meters down the hall before coming to a chamber with a dusty folding chair resting in the middle before a framed photograph affixed to the wall.

"That's just creepy," Colin whispered.

I nodded, about to move toward it, when a distant sound of falling cans came from behind.

We spun and headed back. Heart thudding, I moved closer to the room, seeing the spilt can wall cast in red and orange light. I reached it first and looked around the cathedral seeing nothing.

Nick's bright lights swept the room then froze on a lone figure standing before the far wall, with its back to us.

"Bonjour?" I said, stepping closer. My finger's tightened on Hounacier's horn grip as the figure shuffled, but didn't turn. I couldn't tell if it was male or female, only a human in dust-caked clothes. "Turn around!" I ordered, raising my holy machete.

The figure didn't move.

Nick stepped up beside me. "Don't get any closer."

Just then, the figure turned toward us. The flesh along the left side of its face was gone. Its single milky eye locked onto us and a hissing growl came from its shredded mouth.

More hissing sounded to the right. I turned, bringing my headlamp's beam on two more staggering corpses coming from another passage. Each only had one eye.

"Behind us!" Colin yelled, his voice booming in the stone chamber.

A trio of ghouls scurried out from another tunnel, moving on all fours like long-armed monkeys.

"Circle up!" Nick ordered. He swung his nadziak at the half-faced creature coming toward us, though it was still a good seven feet away. Yanking the weapon back mid-swing like a cracking whip, a shockwave of compressed air shot like a cone from the war pick's tip. The cone struck the creature's shoulder with a loud *thop*, and blew a hole through it like a high-powered rifle. The creature reeled around, its arm coming free at the motion and landing several feet behind it. Nick lunged forward and slammed the pick into the zombie's chest before it could recover. It fell dead to the ground.

Colin stepped beside me, eyes on the circling ghouls, and swinging Saighnean before him in a figure-eight. The blade moved faster and faster, gaining momentum until it was nothing but a whirring blur.

"Mal, take the minions," Nick shouted. "Colin, the demons."

Hounacier in hand, I threw my left palm forward toward the closing zombies. The tattoo's warding eye stretched wide, feeling as if the flesh might rip. The zombies froze their advance, their growling hisses rising even above the sound of Colin's swinging sword. Seizing the opening, I lunged, driving the machete's blade at creature's heart. It brought an arm up, deflecting the blade so that it plunged into the right side of its chest and missing the target. Unfazed, the creature grabbed my forearm.

I screamed. The bones in my arm bent, threatening to crack under the creature's inhuman grip.

Nick moved past me in a blur and buried Ozkareen in the creatures back. Its chest exploded as the pick came though, showering me with rotted gore. "Go for the heart!" he shouted.

A pair of ghouls charged Colin.

One moved as if to lunge, but dashed to the side at the last moment. The other one leapt toward him, claws raised. Colin brought his blurring sword up as it reached him. The ghoul's arms diced apart, the blows striking so fast they seemed simultaneous. Shrieking, the demon fell, blood spurting from its twin stumps. Colin rammed the blade down into its head.

Golden yellow fire ignited along the slain demon's skin and from the severed pieces scattered about the room.

The last zombie was coming for me. My wrist still aching from its near break, I lifted my warding palm, freezing the creature again, then rammed Hounacier up under its ribs and into its dead heart. The zombie fell, nearly yanking me off balance with the sudden weight coming down on the impaling blade.

Yellow firelight danced along the walls. I wrenched Hounacier's blade free in time to see Nick swing Ozkareen in that whip-like fashion, launching another cone of air at a ghoul. The beast dropped to the floor, dodging it. The cone blasted past, dissipating after ten feet.

The demon leaped toward Nick, but he spun out of the way of a slashing claw.

I ran toward it, bringing my warding palm up. The ghoul turned to face me but then froze, shielded its eyes from the displayed tattoo.

Before it could recover, a conical shockwave struck it on the neck, blasting its head nearly off. Golden demon fire sprayed into the wall and the ghoul's corpse fell, its soul burning away.

Colin began swinging Saighnean in another unstopping pattern, its speed quickly accelerating into a blur. The final ghoul moved toward the nearest exit but I ran around to meet it, Hounacier raised and warding palm out.

Without looking at the tattoo, it lurched to the side, but too late before Colin was on it. Spectral flames erupted as the ghoul seemed to come apart into four pieces. Colin grinned as he pulled the sword out from a hunk of burning torso where the blade had finally stopped.

"Looks like you were right, Nick." I turned to see the Armenian standing, pick raised at his side. A figure stood in the passage before him— fat, vaguely feminine, and naked, reminiscent of a Paleolithic Venus. It had no face at all, only a smooth blankness.

Nick stepped closer, nearing the range for Ozkareen's shock missile.

A vertical slit opened along the creatures face like a lipless mouth. The crack lengthened, stretching down its body, between its sagging breasts, and splitting its hanging gut. Then the demon unfolded out like a flower and Nick screamed.

Thousands of eyeballs filled the inside like the seeds of a pomegranate. They rolled and moved in swirling patterns, set to some unheard music. A honey-like aroma flooded the chamber, but beneath that, lurked the eye-watering ammonia stink. Nick's screams ceased. His raised arm lowered and fell limp to his side. Ozkareen slipped from his grip and clanked to the floor.

The demon moved closer. Slender tendrils, rooted at the mass' center, wriggled toward him.

"No!" I charged toward it. I raised my warding eye before me, thrusting it over Nick's shoulder.

The rolling eyes all zeroed in on my palm and then seemed to boil along the flower's surface. The demon flew off like a swimming jellyfish, slinging dust as it surged away into the darkness, tendrils trailing behind it.

Nick's head lolled. I caught him as he stumbled forward and vomited. Colin stepped in and helped me move him to a sitting position, my eyes never leaving the dark passage the demon had fled down.

Nick feebly reached for Ozkareen lying in the dust.

"Here," I said handing it to him. "Are you all right?"

Still panting, Nick nodded. "What…was that?"

"I don't know. I—"

"You're the fucking Librarian," Colin snapped.

Setting my jaw, I pulled off my pack and opened my tablet. He was right, this was my job. They'd killed the demons, while I'd only killed a mindless servant. I scrolled though the record. While the tell-tale smell and resemblance to the Venus were certainly noteworthy, the sheet of eyes reminded me of something I'd read before, something I thought I'd never encounter.

Nick crawled to his feet and stood behind me. Whether real or imagined, I could feel his mounting impatience. It was getting away.

"Here," I said, clicking a file. A crude image of a Japanese screen peppered with eyes filled the top of the page.

"What is it?" Colin asked without taking his gaze from the passage. His free hand touched his chest, feeling the rosary beneath his shirt.

I licked my lips, reviewing the scant description. "A mokumokuren."

"Mokuwhat?"

"Mokumokuren," I repeated. "Extremely rare. Thought to be extinct. Last one reported in Turkey 1892. No mention of stealing eyes, but said to…*entrance its prey with hypnotic patterns of eyes*. Lives in dark places, moves in aquatic fashion, and it can strangle you with its hundred tentacles."

"Lovely."

"What hurts it?" Nick asked, peering closer.

"Pure quartz."

He grunted. "I don't have that."

"I have one shell." I clicked off my screen. "Mixed load, but quartz is in it."

"Just one?" Colin asked.

"Better than nothing," Nick said. "Load it and let's get after that thing."

Quickly, I stored my tablet away and withdrew a lumpy rolled bundle. I unfurled it, revealing a rainbow assortment of hand-loaded shotgun shells. Moving my fingers along the rows I removed a white plastic shell with a red and black band. I clicked open my Remington and switched it out with one of the obsidian loads before putting the bundle away. "Ready."

Nick held out his hand and I gave over the sawed-off. The yellow light flooding the room had begin to wane as the slain ghouls returned to their once human forms. The honey aroma had faded, but the cat piss stink seemed to have gotten worse. Nick took point, with me behind him, Hounacier in hand.

We moved slow, checking each chamber and crevice before going on. The passage wound its way deeper, angling sharply before leveling out. Fueled with paranoia, my heart pounded and sweat beaded my gritty face, despite the cold unmoving air.

Nick moved toward a pit-like vault, but I touched his arm.

He turned toward me and I pointed down at a low crevice in the wall by his feet. The limestone dust before it was rippled like miniature wind-swept dunes.

Instantly, he moved past to the other side, his holy weapon raised. I drew my mirror and angled it at the hole. A tunnel, no more than eighteen inches high and two feet wide extended into darkness.

I nodded to Colin beside me and he lowered his torch, shining the crimson beam along the tight passage. It extended a little over a meter before opening up into another chamber. Relaying this to my partners, I crawled onto the smooth floor.

Nick cracked one of his last glow sticks, filling our tunnel with brilliant orange light, then he hurled it through the shaft before me.

The stick ricocheted off the tight walls, finally bouncing to a stop just a few feet inside the room. The chamber appeared small, but I couldn't see much from my limited view. I extended the mirror's handle to its full length and stretched my arm as far as I could to get a better look.

It wasn't long enough to reach and I had to crawl a little inside, my arm out before me. Rotating the mirror around, I saw no exits. I pushed it out a little further for a better view. Black whip-like strands shot down from the ceiling, wrapping around my mirror and ripping it from my grip.

I cried out in surprise, banging my head as I tried to scramble back. More tendrils fluttered along the top edges of my tunnel, reaching blindly. A palpable waft of sweet nectar filled the passage. Colin seized my belt and dragged me back out.

They didn't have to ask what I'd seen.

"Exits?" Nick mouthed.

I shook my head, panting, then pointed upward. "On the ceiling."

"What do we do?" Colin whispered, his mouth so close I could feel his breath on my ear.

"If we try to crawl in we're dead before we can make it," I replied, looking back down the now empty hole.

Nick crouched beside me, silent as he studied the shaft. He shook his head steadily, seeming to run through our few options.

I licked my dusty lips. "I have an idea."

Nick gave me a look and I pulled off my pack and laid on my back. I drew Hounacier. "Give me my gun. Push me through. Fast."

Colin shook his head.

"It's the only way." I mimed firing the Remington, then hacking the machete.

"No!" Colin mouthed. He looked to Nick for support, but the Armenian nodded instead.

"It'll work. But I'll go. I'm senior knight."

"You don't have this," I said, opening my palm. "Bang," I whispered, miming pulling the trigger, then dropping the gun and rolling my empty palm before me. "I'm the only one that can do it."

Nick's lips tightened. He handed me the sawed-off. "I'll push you through," he mouthed. "Then you," pointing to Colin, "push me. One, two."

I nodded.

Colin look at Nick, then to me. Finally he nodded. "You need earplugs."

"Ah." I reached for my pack and drew out the yellow foam plugs Nick had given us. With those firmly in place, I returned to position, gun and Hounacier against my body and before my face.

"Close your right eye," Nick ordered.

I did.

"Open it after you've fired. Otherwise the flash will leave you blind." He cracked his final glow stick and set it on my stomach. He took position at my feet, crouched in a runner's stance, hands on my boots. Colin squeezed in behind him, mouth tight in an unhappy line.

Right eye clenched, I nodded to Nick and mouthed, "Three... two...one."

I launched forward, rocks scraping my back. The tunnel flew past me in a blur. As my head came into the room I extended the shotgun toward the ceiling. I had only a moment's glimpse of a thousand eyes looming above, black tendrils lashing toward me.

I fired.

The brilliant flash burned my vision and the boom was so loud it jarred my bones. A keening shriek filled the room, audible though my plugged and ringing ears.

Without time to think I rolled to my feet, staying low but still banging my head, and slinging the other glow stick onto the floor. The room was no more than five feet high. Opening my unblinded right eye I saw the demon before me lashing and writhing like an enraged manta ray. Thousands of eyes rolled to focus in my direction. I dropped the smoking shotgun and extended my warding palm. The tattooed lid stretched wide and the beast shrieked again.

I lunged, thrusting Hounacier into the heart of the thrashing mass. Her blade buried deep. I yanked it free and hacked and hacked, shredding rolling eyes as slimy tendrils squirmed and whipped at my face and arms.

Screaming, I rammed the machete's blade back into the twisting folds with both hands, and then slashed to the side, splitting the monster nearly in half.

Brilliant maroon fire spilled from its wounds as the demon crumpled to the chamber floor. Panting, and covered in blood, now burning with cold flames, I noticed Nick beside me. Hounacier twisted in my grip moving like a dowser's rod, her blade coated in flickering fire.

Loosening my grip, I allowed the machete to move, to guide me where she wanted to go. The blade bent, moving in circles. Transferring her to my off-hand, Hounacier dipped toward my now-emptied right. I brought it up to meet her, palm flat. The edge met my skin then bit in with sharp pain. Demon fire surged into the wound and the machete's fighting ceased, her newest gift bestowed. An orange and blue half-lidded eye, similar to the one tattooed in my left palm, glowed within the flesh of my cut hand. Then the image faded.

"Thank you," I breathed.

"What was that?" Nick asked, his voice muted.

"Hounacier telling me to get a new tattoo."I turned as Colin scrambled into the room.

"Thank God," he said, looking at the dead monster. "Everyone all right?"

"Yes ," I replied, closing my bloodied hand. "Let's get some fresh air, and buy Nick a beer."

NO BALANCE BUT IN DEATH

Evan Dicken

The Theban hoplite thrust his broken spear at one of the Athenian ekdromoi surrounding him. The Athenian reflexively raised his shield, but the thrust was only a feint. Twisting at the last moment, the Theban whirled his weapon in a tight arc, stabbing down with the butt-spike to pierce his opponent's sandaled foot. It was a blow that would've hobbled anyone else, but the Athenian only grunted and lashed out with his own weapon.

The other ekdromoi wasted no time in closing the distance, spears stabbing like physicians' lancets. They were equipped as hoplites, but with lighter shields and helms, with armor quilted linen plates rather than heavy bronze. Despite the lighter kit, their moves were awkward, strangely uncoordinated even for citizen levies.

Contorting like a gymnasion acrobat, the Theban released his spear, reaching up two-handed to grab the shaft of one of his attacker's weapons and rip it from the man's grasp. A moment, and the hoplite had recovered his balance, swinging his new spear in a wide circle that set his attackers back on their heels.

"He's good," muttered Damaris, shifting to keep his armor from scraping against the rocky escarpment from where he and his companion were watching the fight.

"Six on one?" Haemon's eyes almost disappeared beneath the shadow of his bushy brows. "He'd need to be Herakles himself."

"Five."

"What?" Haemon frowned.

"That man's nothing but a liability." Damaris thrust his chin at the Athenian trying to work the spear from his ruined foot. "See how the Theban moves to put them in each other's way. He's fought groups of men before or I'm a Persian catamite."

Haemon glanced at the three javelins Damaris had managed to scrounge from the slaughter at Tanagra. "Might be we could even the odds."

"We?" Damaris fixed the wiry Rhodian physician with a slit-eyed stare. "What of your oath to Asclepius?"

Haemon gave an airy wave of his hand. "By we I meant *you*."

Below, two of the ekdromoi charged with wild shouts, stumbling forward as if wine drunk. It made sense, many warriors found courage at the bottom of a flask.

They were driven back by a series of quick thrusts. Another Athenian stabbed in, but the hoplite shifted to take the blow on his breastplate, iron shrieking across bronze.

"We should go." Damaris made to crawl back from the ridge-line. "Before we're noticed."

Haemon's scowl took on an air of distressing intractability. "You took Boeotian coin, mercenary."

"I took *Tanagran* coin," Damaris replied. "And, last I saw, the Athenians had pulled down the city walls. No Tanagra, no contract."

"Tanagra was part of the Boeotian League and so is Thebes. You were paid to fight Athenians." Haemon's gaze flicked to the battle below, his rebuke sharp as a skinning knife. "Well there they are."

"Why do you care?"

Haemon bared his teeth. "I may have been born in Rhodes, but Tanagra was my home."

Damaris grit his teeth. After the League's crushing defeat at Oenophyta and the loss of Tanagra, Athens was poised to overrun all Boeotia. Of the remaining League states, only Thebes had the power to resist.

"You're very brave when gambling with other peoples' lives." Damaris tried to ignore the shouts and clatter from below.

"I am sworn to Asclepius, god of healing." Haemon crossed his arms, his expression a caricature of mock outrage. "I *never* gamble with lives."

Damaris sighed, drawing his short-bladed xiphos. Having a skilled physician for a companion had seemed like a blessing from the gods, but he was quickly coming to regret traveling with Haemon. Javelin in hand, he stood to regard the battle below.

The Athenian with the wounded foot had worked the spear free and joined his fellows, apparently untroubled by the injury. Another of the attackers had been stabbed through his spear arm, but he stood with his companions, using his shield to parry the Theban's thrusts. While Damaris would've expected such bravery from picked men, ekdromoi were usually drawn from the lower ranks. And yet they pressed in, faces red, teeth bared, stumbling forward despite their wounds.

The Theban was clearly near the end of his strength. His dodges came slower, his tired counterthrusts easily deflected by even the ekdromoi's light shields. A few more moments and he would be overwhelmed.

It was common practice for warriors across the Peloponnese to unnerve their opponents with boasts, paeans, and the clatter of war panoply. Often, as in the case of feared fighters such as the Spartan Homoioi or Theban Spartoi, a well-timed war chant could break an enemy before the lines even met.

For his part, Damaris had always preferred a well-timed javelin. His first throw thudded into the padded linothorax covering the nearest ekdromoi's back. The missile's force was blunted by the layers of metal-reinforced linen, but Damaris had not intended the throw to wound, only to get the man's attention.

Damaris released his second javelin before the first had struck home, aiming just slightly higher. As the ekdromoi spun, the oiled iron tip pierced the hollow of his throat – a bit off-center, but close enough to cause the man to stumble back in a spray of bright blood.

Unbelievably, the Athenian kept his feet. With a gurgling shout, the wounded man took a stumbling step up the hill, spear outstretched as if to pinion Damaris to the sky.

Damaris's last javelin thudded into the man's mouth, putting a swift end to his blood-choked cries. The dead man's companions turned to squint into the late afternoon sun, but Damaris was already charging down the hill, xiphos and hatchet at the ready.

Fortunately, the Theban took advantage of his opponents' momentary distraction. His spear-blade glittered, threading the narrow gap between shield and arm to slide into unprotected ribs. Another Athenian collapsed with a strangled grunt. Parched mountain soil drank deeply of the man's blood as he struggled to rise, but whatever drunken fury animated the ekdromoi seemed no proof against deathblows, and at last, the Athenian fell still.

The remaining four ekdromoi moved to lock shields, but Damaris was already among them. Spears might be king in the brutal push of phalanx warfare, but they were as deadly as fresh reeds once you slipped past their point.

Damaris kicked the bottom of the foot-injured man's shield, then hooked the beak of his hatchet over the upper rim to drag it down. The Athenian's face was a mask of rage, eyes bulging, lips flecked with foam. Damaris stabbed with his xiphos, and felt the sharp, double-edge of his shortsword bite into the man's cheek.

He dropped a shoulder into the dying ekdromoi, already turning as the man tumbled back spitting blood and teeth. The Athenian on Damaris's left cast his spear aside to snatch his dagger from its sheath. Damaris dropped to one knee to avoid the blade's upward slash, and buried his hatchet in the meat of the Athenian's inner thigh. Hot blood soaked Damaris's arm as he dragged the blade free only to drive his xiphos up into the man's groin.

Something struck Damaris's helmet, knocking him off balance. He wheeled to see the ekdromoi with the injured arm draw his shield back for another blow.

Damaris tried to stand, but another bash from the shield set him sprawling. Instead of backing off, the Athenian discarded his shield to leap upon Damaris. One arm raised to ward against the rain of heavy fists, Damaris worked the tip of his xiphos between the padded plates of the Athenian's linothorax. Blood spread across the dirty fabric, but the wound seemed only to enrage the man, and he caught Damaris by the throat, smashing his head back against the rocky ground.

Dark suns danced across Damaris's vision, his mouth thick

with blood from where he'd bitten his tongue. He twisted the xiphos, driving it deeper, but the Athenian only slammed him down again, and again, and again. Soon, it was all Damaris could do to keep hold of his weapons, let alone wield them. The Athenian seemed a man possessed, shouting and shrieking in an incoherent babble of foam-flecked rage.

Blood glittered red in the dying light.

With a choking moan, the Athenian released Damaris, hands moving up to explore the spear point that had erupted from the front of his throat. Through blurred vision, Damaris saw the man take hold of the tip as if to pull the spear free.

With a grunt of effort, Damaris gave his xiphos one final twist, and the Athenian shuddered and went limp. Crabbing out from under the dead man, he climbed unsteadily to his feet.

The Theban hoplite pulled his spear from the corpse, stepping to Damaris's side with a tired nod. Together, they turned to face the final Athenian.

Despite being outnumbered, the man did not flee. Muttering and gnashing his teeth, he advanced upon Damaris and the Theban, spear at the ready.

A stone exploded from the Athenian's shield, knocking him back a step. A heartbeat later another rattled from his helmet.

Damaris blinked as Haemon stepped to his side. The physician stooped to snatch another rock from the hillside and fit it into his sling. A quick whirl sped the missile bare inches from Athenian shocked face.

At last, whatever madness had seized the man lifted. He shook his head as if to clear it, seeming to recognize his companions were all dead or dying. With a strangled groan he turned to shamble down the mountain.

Damaris shook his head at Haemon as the physician hurried down to them. "I thought you were sworn to do no harm?"

Haemon shrugged, grinning at the running man. "Does it look like I hurt him?"

"An oversight easily rectified." Damaris pulled one of his javelins from a nearby corpse, but Haemon grasped his arm.

"If he escapes, he'll bring half of Athens down on us." Damaris tried to tug free Haemon's grip, but the little physician was surprisingly strong.

"He ran because of me. If you kill him, it will be my fault."

"Your ethics are as limber as a Spartan gymnopaedia."

"Oh, how I've always *dreamed* of being lectured on morals by a Molossian mercenary." Haemon snorted, releasing Damaris's arm to give his cheek a friendly pat. "Come, we should meet our new friend."

"*Our* new friend?" Damaris turned to regard the Theban.

"I am Ophelos, a Spartos of Thebes." Panting, the man removed his helmet. "And I am in your debt."

Damaris grunted as the reason for Ophelos's skill became clear. The Spartoi were the finest fighters in Boeotia, perhaps in all the Northern Peloponnese. Tasked with defending Thebes, the first Spartoi were said to have been grown from dragon's teeth planted by the city's founder, Cadmus. All Theban nobility claimed descent from these first: 'sown men'.

Divine descent or not, Ophelos's black hair was plastered to his head. Exhaustion ringed his eyes with dark circles and made shadowed hollows of his cheeks.

"Are you fleeing Oenophyta?" Damaris asked. "Were you followed? How quickly do the Athenians advance?"

"I am Haemon of Rhodes, a disciple of Asclepius." Haemon pushed past him, waving a hand as if Damaris were a bad odor to dispel. "And my inquisitive comrade is Damaris of Epirus, a mercenary in the employ of the Boeotian League."

"*Recently* in the employ of the League," Damaris added.

"A physician? Thank the gods." Ophelos glanced skyward. "I am desperate need of your aid."

Haemon cocked his head. "Are you wounded?"

"No, my men are..." Ophelos swallowed, then took a slow breath. "I marched from Seven-Gated Thebes at the head of eighty warriors, picked men all. We planned to follow the mountain trails around Parnitha and take the Athenians by surprise, but somehow they knew our ploy."

Ophelos shook his head. "They fell upon us like wild beasts. You saw their fury, their madness. They must have fallen under the witch's spell."

"Witch?" Damaris made a warding gesture.

"A Persian sorceress, one of many unnatural blights unleashed by Xerxes to vex the Peloponnese," Ophelos replied. "She enchants men, drives them mad and sets them upon their fellows. We thought it merely a rumor, but she is all too real."

"A good reason to avoid the mountains." Damaris glanced at Haemon, but the wiry physician had knelt to examine the Athenian dead.

"Thebes is in danger," Ophelos replied.

"What could three men do against ten thousand?" Damaris sucked air through his teeth. "Besides, we'd have to walk right through the Athenian lines."

"There is another way." Ophelos's words were almost a whisper. "The Parnithan path leads southwest past the Athenians, we would come out just a few miles from Thebes."

"Risk a witch's ire?" Damaris wrinkled his nose. "Not likely."

"Some of my men yet survive," Ophelos replied. "In the mountains there is a shrine to Apollo. I left the wounded in the care of a priest, then went to seek aid."

Haemon glanced up from his work. "We should see to them."

Damaris scowled at the physician. "I can't believe you're seriously considering—"

"Considering aiding an ally? Helping wounded men? Of course I am." Haemon laid a hand on the corpse's brow, then snatched it back. "By Zeus, this man is hot as kiln-fresh clay. His warm humors are rampant."

Damaris took a quick step back. "Is it the plague?"

"Possible." Haemon drew a brass rod from his satchel, using it to poke at the corpse. "The signs are all there – swollen glands, blotchy skin, bilious complexion. And yet I've never known plague victims to exhibit such… vigor."

"So you would oppose not only a witch, but one capable of casting plagues like arrows?" Damaris asked.

Haemon ignored him, addressing Ophelos instead. "I wish to study this disease. I shall come with you."

The Theban gave a grateful nod, then turned to Damaris. "You are a mercenary? I shall fill your helm with silver upon our return to Thebes. Your sandals, too."

Damaris chewed his lip, cursing the mad whims of the gods. All the pay chests had been lost when Tanagra was sacked, and he with little more than a handful of shaved coppers to his name. Ophelos's silver would purchase much in Epirus – herds, hounds, servants, perhaps even a chieftainship.

As if reading his thoughts, the Theban continued. "Journeys pass more smoothly with wealth in hand."

"It will be hard to walk with my sandals full of coins."

"I'll buy you a new pair," Ophelos replied.

Damaris crossed his arms, scowling. "*Two* new pairs."

The Theban's answering grin was tired, but heartfelt.

Damaris ducked as another arrow hissed overhead. Although the twisted, rocky path made it difficult for their pursuers to get a clean shot, the blind curves and sheer drops made for a harrowing traverse. Wan moonlight did little to speed their desperate flight, turning every boulder into a jagged shadow and making the footing even more treacherous.

Rocks skittered from under Ophelos's sandals, and the Theban stumbled to one knee. Haemon would've tripped over him had Damaris not caught his robe, pulling the physician up short. With a grateful nod, Haemon helped the Theban back to his feet, and they continued to hurry along the mountain path.

"How many?" Ophelos's question came between labored gasps. The Theban had traded his spear for a shield and blade taken from the ekdromoi – the armory now slung over his back.

"At least a score." Haemon shot a worried glance over his shoulder. "How did they come upon us so fast?"

"Sorcery. How else?" Damaris scowled. By the gods, he should've taken his chances with the Athenian army.

"The shrine isn't far," Ophelos replied. "It's set back into a mountain cliff. The only way in is a narrow ledge. Numbers will avail them nothing."

As if shaped by the Theban's words, the trail thinned to the width of a goat path, a sheer cliff dropping on one side, bare stone on the other. They were forced to turn sideways, clutching the rock face as they edged around the bend.

"Are you sure this is the way?" Damaris asked.

Ophelos chuckled. "I'll be the first to fall if it isn't."

"Very comforting." Damaris worked his fingers into cracks in the stone, feeling as if the narrow ledge below his feet might give out at any moment. He'd been raised on the slopes of Mount Pindus, scaling cliffs with the other children, but night climbing was sheer madness.

After a teeth-gritting eternity, the ledge widened into what appeared to be some manner of natural cave. Although Damaris could still see some of the stars, the rocky overhang blotted out the moon, turning the cavern into a maze of half-seen shapes.

Something scraped to Damaris's left. A torch flared to life, bonfire-bright after the inky shadows of the mountain. Blinking back tears, Damaris shielded his eyes against the sudden brilliance. As his vision adjusted, his surroundings came into focus. Stone columns supported a ceiling of natural rock that stretched back into the darkness at the rear of the cavern. The pillars were etched with pictures and glyphs Damaris recognized as prayers to Apollo Apotropaeus, the patron god of Thebes. Someone had taken pick or axe to the carvings, prizing out settings and defacing wards.

At the rear of the cavern, a shadowed cave glared like the baleful eye of a cyclops. Damaris noticed worked stone around the edges, rusted brackets that might have once held some manner of gate.

"Help me move this." Ophelos nudged Damaris. Handing his torch to Haemon, the Theban went around one of the pillars. Damaris followed to find a rusted bronze gate leaning against the cavern wall.

"It was shattered when we arrived," Ophelos said. "But might serve its purpose, yet."

Catching Ophelos's intent, Damaris braced himself against one side, and together they dragged the heavy gate to block the entrance to the cavern. Pressed against the rock, only able to advance one at a time, the Athenians would have a hard time finding the leverage to shift several hundred pounds of bronze.

Ophelos retrieved his torch from Haemon and led them deeper into the cave.

Damaris trailed a hand across the inscriptions feeling the rough stone beneath his fingers. "Seems strange to build a temple to the sun god underground."

"The Oracle at Delphi goes beneath the earth to receive her visions." Haemon gave a patronizing nod.

"I see no oracle here." Damaris frowned at the etchings on the cave wall. "And what of these inscriptions? I don't recognize the script."

"*It has not been used in many centuries.*" The voice came from the darkness to their right.

Damaris drew his weapons as a man in patched robes stepped from the gloom. He appeared to be in late-middle years, tall and thin, his back just beginning to bend beneath the weight of age. By the man's sallow complexion, Damaris judged he spent little time beyond the chthonic recesses of his temple.

"This place was already ancient when Troy's walls fell, old when Theseus was cast into the Labyrinth of Crete." The man drew back his hood, shadows from the torch making him seem almost an apparition. "Later builders added, expanded, but the bones still remain."

Damaris pointed his xiphos at the man. "Announce yourself, or your bones will remain here, too."

"Peace, friends." Ophelos held up a hand. "This is Loimos, high priest of this shrine."

"Welcome to my temple, such as it is." The priest's voice was the whisper of wind-rustled parchment. "I fear I cannot greet you as I once would have, but you are welcome to such hospitality as remains mine to give."

"My men?" Ophelos asked.

"In the vault," Loimos replied. "I have been caring for them as best I am able."

"We brought a physician." Ophelos introduced both Haemon and Damaris, who sheathed his weapons, grinning sheepishly.

"A disciple of Asclepius?" The priest bowed low. "Another child of Apollo."

Haemon returned the bow. "I would see the sick."

"Of course, follow me." Loimos gestured to the darkness. "The warriors appear to be afflicted by a surfeit of yellow bile. I have made their surroundings as cool and dry as possible."

The priest led them deeper into the temple. Torches lit a series of stone rooms, each etched with more strange script, all similarly defaced.

"Much has been lost to time and troubles." Loimos offered a tight frown when he noticed Damaris studying the inscriptions. "Not all are as respectful of the gods as one would hope."

Damaris ran a hand along one of the roughly-carved lines, the hair on his arm prickling. "Is this the witch's work?"

"She cannot touch you here." The priest chuckled. "Athenians came but four days ago. They took everything of value and destroyed much of what remained."

A flight of irregular stone stairs opened into another large cavern. Lit by coal braziers the air was nonetheless as cold and dry as Loimos had promised. Like the outer temple, the walls were carved with a twisted web of incantations, the symbols seeming to coil and twist in the firelight.

Perhaps twenty wooden pallets had been arrayed around the chamber, their inhabitants straining feebly in the gloom. Sweat glistened in the torchlight as the men groaned and shifted. The Thebans had been stripped of weapons and armor, and as Damaris approached he saw they had been lashed to the pallets with lengths of stout hemp rope.

"The restraints were necessary to keep them from hurting themselves." Loimos pursed his lips as if searching for words. "And each other."

Haemon gave a grim nod. "We have seen the fever's affects firsthand."

Ophelos stepped forward, jaw tight and shoulders high. His gaze swept over the stricken men, and his face fell. "There was an older man," the Theban said. "Gray-bearded with a scar on his right cheek. He was wounded by a sword-thrust to side. Is he here?"

Loimos shook his head.

"I would see his body," Ophelos said.

"That is not advisable," Loimos replied. "The sickness leaves them somewhat less than… presentable."

"I am no stranger to death, priest. Take me to him."

"As you wish." Loimos inclined his head, then glanced at Haemon and Damaris.

"I shall see to the sick." The physician did not even wait for a response, flitting amidst the pallets like a fly in a butcher's shop.

Damaris gave a sour frown. "Dead or dying, it makes no difference to me."

He followed Ophelos and the priest toward the rear of the cavern where a tunnel wound even deeper into the mountain. The air went from chill to genuinely frigid as Loimos led them along the low passage.

"This place is a temple?" Damaris's breath smoked in the cold air. "It must have been the work of years to carve out."

"Oh, it took far longer than that." The priest returned a thin smile.

"Shouldn't there be a statue?" Damaris asked.

Loimos gave a puzzled frown.

"To Apollo?"

"Oh, yes, a statue." The priest gave a sad shake of his head. "Alas, the Athenians destroyed it."

Damaris was about to ask more when they came to a large rectangular chamber perhaps twenty paces wide and half again as long. The light of Loimos' torch revealed rows of stone plinths, all empty save one, on which lay a linen-wrapped corpse.

"I am sorry for the presentation." Loimos shook his head. "But it was difficult to move him alone."

Ophelos waved away the priest's apologies, moving toward body. He laid a hand upon its shoulder, blinking as a man who wakes from a terrible dream.

Damaris stepped up to lay a hand on the Theban's shoulder. "Now he stands at Herakles's side."

"I want to see his face."

Loimos shook his head. "That would be—"

"I would *see* him." Ophelos's words were a strangled hiss.

The priest nodded. Drawing his belt knife, Ophelos bent over. A few quick slashes and the rope bindings fell free.

Damaris bit back a moan.

What lay within the linen could no longer be called a man. Black ropes of viscera hung loose and liquid over bones the color of wet shale. The corpse's skin was cracked and peeling, the muscle beneath corded like rotten rope. There were no eyes, only hollow pits that seemed filled with feculent shadows. The man's jaw had fallen out of place, gums drawing away from teeth that seemed ragged and sharp in the lamplight. A smell like stagnant water filled the cavern, so thick it seemed to burrow into Damaris's nose.

Even Ophelos flinched back, a move which probably saved the Theban's life.

The corpse shuddered, heels drumming against the stone as it lurched up, reaching for Ophelos with fingers of filth-caked bone. They slashed only air as the Theban threw himself back with a strangled shout.

Great tendrils of blackened viscera lashed from the corpse's ruined chest. Ophelos tried to stumble toward the hall, but one of the oozing loops of flesh tangled in his legs, then drew tight to snatch him from his feet.

Instincts honed by years of battle came bubbling up. Out of pure reflex, he flung a javelin at the shrieking thing. The point struck it in the chest, sliding through the creature to knock it from the plinth. Hatchet in hand, he sprinted to Ophelos's side and hacked down at the rope of greasy viscera looped about the Theban's leg.

Corrupted flesh parted before the sharp edge of Damaris's axe. As the corpse-thing ripped the javelin free, Damaris hauled the Theban to his feet and shoved Ophelos out of reach of the corpse's writhing entrails.

The creature scuttled at them like a maddened spider, bits of corrupted organ sloughing from between its ribs. Damaris could see the vile scraps of flesh clinging to its hooked fingers, and knew that a single scratch would see him bound upon a pallet outside.

He chopped down with his axe, almost severing one of the corpse's grasping hands, but the creature didn't even pause. It stabbed at Damaris with the ruined remains of its arm, hand flopping limply at the end of a jagged wrist bone. Corded flesh slithered snakelike from within its body, and it was all Damaris could do to avoid the writhing innards.

Shield braced, Ophelos charged in. The Theban drove the corpse-thing back, legs pumping, until it was pinned against the far wall. It clawed and spat, but Ophelos was phalanx-trained, and the hoplite kept his head low, his shield firmly braced. Bone scratched across bronze with a sound like a dying cat, but the creature could find no chink in the Theban's armor.

"Damaris, the torch!" Ophelos shouted.

Casting about, Damaris saw Loimos still by the entrance. The priest stood transfixed by the sight of the hideous thing, lips skinned back from his teeth in a rictus snarl.

Damaris snatched the torch from Loimos's hand, then sprinted over to hold the burning brand to the creature's side.

It hissed, snapping at Damaris, but Ophelos kept the corpse pinned until the linen bindings caught. Dark purple-green flames crept along the creature's limbs, silhouetting the bruised hues.

With a shout, Ophelos gave the shield one final shove, then abandoned the writhing corpse to sprint for the entrance to the chamber, Damaris close behind.

He heard the click of bone on stone as the thing stumbled after them, the heat of its burning body warm on the back of Damaris's neck.

With a crack like fresh wood in a fire, the creature's legs gave way. Damaris turned to see it squirm upon the floor, entrails thrashing the air like headless snakes. The stink of burning flesh pressed in around them like a physical presence, and it was all Damaris could do not to gag as the creature finally heaved and lay silent.

"By the gods, what's that commotion?" Haemon jogged up, lantern in hand, only to stop short to stare at the burning remains. "What have you—?"

"Ask him." Damaris pointed his hatchet at the priest.

Loimos shook his head , eyes wide. "She reaches us, even here."

"It's the witch," Ophelos said. "Clearly her evil has tainted even this holy place."

"Long has she troubled my temple." Loimos nodded. "Just as her master, Xerxes, sought to extend his dominion over all the lands, she would enslave all to her power."

"This cannot be allowed," Ophelos said.

"I don't see how we can stop her." Damaris gestured at the still-burning corpse. "Plague isn't a phalanx, we can't just hack our way through."

"Then we must *find* a way." Ophelos's face hardened. He glanced at Haemon. "Have your examinations found anything, physician?"

"The disease is like none I've ever seen," Haemon replied. "Bilious and sanguine, it takes root in the afflicted, spreading through their body and soul. I have attempted to rebalance their humors, but it continues to fester. If it truly is a curse, I fear there is little I can do while the witch lives."

"This witch, do you know where she dwells?" Ophelos asked Loimos.

"Farther up the mountainside on a plateau of bone," the priest replied with a wince, as if the words alone were an affront.

The Theban nodded. "Then we must find and slay her."

"And what of the swarm of blood-crazed Athenians waiting outside?" Damaris asked.

Ophelos sagged like Damaris had stuck a spear in his gut. His gaze flicked back to the smoking ruin of his former comrade, then the bodies beyond.

The weight of the Theban's sorrow seemed to settle upon Damaris's shoulders. He had lost comrades before, their absence around the campfire felt as keenly as a missing finger.

"That man." He nodded at the burnt body. "What was he to you? Friend? Lover?"

Ophelos closed his eyes, swallowing heavily. "He was my father."

Damaris grunted, the reason for the Theban's need for vengeance finally becoming clear.

Other mercenaries swore oaths of iron – strong in battle, but liable to rust over time. But Damaris was a Molossian. His people might be rustic mountain folk, but their promises were gold, never to tarnish or lose their luster. Like it or not, he was Ophelos's man. At least until they reached Thebes.

He turned to Loimos. "The rope you used to bind the bodies of the dead, you have more?"

"*Much* more," the priest replied.

"Ophelos, how are you at climbing?"

"I'm no Molossian." The Theban seemed to regain some of his former spirit. "But I surmounted Mount Cithaeron at twelve summers of age."

"It will have to do." Damaris grinned as Ophelos sputtered. "Haemon, you stay with Loimos and try to keep any more Thebans from journeying to the Underworld."

The physician gave a relieved nod.

"Loimos, gather up the ropes, a hammer, hooks, and iron spikes, too, if you have them." Damaris watched the priest hurry off, then turned to his companions. "We may not be able to take the path, but mountains move in four directions."

"And the witch?" Ophelos asked.

"I doubt she'll be hard to find." Damaris glanced at the ceiling as if his gaze could pierce the countless tons of rock overhead. "Her kind seldom are."

Chips of stone showered Damaris as the rear spike of his hatchet bit into the cliffside. With a grunt of effort he pulled himself up, bracing his feet on the craggy cliff before fitting an iron hook into the crack and hammering it home. Wind plucked at his tunic as he secured the rope to the hook, tested it, and called for Ophelos to advance.

Teeth gritted, the Theban dragged himself up the mountainside. They had been scaling the cliff beyond the temple entrance for the better part of the morning, lashed together with rope in case one should lose their grip. Of the Athenians, there had been little apart from the occasional arrow fired from the ledge far below, but the high angle rendered the missiles more nuisance than threat.

A fall of scree was Damaris's only warning as the rock above gave way beneath Ophelos's weight. As the stones tumbled past on his right, he braced himself against the cliff, gripping his axe tight even as he clung tightly to the stone. A moment later and the Theban tumbled past. Damaris heard the ping of a spike being ripped from the rock, then he was jerked backward. Jagged agony shot up his arms. It seemed like every joint in his torso was being stretched to breaking, but Damaris only grit his teeth and held on.

There was a clatter as Ophelos struck the cliffside. From the metallic noise, it sounded as if the Theban had twisted to take the impact on the shield slung over his back. Blood trickled from Damaris's fingers, dripping upon the hungry stone. He let out a low groan, arms and legs trembling from the strain of bearing the weight of two men.

More rocks rattled below.

"Whatever you're doing, Theban, do it quick!" Just as Damaris's arms seemed ready to bid farewell to his body, the weight lessened.

"I've got a decent grip." There was a bit of a quaver in

Ophelos's voice, although whether it came from exhaustion or nerves, Damaris couldn't hazard. "Cut the rope."

"What?"

"The rope binding us," Ophelos called back. "I'll hold here while you climb the rest of the way. Then you can lower down a line."

Damaris chewed his lip. He didn't like leaving a comrade behind, but the Theban's plan made sense.

An arrow clicked from the rock perhaps ten yards to Damaris's left.

"That settles it." He fumbled for his belt knife. A bit of sawing and the line tumbled loose. Freed of Ophelos's weight, it felt as if Daedalus himself had grafted wings to Damaris's shoulders, and he soon fell into an easy rhythm with axe and climbing spike.

Even so, the sun was near its zenith when at last Damaris hauled himself up onto the ragged plateau above the temple. He spent a good long moment sucking wind before shambling over to loop his rope several times around a nearby outcrop, then lower it so Ophelos could climb up.

The Theban finally collapsed onto the stone. "Gods, I hope the witch isn't nearby," he said, heaving in great gasps. "I'm weak as a starving kitten."

"Lowlanders." Damaris's attempt to play the veteran climber was spoiled by his shaking arms. Truth be told, it had been some time since he'd been off the dirt.

He bound the scrapes on his knuckles with strips of linen, all the while keen for the scrape of sandal on stone or the creak of battle harness that would presage a surprise assault.

It took them a bit of searching to find the goat path Loimos had mentioned, but it seemed to fit the priest's description once they began the ascent.

"I'll take the lead," Ophelos stepped forward, shield braced, a heavy, forward-curving kopis in the other hand.

Damaris frowned. "I've got more experience scouting terrain like this."

"No argument on that score. It's just... I seem to be proof

against the witch's plague." Ophelos shrugged. "Perhaps it is Apollo's blessing, or my Spartoi blood."

"Or pure luck."

The Theban gave a tired grin.

"Let it never be said I stood between a madman and death." Damaris gestured toward the trail. "Lead the way."

The goat path wound up the mountain, a thin line of scrub-covered gravel that occasionally gave way to patches of broken stone. Although the footing was treacherous, it was a jaunt compared to climbing the temple cliff.

At last, the trail leveled. Stone gave way to a carpet of sun-bleached bone as the two advanced onto the plateau. Loimos's description of the Persian sorceress had conjured images of man-eating graeae in Damaris's mind, of skulls and stewpots, and mounds of cracked ribcages, all the marrow sucked dry.

Although there were bones aplenty, they seemed of a wholly mundane sort – birds, and squirrels, and goats, even the occasional lynx. The plateau was a wide and relatively flat expanse, broken only by the occasional tumbled boulder or fall of rock from farther up the mountain. The air smelled of woodsmoke and burnt grease, and more than one of the stones were stained by soot from old cookfires.

The only indication of sorcery was the symbols etched into the stone. Strange words covered every bit of exposed rock in a wild, twisting panoply unbound by line or ledger. Even as Damaris watched, they seemed to crawl like beetles across the stone, tugging at his eyes, drawing him in with the inevitability of an ocean tide.

Ophelos caught his shoulder. "What are you doing?"

Damaris blinked, only just then realizing he'd been calmly ambling toward the stones.

"Sorcery," his muttered excuse earned a tight-lipped frown from Ophelos.

"Just keep your wits about you, Molossian."

Javelin and hatchet in hand, Damaris fell in behind the

Theban. He avoided looking at the stones, instead letting his gaze roam the approaches to either side. Tiny bones crunched beneath their sandals as they moved across the plateau. Each footstep seemed to echo from the rock, loud as battle-drums in the chill silence.

The thrum of a bowstring was Damaris's only warning. Acting on reflex alone, he shoved Ophelos, throwing himself back as the Theban stumbled forward.

An arrow slashed the air where Damaris had been standing. He spun to trace the missile's flight, spying a flicker of movement between two canted boulders just a moment before another arrow came winging toward them.

Adder fast, Ophelos shifted to interpose his shield, and the missile clattered from the hard bronze facing. They dove for a fallen boulder, crouching behind the rock.

Bones skittered as the witch repositioned herself.

"I can't get a clean throw without standing." Damaris risked a peek over the little boulder, and almost received another arrow between the eyes for his trouble.

"How was I to know she'd have a godsdamned bow?" Ophelos flinched as another arrow hissed overhead, followed by a very un-witchlike curse from the distant rocks.

"So, Loimos has dispatched more thralls to end me?" Her voice was clear and strong, far different from the creaky rasp Damaris had expected. "Come and join your brethren."

"My brethren lay within the temple!" Ophelos shouted back. "Warded by the hand of Apollo."

Her response was in a language Damaris didn't recognize, words slipping like smoke through the air.

"Strange," she said. "I sense his touch upon you, but you are not his."

"Keep her talking," Damaris crawled around the stone, careful to stay low.

"We fight for Thebes, and for our comrades!" Ophelos shouted back. "Comrades who have fallen prey to your vile enchantments."

"Vile? You Greeks know nothing of vile." She laughed again. "Pity you won't live long enough for me to educate you."

From the sound of her voice, he could tell she crouched within a fall of boulders perhaps twenty paces away. If he could skirt the plateau without dislodging any bones, he might just be able to get behind her. Before Damaris had crossed half the distance, the witch's voice rose again.

"*Aski kataski lix tetrax damnameneus aisia!*" Her incantation split the silence. "Spirit of the root, come to me – remove these defilers!"

The hairs on Damaris's arms prickled, the air going thin and chill as if he had suddenly ascended to a great height.

Bones clicked and clattered. At first, Damaris thought he had dislodged some animal skeleton, but the bones seemed to move of their own accord. Tumbling over one another as if caught in an invisible gale, they rattled toward the center of the plateau.

They heaped upon one another, tiny femurs threading ribcages, spines and featherless wings lashed together by ropes of dried sinew. Slowly, it formed. First, as tall as a man. Then much, much taller.

What rose from the scattered animal bodies was a thing of nightmares. Vaguely serpentine, its long body was spiked with broken bones. A score of stubby arms jutted from its jagged frame. Assembled from mismatched limbs, they were tipped with lynx claws, eagle talons, even the twisted horn of a mountain goat. Where its head should have been was a mass of tiny skulls, toothless maws spread wide, their eyes glittering with blue-green flame.

The thing reared back, shrieking death from a hundred mouths.

There was a crashing boom as the creature hove itself over the rocks where Ophelos sheltered. Damaris risked a glance back and saw the Theban leap to his feet, hacking at one of the creature's arms. The heavy forward-curved blade of his kopis was made for dismembering, sinew and bone parting like clouds before its razored edge. Talons scraped on bronze as the creature clawed at Ophelos's shield.

The Theban stood firm as Herakles himself, his parries and slashes almost too quick for Damaris to follow. Then, the creature's heavy tail lashed around. Ophelos raised his shield, but muscle-backed bronze could do little against what amounted to an avalanche of bone, and the Theban went tumbling back.

Damaris saw the witch rise from cover only a few paces away. She was younger than he'd expected – middle-aged rather than cronelike, her dark hair shot with streaks of gray, her face weathered but not deeply lined. She wore a Phrygian cap of dark felt, and was clad in breeches and a loose tunic of tanned animal hide.

The creature screeched again.

Somehow, Ophelos had regained his feet. Shieldless, his kopis clutched in both hands he bounded atop a flat rock, gathering his legs beneath him as the demon bore down. With surprise, Damaris realized the fool intended to leap at the thing.

The witch drew her bow, sighting at the Theban.

Abandoning all pretense of stealth, Damaris hurled himself at the woman. His shoulder struck her just below the ribs, and he felt the breath rush out of her as the arrow flew wide. Despite the shock of impact, she reacted quickly, slamming the stock of her bow into Damaris's nose. He felt cartilage buckle, bolts of bright pain streaking through his head even as his eyes began to water.

Swallowing against the blood that filled his throat he dropped his javelin, fingers closing on the witch's tunic. Blindly, he slammed her back against the rock. She twisted to drive a knee into his groin, but Damaris felt the shift in her weight and managed to interpose his thigh – painful but not debilitating. Her fingers scrabbled along his cheek, searching for his eyes, and turned his head even as he slammed her back again.

The second blow seemed to take some of the fight from the witch. Before she could regain her wind, Damaris pressed the blade of his hatchet to her throat.

"Call off your demon." His voice came wet and hoarse, but clear enough.

Through blurred vision he saw her grin. "So you can finish your master's work in peace?"

Behind them, there was a tremendous clatter, furious shrieks mixed with shouts and the hollow thud of iron cleaving bone. Damaris didn't dare risk a glance back, so he increased the pressure on his blade. Blood slicked the edge, trickling down to pool in the hollow of his throat.

"Master?" Damaris frowned.

"Loimos," she replied. "Or do you expect me to believe you weren't dispatched by that ancient blister."

"You lie. He is a priest of Apollo."

"Priest of Apollo?" She snorted. "More like bastard son, cast aside for his wickedness."

Damaris increased the pressure on his blade, but the witch did not flinch.

"Killing me won't save your comrades." Her dark eyes were clear and unafraid, her expression one of anger rather than fear. "In fact, it may doom them."

Damaris grit his teeth. "Your lies shall not bewitch me."

"You have been to Loimos' temple." The axe at her throat whetted the witch's words to an urgent whisper. "You have seen the wards, the sickness, the vile creatures he cultivates. *Think,* fool. Does that accursed place seem like any shrine to Apollo you have ever seen?"

Damaris scowled as the inconsistencies of Loimos's story came clear – the priest's strange affectations, the lack of proper trappings, the strange sigils scratched upon the temple stones.

It felt as if a stone had settled in Damaris's gut; a bone-deep knowing that it was truth that spilled from the witch's lips. "You didn't curse Ophelos's comrades, did you?"

"Curse them?" She seemed genuinely perplexed. "Why would I do that?"

Damaris released her with a tired sigh. "Call off your demon."

She regarded him through slit eyes.

"Please. We want the same thing." He dropped his hatchet, then held up both hands.

Snatching up her bow, the witch scrambled to her feet. She made as if to draw an arrow from the quiver at her side, then scowled, slamming it back with a disgusted grunt. "Are all Greeks so foolish? How Xerxes failed to conquer this misbegotten place I'll never know."

Damaris let out the breath he had been holding. "I am Damaris of Epirus."

"Kasra." She glanced at the battle, lips pursed. Damaris followed her gaze and saw Ophelos clinging to the creature's back just behind its mass of heads. It whipped back and forth, scrabbling to reach him with its stubby claws even as he hacked at the mass of tangled bones.

Kasra bared her teeth. "Gods, I fucking *hate* Spartoi."

"That makes two of us." Damaris's shrug brought a crooked grin to her face, and the witch muttered a low incantation, ending it with a sudden chop of her hand.

The mountain demon dissolved as quickly as it had formed. Sinews unbound, ribs untangling to send Ophelos tumbling headfirst into a pile of long-dead animals. The Theban continued to shout and slash for several long moments, scattering flecks of broken bone across the plateau.

When no new assault seemed forthcoming, he paused to glance around. Damaris would've laughed, but the thought of Haemon alone and unaware of his peril drained all mirth from the moment.

Ophelos pushed to his feet, brushing bits of bone and stone from his tunic. Seeing Damaris and the witch together, he raised his sword unsteadily.

"Stand away!"

"Sheathe your blade, friend." Damaris met the Theban's questioning gaze with a scowl. "It appears we've been lied to."

"She cursed my men. Slew my father!" Ophelos gave a dogged shake of his head. "She is a thing of evil, spreading disease and suffering."

"My sorcery is the same as that of your ancestors, Theban," Kasra replied. "The magic of earth and bone and stone. Look upon me, you know it to be true."

Ophelos's blade lowered a fraction.

"Every moment we waste here is one more that Loimos is alone with Haemon and your companions." Damaris nodded at the witch. "She has done us no harm."

"You perhaps." Ophelos turned to display the collection of ragged scratches upon his arms and legs.

"I'll have Haemon look you over." Damaris felt the hollow in his stomach grow. Damned if he'd come to like the irascible little physician.

"None of us can defeat Loimos alone." Kasra thrust her chin at the scattered bones. "If you're half as good against demons as you are against mountain spirits, that is."

Ophelos chewed his lip, gaze flicking from Damaris to Kasra. "How do I know she's not bewitched you?"

"I bow to no enchantment save that of silver," Damaris replied with a smile. "And you're going to owe me more than a few sandals full when we get back to Thebes."

Ophelos stood still for a moment, then gave a rueful shake of his head. "Damn, I'm not looking forward to climbing back down that godsforsaken cliff."

Kasra raised an eyebrow at the Theban. "I believe I can help with that."

"The temple path is below." Kasra waved her bow at the boulder-strewn hill. Damaris noticed many of the rocks had been etched with arcane sigils, and gave the witch a suspicious glance.

"Wards." Her smile was not the least bit comforting. "To keep Loimos's corruption from spreading up the mountain."

"Would that you had kept it from the valleys as well." Ophelos's voice was tight and angry.

"The lowlands are not my concern."

"I would expect as much from a Persian witch." Ophelos's knuckles whitened on the grip of his shield.

"I seem to remember Thebes fought alongside the invaders," Kasra replied.

"Not out of any love for the Persians. Athens needed to be stopped. Athens *still* needs to be stopped." Ophelos' scowl seemed carved from granite. "I wouldn't be surprised if Xerxes himself set you to bedevil these peaks."

Kasra made a face as if she had just bitten into something sour. "I have more cause to despise Xerxes than any Greek."

Damaris was about to step between the two, but Ophelos seemed taken aback by Kasra's words.

"Who do you think had me exiled to this uncivilized backwater?" Kasra's sneer was sharp as her tongue. Without a word, she turned and began to pick her way down the stony incline. Damaris fancied himself a skilled mountaineer, but Kasra seemed almost to be walking on level ground so easily did she ghost across the broken rock.

Ophelos and Damaris followed with similar speed, if far less grace, dislodging no small number of stones, much to Kasra's mounting fury.

"Quiet! You're almost as bad as Athenians." She spared them a disdainful glance. "Worse, perhaps. At least they can blame their clumsiness on the plague."

Reddening, Ophelos opened his mouth to reply, but Kasra hissed him to silence, crouching behind a cracked lip of stone.

"On the path below," she whispered.

Damaris risked a look over the rock and saw three Athenians stumbling along the narrow trail. They looked as men near death, without helms or weapons, their sandaled feet scuffing long tracks in the gravelly dirt. The heated, sanguine flush that had suffused their skin earlier had been replaced by an ashy pallor, as if their flesh had already begun to mortify.

As Damaris watched, one of the men stumbled with a throaty groan. For a moment, it looked as if he might stumble from the cliff, instead he collapsed, flopping upon the ground like a landed fish as he struggled back to his feet.

"Only three," Ophelos whispered. "Where are the others?"

"They are almost ripe." Kasra's reply came edged with something akin to apprehension. "He calls to them."

"Would not Loimos wish to spread his sickness?" Damaris asked. "It seems foolish to gather the diseased."

"It will spread soon enough," she replied. "The demon has spent centuries locked away in that cave. If not for that band of foolish Athenians thinking to loot the place he would've spent centuries more. Now, he is free to cultivate."

"Cultivate what?" Ophelos asked.

Kasra drew in a deep breath. "His godhood."

"Seems like something we might want to stop." Damaris glanced at Kasra. "Can you summon your spirit?"

She shook her head. "Just as Loimos's foulness cannot pass these boulders, his power keeps mine in check below them."

"Well, then I suppose we'll have to handle this ourselves." Damaris hefted a javelin.

It was a simple plan, but their opponents seemed barely able to see, let alone spot an ambush.

Clashing sword against shield, Ophelos advanced up the path. Like wolves scenting prey, the Athenians turned at his approach. HHHHands crooked into claws, they shuffled toward the Theban with surprising speed.

Kasra's arrow took the first in the throat. The man's skin split like overripe fruit, peeling back to expose a seething mass of corrupted flesh. He stumbled as the wound tore wider. Strands of blackened sinew unwove, curling like spider legs as they scratched and slashed, almost as if the Athenian's skin were a sodden sack they were trying to rip free of.

Suddenly, Damaris's javelin didn't seem quite up to the task.

He dropped the missile, bending to heft one of the larger rocks. With a grunt of effort, he sent the stone plummeting through the air. It struck the flailing man's shoulder, pulping rotten flesh and corrupted bone. The Athenian spun a slow, shocked circle before pitching off the path to land with a wet thud on the rocks below.

Seeing the effect of Damaris's stone, Kasra abandoned her bow to gather up and armful of fist-sized rocks, and together they set another diseased creature tumbling down the cliff. The last Athenian was too close to Ophelos to risk a throw.

Damaris broke cover, drawing his weapons, a move he immediately regretted as his sandals skidded on loose gravel as he stumbled down the mountain, almost beheading himself with his own axe.

Instead of slashing at the creature, Ophelos drove his shield into the man's chest, which yielded with a series of wet pops. Before he could recover, the Theban jerked his shield up so the upper rim smashed into the Athenian's jaw, sending him staggering back.

Now, Ophelos lashed out with his blade, chopping not at the man's body, but his extended leg. The blow didn't quite remove the limb, but was hard enough to break bone. The creature listed like a breached trireme, stumbling directly into Damaris's path.

Half-rotted fingers left greasy trails on Damaris's armor as the thing scrabbled for purchase. He slammed his axe into the side of the creature's head, splitting its skull like rotten wood. At last, the disease-ridden man's grasp slackened, and he fell away.

For a moment, Damaris hung suspended over the cliff edge, body twisted like a festival dancer's, then a strong hand closed around his.

"I thought you Molossians knew your way around mountains." Ophelos dragged him back onto the ledge.

"You call this a mountain?" Damaris laughed to hide the tremble in his voice. Even so, he didn't rick a glance down as they edged along the narrow path that led to the erstwhile temple. As they'd expected, the heavy bronze door had been moved aside, presumably by Loimos's creatures.

The outer temple appeared much as it was, great columns etched with prayers to Apollo that Damaris now knew were wards meant to keep Loimos imprisoned. As they passed the ruined gate, he was struck by the sickly-sweet smell of putrefaction. Damaris grit his teeth against the queasiness in his stomach, and even Ophelos appeared taken aback by the smell, hands tight on his weapons, jaw clenched as if he were fighting nausea.

Kasra muttered under her breath, the words low and unfamiliar. Damaris wasn't sure if she sought to combat Loimos's sorcery or simply the smell, but the chant seemed to quiet Damaris's churning gut.

He snatched a torch from one of the wall sconces, and together they moved through the ancient chambers and down the long stair to the shrine's central cavern.

The cave was unsettlingly quiet. Light from the few remaining braziers showed most of the cots were empty. Those few Thebans who remained lay still and silent, their bonds slack. Damaris did not need to approach to know they were dead.

Ophelos let out a low moan, pained gaze sweeping over the remnants of his command.

"You've returned."

Damaris whirled at the voice, axe raised.

Haemon stood in the gloom. The little physician's robes were stained with old blood and his arms were red to the elbows.

Kasra raised her bow, but Damaris waved a calming hand.

"This is Haemon, a friend and good man." He cocked his head, squinting at the physician. "If you still are a man."

"What else would I be?" Haemon scowled at Kasra, who scrutinized the physician.

"He is untouched." She gave a quick nod. "His god protects him."

"Protects me?" Haemon stepped up to glare at the three of them. "Who in Hades is that? Don't tell me you brought the witch *back*."

"We brought the witch back." Grinning, Damaris clapped the physician on his boney shoulder. "Damn, but I'm glad you survived."

Haemon's bushy brows shaded his eyes. "This isn't my first plague."

"This isn't a plague," Damaris replied, glancing around. "Where is the priest?"

"Loimos? He is preparing the bodies of the dead for burning." The physician glanced at the empty cots, then met Ophelos's gaze. "I'm sorry. I did everything I could, every cure, every remedy, but no sooner did I see improvement than the sickness would blossom elsewhere. It was as if the sickness anticipated my treatments."

"*It did.*" The voice was unmistakably Loimos's, but different, deeper, as if the priest spoke from a dozen throats. "*For it stood at your very shoulder.*"

Stepping to Ophelos's side, Damaris raised his torch, but saw no robed form amidst the shifting gloom.

Kasra let out a low hiss, her aim jumping from shadow to shadow. Unfortunately, the witch seemed as blind as her companions.

"*I want to thank you.*" Loimos's words echoed from all around. "*For bringing me not only a skilled physician, but the witch as well. She has frustrated my work for too long.*"

Kasra loosed an arrow into the darkness. There was a meaty thud, but no grunt of pain or thump of a body hitting the cavern floor.

Loimos chuckled. "*We have slipped the strictures of flesh, of pain, to grow strong in sickness.*"

Now, Damaris saw them.

Pale flesh caught the brazier's light, corrupted lesions glistening with puss and other vile humors. They had not even the form of men, but scuttled like insects around the circle of light. Damaris caught glimpses of limbs twisted beyond recognition, bones broken and reknit by tumorous growths. Eyes like pale river rocks stared from misshapen brows, jagged teeth jutting from slavering, crooked jaws.

There were no Thebans, no Athenians, only monsters.

Damaris had his back to Ophelos's, drawing Haemon into the little circle with a quick jerk.

"By Apollo, what are they?" the physician's voice trembled.

"*Apollo?*" The creatures gave a hissing laugh. "*Father to a thousand bastards, he cares nothing for you, just as the gods care nothing for you. Consumed by petty rivalries, they squat on bejeweled thrones, grown fat upon unblemished hecatombs. I, on the other hand, care deeply for the fate of man.*"

"What of the fate of *my* men?" Ophelos shouted.

"*Wounded in battle, I have given them strength to rise again. Made warriors the likes of which this world has not seen in an age.*" One of the creatures shuffled forward to extend a hooked hand. When it spoke again, the voice was different, older. "*Join us and we shall save our city. Together.*"

Ophelos flinched as if the creature had stabbed him. "You are not my father."

"*I am.*" It straightened, glaring down at the Theban with mismatched eyes. "*But also so much more.*"

"*The push and pull of humors – sickness, ague, health.*" The other creatures spoke with Loimos's voice. "*Haemon and his ilk seek balance, but this is a lie. There is no true balance save in death. Life is war, this world is war.*"

Damaris dropped his torch to unlimber a javelin, drawing comfort from the missile's solid weight. Squinting into the darkness, he caught the faintest glimpse of a robed form among the shuffling throng.

"*Join me. Worship me.*" The creatures chorused. "*Your reward shall be life eternal, freedom from suffering, the strength to cast your enemies down and—*"

Loimos's words were cut off by the *hiss-crack* of one of Haemon's sling stones striking bone. The robed man stumbled back even as the plague creatures recoiled with a strangled hiss.

"That stone speaks for us all." Damaris stepped forward. "But please allow me to add a rebuttal of my own."

It was hard to judge distance in the shifting shadows, but Damaris still managed to plant his javelin in the priest's shoulder.

Kasra shouted a word that blistered the air, kneeling to press one hand against the stone of the cavern. The braziers flared and the chamber was filled with crackling light.

The sudden brightness revealed Loimos's creatures in hideous detail. Spotted with weeping lesions, their bodies were little more than lumps of tumorous flesh bound together by blackened sinew and long ropes of twisted muscle. They contorted and howled as if the light burned them, skin smoking even as they charged.

"If they live, they can be killed." Ophelos struck at the creature that had spoken with his father's voice. The Theban's blade sheared through corrupted flesh, and buboes burst to spatter his shield with black blood. Tears glittered on Ophelos's cheeks as he hacked down again, and again, turning the thing into a red, twitching ruin.

Teeth gritted, Damaris drew his weapons, stepping up to bury his hatchet in the neck of a shrieking abomination. The creature howled and spit at him from half-a-dozen mouths; jagged, broken teeth snapping as it reached for him.

An arrow took it in the eye.

Damaris seized the moment, slashing with his xiphos as the creature stumbled back. The flesh of its torso split to reveal a mass of seething viscera. Before any of the rotted tentacles could lash out, Damaris shifted to kick the thing in its twisted ribs. It stumbled into one of the braziers.

The flames seemed almost to embrace the creature. Flesh boiled from bone even as its skin stretched and cracked. The sight of it writhing like a nest of snakes stole the breath from Damaris's lungs, and he would've been blindsided by another one of the creatures had not one of Haemon's slingstones turned its bulbous head to pulp.

"Loimos is the source of the corruption!" The physician called as one of the creatures caught his arm. "Strike for the priest."

With a roar, Ophelos bowled another of the abominations aside, but only made it two steps toward the priest before more the monsters hurled themselves at him. One of Kasra's arrows flicked past Damaris, striking Loimos in the shoulder.

"*You should know better, witch.*" The priest's face didn't even twitch as he calmly plucked it free. The arrow warped in his hand, twisting into a barbed, scabrous disk of wood and metal. With a sneer, he flung it back at Kasra who dove away. But the twisted weapon seemed imbued with malign bloodlust, and it buzzed in the air, rebounding from the cavern wall to seek the witch again.

With Haemon and Kasra pinned down, and Ophelos surrounded, only Damaris was still able to move. He skirted the edge of the cavern. Dodged the clutching talons of a creature who seemed to be made of two men fused together. Pivoting around the thing's wild grab, he buried his hatchet in the back of its knee, then shoved it into a pair of its fellows.

They fell into a jumbled heap, and Damaris leapt over the seething scrum. Another creature reared from the harsh shadows only to receive a Damaris's hatchet in the side of its bloated head. The blow slammed it against wall of the cavern, and Damaris quickly followed with a chop of his xiphos. Unlike its brethren, this creature's flesh was tough as old rope, and it took several blows to hack through its leathery neck.

He turned, panting, just as Loimos's fist came crashing in.

The blow was hard enough to knock Damaris's helmet free. He felt drunk, balanced on limbs that seemed unable to support his weight. The cavern floor almost knocked the wind from him, and he rolled upon the stone, gasping, as Loimos loomed over him.

The priest had added several feet of height and quite a bit of bulk. Loimos's robe billowed as if caught by unseen wind, fabric twisting and stretching as strange shapes slithered beneath.

Damaris struggled to his knees, only to feel iron-hard fingers close about his sword arm. He was lifted bodily from the ground to dangle from his sword arm, eye-to-eye with Loimos.

Firelight and sickness had made the priest's face a ragged, cadaverous thing with eyes like pools of shadow. Blistered lips drew back from teeth the color of rotten wood as the priest opened his mouth.

"*From struggle, strength. From conflict, wisdom. You Greeks should know that better than any.*" The priest spoke as if his mouth were full of meal. "*I will make of this land a paradise to rival Olympus itself. If you will not serve me willingly, your flesh will suffice.*"

Something moved deep within Loimos's throat, glistening as it squirmed in the darkness.

Damaris swung his hatchet up, grunting as it sunk into the side of Loimos's jaw. The priest's head exploded in a mass of gore-slicked tendrils. One traced a fiery line across Damaris's cheek even as others wrapped around his throat and arms. He could almost feel his flesh curl and blacken at their touch, veins of corruption seeping into muscle and bone.

The priest shuddered as skin and fabric tore away to reveal the horrid, sinuous thing he had become.

Damaris struggled against the demon's terrible strength, but was held fast. He felt something wet slip across his chin, and clenched his jaw as it pressed against his mouth, gagging as it wriggled past his lips to try and slip between his teeth.

Out of the corner of his vision, he saw Ophelos running toward them. The Theban turned, spinning like a discus thrower, once, twice. Bronze flashed across Damaris's vision and the serpentine tendril probing his mouth was knocked away. Something clattered to his left, and he glanced down to see Ophelos's shield rolling upon the ground.

The Theban was not far behind. He brought his blade down, the heavy kopis shearing through the ropes of sinuous flesh binding Damaris's hatchet arm. Damaris responded by applying his weapon liberally to the mass of seething flesh before him.

Shrieking, Loimos flung him away. Impact with the hard stone floor set Damaris's weapons skittering from his grip. He twisted with the fall, turning what would have been a bone-cracking impact to a bruising roll. He stumbled to his feet, casting about for the weapon.

"Molossian!" Haemon's voice rang from Damaris's left. "Stop gawking and help us with this."

Damaris turned to see Haemon and Kasra struggling to lift one of the heavy braziers. He staggered over, wincing as his hands were singed by the hot bronze. Kazra was chanting again, each word seeming to stoke the flames higher.

Loimos appeared to have gotten the better of Ophelos. The Theban was backed against the wall of the cavern, one arm clutched to his side, slashing madly with his sword as the demonic priest closed in.

The smell of his own scorched flesh was sharp in Damaris's nose, but he did not let go as the three of them lifted the brazier high and dumped its blazing contents upon Loimos.

Sorcerous flames crawled across the priest's writhing limbs, corrupted flesh kindling like dry grass. Silhouetted by fire, Loimos shrieked, but although he batted at the flames, it only served to spread the hungry blaze.

Shielding his eyes from the glare, Damaris dragged Ophelos clear, and together they stumbled away from the burning, thrashing monstrosity. Hot air wafted across their backs. As it had with the corpse of Ophelos's father, the flames consumed the priest.

Loimos's creatures shuddered and fell to twitch upon the ground. Whatever bilious animus possessed them seemed to have fled with the destruction of their master.

Soon, the chamber was silent but for the sullen crackle of fire.

Haemon was the first to break the silence. "I've never seen a boil so desperately in need of lancing. Still, it seems we've removed the infection."

"For now," Kasra replied. The witch's cap had fallen off and dried blood matted the hair to one side of her head, but she seemed hale enough. "Sickness always returns, if in a different form."

"Is their naught we can do?" Ophelos asked.

"Perhaps not us." Damaris gave a thin smile. "Kasra, you might want to ask that mountain spirit of yours if it fancies dropping a few tons of rock upon this wretched pit."

Her answering grin had none of the sharpness of earlier. "I believe it could be convinced."

"Well then." He ambled over to retrieve his axe and xiphos, then glanced at the scorched remains of his helmet amidst Loimos's ashes. With a shake of his head, he turned back to Ophelos. "Shall we make for Thebes? I seem to have lost my helmet, but I bet I can find another along the way."

"The bigger the better." Ophelos nodded. The four of them limped up the ancient stairs and through the inner chambers to blink at the morning sun cresting over the mountains.

"Will you accompany us?" Ophelos asked Kasra. "Thebes hates Athens far more than it ever did Persia."

She made a sour face. "I've had enough of cities to last a lifetime. Seek me out if you're ever in these mountains again."

"After the welcome we received this time?" Haemon frowned. "My feet shall remain firmly upon flat soil."

A few nods seemed inadequate to the task of bidding farewell after such a momentous battle, but there was little else to suffice, and dawn saw Damaris, Ophelos, and Haemon picking their way down the mountain trail toward Thebes.

"Keep your eyes sharp," Ophelos said in a tired voice. "It would be our luck to run across Athenian peltasts this close to home." Damaris snorted, thrusting his chin back at the mountains. "After that, I'd welcome a fight with honest soldiers."

Below, men moved across the valley. Little more than specks in the distance, Damaris couldn't tell if they were Athenians or Thebans. He wondered if this was how the gods saw all humanity, but put the thought out of his mind. It did no good to ruminate upon the divine. Damaris was a mercenary, after all.

The gods might be fickle, but silver never disappointed.

SUITS

Steve Lewis

Graves Farmstead, Tau Ceti IV

It was dark, about midnight, when something woke Henry Graves. He sat upright in his bed and looked around, hearing nothing but the gentle breathing of his wife, Beth. He contemplated getting out of bed to check the security grid in the next room... A few seconds later he had no choice; an alarm screeched out and woke everything within a mile.

He was out of bed and into the farmstead's security room in a heartbeat, the monitors flicking to life in response to whatever threats the remote ground and satellite sensors had picked up. He was hoping it was just cattle from his neighbour's property – Jenkins was renowned for being cheap with his fencing – but by the slowing spreading blooms of light on the screens it was clear this was something much worse.

"Hank, what is it?" Beth asked as she entered the room. "Jenkin's cows again?"

"Afraid not, honey," Graves replied. "Looks we have deebees coming in."

"Crap."

"Crap indeed, honey, crap indeed."

Tau Ceti IV had taken decades to colonise, and it was a few years after the planet had been successfully terraformed that the aliens had shown up. Coming through dimensional gateways on and just above the planet's surface, the 'Dimensionial Beings' – or deebees for short – had initially wreaked havoc amongst the unsuspecting colonists. If it wasn't for an armed cruiser passing through for R&R, with heavy screens, armoured hull and batteries of hot lasers, the planet would have been overrun.

The invasion was finally broken, the gateways closing

quickly and the deebees slaughtered with no line of retreat... now it was only a raid every few years, more a nuisance than anything else.

"Looks like a wide pattern," Beth said, looking over Graves' shoulder at the various screens. "Gates opening up all along the ridge and across most of the farmsteads."

Graves nodded. "They should be easy to mop up, scattered out like that," he said. "I'll go suit up, you get on the horn to Jenkins and the others, make sure they're up and armoured before the gates open completely."

He stood and kissed his wife on the forehead as she slid into the seat.

"Looks like we have about 30 minutes before they open enough to let them through, everyone should be ready and mobile by then," he said.

"Get suited while I make some calls," Beth replied. "Let me know if you need anything."

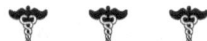

Graves's suit was built around the chassis of an old, four-armed agricultural exoskeleton. With an upgraded power plant, some welded armour and batteries of weapons added each year, *Brutiful* was a family heirloom passed down over the generations. Every farmstead had to have one, and the Graves' family took much pride in the effort they'd taken to maintain their deadly, hulking suit.

As *Brutiful* powered up, Graves got into his combat suit – a second-hand, naval-grade skin-suit, it provided a degree of life support, body armour and communications gear that made piloting the heavy exomech far less uncomfortable than it might otherwise have been. Plugged in and zipped up, he checked the ammunition drums and ran last minute diagnostics tests before strapping himself into the suit's cockpit.

"Beth, I'm in," he said as the heavy armoured glass canopy closed around him. "Systems green across the board, heading out now."

"You're showing green across the board here too, honey," Beth replied, coming through clearly over the suit radio. "Jenkins and the others are all suiting up, should be out before the gates open."

"Roger that," Graves said. "Anyone coordinating this?"

"Afraid not. All of them are interested in defending their own property first, and we'll coordinate a clean-up once the gates close and we can see what's left."

"Fair enough... shouldn't take us long, the gates being spread out like they are."

"And we don't want Jenkins trampling down our fences like he did last time he came over to help." They both laughed, though they hadn't been laughing at the weeks they'd had to spend repairing the downed fence-line and retrieve their roaming livestock.

"Where do you want me, honey?' Graves asked as *Brutiful* got underway and stomped out of the barn and into the night.

"It looks like a cluster of gates will open in the eastern quarter first, counting seven gates. After that, the next opening cluster is another five in the south."

"Eastern quarter it is, on my way."

Graves made good time, the heavy exomech eating up the miles at a rapid pace. With no threat, he set the autopilot and then cycled through his weapon and targeting systems to make sure everything was running smoothly – the diagnostics had indicated everything was green, but he'd long learned the value in checking everything twice, just in case.

By the time he got to the farmstead's eastern fields, some 15 miles away, the gates were beginning to sparkle, the bright inner light of an alien dimension shining through. It was a rare sight, but not one that Graves was overly interested in admiring. Like a lot of things in nature, beautiful also meant dangerous.

He halted his exomech where he could see all seven of the

gates – they were closely bunched – and swung the heavy chain-guns on his right shoulder down, ready for action. The 15mm multi-barrelled autocannons weren't his heaviest weapons, but they were dependable, hard hitting, and could deal with most deebees.

Besides, 15mm ammunition was cheap, and anything he fired came out of the farmstead's operating budget.

"Hank, honey," Beth said," I make the gates opening in three... two... one... now!"

On her mark, a swarm of deebees poured out of each gate, scattering around as they cleared the gate for the aliens follow-ing behind, and searching for a target. *Brutiful's* infra-red scanners picked them out in the darkness and automatically counted them. It had reached 80 by the time the gates' sparkle began to fade, and Graves decided he should open fire before they dispersed too much.

With a whir, the autocannon barrels began to spin, and as they reached their maximum rotation, he fired. Over 600 rounds per minute poured out of the 5-barrelled weapon, cutting into the creatures around the nearest gate.

The 15mm rounds were mostly copper-tipped hollow points, with every 5th round a steel-tipped armour-penetrating round, and every 20th round a tracer round that marked its flight in a glowing red arc – at 1,500 metres per second, they streaked across the landscape, lighting the night sky and easily punching through alien hide, flesh and bone.

His first burst cut down the group around the first gate, then he switched to the second. The deebees had reacted now and were spreading out as they charged towards him. He fired the autocannon in short bursts of 25-30 rounds, taking down the leading aliens as they closed, confident he could whittle them down enough before they got to him.

"Hank?" Beth asked. "Got time for an update?"

"Sure, honey," he replied, "but keep it brief, I got incoming."

"Okay. Jenkins, Anderson and Wright have deployed and engaged, they're all dealing with their own first clusters...Peters,

Donaldson and the Singhs are en route, but their gates are all over the place and they might need a hand with clean-up once we've got the main clusters dealt with."

"Okay," Graves said as he triggered off another burst that dropped a clump of half-dozen aliens as they cleared a fence-line 500 metres in front of him. "You sound like you're coordinating with the other wives. "

"I am," Beth replied. "We're trying to keep each other updated on the back channels, just in case there's a breakthrough somewhere."

"Good." Another burst, another clump falling apart under the autocannon fire. "I'm almost done with this group, moving south soon."

"Roger. Be careful, honey, the next group are bigger gates and they'll likely be fully deployed before you get there."

"Will do!" He triggered his last burst, splashing the last of the deebees across his eastern paddock and then turned the exomech south to deal with the next group.

The eastern paddocks were fallow this season, and if nothing else the alien corpses would make good fertiliser when he got around to ploughing them into the soil.

Wright Farmstead, Tau Ceti IV
Jake Wright hated his exomech and was pretty sure it hated him. *Carnigore* sounded ferocious, but the 'carni' wasn't named after a predator's eating habits – the suit was a built on a mobile amusement park ride, and the old red and white paint job made it look far more 'carnival' than he would have liked.

If maintaining the suit in its original condition hadn't been part of his old man's will, he'd have had it redone and renamed a decade ago.

"Jake," his wife said as he fired his own autocannon into the creatures moving towards him, "you need to get the lead out, that second cluster of gates is opening."

"Helen, I'm doing this as fast as I can," he said, gritting his teeth as he fired another burst. *Carnigore* wasn't a well-padded suit and he swore he felt every jolt of recoil through his bones. "Last group coming up now, I'll head to that second cluster in a moment."

"I hate to nag" she replied, though Jake didn't believe that for an instant, "but Graves and Jenkins have cleared their first gates and are already on route to their second."

"For Christ's sake, Helen, it's not a contest!"

"It never is with you Jake, it never is..."

Wright flicked the mute button on his communication piece and cursed, long and loud, as the last of the deebees died in front of him. He swung *Carnigore* south and headed towards the river, where the second cluster of gates was already opening. He threw in a few curses towards his exomech for good measure, bracing himself for every bump and jolt the insanely grinning suit was going to pass on to him.

Anderson Farmstead, Tau Ceti IV

'Crazy Bill' Anderson was the old man of the colony, a silver-haired widower in his 70s. He'd built his suit himself, turning an obsolete agricultural exomech into a formidable fighting machine. It was a blocky, hulking brute that lacked the sleek lines of newer suits, but he and his *Grampage* had weathered decade after decade of deebee raids without showing any signs of slowing down.

He'd dealt with the first cluster of gates easily enough and was perched on a low hill overlooking the slowing blooming forms of his second cluster. The three gates were very tightly bunched, much tighter than he'd ever seen before, and he waited patiently as they grew. Close-packed like that, the deebees would run out into a withering hail of fire, and he certainly had no problem with that.

Still, the sight bugged him. Gates were always spaced apart, likely to stop them interfering with each other. The energy required to cross the dimensional barrier was stupendous, even if the colonists didn't have a clue as to how it all worked. Anything might happen if the gates actually overlapped.

Graves Farmstead, Tau Ceti IV
"Hank, we have a problem."

"Talk to me Beth."

"The wormholes on the ridges, they're getting stronger."

"How strong?"

"Off-the-chart strong. The satellite view shows them growing every minute."

Brutiful was nearing the second cluster of gates, and in the distance Graves could see them spiralling closed. Whatever deebees had been using the gates had already been dropped off and were spreading out across his property.

"Keep an eye on them, honey, while I deal with this second group, and then I'll go take a look," he said. "And keep the others in the loop; I don't want any surprises coming our way when we get around to mopping up."

"Roger that," Beth replied. "I've got one of the crop-duster drones headed that way, should give us some eyes on the ridge in about ten minutes."

There was a sharp 'ping' as *Brutiful's* sensors picked up something moving his way – fast – and Graves zoomed his suit's cameras towards the motion.

A dozen deebees were headed right for him, and they were close.

"Okay Beth, I have some unwanted guests heading my way, need to focus a little," he said. "I'll let you know when I'm done here, but let me know if anything super-important happens."

"Will do, honey," Beth said. "Be careful."

The deebees swarming towards *Brutiful* were closing from a wide arc, too far spread for his autocannon to sweep them all.

He fired a few bursts at those on his right side anyway though, dropping three of them while he got himself ready.

His left-shoulder weapon was a heavy-barrelled, semi-automatic shotgun, if you could call a weapon with a 4″ bore a shotgun. Twin ammunition belts fed the beast, allowing Graves to fire either fin-stabilised slugs or heavy loads of 8-ounce buckshot. He thumbed the selector for buckshot and put away the autocannon as the aliens closed.

It always disturbed Graves that the deebees looked nothing alike. They were mostly four legged, or six, or occasionally eight; their heads were usually long-snouted, like dogs, though many were round-faced like great cats or sharp-beaked like birds; and their skin was typically thick hide, though many had feathers like soft down, or slabs of chitin that provided some slight armour protection. Some of them had combinations of all of these things, and Graves had long given up wondering how and why the deebees had evolved the way they had.

One thing they all did have in common though was a serious hatred of humans, and every deebee they'd ever seen wanted to do nothing but kill anything human within its reach.

Brutiful's shotgun aligned briefly on a deebee closing fast on the left, and coughed a swarm of tungsten balls...the creature was fast, dodging aside as the weapon spoke, but the spreading cloud of balls covered too large an area. Struck by three balls the creature went down, chest and head ruptured completely, the deebee's equivalent of blood gushing into the dirt.

The creatures continued to close, and Graves backed his exomech away slowly, sending out a cloud of tungsten every six seconds or so – it took that long for the belt to feed the next round, chamber it and align the heavy barrel onto the target. At a kill every six seconds, that was ten dead deebees a minute, but it was going to take them a bit less than that to get to him, and there were more than ten of them out there.

The first of the deebees launched itself at him, a four-legged beast that shimmered with the residual energy of the alien dimension. Its mouth opened wide, showing row after row of gleaming, serrated teeth, and Graves swung his suit's right arm to block it. More by luck than design, he managed to catch it in mid-air, and squeezed the creature as hard as his exomech could.

Trapped in the metal grip, the creature swung its hind legs down and began to rake, long claws gouging chunks of armour of *Brutiful's* thick torso. For a moment Graves thought the creature might get through, but then the suit's grip tightened and the creature exploded into a multi-coloured burst of flesh.

He didn't even see the other one coming. It was big, strong, and travelling at speed, and barrelled the heavy suit over like a man pushing over a child. *Brutiful's* gyro-stabilises shrieked in protest as they tried to correct the unexpected fall, but to no avail. With a loud thud, the exomech went down, the fall stunning Graves for a moment.

When he came to, the creature was on top of him, clawing and biting away at the glass canopy, only a foot or so from his face. The heavy glass was holding for now, but wouldn't for long...Graves needed to end this one quickly and get *Brutiful* back on its feet.

The creature was inside his reach, so his two heavy weapons would be useless. I Instead, he activated the cutting torch on the exomech's smaller right arm. With variable settings for welding or cutting through thick steel, the torch was a legacy of the suit's original purpose, and one he'd never gotten around to replacing.

Pushing the flame against the creatures hide brought a shriek of pain, which did nothing to reduce the creatures frenzied clawing on the glass canopy; in fact, it only seemed to make it worse. He couldn't quite bring the torch to bear on something that might prove vital, and he had to endure the creature's attacks for another 30 seconds before he finally managed to find something important. The creature gave one enormous spasm and then died.

Flicking off the torch, he pushed the creature off him and slowly struggled to rise. The exomech wasn't designed for agility, and it took him a good five minutes to finally get back on his feet. If there'd been any more aliens around, he'd have been dead for sure.

Sweating – the suit generated a lot of heat – he checked his scanners and toggled the radio.

"Honey?"

"Here Hank," Beth replied. "You okay?"

"Scratched up, a little bruised but otherwise okay. How's everything else look?"

"Honey, I think we might have a problem…"

Singh Farmstead, Tau Ceti IV

Unlike the other colonists that ran one small family unit per farmstead, the Singh family were a polygamous family collective that ran a farmstead twice the size of the others. Graves and the others figured there to be three distinct 'marriage arrangements' amongst the Singh farmstead, which gave them a requirement for three exomechs in accordance with the colony's laws.

Crescent Moon was piloted by Jaswant Singh, the elder of the family. Based on the chassis of an old construction suit, it was well suited for the slabs of thick armour and heavy weapons the Singh family had added to it over the years.

The other two suits were *Hawk* and *Eagle*, two much smaller exomechs based on warehousing droids. Fast and nimble, the two light units were built for close-quarters combat only, and spent most of their time keeping *Crescent Moon* clear of deebees so it could do all the long-range killing.

The three suits had cleared their first two clusters of gates, and were advancing on their third, *Hawk* and *Eagle* scouting ahead as *Crescent Moon* followed slowly along. Putting his suit on autopilot gave Jaswant time to update his tactical display from the various sensors around their property and from the satellite above. His update was showing some unusual activity, something he felt warranted caution.

"*Hawk, Eagle,*" he said into the radio, "hold on the next hill… something is amiss here."

"*Hawk* acknowledging," replied Agun, Jaswant's eldest son. "Hill clear, covering left flank."

"*Eagle* acknowledges," replied Kubai, his daughter's husband. "Will clear the peak in fifteen seconds, will cover the right flank."

The two smaller suits took up covering positions atop the hill as *Crescent Moon* trundled slowly up behind them.

"There's nothing here, brother," Agun said. "Should we push on to the next hill?"

"No," Jaswant said. "I need to assess the situation before we get too far from home."

"The place is barren," Kubai replied. "There's nothing to assess."

"Exactly... but there should be."

Jaswant's exomech drew level with the smaller units and looked over the flat, ploughed field below. The next hill was a mile away, and beyond that was the next cluster of gates, which should be opening any minute.

"Our initial reading showed six gates opening beyond that next hill... readings now show only four."

"Fewer gates are a good thing, isn't it?" Kubai asked.

"Gates never just disappear," Jaswant replied. "They open then they close. These ones haven't opened, yet two are missing."

"I don't understand," Agun said.

"Neither do I," Jaswant said, "But now sensors are showing only two."

Graves Farmstead, Tau Ceti IV
"Hank, the gates on top of the ridge are disappearing," Beth said. "Not opening, just disappearing, a few every minute or so."

"Do we have a visual on the ridgeline yet?" Graves replied. "Something might be messing up the sensors."

"I'm sorry, honey, something knocked the drone out." Beth said. "I've powered up another three and having them fitted with cameras now, should be airborne in a few minutes."

"Good thinking, honey. Anything else to report?"

"A little. Jenkins is shutting down his gates, but taking his time about it, and Crazy Bill Anderson wants to know if anyone needs his help…he seems to still have gates open on his property though."

"Jenkins is just taking his time so he won't have to help clear the ridgeline," Graves said with a chuckle, "and Crazy Bill wants to be able to claim ammunition and fuel from the Colony account for helping others."

"Other than that, the Singhs look like they have their area under control, as always, and the others are mopping up as they advance towards the ridge. Oh, and the drones are on their way."

Moments later, *Brutiful's* sensors picked up the flight of crop-dusting drones as they sped towards the ridgeline. As they passed, Beth switched the video feed over directly to the suit and Graves toggled between the three camera views.

At first there was nothing but the well-ploughed fields he expected to see. As the drones moved beyond his property the vegetation grew wilder, mostly tall trees. As the passed over the first growth of forest beyond his fence line, one of the cameras went out.

"Beth, what was that?"

"No idea, honey," Beth replied. "I'll go back over the video feed and check."

The drones were approaching the ridgeline now, and Graves toggled the controls to make them move in a more erratic manner. Even as he did, a second camera went out.

"Honey!"

"Working on it, Hank, working on it!"

The remaining camera made it to the ridgeline, Graves piloting this one manually now to be as erratic as he could make it. The sight wasn't a good one.

The gates *were* disappearing, in a manner of speaking. As Graves watched, two gates slowly expanded until their edges touched, and then they merged into one larger gate. All along the ridgeline, gates were coalescing, and at the rate they were merging they'd be one giant gate before too long.

"Beth, drop whatever you're doing and take a look at this!" he said, urgently. "Take in as much of it as you can, just in case I lose this drone."

There was a moment's silence and Graves could hear Beth's breathing quicken over the radio.

"Oh. My. God!"

"Patch this through to the others, and make sure Crazy Bill and the Singhs acknowledge...if anyone knows what this is about, it'll be one of them."

"Will do, honey!"

"And Beth?"

"Yes, dear?"

"It might be a good time to start powering up the Bunker."

Wright Farmstead, Tau Ceti IV

Carnigore had taken some scratches dealing with the first two gate clusters, but nothing significant. Jake was sure he'd been knocked around more than his exomech, and could feel bruises already forming where his skin had come into contact with hard metal. Not for the first time, he made a promise to himself to get a better combat suit and to put some padding around the cockpit.

He was approaching his third gate cluster, *Carnigore* set on autopilot as he transferred chain-gun ammunition from the bins on the suit's lower back to the internal hoppers.

"Jake?"

"What do you want, Helen?" he asked, annoyed at the interruption. "I'm kinda busy here."

"You'll be busy dodging deebees if you don't pay attention," Helen replied. "I have some video feed from the Graves'."

"Are Hank and Beth in trouble?"

Jake punched the autopilot's 'Off' button, bringing *Carnigore* to a lurching halt. Jake had a lot of time for the Graves family, despite Graves setting some impossibly high standards for Jake to live up to. If the two of them needed his help, things were very bad.

"I think we all might be," Helen replied, some real concern in her voice now. "Patching some video through to you now."

Jake watched the video feed, recognising the ridgeline that marked the southernmost boundary of the colony area. Deebees often had gates up there, giving them time to spread out and consolidate their numbers, but this was looking weird.

There were only three gates now, each enormous and slowly growing. The middle and left gates touched and merged, and then there were only two. Minutes later, the remaining gate was absorbed, leaving one giant gate that covered the entire ridgeline.

"What the hell is that?" he asked.

"I don't know, Jake," Helen replied, "but I'm sure it's not good."

"Any word from the others?"

"Jenkins says he's got gates of his own to worry about, but he'll help out when he deals with those. The Singhs are finishing up their final cluster and are sending some drones to keep an eye on things until they can get over here, and Crazy Bill is on his way to the Graves' farmstead right now."

"He's cleared his clusters already?"

"No, but he thinks this is more important. He's sending his kids over to the Graves' place now, Beth has their bunker powered up and plenty of room."

"You might want to join them."

"I'll be fine," Helen said. "Besides, you need me here to keep an eye on things while you wander around in your giant clown suit."

Jake bit back a curse; his wife always knew how to needle him.

"Suit yourself," he said, after a moment's pause to regain some control. "But if things get out of hand I want you to out of there and on your way to somewhere safe."

"Why Jake Wright, that's the sweetest thing you've said to me in years!"

Graves Farmstead, Tau Ceti IV

Beth ran quickly from the farmhouse control room to the metal and concrete monstrosity standing in the yard behind the house. Affectionately known as 'The Bunker', it was built to military specifications as a fortified command and control facility, a legacy of Graves' grandparents who had the foresight to see that the war with the deebees would last generations.

With its own internal fission pile, water tanks and food supplies, it could easily house a headquarter staff for three months. Add the communication links and self-defence turrets, it was looking like a good place to be right now.

The screens inside had already powered up, showing clearly the video feed from the last remaining drone, plus *Brutiful's* cameras, satellite imagery and live feeds from the various security cameras around the farmstead. She hit the safety switch as she ran inside, dropping the armoured concrete slab that passed for a door into position, and slipped into her own combat suit and command helmet.

"Hank? You reading me, honey?"

"Loud and clear, Beth, loud and clear," Graves replied. "How's it looking?"

"Not good at all. That one giant gate is giving off some ferocious readings, completely off the charts for even the Bunker's sensors."

"I don't have much fine detail on the drone camera," Graves said. "Anything I need to know?"

"I'm getting plenty of flicker, all along the gate, looks like it's ready to open."

"I'm not feeling to particularly happy about this one, Beth—"

The gate opened, and deebees poured out. The overhead satellite tracked their heat sources, counting them automatically, and Beth watched open-mouthed as the counter climbed rapidly. 100. 200. 400. 700. 1000… she tore her eyes from it when it reached four figures.

"Beth?"

"Hank, honey? GET THE HELL OUT OF THERE!"

She could see from *Brutiful's* video feed that it was now moving, walking backwards on autopilot. Graves was too good a pilot to just turn and run, he'd want to keep his guns between him and the enemy.

"Moving now," Graves said, quite calmly. "Where do you need me?"

"Anywhere but there, honey," Beth said. "The sensors are showing 3000 deebees and counting."

There was a moment of silence as that figure registered on Graves…the biggest raid in a generation had been less than 500, and that had stretched the colony to the limit. Many families died that day, and the colony still hadn't recovered.

"Beth, I need you to patch this through to the others, right now…we're going to need all of the exomechs together."

"All right, honey, I'm on it."

Jenkins farmstead, Tau Ceti IV

Keith Jenkins was having a bad day. He hated deebees with a passion…or rather, he hated that they made him have to do things he didn't want to do. He didn't want to be out of the farmhouse today, and certainly didn't want to be in his exomech having to fight.

The only saving grace was that *Shepherd*, once a medium-sized agricultural exomech, was refitted over the years to be big on comfort and big on speed, so he could wander around his farmstead and avoid fighting if he could. Any fool can fight, why be uncomfortable about it?

Shepherd's main armament was a long-ranged, three-barrelled autocannon, firing high-velocity 35mm slugs in three-round bursts. The long barrels severely affected the exomech's centre of gravity, so he had to stand still to fire, but the long range meant that he could deal with deebees from ranges well beyond anything his fellow farmsteaders could match.

Right now he was in a standing in a clump of trees on a hill, taking pot shots at a group of deebees milling around his second cluster of gates a mile and a half away. At this range accuracy wasn't great, but he was getting hits every third burst or so, and the deebees still hadn't worked out where the shots were coming from.

The crackling of his suit's video-comm interrupted as his wife, Jessie, came on-screen.

"Keith, I have an update from the Graves'," she said. "Things are going pear-shaped on the ridgeline, they need you to get down there right now."

"Tell them I'm busy, got problems of my own," he replied, firing another burst. He fist-pumped as he saw at least one of the heavy tungsten rounds strike one of the aliens, splashing it across the soil.

"I think they're serious, Keith," Jessie said. "Most of the others have acknowledged and are already on their way."

"They've dealt with all their clusters already?"

"Nope, leaving them as they are," Jessie replied. "That's what makes me think this is serious."

"Any word from Crazy Bill?"

"Oh, plenty of words from him…mostly to tell you what he's going to do to you if you don't get your arse into gear and join up with the others. Assuming you survive of course."

Jenkins sighed. Crazy Bill was just that. Crazy. And he hated to have to listen to him. Everything 'back then' was bigger, tougher and harder than it was now, and he traded on his age to influence the others. Since when was being old a substitute for being right?

"Tell them I'm engaged right now, will head over as soon as possible," he said. "I've got some suit trouble, don't think I can disengage safely, so I'll have to fight my way clear."

"You have suit trouble? I'm not seeing anything on *Shepherd's* feed."

"No, the suits fine… though they don't need to know that." He fired another burst, missing completely.

"Keith," Jessie said with a sigh, "this looks serious. You might want to consider doing the right thing, just this once."

"You're right," he replied. "I'll consider it."

Peters Farmstead, Tau Ceti IV

Carl Peters hardly knew what hit him. He'd had three clusters of gates on his property, and had cleared them out with minimal bother. His exomech, *Hamfisted*, was a dependable suit with solid armour and reliable weapons, and the deebees hadn't posed much of a threat. The smallest of the farmsteads, squeezed between the southern ridgeline and the Toolong River, his clusters were relatively close, so it didn't take him much time to find and destroy the deebees coming out of his gates.

One minute the screens were clear, then suddenly there was a wall of deebees headed his way. *Hamfisted's* sensors counted what they saw, and Peters stood in shock for valuable seconds as the numbers registered, but it was too late for him to have done anything with those seconds.

He brought *Hamfisted's* chainguns down, firing bursts on his maximum rate of fire, carving swaths through the creatures as they closed. High-speed tungsten carved through alien bodies, but still they came.

So swift was the deebee assault that he didn't have time to get a shot off from any of his other weapons… the wall crashed over him, knocking *Hamfisted* to the ground, stunning him for a moment. Something in the swarm was strong enough to drive an armour-piercing claw all the way through his armoured glass canopy and into his chest, and he died without even a scream.

Or a chance to say goodbye to his wife, who watched the whole thing through *Hamfisted's* video feed.

Donaldson Farmstead, Tau Ceti IV

'Angry' Andy Donaldson was the second to die. His exomech, *Mariner*, was an old combat droid his grandfather had bought and refitted fifty years ago, heavily built with military-grade weapons, it was the family pride and joy.

It was also expensive, and building it and keeping it running had almost bankrupted the family. The other farmsteaders had long forgotten where he'd picked up his nickname, but they all assumed he was still angry at his grandfather for lumbering him with a white elephant of exomechs.

The Donaldson farmstead was also south, much bigger than the adjacent Peters' property, and he'd had two clusters to deal with. His primary weapon was a ridiculously expensive battle laser, firing 3" diameter beams that vaporised almost anything they struck. Designed to fight other heavily armoured units, it was a massive overkill against anything unarmoured, and Donaldson hated it.

The wave of deebees that swept over Peters now came for him, and he knew he'd never make it to anywhere safe. He planted himself on top of a low ridge, giving himself a good field of fire, readied his weapons and began firing.

His laser took time to recharge, and spat a beam of death every four seconds, with enough energy to punch right through the first deebee it struck and go on to the next. From his elevated position, a good shot could kill three or four of them before it dug into the ground. It was effective, but not against a swarm that size.

He wasn't going to make it, and he knew it… time to call his wife.

"Sarah, you there?"

"Yes, Andy, I'm here," Sarah replied.

"I need you to grab your things and get over the Graves' place, get yourself into their bunker."

"Okay," she said, "swing by and pick me up."

"Not this time, Sarah, not this time."

He knew she could see his video feed, could see the wide wall of aliens bearing down on him rapidly, and knew that she knew how this was going to end.

"Andy?"

"Just go!"

"I can't just leave you…"

"Yes you can! Don't make me do this for nothing." He lowered his secondary weapons now, a 4" cannon firing high-explosive rounds, and began targeting tight clumps of aliens with it. He could hardly miss.

Sarah was crying openly now.

"Sarah… say goodbye now, while we still can, then get out."

"Andy… I love you."

"And I love you too." He had the luxury of the battle to keep his emotions in check, but it was all he could do to keep from crying himself.

"Goodbye, Sarah."

He cut the video feed, knowing that she'd stay there as long as she could while he was alive. He knew he was going to die, but wanted her to have as much time as possible to get to the Graves' bunker.

Both weapons were firing now, as fast as they could, and he cut the safety overrides on both to keep their rate up. He knew he was burning out his laser and would soon warp the cannon barrel, but didn't expect it to be a problem for much longer.

At 100 meters, the laser stopped firing, overheated.

At 50 meters, the warped cannon barrel caused a misfeed and jammed.

At 20 meters, he managed to get his close range weapons into action, a pair of 10mm machine guns and a small flame-thrower. The machine guns cut a handful down as they closed, but without the instant-kill of the bigger weapons, the ones he hit just provided mobile armour for the ones behind for a few seconds, which was all it took.

Something from his left struck *Mariner* and knocked him down, and then a swarm of deebees was over him, gouging his armour and looking to get at the human inside. His armour was solid, very solid in fact, but he knew it was a matter of time before something gave.

He had the machine guns on automatic now, but they weren't protected by armour and lasted a few seconds before a deebee claw cut through the metal and put them out of action.

The flamethrower lasted longer, burning anything on his right side to a cinder. It was well protected, housed within *Mariner's* left arm, but a deebee must have sliced deep enough to cut the fuel intake... the flame sputtered and then went out as flamer fuel gushed all around him.

Weaponless now, he could do nothing but thrash around with his armoured fists and feet. They took a toll as well, crushing alien bodies with each solid blow, but the press of creatures above him made it harder and harder to get a decent strike in.

Suddenly, a warning light flickered on. He barely had time to recognise it – something had carved deep into his right arm, striking the laser housing and shorting the small fusion pile – when a spark ignited the flamer fuel pooling around the prone exomech. The explosion was small, but that detonated the unspent high explosive rounds still in his ammunition drums, and that in turn breached the fusion containment cell.

The resulting explosion killed hundreds of deebees, scattering them around the farmstead in shattered chunks. But in a swarm of thousands, it mattered very little indeed.

Graves Farmstead, Tau Ceti IV
Graves stood on a low, wide hill, and looked around.

Brutiful was in the centre of a line of exomechs, with *Carnigore* on his right and *Grampage* on his left. It wasn't much against a horde of killer aliens, but it was the best they could do.

"Hank, honey?" Beth said over the combined command net.

"Here, Beth."

"The Singhs are on their way in, but they'll be a while, and Jenkins is reporting suit damage, not sure when or even if he can get here."

"Suit damage my arse," Crazy Bill said. "He's either chicken-shit lazy or chicken-shit scared."

"Either way, we can't rely on him, so it's just the three of us for now," Graves said. "If we can hold out until the Singhs get here, we might have a chance."

"We could always hole up in your bunker," Wright said. "Plenty of room down there for everyone."

"We'd have to come out eventually," Crazy Bill replied. "Our best chance for the colony is for the exomechs to deal with them now, while we've got them in a bunch."

"I agree," Graves said. "We kill what we can here then fight as we fall back to the Bunker. That should slow them down a little at least."

"The command and control suite has some suggestions for fall-back routes, honey," Beth said. "I'm sending data now for your autopilots."

Brutiful beeped as the data came in, and Graves quickly looked over it before setting it up as his autopilot program.

"Got it, Beth, thanks," he said, as both Wright and Crazy Bill acknowledged receipt of their information packets.

"I have all our drones fitted with cameras now, and Helen Wright has sent hers in as well," Beth continued. "We should have plenty of real-time video coming in, and I'll punch it through as you need it."

"What's the satellite showing?" Wright asked.

"Nothing good," Beth replied. "There's a wall of deebees coming your way, should be in sight in a few minutes, and there are some gates still yet to open."

"Any sight of Peters or Donaldson?" Graves asked. There was a long pause before Beth replied.

"Nothing on the sensors, nothing on satellite, and I can't raise anyone on the radio."

"That's not good."

"No it's not," Beth continued. "And that swarm headed your way would have swept right over their farmsteads."

There was silence as the three men made last minute preparations for the onslaught to come.

Singh Farmstead, Tau Ceti IV

Jaswant Singh stood atop a steep cliff, his *Crescent Moon* raining death into the valley below him. His exomech's main armaments were a pair of long-range 3" cannon on the right arm and a heavy rocket launcher on the left. The cannons each spat out high-explosive shells every six seconds, giving him one round every three, and amidst the swarm of deebees headed his way the bursting charges and their tungsten shrapnel were leaving great gaps in the alien ranks.

The rocket launcher was a box-shaped, 6-tube weapon, capable of firing single rockets or volleys of six. It wasn't as accurate as the cannon, but didn't need to be – a volley of six rockets had enough scatter and burst to fill quite a large area with shrapnel, and close enough was good enough when it came to big explosions.

Its only problem was that it was slow to reload, and he was getting a volley away every five minutes.

Below him, midway up the hill, *Eagle* and *Hawk* waited, both pilots nervous as they watched the swarm approach. Their weapons lacked the long range of *Crescent Moon*, but were lethal at close range… how lethal, and how quickly they could kill swarming deebees in these numbers, was about to be tested.

The aliens were now 50 metres from the base of the hill, and *Crescent Moon* had time for one last volley of rockets before the creatures were too close for Jaswant to use his heavy weapons. All he could do now was pick off the creatures following behind, and hope the other exomechs could handle the rest.

As the deebees closed, *Hawk* and *Eagle* opened fire. Both

arms mounted a pair of linked 15mm machines guns, capable of firing over 800 rounds per minute each and loaded with a mix of solid tungsten slugs and hollowpoint rounds. Each arm could fire independently, and the wall of tungsten that they spread before them stopped the first ranks of the swarm dead in their tracks.

The next waves met the same fate, but as each creature fell it created a small wall for the ones behind. Both exomechs walked slowly backwards up the hill as the wall grew, hoping to maintain some elevation so they could shoot at the creatures massing behind it.

From around both edges of the wall, however, more creatures swarmed, and *Eagle* and *Hawk* turned to face the new threat.

Hawk's heavy weapon was a pair of semi-automatic mortars that fired over the exomech's shoulder. They only had a range of 50 metres, but were able to empty their 5-round clips in a matter of seconds, generating enough firepower to devastate a large target almost instantly.

Agun Singh stomped the foot pedal for his mortars, emptying the clip at the approaching swarm. The mortars were set to target 40 metres away initially, then increase a few metres for each successive shot... the first three rounds from each mortar, all high-explosive, flattened the incoming wave, while the fourth rounds airburst and scattered shards of white phosphorous around.

The creatures beneath the white-hot halo burned as the hot phosphorous dug into the skin. Some collapsed instantly, the shards deep enough to cook them from the inside, but the rest kept coming, despite their horrible wounds.

The fifth rounds were napalm, splashing across the side of the hill and covering anything it touched with intense flame. Very few creatures made it through, and Agun dispatched those that did with tightly controlled burst from *Eagle's* twin machine guns.

Behind him, Kubai deployed *Eagle's* own heavy weapons, a pair of flamethrowers, one over each shoulder. Unlike the smaller flamethrowers on other exomechs, these were military grade, emitting white-hot jets of plasma that incinerated anything they touched. His approach was to let the creatures approach to within 20 metres and then spray them all with gouts of plasma.

They died by the dozens, the dead providing no cover at all as they turned to ash under the incredible heat. *Eagle's* canopy darkened to protect him from the intense glare, which made Kubai blind to what was happening in front of him.

He toggled the camera feed, tapping into *Crescent Moon's* video to get a third-party view of the battle, and adjusted his flame jets to deal with a group that were trying to flank him. They never made it, though the last of them was a charred corpse only a metre or so away.

Jaswant had reloaded his rocket pack now and looked for a target worth expending the high-explosive six-pack on...there was nothing as yet, so he used his time to fire cannon shells into small groups of deebees that were trying to push their way through or over the wall of corpses *Hawk* and *Eagle* had made with their machine guns.

Using his command suite, he checked the ammunition states of his small force. Everything was getting low, and he knew it was going to be close. Soon, the plasma jets would be out of fuel and the machine gun hoppers would be empty, and then they'd be in serious trouble.

Suddenly, it was over. The flank attacks proving futile, the remaining deebees swarmed directly up the hill, clumping together to push through the wall of their dead. It took Jaswant a second to align his rocket pack and fire, and the swarm disappeared as the volley of six rockets detonated amongst them.

The three men sat in their exomechs for a moment, happy to be still alive after the onslaught, and then it was back to the business at hand.

"*Hawk, Eagle*, report," Jaswant said quietly.

"*Hawk* intact," Agun replied. "Heavy weapons empty, gun ammunition at five percent."

"*Eagle* intact," Kubai added. "Plasma gone, gun ammunition at nine percent."

"And *Crescent Moon* intact," Jaswant said. "Rockets gone, six rounds of cannon left."

"We're in no state to fight, father," Agun said. "We don't have enough ammunition to fight through to the Graves' farmstead."

"I concur," Jaswant replied. "Let's head for home."

Toolong River/Donaldson Farmstead, Tau Ceti IV

Sarah Donaldson was still in tears as she left the farmhouse she and her dead husband had turned into a home. She wanted to race to the battle, hoping beyond all hope that Andy was somehow still alive, but she knew it was less than futile…it would be suicide. Andy hadn't been able to stay alive in *Mariner*, she'd have no chance in anything less than a fully-armed exomech.

Racing into the shed, she wheeled out a powerful motorcycle, one of the pair that was always kept fully charged for emergencies. Stuffing her overnight bags into the vehicle's panniers, she climbed aboard and thumbed the starter switch, kicking the electric motor into life.

She had visited the Graves' place regularly, and swung the rapidly accelerating bike onto the dirt road that ran towards the neighbouring farmstead, paralleling the Toolong River. She and Andy had always joked about the name, inherited from the initial survey report a century ago, and this time it really did seem 'too long'.

Ahead was the concrete bridge that Andy's grandfather had built, the old Donaldson crest on all four of the concrete support pillars. As she approached the bridge her eyes misted over again, thinking about grandchildren of her own that she and Andy would never have.

Lost in her thoughts, she didn't notice the rippling surface of the water or the sparkling gleam of alien bodies as they rose from the depths.

Three deebees leapt out of the river just as she pulled onto the bridge, knocking her from the bike and sending her sprawling into one of the concrete pillars. Even if she'd been wearing a helmet, the impact would still have knocked her out and it would have done her no good at all as a swarm of deebees burst out of the river and tore her body to pieces.

She died not even knowing that she was pregnant with Andy's child.

Graves Farmstead, Tau Ceti IV

The three exomechs held the line as best they could, using their long-range guns to slow down the advancing horde as they slowly retreated along the line of hills. Ammunition was quickly becoming an issue though, and they all knew they had fewer rounds than there were deebees.

"Hank, honey?" Beth cut in over the radio.

"Kinda busy, Beth," Graves replied. "Unless you got news worth hearing, I don't have much time to chat."

"I got news, some good, some bad."

"Start with the good," Crazy Bill cut in, "I think we could all use some cheering up right now."

"Okay," Beth said. "Helen has re-routed some of her drones your way, carrying ammunition drums. "

"That *is* good news, honey," Graves said. "I'll be throwing rocks at them if this lasts much longer."

"The drones can't reload for you, only drop the drums close by."

"That's fine, honey, drop them close, we'll do the rest."

The three pilots switched to manual control and drew closer together as their sensors picked up the incoming drones. There were six, two each, and they were coming in slow and low... clearly, Helen had loaded them with as much as they could bear.

Which was good, they were going to need it all.

"Jake, how's your ammo state?" Graves asked.

"Almost out of everything that matters," Wright replied. "I got some close-in stuff left, but was really hoping not to need it."

"Okay, you reload first, Crazy Bill and I will cover you."

"Roger that!"

"And get the lead out," Crazy Bill added. "I'm down to my last rounds as well."

Carnigore fell out of the line, leaving *Brutiful* and *Grampage* to face the horde. Two drones passed over him, dropping heavy drum canisters into the soft ground within a few metres…one struck a rock and burst open, scattering autocannon ammunition everywhere, but the other canisters stayed intact.

One of *Carnigore's* saving graces, as he was just learning, was that it had much nimbler hands than your typical exomech. It was relatively easy to pick up a canister, eject an empty one, and reload the canister directly into the waiting drum feeder. 'Relatively' still meant that it took him minutes however, and he was out of battle during a time when mere seconds were critical.

Graves was very aware of his rapidly diminishing ammunition supply, and was firing controlled burst of 2-3 rounds each. It was never going to make a dint in the oncoming horde, but killing those in the lead would buy them some time… no idea what for, but maybe the Singh's would get there in time to rescue the wives and children locked into the Bunker.

Crazy Bill was firing constantly, preferring his own heavy cannon over his lighter autocannon. The high explosive rounds tore clumps out of the enemy and caused some confusion, which helped slow them down a little. Not enough, but everything helped.

"Hank," he said over the firing, "something just occurred to me."

"What's that Bill?" Graves replied, simultaneously firing a burst from his over-sized shotgun into a clump that was just begging to have a spray of tungsten sent its way. "You leave the gas on?"

"No," Crazy Bill said, chuckling loudly. "That wife of yours, she never gave us the bad news."

"You're right," Graves said. "Beth, honey? You got something else for us?"

"The bad news? You want it now?"

"Sure! What could possibly make anything worse?"

There was a pause, and Graves could hear his wife's sharp intake of breath.

"It's the giant gate on the ridgeline... it's still open."

The three men in the exomechs paused a moment as that sunk in. Gates always closed after they'd dropped off their load of deebees. *Always.*

"Well, shit!" Wright said, trying to push the last of his reload canisters into place.

"And then some," Crazy Bill added.

Singh Farmstead, Tau Ceti IV

The three exomechs stood open, family members working quickly to repair and reload them as best as they could, while the three pilots stood around the tactical display in the farmhouse's security room. The picture looked grim, and they doubted that Graves and the others would last much longer.

"If we move quickly," Agun said, "*Hawk* and *Eagle* might get there in time to be of some help."

Jaswant shook his head. "You'd need *Crescent Moon* to support you, you don't have the firepower to make much of a difference."

"We could give them close defence like we do for you, keep the deebees clear while they clean them out."

"Good idea, brother," Kubai said, "but that would leave *Crescent Moon* without support."

"Someone needs to stay here and guard the families."

That brought a frown from Jaswant, one that silenced his son. "If Graves and the others fall, there's no point guarding anything else." He pointed to the satellite images of deebees pouring towards the distant farmstead. "The colony lives or dies at the Graves farmstead."

"What do we do, father?" Agun asked.

"The best we can my son, the best we can."

Graves Farmstead, Tau Ceti IV

Brutiful's autocannon whirred and clicked as they finally ran out of ammunition. He was down to his last three shotgun rounds and then he'd be useless until the deebees got into close range, and by then it would be all over.

"Hank!" Wright's voice cut over the radio. "I'm reloaded, you're up!"

Carnigore stepped beside him, its clown-face a garish red grin as it opened fire on the aliens. Wright had no concerns at all about ammunition now and was firing it as fast as he could – there were certainly plenty of targets for everything he had to throw at them.

Graves stepped back out of the line and moved quickly to the clump of ammunition canisters the drones had dropped off for him. *Brutiful* was a large exomech, with lots of ammunition storage and he knew it was going to take him a while to get completely reloaded.

"Crap," Crazy Bill cut in, "I'm out too, nothing but close-in guns and my fists!"

"I can hold them," Wright replied, "But you'll need to be quick!"

"Bill, grab your canisters, make for the next hill," Graves said. "We'll cover you, you reload up there and cover us as we move back."

"Roger that!" Crazy Bill picked up his ammunition drums and ran for the next hilltop as fast as *Grampage's* servo-motors would go.

Graves could hear the sounds of firing behind him as he reloaded.

"Hank!" Wright yelled over the radio, "I need you real bad!"

Graves picked up the remaining canisters on *Brutiful's* lower arms and turned back to the line, his heavy shoulder-weapons coming back down, as reloaded as they were going to be.

The swarm was only a few hundred yards away now, and the exomech sensors still showed thousands of creatures out there. True, they could see the swarm was smaller than it was before, but they both knew it wasn't going to be enough.

Graves started firing, autocannon on maximum rate, shotgun blasting out a spread of tungsten as soon it chambered another round. Beside him, *Carnigore* matched him round for round, and the slaughter amongst the deebees was incredible.

But not enough.

"Hank," Wright's voice came through on a private direct channel. "I don't think we're going to make it."

Graves knew he wasn't wrong, but really didn't want to admit it.

"I know," he said softly, "but we'll go down swinging, give the Singhs and the others as best chance we can."

"I guess we will," Wright said, triggering another burst. "I just hope it counts for something."

The two men were silent for a long time, firing rapidly and switching fire to deal with the targets that presented the greatest threat.

"Hank, honey!" Beth's voice cut through urgently, "I need you to both get off the hill, and now!"

"What?"

"Don't argue, just get the hell off there!"

Graves shrugged and powered *Brutiful* off the hill as fast as he could, and a moment later he saw *Carnigore* do the same, with the front ranks of deebees only a dozen or so metres behind and closing.

His suit sensors pinged as they picked up a flight of something coming in fast and low, and he instinctively ducked as something flew overhead. He'd barely made it half-way down the slope when there was an explosion on the other side of the hill, powerful enough to knock both *Carnigore* and *Brutiful* off their feet and send them tumbling down the hill.

Southern Ridgeline/Jenkins Farmstead, Tau Ceti IV

Jenkins day just wasn't getting any better. Jessie was sending him the video and satellite feeds and he knew the colony was well and truly screwed over. There was a small chance Graves and the others could hold the deebees back, and he wanted to still be alive when the battle was over, but sitting back and watching wasn't going to help anybody, including him.

"Keith, I'm picking up movement on the ridgeline," Jessie said. "Big biomass, headed towards Graves' place."

"Well, that's them screwed then," he replied. "Might be best if you start packing some things Jessie and we take our chances in the wild until the next ship arrives."

"Might not be so bad, Keith… that big swarm of deebees isn't showing up on the satellite at all!"

"What now? That son of a bitch Graves took out an entire swarm by himself?"

"No idea," Jessie replied. "Might be worthwhile getting over there though, just in case."

"Good idea, Jessie," Jenkins said. "There should be plenty to claim from the colony account after this."

Turning *Shepherd* southward, he started mentally calculating the claims he was going to be putting in for his defence of the colony… and very, very inflated claims they would be.

Graves Farmstead, Tau Ceti IV

Shaken, Graves struggled to get his exomech back on its feet, but whatever had knocked him down must have had enough force to throw *Brutiful's* gyros out of alignment.

He noticed the ringing in his ears only when he started to get his hearing back, and only when that died down did he hear Beth calling out for him over the radio.

"Hank! Hank! Do you read me?" Her voice was frantic, and Graves had no idea how long he'd been out.

"I'm here, honey," he replied. "Quit yelling and tell me what the hell just happened."

"Oh, Hank, honey!" she said, the relief evident in her voice. "I thought I'd lost you!"

"Nope, still here... what did I miss?"

"You missed a lot! The Singhs came through, the smaller gates are all closed and the two Singh boys are on their way over, should be at the bunker within twenty."

"Just the boys?" Graves asked. "Jaswant didn't make it?"

"Jaswant's fine!" Beth replied. "They stripped the fusion cell out of *Crescent Moon* and sent it in on a drone, rigged to detonate on command."

Graves paused as that sank in... fusion cells were expensive and temperamental, and it would have been fast and risky work to take one out of an exomech and rig it to a crop-dusting drone.

No wonder Beth had wanted him off that hill in a hurry!

"Wait... the Singh's just nuked my back yard?"

"Honey!"

"We'll talk about it later, Beth," he said. "Right now, I need an update on everything else."

"I can't give it to you, honey," Beth replied. "The blast's EMP took out our sensors and all the drones, and our satellite link is going to be down until you get back and fix it."

"Okay... I'll look around here and let you know what's going on."

"Roger that... I'll get this place sorted out and see to the families I have here."

He had to shut down and then reboot the gyros before he could stand up, and then he turned and went back to the top of the hill. The place was a mess.

On the fields below, the deebee swarm was now ash, turned to scorched dust by the force and heat of a fusion explosion. It would take him years to deal with the radiation, and he might have to move to maintain enough land to make a viable homestead, but he was glad to be alive.

He was saddened, however, at the sight of *Carnigore*, lying shattered and twisted at the base of the hill. The blast must have picked the exomech up and hurled it down the slope, and looking at the torn armour the following wave of radiation must have cooked Wright inside his suit.

Hopefully, he'd have been unconscious when the wave hit and he'd died quickly.

There was movement behind him, and he turned to see *Grampage* moving towards him. The exomech waved at him, then the right arm carefully tapped the suit's head, indicating radio failure. *Grampage* would have been well protected from the explosion, but high up on the next hill it would have been quite vulnerable to the EMP.

Crazy Bill came closer, and Graves could see through the armoured glass canopy that he was waving a hand-held radio at him. The hand-helds were standard equipment for all colonists, and it took Graves only a moment to unclip his.

"You okay old-timer?" he asked, smiling to take the sting out of his words.

"Never been better," Crazy Bill replied. "You got a lot of dead deebees on your land, Hank, going to be good fertiliser come next summer."

"Summer in about 300 years you mean," Graves said, "after the radiation dies down."

He could see Crazy Bill laughing at him.

"Don't be foolish, Hank, the deebees will absorb that radiation as they break down."

"Really?"

Crazy Bill was nodding now.

Suddenly, there was an almighty roar, loud enough to shake them both through their armoured exomechs. Looking around, Graves saw a creature that even his worst nightmares wouldn't have thrown at him.

It was a deebee, but like nothing of them had ever seen before. His visual sensors were out, but it towered over the trees it was brushing easily aside, and must have stood at least 30 metres tall at the shoulder. Graves counted six clawed legs, could see from the sheen that it was chitin armoured, and the snout was fanged like a hungry cat.

"What... on... earth... is ... that?" was all he could mutter.

"That," Crazy Bill replied, "is as good a reason as you'll ever need to run the hell back to your bunker."

Nodding, Graves turned his exomech and moved as fast as he could back to his farmstead.

Graves Farmstead, the Bunker, Tau Ceti IV
By the time Graves and Crazy Bill got back to the Bunker, the two light Singh exomechs had arrived, and Beth and Helen were out chatting to the two men. Beth waved happily when Graves arrived, but stopped waving when she saw the state of *Brutiful* and the urgency on her husband's face.

"Hank, honey, what is it?"

"Deebee coming, get back in the Bunker!"

"How many?" Agun asked, strapping himself back into his harness.

"Just one, son," Crazy Bill replied, "just one."

Agun and Kubai frowned as they sealed their exomechs and powered up their sensors – they'd known when the fusion cell was due to detonate and had shut down their systems to avoid the worst of the EMP – but they weren't making much sense of the readings.

"My sensors must be fried," Kubai said.

"Mine too," Agun added. "I'm picking up one signature, of enormous mass."

"There's nothing wrong with your sensors," Graves said. "Just the one, and it's the size of a deep-space shuttle."

The creature appeared at that moment, towering over the trees, and Beth and Helen both ran for the safety of the Bunker. Moving at great speed, the deebee headed towards them and Graves barely had enough time to reload the last of his ammunition canisters before the thing broke through the electric fence surrounding the farmstead. Built to keep out cattle, it barely registered on the behemoth above them.

The Bunker was equipped with a pair of 200mm cannon, capable of firing both high-explosive and anti-armour rounds. The ammunition hoppers were always filled with high-explosive, and Beth was firing them at the rapid rate, hoping to bring the creature down under a hail of fire. Against the thick chitin armour, however, the rounds did nothing.

Brutiful's autocannon had much the same effect, bouncing harmlessly off or exploding on impact without troubling the creature at all. He didn't even bother firing the shotgun, knowing the lower-velocity rounds would do nothing.

The Singhs charged in, *Hawk* and *Eagle* moving swiftly around the creature, firing their machine guns hoping to find a weak spot. The creature didn't appear to have any, and the rounds did little more than distract it.

Kubai's flamethrowers did little better, managing to infuriate it, and the creature reared up on its four hind legs and brought its fore-paws crashing down…

Both of the lighter exomechs managed to dodge, though only just.

The Bunker's twin cannon were still firing, and still having no effect at all.

"Beth," Graves said as he moved *Brutiful* around to the giant deebee's right side, "quit wasting the hi-ex. I need you to unload as fast as you can and reload with the anti-armour rounds."

"Hank, honey," Beth replied, "what do you think I'm doing?"

Graves conceded that she had a point… unloading manually would have taken much longer than just firing it all off.

"Okay," he said. "Let me know when you've got a few anti-armour rounds loaded, we'll try to keep the thing off the bunker until you do."

"Roger that!"

Eagle and *Hawk* were running between the creature's legs now, still firing, and it didn't seem to like it much. It reared up again, this time on its rearmost pair of legs, and brought its whole body down.

This time *Eagle* wasn't so lucky, and a descending claw caught it and pressed it to the ground. The giant head came around, jaws open, and then the creature's teeth crushed and tore into the exomech and the pilot within. Graves winced as he heard Agun's screams, and then there was silence.

"Brother!" Kubai yelled, and darted forward to avenge his fallen kinsman. The creature was grinding the suit between its teeth, shredding the armour and Agun's remains. Ignoring his other weapons, Kubai slammed *Hawk* directly into the deebee's head, using the suit's armoured shoulders as a battering ram.

The impact was incredible, and Graves saw teeth fly out of the mouth as the creature sagged for a moment, and Kubai took the opportunity to slam *Hawk's* fists into the creature's head, massive roundhouse blows with power and weight behind them that only an exomech could generate.

The creature's exoskeletal armour began to break apart, and Kubai dug his suit's hands deep into a crack and heaved… Armour pulled away, revealing bright pink and yellow flesh beneath. He shoved his right arm into the hole and fired a burst from his twin machine guns, digging deep as the rounds finally punched into something vital.

The creature roared in agony and lifted its body, dragging *Hawk* with it. Kubai used his left arm to hang on and continued firing as the creature shook his head frantically in an effort to dislodge him.

"Hank, honey!" Beth cut in. "I have six anti-armour rounds loaded, ready to fire!"

"Roger that," Graves replied. "Kubai, drop clear!"

"Negative, Henry Graves," Kubai said. "You know the saying about riding the tiger."

Graves did indeed – there was no getting off once you started.

"Beth, Kubai can't get clear… I'll try to turn it so you can get a clean shot."

"Negative again," Kubai said. "Beth Graves, take your shot now, while I have it distracted."

"Hank, honey?"

"He's right, Beth, take the shot. Try to aim low, and be sure not to miss."

Graves watched as the twin cannon slewed around and then dropped, aiming right for the creature's chest, and fired three rounds from each barrel. At that range, they couldn't miss.

The anti-tank rounds were a tungsten slug with a hollow charge, that turned into a shaped charge on impact…striking the creature, they formed and detonated, with enough heat to melt the tungsten and fire it at supersonic speeds into the target. The six rounds struck in quick succession, each a metre or so apart, and the resultant explosions turned the creature's torso to pulp.

It rose up in its death throes and thrashed around uncontrollably… Kubai couldn't maintain his grip and *Hawk* fell, landing heavily on its back, only to have the creature fall on top of him, its sheer weight crushing the exomech and cracking open plates of armour.

And then it died.

Graves Farmstead, Tau Ceti, IV, Aftermath
Graves, Jaswant Singh, Crazy Bill and Keith Jenkins stood outside the Bunker as the other colonists cleaned up the mess, which included cutting up and dragging away the corpse of the giant deebee.

With a lot of families dead, there'd be room for more colonists. The Donaldsons were gone, so their farmstead was vacant land, and Peters' wife and family had decided to leave Tau Ceti and head home to Earth, which freed up that land as well.

They managed to drag Kubai Singh out of his exomech's wreckage… he was still alive, but had lost both legs and an arm, and would require expensive prosthetics, which the Colony account would happily pay. Likewise, replacement exomechs for the Singhs, who had lost all three of their suits, would come from the Colony account.

Jenkins had put in claims for damages and repairs that they all knew were ridiculous, but no-one had the energy to argue – he'd survived, that counted for something, and they needed everyone to move forward together. Jaswant Singh had suggested giving Jenkins the deeds to the Donaldson and Peters farmsteads, in exchange for his own, as payment for his efforts, and the others had reluctantly agreed – the Singhs had lost too much for them to deny any reasonable requests right now. Graves could see Jenkins mentally rubbing his hands together in glee, and it sickened him.

The really good news was that Jake Wright had survived after all. Despite his complaints about his exomech, *Carnigore* had one feature no-one had counted on – it had more radiation shielding than any of them had ever seen, likely as a measure to protect patrons from radiation leaks from when it was still an amusement ride droid. It was a wreck and would need replacing, but Jake was okay.

And that left the giant gate on the ridgeline. It lacked the sparkle that indicated an open gateway back the deebee's home dimension, but it was still there. None of them had any idea what to do about it, other than to arm up, stay vigilant, and invest heavily in defences. It was going to be expensive and hard work, and it dawned on Graves that Jenkins new farmstead would be right in the path of any further attacks... Jaswant Singh was much wilier than he'd given him credit.

With the creature dragged away and the other colonists gone, Graves and his wife surveyed the land they'd fought hard to defend. It never occurred to them to pack up and leave, to head to somewhere safer. This was home, and alien invasion or no, this was where they were going to stay.

HERE THERE BE MONSTERS

Dave Beynon

Are you done yet?"

Falstaff wore his usual roll-eyed expression of impatience. He tapped his foot, checked his watch and looked theatrically at the column of soldiers moving out.

"Almost," I said, scribbling co-ordinates and notations in my notebook. "If the army allowed me a crew, this would all be going so much faster, Sergeant."

"No crew. Just lucky old me, but you know the drill: we move in, we secure, you map – *quickly* – then we move out. That's the way it is."

I muttered under my breath.

"Did you just say 'Invasion on a budget' again?"

I nodded. I was indeed a broken record when it came to my need for a crew. Sgt Falstaff was as fine a person as you would meet in the soldiering profession but he lacked the temperament for surveying and mapmaking. You'd think a soldier would be good at standing still and holding a rangefinder or an elevation target but sadly, no. I'd had soldiers assisting me for the last twenty years and there wasn't a one of them who didn't sway.

"You know, in the old days…"

"Yes, I do know. In the old days, there would be a corps of engineers dispatched with each unit blah, blah, blah. I know. I almost sympathize. I really do. We soldiers, however, have a job to do. Do you think these indigenous people are going to quell themselves?"

I glanced back along the narrow roadway I was mapping toward the village. The old man who spoke for the village had told Murray, our IPLO – Indigenous Persons Liaison Officer – that the name of the place was *Ithalaco*. That was Murray's best guess at how it was phonetically spelled, given the dialect was hard for a human tongue to negotiate. Murray did her best, but even a linguist of her skill had difficulty reproducing the sounds the locals' beaks created. Well, *Ithalaco* was what was on the map now.

At the edge of the village, I'd placed a pair of markers. A traditional iron surveyor's spike was hammered deep into the ground. The other marker was an elevated solar-powered beacon. I'd set it in the hope that one day there'd be a GPS satellite placed in orbit around this godforsaken world. A half-dozen local children moved cautiously around the two metre tall post, daring each other to touch it.

"There doesn't seem to be a lot of quelling needed. They seem a pretty cowed population. Maybe just this once I could have enough time to double-check my measurements before we move on?"

"We don't camp in the villages. The captain wants us five klicks into the jungle before we camp for the night. Can we go?"

"Fine," I said, not yet packing up my transit, the main measuring device I use for calculating distance, elevation and location. "First I need you to take your marker and stand over by that tree. And try to hold it steady for once. God, what I wouldn't give for just one set of measurements that made sense at the end of the day."

I made the last of my notes then wrapped the notebook in good old fashioned oilskin. In the humidity of the jungle – any world's jungle – portable computers were notoriously unreliable. Almost all of my equipment, from my optical sextant and transit right down to my pens, pencils and paper, was analog. My camera was digital, a bulky thing of neoprene, glass and plastic that seldom came out of its waterproof carrying case. It was so bulky I made sure Sgt Falstaff always ended up with it in his pack along with stakes, beacons, tapes and markers. I might not get a crew, but I was determined to make the good sergeant my own personal packhorse.

I gave the village one last glance as I collapsed my tripod. The village elder who had spoken with Murray came to the edge of the village and chased away the children. He looked at me, raised his two left hands and pointed toward the jungle the troop was entering. With an oddly human gesture, he shook his head and then dropped his gaze to the ground. I would have asked him what he was trying to tell me but I'd only picked up a handful of words and most of those had to do with food. Murray had moved on at the head of the march. I smiled, careful not to show teeth, and waved to the old man. He shook his head in response and returned to the village.

"While we're young, Wilson," said Falstaff. "You know how you want time to double-check your measurements? Just once, I don't want to be bringing up the rear."

I packed away the transit and secured my tripod to my pack. "What are you complaining about? In twenty years of following the army around making maps, I've never once had to set up a tent or prepare the evening meal." I shouldered my pack and nodded toward the swath our trailblazers' machetes had cut into the jungle. "And neither has my sergeant."

Falstaff smiled at that. "You might just have a point, Engineer Wilson."

True to form, five kilometres from the village, measured by my boot-mounted pedometer, Falstaff and I found the camp. Dinner was well underway. A rehydrated salad and a soybean brick augmented with vitamins and minerals made for a nutritional-ly-balanced meal. How could it be that humanity managed to master faster-than-light travel but was hopelessly stymied when it came to infusing anything approaching flavor into a soybean brick?

I took my foil plate and sat next to Murray.

"Ted," she said. "Nice to see you found us."

"Always nice to see you, too, Lisa. It doesn't take a mapmaker to follow the trail this bunch leaves. Chicken tonight?"

Murray lifted the edge of her nutrition block and shrugged.

"I've no idea what kind of meat they tried to simulate with this one. They failed. Again."

"I've been eating this stuff for twenty years. A few years back there were a half dozen bricks that tasted just like smoked salmon. I think they *were* labelled as chicken. Never tasted anything so good before or since out of a ration pack." I swallowed a chalky mouthful. "So, has the captain figured where we're going tomorrow?"

"I think we are exploring from here on. The village elder told me his village stood on the frontier. No other people heading... which way are we heading anyway?"

I didn't need to check my compass. "West. Well, west-*ish*. The magnetic north on this world is offset from the rotational axis by twenty-six degrees so your angle of—"I stopped myself. I'd long ago discovered the details of my profession made for snooze-worthy dinner conversation. "We're kind of heading west."

"Chokohn – that's the elder's name – he told me there's a string of villages that run the equivalent of north and south in a straight line along the edge of this denser jungle. He said they never come in here."

"Never? I know this jungle's dense but Falstaff and I passed a ton of what looks like edible fruit on our way here."

She shrugged. "He said 'never'."

"Maybe that explains it."

"Explains what?"

I described the elder's actions and gestures as I was packing up to leave.

"You've always got to be careful, Ted. You can't assign human meaning to alien gestures. Jesus, there's not universal consistency across human cultures, let alone alien ones."

"Well, it sure looked like he was trying to tell me not to come out here."

Murray shrugged. "They're a primitive culture. Limited agriculture. Just starting to smelt metals. Maybe jungle represents the unknown and they're naturally afraid of it."

"I guess. But for a fledgling culture, this jungle also represents new resources, right? Hey, that's why we're out here. But the old man said they don't come out here at all? Not even to hunt? Not even those kids I saw poking around my beacon?"

Murray shook her head. "This whole area is taboo. Because it's taboo, there's naturally superstition surrounding it."

"Boogeymen?"

She laughed. I always liked it when I was able to coax a laugh from Murray.

"Pretty much. But his word, if I'm right, translates to 'The Others'."

"How ominous. Wait a minute. I thought that's what the indigenous people called us."

"That's what I thought they were calling us. They call us Jahahlla." The word ended in a delightful trill that brought out Murray's laugh lines. "I thought that meant 'others' until today. The elder explained the difference. I now know it means 'visitors' or 'travellers'."

"So how do you say 'others'?"

There was nothing at all delightful about the guttural clack that came out of Murray's mouth.

"Oh... that doesn't sound very friendly, does it?"

"No. Chokohn told me we shouldn't come out here. I explained to him as best I could that we're mapping the area so that when more visitors arrive they'll know where everything is. He told me we didn't want to know what was in the jungle. He said we could just end our map at the edge of his village and go back the way we came."

"I wish. I can't believe I'm about to say this but I could really go for the relative luxury of a spaceship right about now. We've been here for over a month now. This traipsing through the wilderness following soldiers is a young person's game."

"You whine and complain but you love it. Besides, on a civilized world there's no need for mapmakers."

"Or linguists. Not on the civilized ones."

"Too true," she said. "It's weird. Usually the locals are only too ready to have us push on."

"Not this time?"

"No. Chokohn invited us to stay, rather than have us press on into the jungle. He said they'd hold a feast for us, if only we promised to go back the way we came."

"They really don't want us out here, do they? Do you think they're really concerned with us running into these Others you mentioned?"

Murray picked at the last of her lettuce but made no motion to move that sad leaf to her mouth. "We hear things like this on other worlds. You know that. *Oh, don't go out there. Bad things are out there.*" She inclined her head toward where the captain sat, eating and talking with her officers. "More often than not the locals are simply trying to keep our soldiers from finding some place of religious or cultural significance. Or from uncovering some nearby resources – resources they'd like to keep for themselves."

"You can hardly blame them. After all, it is their planet."

Murray placed her hand on my arm. "What a naïve notion, Cartographer First Class Wilson." Her tone was good-natured, but there was a bitter undercurrent I wasn't sure she'd intended to share. She lowered her voice a shade. "It's their world until we find something useful. Then it becomes annexed. For their own protection, of course."

"Of course," I said. "We're all just one big happy galactic family."

Sgt Falstaff approached with his tray, eying his food brick dubiously.

"Chicken?" he asked as he took a seat.

"Chicken*ish*," said Murray. "So, what is the captain saying about tomorrow's adventure. We'll continue to the west?"

"That's her plan," said Falstaff. "We'll break camp at dawn then press on until we find a big enough gap in the tree canopy to launch a drone to scout ahead. We'll reassess the situation then."

As it turned out, we never had a chance to launch that drone and only some of us ever got the chance to reassess the situation.

I've marched on more than three dozen worlds, through terrain far more varied than anything found in earth's solar system. Each ecosystem brings its own challenges, and the only thing worse to march through than jungle is swamp. After hacking our way for three hours without a break, the jungle abruptly opened into a vast misty wetland shrouded with a fetid layer of yellowish fog.

"Private Ho, let's have an atmospheric test before we press on," the captain called out from the front of the line. I heard one of the soldiers moving through the ranks, though I couldn't see her. I was reaching for the respirator in the pouch on my hip when the captain called the all clear. "No toxins."

Those were the last words spoken before everything went to hell.

The fog drifted to the edge of the jungle, enveloping us and reducing our visibility. Falstaff stood two metres away. I could barely see him. From the wetlands, I heard what sounded like a breaking wave accompanied by a locust swarm's worth of fluttering.

Two quick shots were fired from the front of the line, followed by a wet slap and a loud crack. A rapid burst of gunfire, a scream and then the sound of branches snapping as something flew through the jungle to my left, landing with a meaty thump. As part of the Cartography Corp, I carry no weapon, yet I found myself instinctively reaching for one at my hip. Falstaff, long a soldier before he became my assistant, reached for a weapon he did not have. He unclasped the marker staff, brandishing it like a spear.

I raised my hand and was about to speak when something leathery, grey and moist reached out of the fog and dragged Falstaff away. The marker staff fell to the ground. As I reached for his foot, a length of ropy, slime-coated tentacle slapped against my cheek. The tentacle's tip was just below my eye. It terminated in a glistening thorny claw that dripped a pus-like yellow venom.

A quick jab just below my left eye, then oblivion.

An alien insect crawling across my eyelid startled me awake. My mouth seemed full of ash. As I opened my eyes, I realized the left one was swollen shut, save for a crusty sliver. When I tried to lift a hand to determine the extent of the swelling I realized I'd been bound.

I was naked. Sitting. My outstretched legs were tightly secured with braided jungle vines lined with tiny nettles that irritated my skin. Behind me, my hands were tied with the same type of vine. Like guy-wires securing an upright post, three lengths of vine kept me from slumping onto my side. Whatever had taken us had dragged us to a boggy clearing. On the ground before me, my clothing and gear was laid out, neat and orderly. Everything had been examined and lined up. My notebooks lay open and my hand-drawn maps were unfurled next to their waterproof cylinders.

"Ted."

Murray's voice came from my left. I turned my head and immediately regretted it. My head swam with vertigo and I tasted bile. I tried to focus through my left eye.

"Lisa," I said, "what happened?"

"Don't know. Something took us. Your eye? Can you see out of it?"

"Not especially. Does it look as bad as it feels?"

I got a vague sense of movement and interpreted it as a nod. "It's swollen and there's a crusty scab on your cheek. Is this the first time you've gained consciousness?"

"As far as I can remember. You?"

"I woke… a while ago… to someone screaming in the distance. I panicked and tried to pull free of these vines. I guess I exerted myself too much. Tunnel vision then I passed out. I woke up a few minutes ago and have been calling to you."

I had a touch of tunnel vision myself and the pasty taste in my mouth had me on the edge of throwing up. I flexed my arms.

There was a little give, yet not enough to work my hands free. Besides, with each flex the nettles bit into my flesh, telling me that struggling was not in the cards.

"How many of us are here?" I seemed to be the end of the line, if there was a line, with Murray and any others to my left, invisible to my swollen eye. "More than just you and me?"

"Falstaff is a little ways off. Kind of by himself. The rest of our soldiers are farther away – those that are still with us, anyway. There's only six or seven. The captain's at the very end."

"That's all?" Thirty-six people had broken camp that morning. "Jesus. Did you get a look at what attacked us?"

The vision in my left eye was starting to clear. I could actually see her nod this time. "I mostly saw their handiwork. Jesus, Ted, they tore our people apart. Private Ho was just ahead of me before that fog rolled in. She screamed. Jesus. Then… pieces of her started hitting me and landing all around. Half of Private Martinez hit the ground next to me. His mouth was still moving. Something like a lobster claw pulled me to the ground… then I woke up here."

"A claw? Like a crustacean?"

"Yeah. Like a crab or a lobster or the Kiloko people on Chara. Only bigger than any claw you've ever seen."

"I was taken down by a tentacle."

"A… tentacle? More than one species? Working together?"

I could only shrug.

"Lisa? All of my stuff has been arranged near my feet. I can't see too clearly over your way yet. Is everyone's gear down by their feet?"

"Yeah," she said. "It's weird. It's so neatly stacked. The soldiers' armor and weaponry are separate from their food and kit. My clothes are apart from my notebooks and recording equipment and from what I can tell one of my voice recorders is missing. It looks like Falstaff confused them a bit."

"Why?"

"Well, it looks like we've been grouped by function. The soldiers with their armor and weapons are all in one group. You

298

and I – the record keepers and note-takers – are over here. But Falstaff is all by himself in the middle. He wears armor and a uniform like any soldier and they're piled like everyone else's armor and uniform. His food and kit are stacked to one side. In the middle, where the other soldiers have weapons, Falstaff has that marking stick you make him carry, those beacons of yours, some iron spikes, a hammer and a big empty waterproof case."

"Empty? My camera was in that case."

"That's odd. Two different types of recording devices are missing."

I shifted, trying in vain to become more comfortable. Impossible. I forced my left eye to open wider. I was rewarded with pain and added focus. I nodded.

"I can see a little more clearly now," I said. "Do you think that whoever took us understands how to use our devices?"

Murray nodded.

"I'd bet money we're being recorded right now."

"By who? Whom?"

"Whom. And that's the question."

The days on this planet lasted just over thirty-eight earth hours. The sun stood high in the sky when the captain finally regained consciousness.

Captain Najafi, after straining heroically against her bonds with no success, ordered a roll call.

"What do we know, people?"

Each of us relayed our experience prior to capture. Each described an attack by a different creature, though barbed tentacles seemed a common theme. Captain Najafi listened without comment until Murray mentioned our missing equipment.

"We're obviously dealing with intelligence. Specialist Murray, do the actions of our abductors jive with what we know of the indigenous people of this planet?"

Murray shook her head. "Not at all. These are a peaceful, timid people. They're not aggressive at all."

"So we're looking at another race?"

"Another species. More than one. But it doesn't feel right."

"What do you mean, Specialist?"

"My experience shows that where two sentient species evolve on the same planet, there's more similarity – in culture, behavior and physically, as well – than we've seen here. It's almost as if we're dealing with something alien out here."

As it turned out we were dealing with something alien, but not in the way Murray meant. Between the people trussed up in that clearing we had over two hundred years of experience in a score of disciplines honed on over five dozen planets. None of it prepared us for what happened next.

A patch of bog a dozen metres away began to pulse with a glow usually reserved for the bioluminescence of a creature dwelling in a very deep ocean. The ground heaved, accompanied by a mucky sucking sound. The air seemed charged with ozone and a metallic taste filled my mouth. A leathery grey hand rose from the centre of the pulsing patch of earth, each of its eight long fingers ended in a dirt-crusted claw. A narrow, lanky arm followed the hand. Another hand and arm followed. Then another. In all, six spidery arms and hands reached out and dragged the creature from the ground.

Spindly and creased, it towered over us. Folds of seemingly mummified skin stretched over bones that looked as if they'd snap with any hint of pressure. Four fleshy legs coated in a layer of sickly yellow quills supported a torso that looked more insect than animal. Each leg ended in what looked like a cloven hoof.

Atop the torso was a tapered, scaly head. Filled with needle-like teeth, a vertical maw opened and closed with the same rhythmic pulse as the luminescent earth. Lining each side of the maw were four unblinking eyes, glassy as marbles and as black as space.

Head pivoting on a pencil-thin neck, the gaze of those eight eyes settled first on the captain, then on Murray.

Sounds, harsh and crisp, slid past all those wicked teeth. It sounded like the language of the villagers only with a hard edge, decidedly nastier.

Murray's eyes grew wide. Clearing her throat, she answered in the natives' language. Anticipating everyone's unasked question, she supplied a translation.

"It asked me if I was the one who was good with language," she said. "I told it I was."

The creature rattled off more words and gestured toward the captain with half of its arms. Murray spoke considerably less. If a smile is possible on a vertical mouth, the thing grinned and made a sweeping gesture that encompassed all of us.

"It… it encourages me to translate everything. It seems interested in the captain. It wants to know if you are our chieftain, Captain Najafi. What should I tell it?"

Najafi sat taller. "Tell it that I am and I demand to be released. That all of us must be released. Now."

Murray spoke the words. The top and bottom of the maw curled, showing mottled gums. A rapid string of words was followed by the clacking of the claws on one of the creature's hands.

As Murray opened her mouth to translate, a ball of dark fur about a metre in diameter fell from one of the trees that surrounded the clearing. It landed silently, then chattered as dozens of hook-footed legs pushed out of the fur. The feet scuttled it closer to the captain. As it turned, the fur parted, revealing a thin-lipped mouth lined with broken, jagged fangs. It stopped just short of Najafi and snapped those teeth twice in her direction.

"It says… it says you will be freed, Captain. I'm assuming this other… lifeform is to free you."

In a blur, the furred creature sped around the captain, snarling and snapping. Like a flea, it hopped back. The vines securing Najafi lay in tatters around her. Naked, she rose defiantly to her feet.

The spindly creature smacked its top two fists against its torso and spat a handful of words. Then it gestured to the ground in front of Najafi. The head pivoted to Murray.

"It says that it is chieftain of its people as you are of yours. It wants you to put on your… the word it used was the one the villagers use for the thin fibre wrap they wear, but I think it means your armor. It wants you to put on your armor."

Captain Najafi glared at the creature.

"Specialist Murray, do you know the local vernacular for 'go fuck yourself'? Tell it I do not take orders from aggressors."

Murray swallowed, then spoke to the creature. It bobbed its head, curiously like a nod. It clacked its fingertips together.

From the darkened edge of the clearing, one of the shadows detached itself from the others and slid silently across the ground. As it grew closer the shadow coalesced, drawing darkness into itself and taking bipedal form. Featureless at first with tar-like glossy black skin, it took on approximately human proportions. On feet that didn't seem to quite touch the ground, it strode over to Corporal Tsang. Silently, the shadow creature grabbed Tsang's hair with one hand and peeled off his right ear with the other. As Tsang screamed, ink black fingers flung his ear to the ground. Before it landed, the furry creature skittered and leapt, catching the ear and devouring it with a snap and a snarl.

The chieftain spat some words at Murray.

"Captain," she said, "it wants you to put on the armor. It says… it says that Corporal Tsang has lots of parts that might be ripped free if you decline."

Najafi was already reaching for her breastplate. As she strapped on her armor, Najafi glared at the chieftain. After pulling on her helmet, she glanced at Murray.

"Fine. Now what does this son of a bitch want?"

Murray translated.

The chieftain pointed with half its hands at Captain Najafi's rifle. It made a motion of grabbing and pulling. It spoke, but Murray hardly needed to translate.

"It is telling you to take your rifle."

Najafi smiled, showing teeth.

"Big mistake."

She casually walked toward her gun. At the last second she rolled, scooped up the rifle, knelt and fired. A burst – six or seven rapid shots – blasted the chieftain off all four feet. Najafi turned her sites on the shadow creature. Before she could fire it dissipated, like smoke caught in a sudden gust. In a heartbeat she sought and found the furred creature, firing a pair of shots at it as those dozens of tiny legs launched it into the foliage.

"Chew on that," she said. "Keep calm, Corporal. I'll have you all freed in a jif—"

The captain fell silent. A series of rapid huffs came from the prone chieftain. The huffs became louder and more frequent.

"Murray," I said, "is that thing still alive? Is it having trouble breathing?"

Murray's face was slack. She bit her lip and hung her head.

"It's laughing. Jesus Christ, Ted, it's laughing at us."

The staccato of exhalations grew louder as the chieftain rose. All six of Najafi's bullets had found their mark, leaving considerable holes in the creature's carapace-like torso. Black ichor oozed from the wounds. When a viscous dollop hit the earth, the ground smouldered and the vegetation nearby withered. As we watched, the ichor congealed at the edges of the wounds, sealing them.

The chieftain raised all six arms. Now it sounded like laughter to all of us. The tapered head turned to Murray and barked a few words.

"We are tiny," she translated. "Tiny and weak."

Captain Najafi emptied her clip.

A standard issue assault rifle holds thirty-eight shots in its clip. Najafi was so close that the remaining thirty must all have struck true. Throughout the barrage, the chieftain stood its ground, all four legs bracing and straining against impact. When the echo of the last gunshot faded, amid the shifting smoke of gunpowder, impossibly the chieftain still stood.

Its torso, head and arms were a slaughterhouse of trauma. Like a hypnotised person, I watched slack-jawed as all of that trauma folded in on itself and healed. The chieftain laughed and barked a single word, then it launched itself at our captain.

Nanocarbonfibre armor – a miracle material that requires extreme temperature and special tools to cut – lay shredded on the ground. All of the claws on the ends of all of those fingers on each of those six arms surrounded Captain Najafi in a whirlwind of motion. Before Najafi began to scream, the chieftain stepped back to regard its handiwork with those eight hard eyes.

In less time than it took to shred her armor, the chieftain had flayed our captain. As I reflect, I like to think that shock took her, then and there, shielding her from the agony. I like to think that. I just wish I could believe it. I can't. As she fell, I saw her eyes.

Before she hit the ground, a carpet of *things* rattled from the tall grass at the edge of the clearing. No two seemed exactly alike. Some slithered faster than any snake. Some scuttled, sideways and crablike. Others lurched, or crawled or scampered. However they moved, all were lightning fast and all shared a common goal.

The creatures converged on Captain Najafi, blanketing her in an undulating, writhing, nightmare mass. Her muffled screams ended, replaced by crunching and the unwholesome chewing sounds of a thousand tiny mouths. We sat in horrified silence until the mass of creatures swept back to the tall grass, moving across the ground like a blanket of cockroaches confronted by a sudden light.

Not content with simply eating Captain Najafi, the creatures left an oval depression where she had fallen, devouring every hint of her, down to the tiniest drop of blood that might have soaked into the soil.

When I looked at Murray, she was shaking. All of us were. From the IPLO and the mapmaker, to the battle-hardened soldiers, each of us wept. Corporal Tsang, his lost ear forgotten, stared at the shallow void where our captain had been. Next to him sat Private Verne and Private Jimenez. Too far apart for physical consolation, they stared at each other, trying to give emotional support. They tried to be brave, but their features betrayed them. Fear was winning.

I didn't really know the next three privates. They'd rotated in a month ago, just before we'd been dropped on this world. I wish I could tell you their names and what sort of people they were in life. I can't. I can only tell you they died as well as circumstances allowed, which wasn't well at all. Terrified and crying and often on their knees, they begged for mercy from the merciless with exactly the results you'd expect.

Falstaff, segregated for no reason other than his equipment, suffered alone, waiting for what came next.

In a daze, I asked Murray a question.

She turned to me. "Wh-what?"

"Before... before what happened... the chieftain... it said something. It sounded like just one word."

"I don't want to say, Ted. Really. You don't want to know."

"Please. Share it, Lisa. Tell me and share it. What did that thing say just before it skinned our captain?"

"Jesus, Ted. I've only heard that word a couple of times among the indigenous people and only ever among the children."

"The children..."

"Once in a while, one of the privates will share some chocolate ration or a cookie pack with one of the indigenous kids. That thing over there said the same word the children say when they're anticipating a treat."

"Share it, Lisa. What did that thing say just before it tore into Captain Najafi?"

"It said 'yummy'."

The chieftain refrained from dirtying its hands murdering any more of our number. Instead, it whooped and laughed and clapped as every few hours a fresh nightmare would detach itself from the shadows, slither from the grass, drop down from the trees, rise from the fetid swamp or crash from the jungle into the clearing. Starting with Corporal Tsang, these new creatures, each just as horrible and twisted as the next, worked their way down the line of soldiers. Twice, the kill was as swift as Captain Najafi. The rest were not so fortunate. One of the privates I didn't know must have taken an hour to die, all the time tormented by a tentacled thing whose touch burned like acid.

Each time a new horror entered the clearing, the chieftain spoke to Murray. It told her the rest of us must watch. If we looked away, the shadowy thing reappeared and began slicing off pieces of the next person in line. When the last private finally died and was devoured, the chieftain strode across the clearing to Falstaff.

It took his face into one of its eight-fingered hands. It seemed to size him up, then looked down at his gear. It turned to Murray and spoke.

"It says you're different from the other soldiers, Falstaff," Murray said. "It is asking me why you wear armor but carry no weapon."

The chieftain nudged the hammer and stakes with one of its hooves. Murray barked a long string of words.

"I just told it those aren't weapons. That they're used to mark location – territory is the word the indigenous people use. I told it you assist Ted, Falstaff. I don't know what it wants."

The chieftain approached me. The maw opened and closed as it drew near. The fingertip claws clacked with each step. It regarded me with those cold, glassy eyes. I felt like some scientific specimen wriggling on a pin. It levelled a claw in my direction and spoke at length with Murray.

She nodded at the end and took a deep breath.

"These creatures did take your camera and my voice recorder. When I asked it why it said, 'So that we can relive the moments again and again after you are used up.'"

"*Used up?* Jesus…"

"I think 'used up' actually means 'gone' but I'm not entirely sure. Given what we've been through… It was very interested in why we are here. I explained as best I could. Then it wanted to know about you."

I swallowed hard. "Me?"

"It says it wants to talk to you about your maps."

The furry creature with all the legs and the snapping teeth dropped from the trees and sped toward me. I felt hot breath as it snarled and circled me, freeing me from the vines amid a tornado of flashing, broken ivory. As it scuttled a few metres away, it clacked its teeth at me.

The chieftain crouched and placed a fingertip beneath my chin. It lifted my head so I would have to look into its maw as it spoke. After a dozen or so words, it seemed to smile and released my chin.

"It wants you to be cooperative. If… if you aren't… the Shadowman will hurt me."

I nodded. "Tell it that I'll do as I'm told."

"Fuck that," yelled Falstaff. "It's just going to kill us all as soon as it gets what it wants. Don't you dare help it, Ted."

The Shadowman appeared behind Falstaff and silently reached toward his ear.

"Stop!" I raised a hand and pointed at the chieftain. To my surprise, the Shadowman actually hesitated. "Don't you dare let that thing hurt him. Lisa, tell it if that… that Shadowman lays a finger on Falstaff there's no way in hell I'll do what it wants."

Alien words tumbled frantically from Lisa's mouth. The chieftain laughed and dismissively waved three of its hands. The Shadowman drifted back a few metres, but like a bad dream didn't dissipate entirely.

I dipped my head to the chieftain. "Thank you," I said. "Falstaff, please stay quiet. I think the Shadowman behind you is just itching to rip you apart the next time you open your mouth. Lisa, what does it want from me?"

The chieftain gathered my maps and rolled them out on the ground. It placed different bits of our gear on the corners to keep the papers from curling up. Murray translated back and forth as we spoke.

"These are pictures of this world?" the chieftain said.

"Yes. I've shown where there's water and land. This shade of green is the jungle. Villages are marked. These lines are elevation – how high or low the land goes. See?"

A crusted talon tapped a dot on the map.

"This place here. That is the village of Chokohn, yes?"

I nodded. "It is. You know of Chokohn? Of his village?"

"I visit him in his dreams." The smile appeared on the maw. "In his nightmares." The chieftain's other hands moved to all the other village dots on all three maps. "I visit them all in their nightmares. They know better than to come out here looking for us. I am surprised old Chokohn did not warn you to stay away."

We all lowered our heads. Understanding the gesture, the chieftain laughed.

"He is a wise man. You should always listen to wise men. Wise men know this territory–" one of its hands spread out over the blank area of the map that represented where we were "–all of this territory belongs to me and mine. We have now taught you – as we once taught their ancestors – this place is not for you. Like their ancestors, we shall allow some of you to go so that you may pass down the notion that this is an unpleasant place to visit." It tapped the map, then pointed at me. "We let *you* go specifically to mark that on your picture. A warning that your people may be wise enough to heed. A warning so your people will *always* know what awaits them when foolish enough to come this way."

The chieftain rose, clacking its fingertips twice. The furry creature whirled around Murray, then Falstaff, freeing them both. We all stood naked in the clearing. The chieftain turned to leave, then hesitated. It clacked its fingers one last time. The Shadowman appeared at Falstaff's side, seized his left hand and twisted off his little finger. As Falstaff slumped to his knees, holding his hand to staunch the bleeding, the chieftain spoke its last words.

"Do as I ask," it said, "or I shall send the Shadowman for the rest of them."

Dropping to my knees, I scrambled to open the case that held my pens. I outlined the area the chieftain had indicated in black and crosshatched the edges of the lines for emphasis. With a trembling hand, I made the notation.

"What have you written?" Murray asked.

"The only thing that makes sense," I told her. "Here There Be Monsters."

CLAWS, TEETH, AND FEATHERS

A Kharrn Story
Charles R. Rutledge

Shit, we've lost power," Captain Sean Strickland said as the lights inside the Blackhawk helicopter went dark.

Sergeant Mike Calvin leaned forward in his jump seat and looked toward the front of the 'copter. The pilot, Lieutenant Owen Tyler, was calmly checking his lightless instrument panel. Calvin knew a 'copter could be safely landed without engine power through auto-rotation, but he didn't much like the idea of being in a flying machine with no juice. It was one of the reasons he'd been infantry when he'd belonged to the regular military.

"Tyler knows what he's doing," Sergeant Abner Milton said from beside Calvin. Milton was the team medic. He was a wiry man with Harry Potter glasses. He was rarely seen without a book, and he seemed to know everything.

Then again, Milton didn't know any more about what they were doing in a powerless chopper, about thirty miles northwest of Holloman Air force base in New Mexico, than Calvin.

The Blackhawk lurched as a crosswind hit them. Calvin didn't completely understand the auto-rotation technique. Something about angling the rotor blades to get maximum upward airflow to keep the chopper aloft until it could glide in for a landing. Whatever he was supposed to be doing, Tyler seemed to be doing it. They were making a controlled descent.

The sun had been up for about half an hour, so visibility wasn't an issue. The vast, flat landscape of the desert was all around them. Calvin glanced at the row of seats opposite him and Milton, where Strickland and the fourth member of the team were seated.

Master Sergeant Tony Brent was the only one of their number Calvin had never worked with. Team members rotated out, Captain Strickland being the only constant. Calvin hadn't exchanged half a dozen words with Brent so far. The man had shown up in the ready room at Holloman for the briefing in the middle of the night like the rest of them. Brent was a big guy with a buzz cut.

"At least we won't have to walk far if we survive the landing," Milton said, pointing out the open bay door. "There's our target."

Looking to where Milton indicated, Calvin spotted several low, flat buildings inside a high chain-link fence. There were also a couple of towers of odd design behind the buildings. Something like cell towers. Far off in the distance, the Sangre de Cristo Mountains loomed in the haze.

There was no dramatic moment of touchdown. Tyler didn't yell out for everyone to brace for impact like in the movies. There was just a sudden thump and they were down.

"Nice work, Tyler, "Strickland said. He fumbled in one of the pockets of his flak jacket and pulled out a cell phone then glared at the screen. "This thing's as dead as the radio."

The five men began checking various pieces of equipment. Brent flipped the switch on some night vision goggles. Nothing. Batteries were apparently as dead as everything else.

Strickland said, "Okay, so nothing with juice works. We've still got a job to do. Get your basic gear together and leave anything with batteries. I didn't get much time to brief you in the ready room, but here's the Reader's Digest version."

"Reader's what?" said Tyler.

"Before your time. Anyway, this is a defense research lab. I don't know precisely what they were working on, and if I did, I probably couldn't tell you. All contact was lost with the lab last night. I think we can see why now."

"Maybe it was some sort of power damper," Milton said. "Like an EMP."

Strickland said, "Possibly. Whatever it is, it must be a big secret or the brass would have sent the local military for recon instead of calling us in."

"If they called in the spook show," Milton said, "means whatever research was going on, it was something unusual."

Strickland shrugged. There was no point in arguing. As far as Calvin knew, every member of this revolving military unit had been recruited after some sort of run-in with the paranormal. In several cases, like his own, the member had already returned to civilian life. Calvin had been part of a SWAT team in the rural Georgia town where he had grown up.

Calvin had been approached after his brush with the supernatural, and made an offer he couldn't refuse, so he had re-upped. They weren't attached to any specific branch of the military and were treated as a reserve unit. The duty was easy, and the pay was phenomenal. The only drawback was the likelihood of a quick and messy death. Or worse, a slow and messy death. They had no official name, but team members had taken to referring to themselves as the spook show.

Strickland said, "As always, our main mission is recon. Assess the situation, but don't engage any enemy unless we have to."

"Do we think there is an enemy?" Brent said.

"We'll know soon enough. Let's get moving."

Tyler stayed with the Blackhawk, and the other four men scrambled out of the aircraft and started across the quarter mile or so of desert between them and the lab. It was early October and the morning was cold. Calvin had read somewhere that desert nights were cold, even during the hot season.

Of course New Mexico, at least this part of it, didn't look much like his idea of a desert. It wasn't just a lot of sand. There was a heavy growth of bushes and of scrub pine trees. A grove of big cottonwoods grew near a small stream close to the lab's fence. The trees' yellow leaves blazed with a fiery light in the morning sun.

A narrow, rutted, gravel road led up to the front gate of the facility. A security station stood unoccupied. The front gate was open. Beyond it, Calvin could see two jeeps and an old pickup.

"Gate might have popped when they lost power," said Milton.

"How many people work here at night?" Brent said.

Strickland said, "Fifteen, according to the roster. About half of those were military personnel and the others were contractors."

Calvin noticed a darker area of sand near the security box. He stepped over and crouched for a better look. Something had soaked into the ground there. Something that had once been red.

"Looks like blood over here, Captain," Calvin said. "A lot of it."

Lieutenant Owen Tyler knew there was little point in opening the Blackhawk's engine compartment. This wasn't mechanical failure. It was something weird. And yet, the mechanic in him wanted a look, so he opened the front panel and stood staring at the chopper's inner workings. As suspected, he didn't see anything amiss.

He pulled out his cell phone. No power, just like everything else. He doubted he would have been able to get a signal this far out anyway.

Tyler heard a sort of scrabbling sound, like someone moving in the sand on the other side of the Blackhawk. He cursed under his breath. He shouldn't have allowed himself to become distracted. As team pilot, he rarely had to go into the real action on the ground, but he was supposed to be a pro, and here he was checking his ride like he'd been out for a Sunday drive.

Tyler's M4A1 rifle was in the 'copter, but he slid his Beretta M9 from its holster as he moved to a position where he would be able to see behind the Blackhawk, but still have the fuselage as cover.

The last thing he ever saw, as he leaned out from the front of the chopper, was a wide mouth full of sharp teeth. Then he felt twin bolts of agony in his shoulders just as the mouth closed over his head.

"Some weird tracks here too," Calvin said.

The tracks had two toes and were maybe ten inches long. There were several of them scattered around the edge of the security box. They seemed to head toward the gravel parking lot where they soon became lost on the rocky surface.

Strickland stepped over to where Calvin was crouched near the bloodstain. "Milton, have a look at this. Brent, you watch the perimeter."

Milton joined the other two men looking at the ground. He went to one knee and touched the edge of the track, which crumbled slightly. "Jesus."

"What is it?" Strickland said.

Milton said, "I thought it was a fossil until I touched it. Whatever made this is supposed to be extinct."

"What are you talking about, Milton?"

"These look like the tracks of a dromaeosaur."

"A what?"

Brent said, "Sir, there's something coming this way."

All three men were instantly on their feet, bringing their rifles into ready position. Now Calvin could hear what Brent had heard while the other three were distracted. Something was crunching on the gravel.

A second later Calvin found out was a dromaeosaur was.

There were three of them and they were huge, about the size of grizzly bears. They looked like… dinosaurs of some sort. They ran on two legs and had muscular arms with big, three-clawed hands. Their heads were long and narrow with the eyes set on the sides of the skull like birds. And like birds they were covered with a thick layer of deep gray feathers.

The creatures came pounding across the space between the closest building and the gate, spewing gravel with each step of their huge feet. The things made a sort of bellowing shriek as they came, mouths spread wide, showing rows of sharp teeth. This close, Calvin could see that while the creatures' feet indeed had two toes that touched the ground, they had a third toe tipped with a great, hooked, claw.

This all felt too familiar to Calvin. His brush with the paranormal had been at a manufacturing plant in the Georgia mountains, where his SWAT team had been decimated by things that shouldn't exist. He had relived that battle in his thoughts and dreams a thousand times. This one wasn't going to end that way if he could help it.

Calvin focused on the center mass of the closest dinosaur and fired three, rapid shots. Gouts of blood blossomed on the thing's chest, but it was still closing the distance.

Switching to fully automatic, he fired again, aware that his three comrades were also shooting. The three monsters stumbled, and Calvin fired until the rifle clicked empty. The dromaeosaurs finally fell, only a few feet from the four men.

Calvin immediately popped the rifle's 30-round magazine out and replaced it. That left him with one more clip in his flak jacket. Whatever these bastards were, they were hard to kill.

"This isn't possible," Milton said, kneeling by one of the fallen creatures.

"Is it what you thought," Strickland said, "One of those dromo things?" Milton ran his hand across the feathers in a motion that was almost a caress. "Yes. I think it's a Utahraptor. I mean, no one has ever seen a live one, but from its size, and the skull shape and type of claws, I'd say that's the most likely identification. It could always be something that's not in the fossil record."

Strickland said, "Whatever it is, it took four men firing on full auto to kill three of them. We'd better hope there aren't many more."

Brent said, "Speaking of which, we should probably go warn Tyler. He'll have heard the gunfire."

"Yeah, we…" Strickland broke off as he turned to look back toward the Blackhawk.

Calvin followed his gaze. Two more of the monsters were running their way from the direction of the helicopter. That didn't bode well for Owen Tyler.

"Shit!" Strickland said. "Find some cover. Everyone head for that building!"

Strickland led the men to the closer of the two buildings. The place was long and wide and had two floors. It was built of some sand-colored stone Calvin didn't recognize. The two pursuing dinosaurs had passed the gate and were bearing down on the men even as they found a door on one side of the building.

Strickland reached the door first and was grabbing for the handle when another of the dromos lurched around the corner of the building and launched itself at him. He didn't have a chance to bring his rifle to bear before the thing slammed into him.

Calvin had thought the creature might use the big claws to tear into the captain, but instead the dromo used them as hooks, digging into Strickland's back and keeping him from pulling away as the wide mouth descended. Blood spattered as the thing literally bit Strickland's face off.

It had all happened in a matter of seconds. Brent was the first one to bring up his rifle. He took aim and put three rounds into the dinosaur's skull. It toppled over, covering Strickland with its feathered body.

Calvin heard a shriek and spun to see the other two dromos were almost on top of them. Then the door behind them swung open and a huge man leaned out.

"Hurry and get in here. I had to clear the barricade."

Brent stared at the man and said, "You!"

"Yeah, me. Now hurry up or I'll leave you out there."

"Come on," Calvin said, pushing Brent toward the door.

The three men were barely through when the giant man slammed it shut. He hurried to a big steel cabinet that Calvin would have sworn he and both his comrades couldn't have budged, and shoved it in front of the door. Several other massive pieces of equipment followed. Even as the big man was wedging them tight against the door, the panel shuddered with a crashing impact.

The giant leaned against the barricade, as twice more something slammed against the door. After a few seconds he turned and looked at the three men. "Short attention spans."

"What are you doing here?" Brent said. "And what the fuck is going on?"

Closer now, Calvin saw that the man had long, dark hair, and a closely trimmed beard. Hie eyes were a startling clear blue, and an old, white scar ran down on side of his face. He had to be seven feet tall.

"There's someone in the next room that can explain the situation better than I can," the man said. "As for what I'm doing here, the same thing I was doing on that island where you last saw me. Trying to stop a bunch of idiots from ending the world."

Milton, who was still visibly shaken, said, "Mind giving the rest of us a clue, Brent? Since, you know, one of those things just killed our CO. And probably Sergeant Tyler."

"When I ran into... the creatures that got me this job, this guy was there."

"I was," the man said. "In fact, I'm the one who recommended you for the spook show."

Brent looked stunned. Before he could say anything else, Calvin said, "Okay, so you know who we are. Who the hell are you?"

"I'm Kharrn."

"That your first or last name?"

"Yes. Now come on. Doctor Kirby will fill you in, as best she can."

Kharrn turned and stalked away without waiting for an answer. He seemed to be someone used to being obeyed.

"You really know this guy?" Calvin said to Brent in a low voice.

"No, I just ran into him the one time, during a mission that went very bad. I thought he was going to kill me." Brent shook his head. "Now he says he's the one who recommended me for the team."

Kharrn led the men down a hallway, deeper into the building. They entered an area of offices and the big man steered them toward one of the rooms. An attractive woman with red hair looked up from a stack of papers as they entered.

"Reinforcements?" she said.

"Something like that," said Kharrn.

Milton said, "I'm Sergeant Milton, and this is Sergeant Calvin and Sergeant Brent."

"No CO?" the woman said.

"He's dead," said Milton.

"I'm sorry. I'm Janet Kirby. Head of research here."

"Can you tell us what's going on?"

"Yes and no. I know more or less why those creatures are out there. I just don't know exactly what to do about it."

"Give us what you can," Milton said. "Was this some sort of time travel experiment?"

Janet said, "Far from it. We were working on, for lack of a better term, a force field."

"No shit?" said Brent.

"None. We've been studying electromagnetic fields, looking for a way to generate a defensive energy shield. We were testing it last night about sundown and we had some sort of power surge. Somehow the juxtaposing energy fields opened a rift. I don't know if it leads to the past or an alternate reality or what."

The sun was well up and it was starting to feel a little warm in the office. Without power there was no airflow in the building. Calvin reminded himself that lack of air conditioning was pretty damn far down on their list of problems.

"What about the dinosaurs?"

"About an hour after we opened the rift, they began to come through," she said, reshuffling some of her papers. "Most of us were outside at the towers, trying to figure out what was happening, and we were overrun before we could get back to the buildings. I wouldn't have made it back if Kharrn hadn't show up when he did." Her pause was slight. "There could be some survivors in building two."

"Is it just the Utahraptors or have you seen anything else?"

"Just them. We must have disturbed a flock of them or something."

Milton said, "This would be a field day for some of my pale-ontologist friends... if we weren't all likely to die."

Janet said, "As you've no doubt noticed, the field we generated also has the effect of dampening all electrical power within its radius."

"Yeah, we almost wrecked our transport," Calvin said. "So I guess the big question is, is the rift still open?"

"It seems to be. The towers are holding it open."

"How does that work?" Milton said, taking a seat on the edge of a nearby desk. "If there's no electricity, how are the towers still functioning?"

"Truthfully, I don't know," she said, a sigh escaping. "My theory is they're somehow drawing energy from the rift itself."

"So it's a loop," Milton said. "If we took out either of your towers would that close the loop?"

"Theoretically." Janet pointed at the papers on her desk. "I was making some calculations on that very thing. But since I don't know the precise nature of the energy source, I can't predict what will happen."

Brent said, "If we don't take some action, more people will come to check on the facility and probably get killed too."

"It's worse than that," Janet said. "I think the rift is growing. If it spreads unchecked, this power dampening field is a menace to everything. We're not that far from civilization."

Milton turned to Kharrn. "Brent says you've had some run-ins with the paranormal. What's your take?"

"I was thinking the same as you. Take out the tower."

"Which means getting past the Utahraptors," said Brent.

Milton said, "Does it matter which tower we hit, Dr Kirby?"

"No, just so long as one is destroyed. I think that will disengage whatever power our field generators have linked to. I hope so anyway."

Kharrn said, "I was studying a map of the place when I heard you men outside. If we go out the rear entrance of this place, one of the towers is maybe two hundred yards away. But it's all open ground. No cover."

Brent said, "We've got enough ammo left to maybe hold the things back until we can get to the tower, but how do we bring it down?"

"Yeah, this was a recon mission," Calvin said. "We didn't bring explosives."

Kharrn said, "The tower is fairly lightweight in terms of construction. It's only about four feet square, and hollow. I can chop it down with this."

The big man reached behind the table where he'd been studying the map, and lifted a wide, flat, leather case. He unzipped the case and brought out a big, double-bladed ax.

"Jesus Christ," Milton said. "You figure you can cut through the tower with that?"

"I can," said Kharrn.

"He can," said Brent. "I've seen him use the thing."

"There's one other thing," Janet said, holding up a hand. "We're dealing with an alien energy source here. If you break the loop there could be some sort of feedback. I don't know what that could do. It could be fatal."

Kharrn hefted the ax. "We don't have much choice. Sooner or later one of those bird-things or something worse is going to get in here."

Milton said, "He's right. And you said yourself this rift could spread. It's worth a shot. If you're willing to try it, big man, I'll back your play."

"Same," said Calvin.

Brent sighed. "Yeah, I'm in. But if we're all probably going to die, answer me one question, Kharrn. What are you? I've seen what you can do."

Kharrn grinned. "I'm a twelve-thousand-year-old barbarian from before recorded history."

"No shit?"

"None. Now let's get moving."

Janet stood, and Calvin couldn't help but notice a slight tremble in her hands. "Good luck sounds kind of hollow, but be careful out there, guys."

Kharrn gave a quick nod, then turned and left the office. The three spook show soldiers followed. When they reached the back door, Calvin saw there was a barricade there as well.

Kharrn said, "Have your rifles ready. If there are any of the bird-things close by they may hear me dismantling the barricade."

"Want any help?" Calvin said.

"It will go faster if I do it alone."

Kharrn leaned his ax against a wall and began manhandling pieces of furniture. Calvin saw what he meant about not needing help. Some of the stuff probably weighed three or four hundred pounds, but the big man threw it all aside in a matter of moments.

Nothing tried to come through the door.

Kharrn retrieved his ax and eased the door open. He made a quick look outside, then stepped over the threshold. "Move quick, and don't shoot me."

The three soldiers went out the door fast and immediately began scanning their surroundings, rifles at the ready. They didn't have long to wait before they heard the familiar shrieks of the Utahraptors. Three of the dromos came rushing from different directions. Following Brent's lead, Calvin aimed for the head of the monster closest to him and fired three shots.

The thing's movements were erratic and only one of the rounds scored, but it staggered the dromo. It was still heading his way, but slower. He put two more rounds into the skull and the thing fell.

"Go, Kharrn!" Calvin yelled. "We got this."

The big man sprinted for the tower, moving far faster than Calvin figured someone of his size could move. But a fourth Utahraptor came seemingly from nowhere and bore down on Kharrn. Had it just stepped through the rift? And where the hell was the rift exactly?

Brent and Milton were mowing down the other two dromos. Calvin tried sighting on the new arrival, but Kharrn was between him and the creature. The giant man didn't slow his run. He merely changed direction, heading right at the Utahraptor. Was he out of his mind?

Calvin saw the dromo spring, just as it had at the late Captain Strickland, hooked claws extended to seize its target. *That's how eagles attack.* Calvin had seen it on a documentary. They used those big claws to pin their prey so they could savage it with their beak. This thing didn't have a beak. It had a mouthful of teeth.

A second later, it didn't have most of its skull. Kharrn stepped into the attack and drove the ax straight down on the dromo's head. Then he slammed into the dead creature with his shoulder, knocking it out of his path. The guy couldn't be human.

"Jesus, what a wrecking machine," Milton said, stepping up beside Calvin.

Brent joined them and the three moved in a tight formation, scanning in all directions.

"I'm almost out of ammo," Brent said.

"I have most of my second clip," Calvin said. "You can take my last one." He passed the magazine to Brent.

"Kharrn's almost at the tower," Milton said, stepping forward. "Let's get over there and give him time to..."

The air just to the right left of the tower shimmered like a heat mirage and something appeared out of nowhere. Something big. It stepped into the desert air and released a thundering bellow.

The thing was probably thirty feet long from nose to tip of tail. It wasn't a Tyrannosaurus. Calvin knew enough about dinosaurs to know that its arms were too big. But it was a similar shape.

Calvin froze. The Utahraptors had been hard enough to come to terms with, but at least they were only about the size of horses. This? *This* was a dinosaur. A goddamn dinosaur. Something that a human being was never supposed to see.

"Allosaurus," Milton said in a quiet voice. "It's an Allosaurus."

As if it heard its name, the dinosaur turned to glare at the three men. It lowered its head and charged. It was fast. So unbelievably fast. It covered the ground between them so quickly that Milton only got off a couple of shots before the creature bit him in half.

Calvin backpedaled from the thing, which had paused a moment to chew its food. He leveled the M4A1 and depressed the trigger on full auto, emptying his last magazine into the

Allosaurus. The dinosaur reared in pain, spitting out chunks of Milton as it whirled toward Calvin.

Calvin could hear Brent firing as the Allosaurus surged his way; saw the mouth open wide, rivulets of blood and gore trailing from the serrated teeth.

Calvin caught a glint of metal out of his peripheral vision and then Kharrn's huge ax crunched into the side of the dinosaur's head. The Allosaurus twisted away from Calvin and staggered to one side. But then it lunged back toward the big man, clamping its jaws over his left arm and shoulder. The ax flew away.

Kharrn yelled an inarticulate curse as the Allosaurus lifted him off the ground. His right hand came up and he reached up and tore the dinosaur's eye out. The monster's mouth snapped open and Kharrn fell. He lurched to his feet almost as soon as he hit the ground. He'd lost most of his shirt, and Calvin could see his left side was dotted with puncture wounds where the teeth had penetrated, and his left arm hung useless.

Calvin looked over at Brent, who hefted his rifle and shook his head. Empty. Brent fumbled for his M9 sidearm, but even as he got the 9mm pistol free, Kharrn picked up his ax in his good hand, and loped back toward the Allosaurus. The man really was crazy.

The Allosaurus bellowed in pain and rage and rushed to meet the giant man's charge. Just as it looked like the monster was about to bite Kharrn again, the big man slipped to one side and swung the ax in a murderous arc. The blade sank deep into the creature's knee and the Allosaurus stumbled and fell.

The dinosaur went nuts, thrashing around on the ground and trying to get up, but each time it put weight on the injured limb, the knee buckled. Kharrn waited just outside its reach, looking for an opening. When the Allosaurus fell for a third time, Kharrn hefted the ax in both hands and swung at the dinosaur's neck.

The Allosaurus gave a last spasm as the heavy ax cut most of the way through, almost severing the head, but not quite. Still, almost was enough, and the dinosaur lay still. Kharrn turned without hesitation and ran toward the tower.

"You weren't kidding about that guy, Brent," Calvin said.

"No. Did you see how quickly he got the use of his left arm back?"

"Yeah. What the hell?"

When Kharrn reached the tower, it only took three strokes of the great ax to bring the structure down. Weird purple sparks flashed around the metal. It fell with a loud crash, sending up clouds of sand and gravel as it hit the ground.

Calvin saw some lights come on in the closest building almost as soon as the tower fell. The power was back on, which meant the dampening field was down, and hopefully the rift was closed.

Calvin and Brent walked over to Kharrn. The big man was just standing there, his massive chest rising and falling. His shirt was mostly gone now, and Calvin saw that the puncture wounds, while still visible, had stopped bleeding already.

"You weren't just messing with us, were you?" said Calvin, "About being immortal?"

Kharrn grinned. "No, I wasn't messing with you, Calvin."

"But you're not invulnerable," said Brent.

Kharrn shook his head. "Enough damage would kill me, but it would take a lot, and I heal fast."

"We can see that."

Kharrn said, "You two should go see if there are any more survivors, and check on Dr Kirby."

"What are you going to do?" said Calvin.

"The rift is closed, but a few of those bird-things may still be around. If so, I'll find them."

"You got a ride home?" Brent said.

"You're not worried about me, are you, Sergeant?"

"Fuck no."

"I'll get home. You men go see to your dead and help the living."

Without another word, the giant man turned and walked toward the gate.

GROUND ZERO

An Alpha Unit Story
Kirsten Cross

IND THE GAP! MIND THE GAP!"
The perfectly enunciated voice boomed through the station.
Authoritative, masculine, and tinged with a fat dollop of 'don't fuck with me' undertones, it had cowed an entire generation of commuters into compliance. You could practically hear it pronounce the exclamation marks. But it was almost drowned out by the teeth-clenching squealing of brakes and the pulse of stale air that always announced the arrival of a tube train at Highgate station. Waiting commuters got shotblasted by a cloud of dust and grit as the train burst out of a pitch-black tunnel and into the fluorescent glare of Platform Two. It sounded like a king-sized tin of thundery whoop-ass had been given a damn good shake and then opened in a confined space, accompanied by all the screaming, tormented souls of Hell.

The train squawked to a halt with all the grace of a car in a crusher, as metal wheels with metal brakes made contact on metal rails. It even threw up a few sparks for effect. Doors hissed open and a high-pitched bleep ticked down the seconds before exiting or entering the carriage would become much more of a challenge than it already was. A surge of humanity broke onto the shoreline of the carriage like well-dressed flotsam and flowed into the garishly bright interior, where the fittest and fastest plonked their arses into still-warm seats.

Alpha Unit moved with the flow of the mob, guiding a couple of stubborn civvies out of the way through the careful application of subtle but painful pressure to various points on the body, carefully disguised under the cover of a crowd crush. Each team member knew exactly where they needed to be. They'd planned this dekko just as meticulously as if it were a live-rounds assault. This particular theatre, though, was packed full of non-combatants. And that was always a problem.

Subtlety was the name of the game today. Black ops didn't always have to be flash-bang-wallop, gun-toting mayhem. Sometimes, it could be a sneaky-peaky before things got up close and personal with the organophosphor rounds later on. It's all very well kicking in metaphorical doors, but Alpha Team knew it helped to know *which* damn doors to kick before you started lacing up your boots.

They had basic kit with them, stowed in the large holdall Gary Parks carried. They hadn't really come for a fight, but it paid to have at least a little bit of kit with you, just in case. They'd come to find out just how bad the Highgate infestation had become, and how much of a threat this particular nest of Taints were to the local food source. Or 'Northern Line commuters', as the poor, unfortunate bastards were known.

The four-man team positioned themselves strategically throughout the carriage. Gary Parks, in a very real sense of the word, 'occupied' the space next to the far exit. He entertained himself for a few seconds by staring intensely at a scrawny little skinhead sporting a piss-poor home-made 'White Power' tattoo. The skinhead, now nose-to-nose with a huge black man encroaching on his 'personal space', suddenly looked like he felt very alone in the world.

Yolanda Jaeger propped herself in a corner by the central doors. From here she could see both Gary Parks and the other end of the carriage, occupied by Colby Flynn and the interminable Micky Cox – master of electronics and generalised mayhem. The Unit's former SAS and REME make-it-happen guy was currently staring at a smartphone like a good little commuter.

Three of the team blended in relatively seamlessly with the surrounding hoi polloi. Gary Parks, however, looked like a rhino gatecrashing a tea party.

"For chrissake, Gary, try to look a bit more commuter-y, will you?" Yolanda hissed into a Bluetooth device. The smartphone revolution meant appearing to talk to yourself was now part of digital life, making it almost impossible to tell the nutjobs from a crack team of SF soldiers on a dekko. Of course, there were those who claimed the two were not mutually exclusive.

Gary responded to Yolanda's comment, avoiding any obvious eye contact as per oppo protocol. *"As opposed to what, exactly, boss?"*

"As opposed to a bag of footballs in a suit. Damn it man, I can see the outline of your Glock from here – and no, Micky, before you chip in your five-pennyworth, that is *not* a euphemism! Seriously, Gary, didn't the QM have anything that actually fitted you?"

Colby Flynn's voice crackled over the comms. *"Yol, c'mon, cut him some slack. His tailor sure as hell can't."*

"Fuck off." Gary frowned at the skinhead, who assumed the comment was meant for him and did everything he possibly could to comply.

Colby grinned and notched it up a turn. *"Seriously. The poor guy's a medical freak. He gets his underpants from Marquees-R-Us, you know."*

Gary's frown turned into a full-power scowl. *"Come down here and say that to my kneecaps, puny little man."* He forgot ops protocol for a second and glowered up the carriage towards the definitely-not-puny Colby Flynn.

Flynn simply grinned back and flipped Gary the finger. *"Hulk smash!"*

"Fuck... off!"

Yolanda stopped the banter in its tracks. "Gentlemen, cease and desist, please. Gary, quit intimidating the racist, would you? There's a good chap. Flynn, eyes on, you reprobate, and stop tormenting the giant man in the bad suit. Micky, are we ready?"

"Ready, boss. I'm plugged into the train's electronic control system. I've by-passed the safety protocols and remotely disengaged the Dead Man's Handle. Should be pretty straightforward to interrupt the power."

"I'm so very, very proud of you, you clever boy. A simple

'yes boss' would have sufficed. Just kill the damn power on my mark." Yolanda pressed closer to the door to try and cancel out the reflection of the carriage interior. She peered out into the darkness as it blurred past the windows. "Three, two, one, mark!"

Micky stabbed at his smartphone and the tube train squealed, slowed, and finally juddered to a halt. A few seconds later a nasally voice mumbled over the tannoy. *"Good morning ladies and gentlemen, this is your driver speaking. We seem to have suffered some kind of electrical malfunction. No need to worry, we should have you moving again in a few minutes. Thank you."* A rousing chorus of very British tutting clicked through the carriage in response.

Yolanda checked the carriage and then spoke into the Bluetooth again. "Now the lights if you would, please, Mick."

Micky stabbed at the smartphone again, and frowned. The carriage lights stayed resolutely on. Yolanda turned and raised an eyebrow in Micky's direction. "In your own time, Mister Cox."

"Trying, boss. Let me rotate the frequency, see if I can hit the sweet spot."

"Micky, I genuinely don't care what you rotate, just get those bloody lights turned out."

The lights flickered and then went out, and the only illumination in the carriage came from dozens of smartphone screens. London's hardy commuters again clicked and tutted their annoyance like a pod of angry dolphins. In between signal dropouts they relentlessly carried on tweeting, texting and face-timing, unaware they were witnesses to a black op happening right in front of their noses.

"Anything?" Yolanda ignored the winter-wonderland twinkle of smartphone backlights and stared out into the gloom. The tunnel was much wider here, with columns, arches and walkways intersecting the various lines. This was a major junction, and they were also very close to the old abandoned Highgate tunnels.

Perfect Taint territory.

"We've got movement." Gary's deep voice came through the comms. *"Yep, they're out there all right. They're taking the bait. Cheeky little fuckers, too. Didn't expect 'em to be this close."*

"Flynn?"

"Nothing this end… wait, nope, scratch that. We've got action here too, Yol. And they're moving in."

"Wait out. Remember this is recon only. We are not to engage, repeat, *not* to engage unless absolutely necessary."

Micky Cox's voice chimed in. *"And by absolutely necessary, boss, you mean…"*

"If they clamber on board and start eating commuters, what the bloody hell do you think I mean, Mick?"

"Judging by the amount of eyeshine out there, that's a deffo probable in the very near future, Yol. Twelve o'clock. I count at least five, possibly six." All the earlier brevity had evaporated from Colby's gravely voice, replaced by a much more serious tone.

"A minimum of six here too, boss." Gary glared out into the darkness.

Yolanda cursed. "Oh, bollocks! I bloody *knew* this was gonna go sideways. Wait out." She slid her right hand slowly back underneath her jacket, and her fingers curled around the butt of the adapted Glock. The object of this operation was to assess a possible nest and see just how close they were willing to get to the trains as they passed through the tunnel. Okay, it meant using a train full of commuters as bait, but it was a necessary part of the operation.

And now it looked like they had their answer.

Bloody close.

A scrabbling outside the doors made Yolanda tighten her grip on the Glock and flip the safety catch to 'off'.

Okay. Make that *too fucking close.*

A swarm of hungry and emboldened Taints were now just inches away from the commuters, separated from 'lunch' by nothing but a flimsy metal door. The genetically enhanced vampires with a less-than sunny disposition and a voracious appetite were single-minded, relentless and fearless. Their exceptional strength and speed meant the doors on a thirty-year-old tube train would pose no problem for their venom-tipped fingers. If one of them got purchase on a gap and put their shoulder into it, they could have the doors open in a heartbeat.

So effectively, all that stood between biblical carnage and a tube full of commuters was a thin metal shell, four Special Ops soldiers with a very limited supply of ammo, and the good will of the Northern Line gods.

Yolanda prepared to repel borders by shooting an organophosphor round into the face of the first bastard that came through the door. That would definitely catch the commuters' attention, and would instantly turn what was supposed to be a low-key surveillance operation into a Twitterverse 'trending' topic. And that would not please the Colonel. It pretty much defeated the whole 'black ops' ethos if the damn thing immediately got its own hashtag and went viral.

Further up the carriage, Flynn had eyes-on with a Taint of his own. The drooling, snarling mutant was worrying away at the outside of the carriage. The scrabbling of talon against metal caught the attention of a young woman and she looked up from her smartphone. Colby gave her a friendly smile and nodded towards the door. "Rats."

The girl shuddered. "Ugh. I hate rats."

"Don't worry. They can't get in."

"Oh. Good." The girl immediately lost interest in the rat-slash-slavering, ravenous, genetically altered vampire, and went back to playing a game. Micky craned to look at the girl's screen and then shook his head. She was playing 'Vampire Hunter'.

Yolanda had seen enough. "Micky, I think about now would be a good time to restore power and get both us and these nice, vulnerable commuters the hell out of here, don't you?"

"*Copy that.*" Micky stabbed at the screen.

The lights flickered on and off again.

"Um, Micky?"

"*Trying, boss. Bear with me…*" There was a waver of anxiety in Micky's voice.

"Tell that to Bitey McBiteface out there, Cox. These fuckers are working to their own timetable, fella, and it's deffo on the hurry-up!" Gary's hand tensed around his own Glock. *"Boss…"*

"I said wait out!"

"Yol, I've got a damn talon here…" Colby put the sole of his boot against the needle-sharp talon that protruded through the gap in the door, and crunched down hard. The resulting yelp made the girl look up again, and Colby did a quick impression of a buck-toothed rat, complete with ears and comic-effect "Eek!" for emphasis.

The girl rolled her eyes, muttered a quick "Weirdo!" at Colby, refocused on her screen and updated her status.

Flynn threw a look to the heavens in thanks, and then double-checked the venom-filled talon had withdrawn. He peered into the darkness and watched the Taint scuttle back into the shadows, cradling its hand. They were getting much, *much* too bold. He glanced down the carriage towards Yolanda. She was eyes-on and totally focused, but he could see the tension in her face even at this distance. This was bad. This was very bad. His own spidey-senses screamed blue bloody murder. He reached back to where his adapted Glock sat in its holster and unclipped the retaining catch.

Halfway down the carriage, Yolanda stared out into the tunnel, watching the Taints move into position for a full-on attack. The onslaught was imminent. The muscle in her jaw twitched. "Micky? I hate to rush you, fella, but now would be good. I would be really *very* pleased with *now!*"

"Damn it, boss, I'm trying!"

"Try *harder!*"

"Wait, wait, yep, okay, I got it!" Micky stabbed at the screen and the train's lights blazed once again. The carriage jerked forward, accompanied by the traditional 'About bloody time!' round of tutting from the commuters. Not one of them had any idea they'd been just seconds from the worst start to a Monday anyone could possibly have.

The train finally pulled into Archway station and screeched to a stop. The doors hissed open and the team surfed the wave of humanity out onto the platform. They reconvened in the centre, letting the commuters flow around them.

Yolanda ignored the swirling and buffeting as the whole in/ out/shake-it-all-about commuter dance played out once again. The four of them stood just to the side of the entrance to the carriage so they could assess and do a field debrief without interruption. "Well, *that* was a hoot and a half, wasn't it? Right then, opinions and options, please."

"We've definitely got a problem, Yol. And sooner or later someone who isn't us is gonna notice there's something distinctly moody going on down here. Then there's going to be full-on panic. Cop an eyeful." Colby nodded at the side of the carriage. Tramline scrapes were etched deep into the metal around the door, and a streak of black blood where Flynn had given the Taint an impromptu manicure was obvious. Thankfully, to the untrained eye it simply looked like a smear of oil, and none of the commuters were close enough to notice the acrid chemical tang either.

"Bugger. That *was* close." Yolanda pointed her phone at the door and snapped a succession of photographs. The Colonel would need documentary evidence if they were going to risk going into the tunnels for a seek-and-destroy op, but she didn't want to alarm any of the commuters still milling around. Sneaky-peaky. Keep it off the radar and don't alarm the herd. The last thing they wanted was a stampede. "I need to get a swab of that for the forensics team before this train buggers off. Gentlemen, would you mind awfully giving me a bit of cover, so the civvies don't get freaked out by the crazy lady taking DNA swabs off a train carriage door, please? Thank you."

The team moved to shield Yolanda from view as she took a swab of the blackened blood. She stood, dropped the cotton-tipped bud into a plastic tube and snapped on the lid. The tube was deposited into a plastic zip bag and secreted into a jacket pocket with all the dexterity of a street magician pulling a card trick. Not a single 'civvy' noticed.

Taints were continually evolving, and the swab would give

the team a chemical blueprint of their current stage of development. It would probably be bad. It usually was with Taints.

"Right then, let's get this back to base." Yolanda nodded towards the exit, and Micky, Colby and Gary set off at a brisk walk towards the stairs, dropping instinctively into the standard staggered two-two formation, even in this supposedly 'safe' environment. It was hard-wired into their DNA through years of training, operations and that overriding instinct to stay the fuck alive. So far, it had worked rather well.

Colby paused and turned, aware that Yolanda had dropped back. She was still standing in the middle of the platform, a puzzled frown creasing her forehead. "Yol?" He walked back towards her and laid a hand on her arm. "You've got that 'look' again. 'Sup?"

Yolanda turned and looked behind her. At the far end of the platform, and right in the CCTV's blind spot stood a massive figure. It ignored the commuters that flowed around it. Unusually for Londoners, they didn't jostle or push past, but gave the looming figure a wide berth, repelled from making actual physical contact with him by some internal survival instinct. Colby snorted a laugh and shook his head. "Damn, that dude's bigger than Gary!" He looked at Yolanda. "Yol? Hey, c'mon, you're starting to freak me out. You okay?"

"Yeah. Big lad, isn't he? Now look closer, Flynn." Yolanda's gaze never left the figure at the end of the platform. "Remind you of anyone?"

Colby looked at the hulking figure and frowned. Then a look of recognition finally spread across his face. "Oh, *hell* no!"

Yolanda nodded. "Yep. And *there* it is..."

Colby reached for his Glock in one smooth, flowing move.

Yolanda grabbed his wrist and shook her head. "Stand down, Flynn." For a split second she battled with him. "I *said*, stand down!"

Colby glared at her. "He's right there, Yol! He's *right fucking there!*"

"And so are god-knows how many civilians! We start shooting now, all hell breaks loose, we are royally burned, and people die. And if two blocks of C4 in Tokat couldn't take the bugger out, do you honestly think a single clip of organo jackets'll do the trick? Now, stand *down!*"

Colby relented, but didn't take his eyes off the figure at the end of the platform. "Okay, but we need to bang out of here sharpish and call in a lock-down team. *Now.*"

"Not until I know that every civvy in here is out safely. We wait."

"Are you actually kidding me? I am *not* just standing here playing platform chicken with that son of a bitch!"

"I said, we *wait!*" Yolanda's gaze never left the brooding figure in front of her. She clicked the Bluetooth. "Micky. Find the station manager. Close the station. *Now.* Then call in containment. I want all trains on this line stopped immediately. Usual 'suspect package' or 'major emergency engineering works' bullshit, you choose. Gary, get your arse back down here. FUBAR. FUBAR like you wouldn't bloody believe. I need you and your bag of tricks here. Move."

Two voices responded in sequence: *"Copy that."*

Yolanda refocused on the figure in front of them. It wasn't just the size that was so intimidating. It was the way that his mere presence seemed to suck the very light out of the air. And those teeth. Man, those teeth! He smiled slowly, revealing a mouthful of dazzlingly white and needle-sharp dentistry.

Vlad.

In London.

In the middle of the morning rush hour, on platform two of Archway Underground station.

One of the most savage and evil monsters ever to walk the face of the earth was currently standing casually on a London underground platform as if it were the most natural thing in the world, dressed in normal clothes, and looking every inch like a bog-standard commuter. A hidden horror, right there, in plain sight. And nobody except the two soldiers had the faintest idea what ancient evil had wandered, unseen and unchallenged, slap-bang into the normalcy of everyday London life.

Tinted glasses masked his distinctive golden eyes from the gaze of his human fellow travellers. But nothing could hide who he really was to Colby and Yolanda. And he was about as welcome as finding a scorpion in your boot.

He stood there, a snarling smile taunting the two soldiers.

Then, from the same carriage stepped another figure. Almost as tall as Vlad, he was lithe and wiry, not as muscular but certainly a contender for ugliest Northern Line commuter of the day. He stood slightly behind Vlad, subservient to the monster. Yet there was a quiet, confident menace that permeated from the creature. He had authority. He had standing. He had a connection with Vlad that went beyond that of a mere 'foot soldier'. This was a Taint of some importance.

Colby glanced at Yolanda. "Like father like son?"

Yolanda's eyes didn't leave the two figures. She shook her head. "More likely one of his Lieutenants. Remember, Col, this bastard may be a monster now, but he was a military man once. And a great one at that. He'll have his own chain of command."

Colby scowled. "Great. So we've got a second tango to deal with. This day just keeps getting better and fucking better, doesn't it?"

"Focus on the primary, Col. If the secondary advances, engage and shoot the fucker in the face. And keep shooting until it goes down and *stays* down." Yolanda's hand tightened around the grip of her Glock.

Okay.

So this could go either way…

Vlad glanced sideways as a pretty blonde, wrapped in her own little commuter-world full of bland pop music, LOL texts from 'Angie' and wearing the standard-issue officeware of white blouse, dark pencil skirt and cheap, clattery high heels, tried to squeeze past. He sensed Colby and Yolanda holding their breath as they watched his fingers flex and ripple.

Motionless and still smiling, Vlad gazed at the woman, sensing every fluttering beat of her heart as she manoeuvred past him.

Then her perfume hit him.

Like a storm surge, it sent a wave of ancient memories crashing into his mind, overwhelming him for a second. He didn't care about the insignificant life of this woman. He had taken thousands – hundreds of thousands – of lives over the centuries. One more wouldn't make him any more evil than he already was. Sparing her would not redeem him either.

But that perfume...

It was the scent of lilacs on a soft, summer evening. It was the scent *she* had worn, all those centuries ago.

Brief seconds slowed to the speed of dripping molasses. Vlad watched the girl move past him in slow motion and took in every detail. Her red lips. Her silken blond hair. But above all, that dizzying perfume that had the power to stir such a fire in his blackened heart. She turned and looked at him, and for a split second he could have sworn the girl's face transformed into *her* face. His love. His sweet love.

Taken from him by soldiers.

Soldiers who had wanted to make sure his dark legacy ended at Tokat. There would be no more children. No more sons. They had gutted her like a fish. Soldiers had butchered his love in front of him. Soldiers had tainted the sweet scent of lilacs with the coppery tang of *her* blood.

And now, this vapid... *child*, tottering past him on ridiculous heels, had the audacity to wear the same perfume as *she* did? Vlad's mind reeled and insanity roared inside him. It warped and twisted that brief flutter of clarity – of light, of beauty – and morphed it back into a black, blood-soaked chasm of hatred. How *dare* she walk on this earth, while his love rotted in the ground! How *dare* she!

Vlad's madness, fuelled by the scent of his long-dead love, boiled. For a moment, his focus had shifted away from the soldiers standing just a few feet from him. The girl and her perfume had filled his world.

His lieutenant saw the black madness in his master's eyes and twitched his finger. It was enough to bring Vlad's attention sharply back into focus.

The girl was nothing more than an impostor.

A mere memory of his love.

A haunting reflection, stimulated by the scent of lilacs.

But the soldiers… Ah, now *they* were something else.

They were toys to be played with, before he unleashed his lieutenant and his pack of slathering Taints on them.

But not yet. Not yet…

The grandfather of all vampires studied his opponents, taking in every micro-expression, feeling every hammer-blow of their hearts, and hearing the blood rushing through their bodies. He could almost taste the fear-tinged frustration they felt at being so close yet so far away from protecting an 'innocent'.

It delighted him.

Watching the impotent rage boil and churn in the bellies of his enemies was exquisite. He relished the thought that for the rest of their probably very short lives the two soldiers would have that gut-punch of shame every time they remembered they had had no choice but to simply stand and watch a monster decide the fate of an innocent girl. In the most normal of surroundings. Where the girl was supposed to be safe.

But this was a tactical confrontation, too. A chance to see how his enemy reacted. How they moved. How they prioritised potential collateral damage. Examine their weaknesses.

Vlad chuckled quietly. Time to take things up a level. He nodded to the lieutenant, who bowed slightly and smoothly stepped back on board the train. Inside, a handful of oblivious passengers sat starting at their smartphones, unaware of what stalked their carriage.

The two soldiers instinctively reacted by stepping forward a couple of paces. Vlad held up a finger and wagged it from side to side. They froze again, closer to the door yet not quite close enough to make a difference.

Colby snarled at Vlad, that taunting laugh sending a pulse of fury through him. He hissed. "Fuck. Yol, we need to get that bastard off of that train. *Yol…*"

"I know. I know, damn it." Yolanda ground her teeth in frustration. *Oh, you clever bastard, Vlad. You clever, clever bastard! Split your targets. See how we prioritise. You son of a bitch, you're on as much of a dekko as we are, aren't you, you fucker?*

An ear-splitting beeping warned of the impending departure of the train. The two soldiers knew those passengers were trapped now. Trapped inside a tin can with one of Vlads lieutenants. And there was nothing, *nothing* they could do.

"Fuck! *Fuck!* Yol, we have to stop that train!" Colby's voice cracked with pent-up fury.

"Damn it!" Yolanda watched as the lieutenant sat beside an elderly woman. He glanced back towards Colby and Yolanda and smiled a vicious, spiteful smile, and draped his arm around the back of the seat.

Yolanda glared back at the lieutenant, clicked the Bluetooth and hissed into it. "Micky, get them to stop the train! Stop the *damn train!*"

Static. Fucking static. *Shit!* Those few steps they'd taken towards Vlad and his lieutenant must have put them slap-bang into a dead spot. She knew that if she moved a muscle, she could instigate a reaction from Vlad. And that would be bad for the long-term prospects of blondie in her clattery heels and tight pencil skirt. "Micky! *Micky!*"

Still nothing but the tormenting hiss of dead air. *"Fuck!"*

Back on the platform, Vlad snarled, and reached out. His long, sinewy fingers brushed the woman's hair as she passed by, a caress as gentle as a lover's touch, as delicate as a butterfly – and filled with so much potential for violence. All he had to do was change that caress into a snatch, wind his fingers in the girl's hair and drag her towards him...

The electric motors of the tube train whined into life and the carriages started to move. Out of the corner of her eye Yolanda saw the lieutenant give her a little wave and then lean in towards the old woman. The last thing Yolanda saw as the carriage started to blur past was a sweet little old lady strike up a conversation with a 'nice young man'...

The noise grew into a mechanical roar, and the air pressure increased. Garish fluorescent lights flickered, combining with the flashing tube train to create a violent strobe effect. The air blasted along the platform, turning the girl's blonde hair into dancing strands and tangling them around Vlad's fingers.

"Yol!" Colby couldn't hold back any more.

Screw this.

"Engage!"

Screw the whole 'low-key' bullshit. They couldn't just stand there impotent and motionless any more. They were burned. Might as well make it official, then. Their Glocks flipped out and the business end of two adapted G17s pointed straight towards where Vlad—

—Wasn't.

Colby cursed long, loud and passionately. "Shit! Shit! *Shit!* Oh, you sneaky, mother-fucking, greasy, undead son of a *bitch!*"

Still holding the Glocks out in front of them, Colby and Yolanda moved forward at a rapid scuttle, ready to start blasting at anything that didn't look like a commuter.

The girl stood alone, alive and paralysed with fear as two grim-faced, gun-toting figures moved smoothly towards her. They were using that feline, cross-step gait that always hinted at extreme violence and explosive power bubbling just below the surface. What were they, Special Forces? Police? Security Services? What? Whoever they were they looked like they'd shoot her in a heartbeat. She stood, frozen with fear, hot tears of terror rolling down her cheeks. "Please! Please don't kill me! Please!"

"Get out. Move. *Move!*" Yolanda moved past the girl, reached back with her left hand and shoved her hard in the back, not wasting time with nice reassurances or any of that touchy-feely shit. The girl didn't need telling twice. She staggered under the surprising power from Yolanda's shove, regained her balance and then clattered her way along the platform towards the exit, where she saw another huge man running down the stairs with a menacing look and equally menacing Glock. Her tears started to dissolve the cheap mascara she wore, and it ran down her face in two gritty black streaks. This was *not* a normal workday commute.

The back end of the train disappeared into the far tunnel behind them, and Yolanda stopped at the point where the platform ended and black oblivion began. She lowered the Glock and unleashed a shit-ton of real passion into an uncharacteristic outburst of cursing. "Fuck! *Fuck!*"

Colby jumped down onto the tracks and started to move towards the darkness.

Gary dumped the kit bag on the floor, looked over Yolanda's shoulder and watched his best friend heading purposefully towards the tunnel entrance. "Colby, you daft bastard, stop! There's an entire army of Taints in there, and the next train is about a minute away from turning you into a smear! Colby! *Colby!*" He glowered at his friend's back and muttered. "God *damn it,* you stubborn…" Gary, still questioning Colby's parentage under his breath, turned and took up position behind Yolanda. He kept his back to his team, eyes fixed firmly on the other end of the tunnel, just in case the Taints tried a pincer move on them.

Yolanda raised the gun, targeting the nose of the Glock straight at Colby's back. She scowled down the barrel and her sharp voice echoed through the station like broken glass. "*Mister Flynn!* You will stand down *immediately* or so help me, I *will* shoot you in the back!"

Flynn stopped, and slowly lowered his gun. He glared into the blackness, trying to ignore the itchy sensation between his shoulder blades. He could practically feel the green dot from Yolanda's sighting laser. She probably wouldn't shoot him, he knew that. Well, probably. *Possibly.* Actually? Thinking about it, she might squeeze the bloody trigger just to prove a point, the crazy bint. But that was just Yol's way. And that's why he loved her. It was nothing personal, just Yol trying to save his stupid, hot-headed idiot self from dying a wasteful, pointless death.

She was right, of course.

The Jaeger family had been hunting and killing vampires across Europe for generations. Even the name meant 'Hunter' in German. There was also the small technicality that when they were on duty Yolanda Jaeger was Flynn's CO too.

So he complied. Not doing so would mean the mother of all arse-kickings in the training gym later. The bloody woman fought dirty. But she'd also stayed alive by knowing which battles to pick, and which to walk away from. It was a lesson he was finally starting to understand. And this was definitely one of those 'walk away' times, no matter how much that pinpoint of fury currently burning its way through his chest told him to chase his quarry down and end this once and for all.

Colby stood motionless, staring into the black of beyond. The clustered eyeshine of at least a dozen Taints winked and twinkled back at him, taunting him, daring him to run away from the safety of the bright platform and into their dark, death-ridden world. A pulse of warm air throbbed down the tunnel, indicating that he had about fifteen seconds to get back to the platform before thirty tons of London Underground rolling stock really fucked up his day.

"Vlad?" Colonel North's voice was sharp.

"Yes, sir." Yolanda nodded. She paced the platform with the phone pressed to her ear. Colby sat on the bench, glowering at the darkness. Micky Cox had got a reluctant official to close the station due to a 'suspect package', so the team were currently alone in a deserted tube station. All Northern Line trains were at a standstill. Gary Parks stood sentry at one end of the platform, a fully loaded shotgun pointed at the north tunnel, while Micky patrolled the south end.

"You're sure?"

"Yes, sir."

"In the middle of the bloody day?"

"Well, technically, it was the morning rush hour, but yes, sir."

"You're absolutely certain it was him?"

"Yes, sir. I'd know that bastard anywhere. It was him. And I'm pretty sure he knew who we were too. His lieutenant hopped back onto the train before it left. We couldn't contain both of them. I'm sorry, sir."

"*You did what you could, Captain. This was supposed to be a rekko, not a damn meet and greet. The fault is not yours, Yollie. It's Vlad's. Always remember that.*" Colonel North sighed. "*Okay. So what's your appraisal of the situation?*"

Yolanda answered quickly and succinctly. "The tunnel between Highgate and Archway is infested, sir. Looks like it's ground zero for this particular nest. London Underground is uber-pissed about us limiting access to the Northern Line between the two stations, but we've pulled our usual 'national security' number on them, so they've been forced to comply. We've got a lot of angry, inconvenienced commuters, but that's nothing new."

"Good. I'd rather they were annoyed and alive than happy and dead."

"Nobody who travels the Northern Line is happy, sir."

"True. Right then. Solutions?"

"We're already on the ground. The station's closed and we're ready to go in and evict the little buggers with extreme prejudice. If you could have Terry Warner and Bravo Unit suited up for a bug hunt and to us with supplies asap, we can try and do a seek and destroy right now. I'd like to keep Vlad off balance by hitting hard and fast. We may not be able to take Vlad out now, but we can certainly show him we're not just going to roll over…"

Yolanda's report was interrupted by a loud bang. She instinctively flinched then spun to face the southern end of the tunnel, where Micky Cox was pointing the smoking barrel of a 12-bore pump-action shotgun into the darkness. Yolanda rolled her eyes. "Jesus! What the hell, Micky?"

Micky turned, grinned, and re-primed his shotgun, ignoring the screaming, thrashing, heel-drumming Taint behind him. "Sorry, boss. Little bugger got a bit lunge-y at me." There was a *'wuuumph!'* sound and a cloud of ash floated gently down onto Micky's shoulders. He casually brushed it off and shrugged.

Yolanda shook her head. "Eyes on, Mick." She returned her attention to the Colonel. "Sorry about that sir."

"Everything all right, Captain?"

"Yes, sir. Just Micky getting trigger happy with a Taint. But that just goes to show how bold they're getting."

"Hmm. They are getting a bit cheeky, aren't they? Anything else?"

"Yes, sir. I'd like permission to go after that damn lieutenant of his if possible, too. I don't like the look of that bastard." Yolanda paused. "Sir, we need to move quickly on this if we're going to keep it under the radar. If the press get hold of it we're going to face an epic shitstorm, and right now I'd rather keep this on a need to know basis."

Colonel North responded with a grunt. *"Agreed. I'll have Corporal Warner and Bravo Unit en route to you in fifteen. Good hunting, Yollie."*

"Thank you, sir. I'll keep you updated." Yolanda ended the call and put the phone in her pocket. She glanced up. "Upstairs, chaps. We're meeting Terry and Bravo team in the ticket area." A nasty smile crept over her face. "We've got ourselves a bug hunt, lads."

Micky and Gary grinned back. Colby merely stared into the blackness of the tunnel and glowered at the blinking, winking eyeshine.

He wanted that lieutenant. He wanted him *bad*.

There was something about that nasty little bastard that made Colby's skin prickle…

Outside the tube station's locked metal gates a throng of commuters milled about. A single London Underground employee, resplendent in a hi-viz jacket and with absolutely no clue as to what was really happening, tried to shepherd the muttering masses towards the nearest bus stop. A scribbled note stuck to a sandwich board apologised for the inconvenience, while the hi-viz employee reassured passengers that yes, the station would probably reopen shortly. Even *he* didn't believe that bullshit line.

Terry Warner walked up to the guy and flashed an ID. "Clean up crew. Open up."

The man – currently engaged in telling an officious, besuited commuter that no, he didn't have any further information and no, he didn't know or in fact *care* who the man was, he'd have to wait like everyone else – flickered his attention towards the ID. He puffed up his chest and looked as 'official' as he could. "Suspicious package. Security alert. Nobody gets in."

Terry carefully pulled his boilersuit open so hi-viz guy could just see the butt of a Glock 17 tucked under his armpit. He made damn sure the stroppy commuter couldn't see anything. His blue eyes hardened and he stared intently at hi-viz guy. "Listen, fella. I have neither the time nor the crayons to explain this to you in any detail. I *said*, clean… up… crew. Translation, open the *damn* gate. *Now*."

Hi-viz guy, now completely ignoring the still-stroppy commuter, focused on the 'clean up team' and, in particular, the tall, fierce-looking man carrying the Glock 17. They were the most evil-looking bunch of 'cleaners' he'd ever seen. They were all powerfully built, probably heavily armed too, and scanning the crowd like a bunch of SAS soldiers on an operat… oh. *Shit…*

Realisation kicked in and hi-viz guy gulped. He quickly decided pursuing any kind of argument he might have about who was allowed where and when was probably trumped by the sheer amount of ordnance this 'clean up crew' were packing. He fumbled with a key and unlocked the gate, opening it just wide enough for the team to squeeze through.

As Danny Smith walked past the man he stopped for a moment. He kept his voice low, so as not to alarm the civvies. "Listen, fella. Things are going to get a little bit *urgent* in a while. So when you hear screaming and a shit-load of people stampeding up the stairs, you open this damn gate and you let them out. Got it?" He gave hi-viz guy what he thought was a reassuring smile.

"I… I… I…"

"I *said*, got it?" Danny's smile melted away.

"Y-yes. Yeah. I got it. Sure. Why the hell not?" Hi-viz guy nodded. He really regretted not calling in sick this morning.

"Adda boy." Danny patted the man on the shoulder just a tiny bit harder than he needed to, and followed his team into the bowels of the station and out of sight of the crowds outside.

Inside, a lone London Underground official stood shaking in a corner. Watching the team pull balaclavas over their faces, wrapping throat comms around their necks, and opening up bags filled with automatic weapons did nothing to rebalance his peace of mind. He let out a little yelp.

A pair of hard, steely eyes immediately connected with his own. He could tell the face was scowling underneath the black fabric. Terry barked out two words. "Which platform?"

The official pointed a shaking finger towards the escalator. "P-p-platform two…"

Terry gave a curt nod. "Thank you. Now fuck off."

The man fucked off at a rapid scuttle, and Terry motioned to Bravo Unit. "Move out." Time to tie up with the boss…

"You're late."

"You're welcome!"

Terry gave Micky the finger and threw a kit bag at him. Micky Cox caught it with all the grace and dexterity of a one-armed blind man in a dark room. Terry chuckled. "Careful, fella. That's the bag with the UV flash bangs."

Micky plonked the bag down and crouched next to it. He unzipped the bag and pulled it open. "Okay. Wadda we got, then? Big, honking great bullet chuckers?"

"Check."

"Spare organo FMJs?"

"Check."

"Sneaking-around black ninja outfits with anti-Taint kevlar weave?"

Gary Parks glanced over and primed his Remington 870 shotgun as an underline, before attaching it to a lanyard and picking up a C8. "Micky, we are not doing sneaking-around ninja shit. We're going in dressed as a team of London Underground Northern Line fluffers who've had all the love, hope and faith in humanity sucked out of them through years of working in one of the city's shittiest hellholes. So it's regulation boilersuits, boots and beanies. No ninja shit."

Micky looked puzzled and glanced over at Yolanda, who was busy checking the recoil on her Glock. "Um, boss? Question?"

Without even looking at him, Yolanda immediately responded. "Fluffers are teams who clean the underground tracks."

"Oh, so they're not…"

"No, Micky. No. They're really not. You bloody pervert."

Gary laughed. "Mate, you watch far too much porn, you know that?"

"Yeah. Porn with your mama in it."

Gary gave Micky a blank look. "Seriously? Did you actually just throw down with a 'yo mama' joke at me?"

Terry Warner turned to Colby. "Are they always like this?"

Colby grinned. "These two? Fella, this is a good day. They're usually going at each other like an old married couple." Colby dropped the magazine out of the C8, tapped it, checked and re-inserted it with a snap. He primed and checked the primary holographic sighting, making absolutely sure that he hadn't accidentally knocked the switch from 'Safe' to 'Rapid' – or 'NoKill' to 'Parp', as Micky liked to call it. The team were using the more compact 10-inch barrel version. The 16-inch barrel might be more accurate, but when you were going in up-close-and-personal with a grabby Taint full of bad intentions, then the longer barrel tended to snag and get in the way. There was no point attaching the standard bayonet either. That would just tangle you up even more, and if you were using a bayonet against a Taint then you were probably *way* too up-close-and-personal already.

A clatter of heavy boots announced the arrival of a worried-looking Danny Smith. He was carrying a tablet in one hand and a C8 in the other. "Boss, you better see this." He spoke rapidly. "Came in via our covert channels about three minutes ago. It was addressed to the team." He glanced at Colby. "Personally."

The team gathered around the tablet and studied the flickering, jerky picture. Yolanda squinted at the screen. "That picture is piss-poor, fella. What are we looking at?"

"Hang on…" Danny pointed at the screen. "There."

Gary groaned. "Oh, now, *this* isn't good." On the screen was a figure that, while the face may have been blurry and grainy, there was no question as to whom it was.

Vlad's lieutenant sat among a train full of oblivious commuters and stared up at the CCTV, a smirk tugging at the corner of his mouth. Next to him, the old lady had her head down on her chest, looking for all the world like she was simply having a quick nana-nap in-between stops. The team, however, knew immediately that she wasn't asleep. They could all see a dark mark on the side of her neck; a small wound with the tiniest trickle of blood running from it. That was one 'nana-nap' the old girl wouldn't be waking up from, bless her heart…

Gary glared at the screen. "Mother*fucker!*"

Yolanda stared at the screen. "Is he sending us this via live feed?"

Danny nodded. "Yes, boss. The train's been held in the tunnel next to Tufnell Park on an emergency 'suspect package' order. The entire Northern Line this side of the water is at a standstill. The commuters are getting majorly angsty, and I'm guessing Vlad's lieutenant is just a finger-snap away from unleashing that pack of Taints you saw and turning that train into an all-you-can-eat buffet." Danny paused. "Boss, there're a lot of people on that train. A lot. And we've basically put them slap-bang in the middle of a potential feeding frenzy."

Yolanda nodded. She pushed the Glock back into her leg holster. "Get the train moved back here and hold it. Doors shut. We move. Now." The steel in her voice told the team it wasn't a suggestion. It was an order.

They grabbed their kit. The time for a bit of pre-op, barrack-room banter was well and truly over.

The team had picked a quiet spot well away from prying eyes and in the station's CCTV dead spot. Nobody needed to know what was going on down here, least of all some jobsworth security 'spotter' in a grey room somewhere. They were here to clear the nest, get the civilians to safety with minimum collateral, and take out the lieutenant at the very least. Not provide some bored security guard with an impromptu reality show.

Yolanda sniffed sharply, and looked straight at Colby. "Right then. What's his end game here, Col?"

"Fuck knows."

Colby was concentrating on balling that churning knot of fury he had twisting his insides up into a focused and precise pinpoint. Random, uncontrolled rage was useless. It would probably get you killed. Focus and you released the true killer inside. It was a side of his personality Colby didn't particularly like, but it had kept him alive up to now, so he had learned to embrace it and use it when necessary.

Combat wasn't just about training. It was about unleashing the monster within that everyone has but nobody wants to acknowledge. And doing it in such a way that allowed you to achieve your objective without thinking about the blood and carnage you were inflicting. You needed to disassociate yourself from that side of combat. Otherwise you'd freeze. And if you froze, you died. Really quickly.

Combat was a means to an end. It was about protecting your team. Protecting yourself. And protecting those who couldn't defend themselves.

And it was about royally fucking up enemy combatants with pointy teeth and centuries of hatred twisting up their intestines.

But now wasn't the time for navel-gazing or introspection on the Art of War. Yolanda studied her oppo and brought him back to the here and now with a bump. "Fuck knows isn't an answer, Flynn."

Colby looked up and shook his head. "Yol, you know more about vampires than any of us. Just because I got up close and personal with Vlad in Tokat doesn't mean I've got an inside on his chain of command or their reasoning."

Yolanda scowled. "Bullshit. You're our strategist and battle-field tactician. That's what you do. And you're damn good at it. So start bloody strategizing! I need to know what his game play is, and what we have to do to make whatever he wants to happen *not* happen." She ignored the slightly puzzled look from Terry Warner. "From my perspective, Old World vamps want one thing. Power. I'll put a week's pay on Vlad not showing his face openly to us again. One exposure was a meet-n-greet. Two would be pushing it and he's not stupid enough to expose himself to any potential risk if he thinks we're ready for him. So I'll guess we'll be going up against that lieutenant and his squad, not Vlad."

Colby nodded. "Agreed. Which at least means we should get a kill out of this shitstorm at the least."

Gary chipped in. "Would Vlad risk one of his top people against us? I mean, like you said, he's a general. He values good lieutenants."

"Not enough to avoid sending them up against us, Gary," said Yolanda. "Nah. As important as this bugger might be to Vlad, he's not irreplaceable. He'll be a tough bastard, so expect a fight. But he can be killed. Remember that, no matter how ugly it gets."

Colby nodded. "Yol's right. This is a game of chess to him. He's a strategist, and a damn good one, too. Don't ever, *ever* underestimate this guy. Look, if you're planning any kind of whacko world domination shit, you take out your enemy's strongest keystone first, right? As far as Vlad's concerned, the primary threat is us. So he's gonna throw one of his lieutenants at us and see how we do. If we lose, he's golden. If we win then okay, Vlad's lost a link in his armour, but it's not as if he can't get a replacement." Colby sniffed. "It also helps if you spread a bit of panic among the general populous at the same time, too. Makes it harder for the military to contain the situation and mount a counter-offensive. Hearts and minds can be used in a negative context too, you know."

Micky scowled. "So, okay, what is it then, Col? Whacko

world domination shit? Revenge for Tokat? Sheer bloody mind-edness? Indigestion?"

"Honestly, who the fuck actually cares right now? We've got a train full of commuters that matey's got lined up as today's chef's special, and no plan other than going in and giving him the biggest beasting we can while minimising collateral." Colby looked at Yolanda. "Back-up?"

"If you're asking if there's a plan B, that would be a no. Like you said, we've barely got a plan A. Back-up is at least another fifteen minutes out." She shook her head. "We're on our own with this one."

"Perfect. So Vlad's Rupert, plus guests, plus a shit-load of panicked collateral in the way, in a confined space, and a team of eight with limited ammo. Oh, happy fucking days." Terry shook his head. "Ah well, more to go around, I guess."

"Yeah. The one with the least number of kills buys the pizza." Gary primed his C8 carbine…

They stopped on the last broad landing before the steps reached the platform. Crouching on either side with their backs to the wall, they were all ready and waiting for the go from Yolanda. She nodded. "Right then. We all know what we're doing. Watch your backs. Objectives. One, get the civvies out and clear. Two, eliminate the nest. Three, take out that lieutenant with extreme prejudice. Four, bang out sharpish and let the cleaners in to bag and tag. No collateral, and I mean *none*. Everyone gets out. Except that arrogant little fucker. Are we clear?"

The entire team answered as one. "Crystal!"

Yolanda glanced at her watch. "Right then, gentlemen. We're on the clock here. Let's go to work, shall we?" She gave them a dark little smile.

They all knew what that meant.

Bug hunt time…

Alpha and Bravo Unit moved silently down the stairs

towards platform two. Everyone knew their role. Staggered two-two formation. Two teams of four. Minimum comms. Chain of command was Yolanda as primary point of contact, Colby leading Alpha team, and Terry Warner leading Bravo.

They'd practised this a thousand times in the old Charing Cross tube station on the Jubilee line, selected as a kill house because it was the most recently abandoned station and had the most up-to-date layout. Now they had to put that training into real-time action, but with both warm bodies and a shit-ton of civilians adding an unknown element into the mix.

The plan, if there was such a thing, was simple. Kill the lights. Bravo team led by Terry Warner would hit the tunnel end and take out any close proximity Taints. Alpha team would take the platform to lay down cover if needed while Colby and Danny dropped down and used Primacord blasting cord to daisychain a series of detonations on the train doors. Create a series of small, contained explosions that would be enough to blow the doors open, cause maximum diversion and allow the passengers to get the hell out of Dodge on the hurry-up. Bravo team would get the civvies out. Alpha team would breach and attempt to take out the tango with extreme prejudice. As fast as Vlad's lieutenant was, even he wouldn't be able to contain an entire tube carriage of stampeding London commuters *and* take on a determined and highly-trained Special Ops team at the same time. Plan A just might work.

Well, that was the theory, anyway.

The teams stopped at the bottom of the stairs, just out of sight of the stationary tube train. The darkened platform wasn't entirely pitch black, but there was more than enough deep shadow to mask their movements. Yolanda turned to Danny and Flynn, keeping the commands to a minimum, delivered in a sharp whisper. "Doors. Go." She turned to Terry and the rest of Bravo team. "Tunnel. Go." Finally, she glanced to her left. "Micky. Exit point. Go."

Danny and Colby hunched up and scuttled along the length of the train, staying tight against the metal skin and expertly positioning a series of Primacord strips on each set of doors. As they placed each strip, they cautiously checked for commuters standing too close to the doors, and waved them back. The orange Primacord2 had a central core of 2.1 grams of PETN explosive per meter of cord, which shouldn't be enough to actually kill anyone, even close up. But an injured commuter could slow the extraction process. This needed to be fast, furious and with minimum casualties. And the entire team knew that 'minimum' in Yolanda's book meant no fucking casualties at all.

A link cord connected the blasting caps on each strip, and led back to the detonation button cradled in Yolanda's gloved hand. She was conscious to keep her finger well away from the button at this point. It might not be enough to kill, but the Primacord could certainly take a hand off at the wrist.

Danny and Colby took up position at the far end and gave the 'Ready' signal. Yolanda nodded and glanced back towards the tunnel, where Terry nodded and gave another 'Ready' signal. Micky nodded and made it three-for-three. The whole thing had taken less than a minute.

She held up three fingers, ensuring all the teams could see.

Stand by.

Three… two… one…

Yolanda flipped up the cover switch and pressed the detonator.

The teams recoiled from the daisychain of blasts that ripped through the station. The tube train doors tore open, accompanied by screams and shrieks from dozens of terrified commuters.

In the tunnel, Terry and Bravo team unleashed an organophosphor shit-storm towards the glistening eyeshine. The waiting pack of Taints were mowed down in a heel-drumming firework display. The organophosphor payloads sent their bodies into overdrive, coursing through their veins like lava and igniting into an explosion of guts and body parts. An intense fire consumed every last one of the bastards, sending clouds of hot ash cascading and tumbling into eddies and whirls, which pulsed down the tunnels and sent the ex-Taints spiralling into oblivion.

A series of double taps took out the last stragglers, including one that lunged towards Terry's face, slashing at him with a freshly mutilated hand. Terry calmly grouped two FMJs in the centre of the bastard's chest, and watched the creature thrash on the floor. This must've been the one Colby stomped on earlier. "Manicure *that*, motherfucker!" Without even a hint of a reflexive flinch, he grinned as the Taint exploded. Terry shouldered the C8 carbine and did a quick double check. "Tunnel clear."

"Get the civvies out." Yolanda kept her instructions minimal and crystal clear. She trusted every one of her team to do their job. They didn't need babysitting.

Terry responded. "Copy that," and motioned to Bravo team. He stabbed a finger towards the train. "Civvies! Out!" The team sprinted back up the tracks and up onto the platform, each taking a carriage and shouting at the terrified passengers to *"MOVE!"* First one and then a flood of commuters poured out of the carriages. They were shoved unceremoniously towards the exit by Bravo Team. Micky Cox stood on the stairs, ushering the flow of terrified humanity up the stairs and to safety.

From the end carriage a screaming, rolling roar of fury echoed around the platform, amplified by the station's acoustics. It stopped everyone dead in their tracks – civilian and squaddie alike. Something deep inside every man, woman and child's soul sat up and screamed in terror.

It was a primeval sensation that stripped away the cosy blanket of safety from an ultra-modern world, like the growl of a wolf next to your ear, or the brush of talons on the back of your neck. It spoke of vast, dark forests and starlit, shadow-filled nights, the sharp tin tang of snow in the air and the metallic taste of your own blood bubbling up in your throat.

It promised nothing but death.

And it was pissed. *Man*, it was *pissed...*

Yolanda barked commands, breaking the stunned silence. "Danny! Colby! Fall back! *Now!*" She threw a quick glance towards Terry and Mick. "Get those bloody civilians out of here! Move!"

Danny and Colby moved carefully backwards towards Yolanda, their C8s trained in front of them, waiting for the sinewy shape of the lieutenant to emerge from the end carriage. Colby's sighting laser didn't waver, and Danny targeted his own so the two grouped tightly together. "Don't cross the streams," Danny muttered, prompting a snort from Colby.

"That would be bad. That would be very bad."

They cross-stepped their way back towards the exit point. "Where the fuck is he? Where is he, Col?"

"Focus, Dan. He'll pop up any second now. We've pissed him off. He might not engage this time, but he's sure as hell gonna show himself, you can bet on it."

The Taint didn't disappoint. Right on cue, he emerged from the end carriage, dominating the platform. He turned and faced his challengers, a vicious snarl curling his lips back from those teeth. He held up his right hand.

Danny squinted towards the monster. "What the hell is that motherfucker holding, Col?"

Colby peered through the darkness, and nearly threw up on the spot.

Dangling from its bloody fingers was a severed head that had quite clearly been forcibly torn from its body. Blood pooled at the vampire's feet, dripping like a broken tap and bouncing off the tiled floor. The grey curls were tangled in his fingers, and the head swung gently in the hot breeze that wafted through the tunnel. Tendons and nerves dangled from the shredded neck, and two streaks of black and red ran down the cheeks, a combination of cheap, gritty mascara and blood.

The Taint threw his head back and laughed – a cruel, dangerous sound that spoke of violence yet to come. He tossed the head casually down the platform like a bowler aiming for a ten-pin strike. It rolled and bounced, coming to a stop at Colby's feet.

Colby looked down at the once-gentle face and then back at the vampire. Sheer rage overtook him. He aimed the green laser at the thing's chest and roared. "FIRE!"

Danny and Colby unleashed a swarm of organophosphor FMJs straight at the Taint.

He didn't explode. He didn't twitch and writhe as fire consumed his body. He didn't scream and drop to the floor, heels drumming and body twisting. He merely threw his arms wide open as if welcoming the bullets into his loving embrace. His body took impact after impact.

Nothing.

The bastard didn't even bleed.

"CEASE FIRE! CEASE FIRE, DAMN IT!" Yolanda's voice cut through the cacophony of noise and gunfire. The last shot echoed around the tunnel and finally, silence fell.

Danny and Colby stood motionless, their fingers still on the triggers of the C8s. There was no point wasting any more ammo on this son of a bitch.

"Fall back!" Yolanda, Terry and Micky gave cover as the two men slowly moved back.

The team regrouped by the stairwell, a veritable clusterfuck of ordnance pointing straight at the lieutenant. Yolanda barked an order. "Danny? If you wouldn't mind?"

Danny grinned, stepped forward and hoisted an AT4 Anti-tank weapon onto his shoulder. Designed specifically for confined spaces and urban warfare, it fired an 84mm round of death and destruction at anything you pointed the bastard at.

Gary turned to Colby and grinned. "Man, you gotta love those Swedes. They might be neutral, but they make seriously funky ATWs!"

Colby grinned back. "Yeah. Let's see the bastard catch this and still smile." He glanced up at Danny. "Fuck his day up, mate!"

"Boss?"

"Fire at will, Dan. Like Col said. Fuck his day up, there's a good chap." Yolanda glared at the smirking lieutenant, and suddenly gave him a bright smile and a wink. "Hey! Toothy! Catch!"

Danny took aim, and squeezed the trigger. The projectile exploded from the smooth-bore barrel and fizzed like a firework along the length of the platform.

Too late, the lieutenant realised the missile was considerably bigger than the FMJs he'd batted away like bees. His mouth formed an 'O' as the missile hit him directly in the chest.

The entire team flinched back from the blast. Even though the AT4 was designed for use in close quarters, the blast was still a little *too* close for comfort this time.

As the smoke and dust cleared, the all looked towards where Vlad's lieutenant had stood. All that was left was a dark, sooty mark on the floor and a pile of ashes that danced and whirled in the backdraft from the tunnel entrance.

There was no heel drumming.

No thrashing.

No fireworks.

The fucker simply vaporised on impact. As did a bench, three advertising hoardings, a 'NO ENTRY' sign and every single tile on the end of the platform wall.

Danny lowered the AT4 and sniffed. "I ain't payin' for the damage, boss. Not on my wages."

Yolanda stood and walked towards the end of the platform. She stopped and crouched where the old lady's head lay, discarded and bloody. She unzipped her jacket and took it off, carefully covering the old woman's remains.

She looked up and into the darkness of the tunnel, and quietly spoke.

"I'm coming for you, Vlad. I'm *coming for you...*"

THE DEICIDE MACHINE

Justin Coates

The Chicago front was in the process of collapsing when the *Andrada Ascendent* arrived. The *Montgomery*-class super tank rolled over a field of corpses, crushing them to dust beneath her gargantuan frame. The ragged survivors of III Army Corps, barely half of the 250,000 that had marched to war a month ago, cheered for the magnificent war machine. She was 10,000 tonnes of steel and murderous intent, her 85-meter tall frame instantly attracting the bulk of enemy small arms fire. The alien weapons glanced harmlessly off her scorched armor as she crossed over the trenches and into the ruins of the city.

Her captain, PSICOM officer Mercy Ubuntu, watched tactical data flow across her comscreen from the handful of surveillance drones still airborne. The situation was worse than her superiors knew. III Army Corps had held the enemy back, but at an unspeakably high cost. Chicago was reduced to a smoldering ruin, cloaked in a vast cloud of ash and dust.

The city was lost, but III Corps might be able to withdraw if the *Ascendent* could cover their retreat.

It's up to us, Ubuntu thought, before addressing her gunnery officer. "Commander Nguyen. Ensure the Voidborn know we are here."

"My pleasure, ma'am. *All conventional platforms, fire for effect.*"

The *Asecendent* woke, and the earth shook. 120mm mortar platforms along her spine hurled white phosphorus rounds at enemy positions. Sponson-mounted 25mm Bushmaster cannons filled the air with depleted uranium rounds. Nearby battalions fell back to safety, dragging their dead and wounded by the furious light of her howitzer and missile batteries.

Her artillery batteries ruptured gibbering N'nogug bio-tanks as they slithered among the ruins, reducing them to stinking black smears on the war-struck earth. Unprepared for the sheer violence and rapidity of the armored assault, two entire companies of squid-like Voidborn clones were caught in the open and fell in their hundreds to the *Ascendent's* scything broadsides. Her rockets punched through hive-bunkers and armored reefs, incinerating dug-in enemy artillery in titanic eruptions of smoke and fire. Her main guns, two massive 50-inch Void Eater cannons, each hurled 7-ton psychoreactive shells that vaporized enemy bio-armor reinforcements nearly twenty kilometers away.

"Enemy advance is stalling," Commander Burley said. The navigation officer turned to look back at her captain. "We've blunted the assault across five kilometers."

"My regards to the weapon crews," Ubuntu replied.

It was difficult to stay professional with the *Ascendent* grumbling violence in her mind. The product of a union between strange science and even stranger sorceries, the *Ascendent* was described as 'semi-sentient' in PSICOM training manuals.

Ubuntu knew better. There was nothing 'semi' about it, and the *Ascendent* found no satisfaction in killing mortals (alien as they were). It hungered for worthier prey.

"Incoming plasma barrages detected," Burley said. "Deploying countermeasures."

Multiple jets of superheated gas struck the prow of the land cruiser. Electromagnetic pulse defenses dispersed the worst of it, but Ubuntu could physically feel an outer layer of armor strip away through her connection to the tank.

The *Ascendent* rocked sideways, but her hundreds of crew members were well trained. Loading teams kept up with her voracious demand for ammunition. Command and signal units, located on her uppermost decks, swiftly abandoned damaged stations for redundant platforms deeper inside the vessel, even as security teams escorted welders and mechanics to repair internal damage. Burley's superlative helmsman skills kept the assault moving forward, and that mattered most of all.

"I want those plasma cannons gone, Commander Nguyen," Ubuntu said, effortlessly overseeing both the battlefield and the *Ascendent's* interior operations.

"Working on it," Nguyen replied, her fingers dancing across her comscreen.

"Commander Burley, inform Phantom 6 to continue a fighting withdrawal from the city limits. We will cover their retreat."

"Yes, ma'am," Burley said, hastily firing off the messages via comscreen. "Be advised: I'm picking up dispersion rates above .6 in multiple locations."

"How many are stable enough for a breach?"

"Over a dozen."

"Plot coordinates for those closest to us. We will strike them as they deploy from the noosphere."

The *Ascendent's* atomic heart rumbled with barely-restrained impatience as Burley charged the nearest dispersion point. Ubuntu took a breath to center herself, then opened her invisible third eye to the swirling hell of the Otherworld. She could see the thin spots between realms as pulsing lights on the battlefield. Some were brighter than others, and from these she knew the dreadful deities of the Voidborn might emerge. These alien gods were titans in their own right, hideous constructs of flesh, machine, and insatiable hunger.

There was already a god on the battlefield, however. The *Ascendent* lurked just behind her, speaking in furious, bloody whispers that Ubuntu knew better than to heed.

Those deific whispers caught the attention of beings lurking on the other side of reality. Entities made of fanged nightmares turned their baleful gaze toward her. One of them, older and hungrier than its kindred, snarled in a language that made Ubuntu nauseous.

The *Ascendent* howled in response. Ubuntu closed her third eye, shivering from the awful rage bound up in the war machine's heart.

"Dispersion spikes in three locations," Burley said. "We're at .75 and climbing."

"That got their attention," Nguyen said. "Permission to prep tactical sleds."

"Granted, but hold for my signal," Ubuntu said. "I don't want to destroy any more of this city than we have to."

They rumbled through the barren New City district. Voidborn small arms fire all but ceased, though the *Ascendent* herself continued to punish any enemy ground forces with the temerity to occupy her battlespace. The tank's restless spirit made its impatience known through groaning treads and spiking reactor heat output. A whisper, one Ubuntu knew only she could hear, hissed across the net.

Is it time?

Burley called out a warning. "Dispersion rate of 1 detected! Breach initiating!"

A portal between dimensions opened six hundred meters to their west and stayed open just long enough to spit out a spindly-limbed void hound. The alien demon gibbered through a hundred fanged proboscises. Particle cannons, crudely sutured to its rigid exoskeleton, flashed a vivid blue through the dust clouds.

"Concentrate howitzer fire on the target," Ubuntu ordered. "Commander Burley, bring us close enough for the tridents."

Plasma bombardments hammered down around them. The comscreens stuttered in and out. Messages between maintenance crews flew back and forth across the net with a renewed sense of urgency.

"I want that enemy artillery dealt with, Nguyen!"

The void hound trumpeted and charged. Its cannon struck their armored prow. Ubuntu grit her teeth. Despite no visible wounds, she felt as though a hot iron was scalding her flesh. An auto-generated report revealed damage to the tank's superstructure on her uppermost levels.

"Fire the first trident," the captain ordered.

"Trident away," Nguyen replied.

The massive harpoon soared through the air, launched from a rocket-assist platform along the *Ascendent*'s spine. It slammed into the hound just below its right shoulder. The meter-thick cable tightened, pulling the extradimensional horror off balance.

"A fine shot, Nguyen," Ubuntu said. "Reel it in, Commander Burley."

The *Ascendent* dragged the hound through the steeple of a church. The super tank swerved, dragging the beast through burning ruins. It shrieked, its cannon discharging wildly into the air, the ground.

"All howitzer batteries, fire for effect," Nguyen ordered.

Twenty-one 105mm cannon shells and a dozen 8-inch high-explosive penetrator rounds struck the creature around its face and forelegs. It turned, snarling, only for a double volley from the *Ascendent's* massive pair of 50-inch 'Void-Eater' guns to strike it midsection. Its torso vaporized in a spray of acidic blood. The trident snapped off, the cable whipping through the air in the vessel's wake.

Prow-mounted horns on the *Ascendent* blared a victory anthem. Her crew members cheered and stamped their feet. Back at the front, the survivors of III Army paused in their consolidation efforts to join the battle cry.

Burley shouted, "God kill confirmed!" Then, louder, her voice rising in pitch: "Breach imminent! Brace for—"

Something hard and heavy slammed onto their right flank.

Ubuntu cursed. Connected as she was, Ubuntu could feel talons made of otherworldly material raking across her ribs. Vile fluids poured through her rent armor, damaging internal systems.

"Void Crawler," Nguyen stated, her voice calm. "Bastard is trying to gut us."

"Get it off, Commander Burley," Ubuntu ordered.

The *Ascendent* roared through an overpass. Concrete and asphalt shattered on the war machine. The cackling demon on her flank paid the debris no heed. Its mandibles dug deep into the vessel, ripping chunks away and vomiting venom into the tank's interior.

"Fires on Decks 3 and 4," Burley said. "Fire suppression systems are damaged. We're open to the air in nine locations."

"Send security teams to defend possible entry points and compartmentalize damaged sections." Ubuntu breathed through the pain, eying a series of office buildings ahead. Most were ruined skeletons, but a few – taller than the *Ascendent* – looked to be mostly intact.

"Commander Burley, all ahead full through those buildings."

"We risk tremendous damage to the structural integrity of our prow," Burley said, even as she ceded more power to the engines.

"Then you'd best double-check your restraints," Ubuntu said, ensuring hers were tight across her chest. "Let's see the bastard hold on through this."

They were going nearly 120 kilometers an hour when they hit the first building. The structure turned to a moving wall of debris, crashing into the next just moments ahead of the *Ascendent*. Ubuntu clutched at her arm rests, fighting through the pain of her chest being struck with sledgehammers. She spit onto the floor of the bridge, wiping away a trickle of blood from her nose.

Surviving external cameras showed the crawler digging its thousand claws into the vessel's flanks. The *Ascendent* roared, not in pain, but outrage at such audacity. Perhaps showing some latent psychic connection to the warmachine's spirit, Burley accelerated further, coaxing even more energy from the strained reactor, grinding the alien demi-god through thousands of tons of debris.

"It's off!" Burley said, sparks flying from her console as the world shook apart. The *Ascendent* emerged from a titanic dust cloud, smashing abandoned homes beneath her treads. "Enemy is clear!"

"Direct all Hellfires to fire for effect," Ubuntu said. "Fire for effect. ***Fire. Burn these motherfuckers and eat the ashes.***"

The voice that came through her lips was inhuman: the sound of the wounded and dying in the midst of ceaseless artillery bombardment, if such noise could be turned to speech. Nguyen turned to her, hesitating, fear reflected in her eyes.

Get back, you bitch, Ubuntu snarled, shoving the *Ascendent*'s psychic will away from her mind. *Your hour isn't here yet.*

Ubuntu met Nguyen's gaze. "It's me, Leesh. Launch the Hellfires."

Nguyen nodded, relieved. "Hellfires away."

A flight of missiles burst from sixty vertical launch platforms near the *Ascendent*'s stern. They arched briefly through the air before screaming toward the shrieking void crawler. The thermobaric weapons blistered its alien form. The abomination caught fire. Strips of smoking flesh peeled from its body. It shuddered, curling up on itself like a dying insect, and lay still.

"God kill confirmed!" Burley declared.

Nguyen thumped her small fist into her tactical console, shouting, "burn, you bastard!"

The *Ascendent* howled her victory anthem again, but Burley's voice cut quickly through the noise. "Captain, we've got three squid swarms heading this way. Estimate 1,200 enemy infantry in the open."

"What's our armor integrity?" Ubuntu asked.

"Compromised. If they get past the Bushmaster cannons, we *will* be boarded."

"That's a big if," Nguyen said, updating firing plans for the sponson guns. She pointed to a pulsing icon on her display, growing closer to them by the second. "Last target is inbound. We'll need to use the sleds."

"That is absolutely out of the question," Burley said. "We'll kill our own crew and cause additional and unnecessary damage to the *Ascendent*."

"Irrelevant," Nguyen replied, her voice sharp. "Our mission is to cover III Corps' retreat."

"III Corps is made of men," Burley insisted. "But the *Ascendent*..."

"Is made *by* men, *for* men. Our mission is paramount. Should she be lost, others can be built to replace her."

"There is only one *Ascendent*," Burley said stiffly. "And the loss of this vessel is too high a price."

"I'm the judge of that, Commander," Ubuntu said, the slightest raise of her voice signal to her subordinates that she would brook no argument. "As it stands, I've no intention of surrendering the *Ascendent* or the battlefield to the enemy."

A warning klaxxon sounded on their comscreens. The tides of the Otherworld rippled out of a yet-invisible dispersion point.

Burley's shouted warning was entirely unnecessary. The hair on the back of Ubuntu's neck stood up. Weird, alien whispers filled the net. Impossible glyphs flashed across the comscreen, then disappeared.

Ubuntu switched her radio channel to address every human unit that could hear her. Her throat was dry; she swallowed, trying to still the twisting knot of terror and anticipation in her gut.

"All elements, this is the *Andrada Ascendent*. A MIDNIGHT-Level event is occurring. Break." She hesitated, then added, "Use of atomics on the battlefield is imminent. Break. All units are advised to withdraw. Godspeed, and *Contre Noctem*"

"*Contre Noctem*," the two commanders muttered. Nguyen genuflected.

The shrieking klaxxon grew louder. The *Ascendent's* psychic growling grew with it. Two of the dispersion points collided. The breach appeared as a brilliant sphere of light on the battlefield. Ruins near it began levitating strangely, the tides of gravity warped by such aberrant, otherworldly power.

The breach swelled in an obscene parody of birth, and a true Voidborn god tore its way out of the madness of the Otherworld. Even at a distance Ubuntu could see how it towered over the *Ascendent*, supported on bulging tentacles and vaguely simian legs. Psychic assimilation devices of bone and sinew, their method a mystery to even the most brilliant minds of PSICOM, spun wildly as they soaked up the energy from the breach.

The name of the god was written with glittering alien runes on each of its titanium scales. The squid infantry advancing on the *Ascendent* took up that name as a battle cry, even as the deity itself roared the name into the mind of every living being within twenty square kilometers.

UZHAIOGACH!

Nguyen whistled. "That's a big fish."

"Captain Nguyen, hold sled fire for my signal," Ubuntu said. "All other systems are yours."

"Yes ma'am. All howitzers batteries, fire for effect!"

Four kilometers of ruins lay between the *Ascendent* and Uzhaiogach. Every one of her guns covered that distance in a heartbeat.

"Rocket pods 1-20, fire for effect!"

200 Hydra 70 rockets screamed from their launch pods. The demon roared, recoiling from the heat and pressure of the multiple blast waves.

"Mortar batteries, bracketing fire from the following coordinates! Exhaust all ammunition!"

The 120mm mortars fired at high angle, raining down burning white phosphorus as close as 200 meters away. The flames spread quickly, punishing the advancing enemy infantry and creating a field of fire that Uzhaiogach would have to cross.

The demon regarded them for a moment. Ubuntu could taste its thoughts: brackish and alien, possessed of unfathomable purpose. Its mere presence drove the *Ascendent* into blind fury. The ghost in the machine struck at Ubuntu as though she were an enemy. For a terrifying moment Ubuntu thought she would be lost, her mind soaked into the vessel's pulsing reactor heart, but her own stubborn refusal to cede control to a damn vehicle kept her conscious.

"Not yet," she hissed through clenched teeth, heedless of the concerned looks both Nguyen and Burley gave her. "Not bloody yet."

The demon god boomed with laughter. Its slime-covered tentacles pushed it faster toward the *Ascendent*.

"Noospheric spike detected!" Burley shouted. "Brace for impact!"

The demon's psychic attack hit the tank hard enough to push it sideways on its tracks. Sparks flew from the bridge's command screens.

The *Ascendent* screamed, and Ubuntu screamed with her. An

invisible spear pierced through her ribs, its cold touch profaning her organs. She could *feel* cancerous tumors sprouting inside her lungs and liver, sprouting in stigmatic sympathy with the tank's injuries.

"Major hull breaches on the second, third, and fourth decks," Burley said. Blood oozed from a wound on her forehead. Nguyen was silent, her head lolling on her chest. "Enemy dismounts are boarding on the fourth. We've lost all sponson guns on our starboard side. Locomotion failing. Reactor close to critical."

"Prepping remaining Trident missiles," Ubuntu said, taking over Nguyen's responsibilities. "Once they've fired, the bridge is yours." Then, though the words were her own, the voice was once again that of the *Ascendent*. "*Don't let that bastard get away from us.*"

Burley gave a crisp salute. Her eyes shone with near-cultic fervor. "*Contre Noctem.* It has been my honor, and privilege, to serve You."

Ubuntu opened her third eye and turned to behold the *Ascendent*. It was a column of atomic fire, a towering psychic whirlwind that was at once familiar and more alien than even the Voidborn.

Is it time? The god demanded.

Ubuntu nodded. "Yes. It is time."

There was no hesitation. The *Ascendent* took Ubuntu, bringing her into the heart of the tempest until She and her were one.

Burley's voice seemed to come from a thousand miles away. "*Tridents away. Happy hunting, Captain.*"

The metal goddess drove her talons into the demon. Three of them failed to penetrate, but a fourth stuck in a gap between its armored scales. Burley accelerated at a tight angle, yanking it toward them.

Squid clones crawled over and inside her. Security teams with shotguns and riot shields battled next to ammunition chambers and fuel supplies, making the enemy bleed for each step.

Integral systems failed. Coolant lines evaporated. Locomotion systems shuddered and threatened to go dark forever.

Together, Ubuntu and the *Ascendent* held on. The strain was tearing her apart, but she forced her atomic heart to stay online, to continue working with what limited power it had.

The part of her that was still Ubuntu shouted: *Come on! We aren't finished yet!*

They turned. Uzhaiogach came on. They collided like mobile mountain ranges, two gods of war desperate to consume the other. The buildings between them were reduced to dust and ashen embers.

Its mantis limbs hacked deep into her spine. She pummeled it with her howitzers and remaining 25mm Bushmaster cannons. Her Void-Eater cannons blasted meters-thick chunks of armored plating from its eldritch form. It seized the yawning barrels in its jaws, chewing through the explosion of the gun's magazine.

Uzhaiogach swung her around. She dug in, her treads roaring, then pushed back. The demon slithered backward, prevented from disengaging by the trident embedded in its torso. The phosphorus firestorm scorched alien and human god alike.

I will devour you, the *Ascendent* seethed. ***And shit you out my exhaust pipes.***

They roared from the flames and into the frigid waters of Lake Michigan. The sky overhead broke with forks of green lightning. Downed alien craft drifted in the cursed waves battering the shore.

The trident snapped free. Uzhaiogach broke away, lumbering down the rocky beach. It sucked in energy from the noosphere, preparing itself for another brutal psychic attack. Bleeding from one hundred thousand wounds, the *Ascendent* pivoted, feeling the fusion reactor in her heart beginning to flicker.

She charged the enemy, hurling her remaining rockets and howitzer rounds. She slammed into its crustacean torso as its main weapon fired. It scoured her back, peeling off her mortar platforms and drone landing pads, but did not pierce her heart.

She did not notice the pain. Her momentum was unrelenting. She rammed Uzhaiogach, piercing it on her armored prow. The god machine forced the demon back into the ruins, through the flames, through a kilometer of pitched battlefield.

She was screaming by the time she shoved Uzhaiogach into the rusted remains of a toppled skyscraper. Dozens of massive structural beams burst through its chest. The *Ascendent* hurled herself into reverse, her treads shredding on razor-sharp debris. For a moment she was stuck, battered by the howling demon's claws and teeth, her cannons and missile systems reduced to sparking wrecks.

Burley came through in the end.

They limped away, fires spreading on multiple decks, smoke pouring from the wounds in her armor.

I am the memory of the great Andrada.

Squid infantry poured through her hallways and corridors. Security teams fought to give loading crews and engineers time to complete their tasks before being overrun by alien horrors. Uzhaiogach pulled itself free, emerging from the rubble of the collapsing skyscraper with hellfire in its crushing claws.

I am a child of the all mighty Behemoth.

She activated her recoilless sleds at last. The devices hurled twin M-422 bombs at Uzhaiogach. The projectiles opened seconds before impact, revealing dozens of fin-steered devices that aimed right for the alien's heart.

The ensuing detonation formed a nuclear fireball nearly 60 meters wide. A newborn sun kissed the earth, sucking in fountains of irradiated ash and spewing it into the air. The blast-wave formed a toxic cyclone that pummeled the *Ascendent* and her foe.

Uzhaiogach burned.

The elemental fury of sundered atoms torched its otherworldly frame. Its accumulated psychic energy ran out of control, mutating and warping its flesh in great heaving loops. Its compound eyes burst. It screamed, and collapsed under the weight of its own mutation, rapidly dissolving into stinking, purple flames.

Ubuntu and the *Ascendent* were one, and then they were two again. Ubuntu gasped, her fingers curled from the agony of her wounds. A thousand warning sirens sounded from multiple systems throughout the *Ascendent*.

Burley held an emergency oxygen mask to Ubuntu's face. Nguyen was still in her chair, barely conscious, clutching a pistol and staring at the door leading out of the bridge.

"God kill confirmed," Burley said. "Ironside 6 is reporting a full withdrawal. III Corps lives to fight another day."

Ubuntu's cracked lips opened.

"Boarders?"

Screams, shotgun blasts, and the gibbering of Voidborn clones on the other side of the bridge's blast doors answered her question. Ubuntu got to her feet, waving away Burley's protest. She reached out her hand; after a moment of hesitation, Burley armed her with a stout pump-action shotgun. Ubuntu racked the chamber.

"Get us off this battlefield, Commander."

Wincing, Ubuntu leaned against Nguyen's chair for support. The *Ascendent* whispered through the rumble of the engines and the ceaseless work of the surviving crew members. A voice that was once bellicose and challenging now seemed almost grateful, ready to lend its strength for the battle to come.

The door to the bridge shook. Burley shouted orders across the net. Slowly, torturously, the god of steel and fire turned away from the irradiated remains of its foe.

Ubuntu aimed her shotgun at the door and whispered, "The honor is mine, my friend."

CLOSING WORDS

Geoff Brown, Amanda J Spedding

First off, we'd like to send out a big thank you to Charles R Rutledge, Greig Beck, Alan Baxter and Evan Dicken, who gave generously of their time to donate original fiction for this volume.

Another special thank you to Dean Samed for his donation of such a fantastic cover design, and to Amanda (AJ) Spedding for her donation of editing for the volume (any errors in proof-reading lie with Geoff, not AJ).

Additional thanks go to Richard Johnson, Jeremy Robinson, Kane Gilmour, Seth Skorkowsky, Steve Lewis, Dave Beynon, Kirsten 'Kes' Cross, and Justin Coates. Not one of them hesitated to allow us to add their tales to this volume, and it means a lot to us, and to Jim.

Thank you all. And everyone reading this, go buy more of their writing. It won't disappoint you.

What can I say about James A Moore?

First, and above all, Jim is my friend, the brother I never had. In the time I've known him, Jim has always been a true gentleman, and my respect and love for the man is endless.

I first met Jim online (I've never had the pleasure of meeting him in real life, although I hope to some day) at the Horror Mall messageboards, back in the days there was no social media.

Jim's an amazing writer, and one of the moderators of 'The Mall', Larry Roberts of Bloodletting Press, was publishing Jim's stories featuring the iconic character Jonathan Crowley. Jim being who he is, he spent a lot of time interacting with readers and fans in that forum, and it was there we forged a bond that

369

will last as long as we do. I don't think I've ever met a creator who is so generous with his time, yet so productive in his craft.

When I started Cohesion Press, I did so with the concept of publishing the first SNAFU anthology. I was a freelance editor back then, and I spent a lot of time working on other people's writing. I complained to my wife that I wasn't getting jobs working on the fast-paced military horror I enjoyed reading. Her response? Just publish it yourself, then.

My original go-to when it came to thinking about authors for the first SNAFU was Jim. He said yes without a moment's hesitation. He's been a Cohesion author ever since. Always the first to offer his time and his stories to us, without hesitation. We've been family for as long as I've known him, so when I heard of his medical issues last year, we wanted to do something to help. You are holding that something (either physically or virtually) right now.

Every cent of income from this release will go to Jim, to help with his medical bills, and to help him maintain his family and his home during these trying times. We could do no less., and I know that if the situation was reversed, he would do the same for any one of us in a second.

We love you, Jim. And we're here for you.

Geoff

I love Jim. It's simple and it's true. We "met" about eight years ago when I reached out, rather tentatively, after reading some very kind words he'd written about a story of mine. Little did I know that the conversation that followed was the start of a friendship I can't imagine being without. It mattered little that we lived on the other side of the world from each other... until it mattered a lot. Distance is a bitch when those you care for are in the fight of their lives.

A rallying cry went up from those closest to Jim, and the writing community answered the call. Auctions and GoFundMe and offers of help flooded in for one of our own. And not just anyone. This was Jim. And Jim needed our help. It's a testament to who Jim is that so many put up their hands and dug into their wallets to make sure that financial stress wasn't something he had to endure during his fight.

Back on the other side of the world, we decided to put our hand up as well. So *SNAFU: Medivac* was born. Before we at Cohesion Press had much of an idea (beyond a title), we had offers from authors for original stories for this edition – anything to help Jim. This edition was always going to be a mix of original and previously published, I mean how could we put this out without a James A Moore story? How could that not be joined by one from his brother, Charles R Rutledge?

We were humbled by the offers, humbled again by the original cover from Dean Samed, and the overwhelming 'hell yes' we received from all the authors whose tales appear in this anthology – you legends.

You see, *SNAFU: Medivac* is more than just a collection of stories, it's mateship at its finest. It's a coming together for a cause greater than ourselves. It's for Jim – the kindest of kind sirs.

Amanda